CLAIM & PROTECT

RHENNA MORGAN

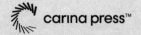

carina press™

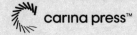

ISBN-13: 978-1-335-00707-0

Claim & Protect

Copyright © 2017 by Rhenna Morgan

www.CarinaPress.com

Printed in U.S.A.

Recycling programs
for this product may
not exist in your area.

To Stephanie. I am so honored and blessed
to have you in my life. You said you wanted Trevor,
and while I can't take him away from Natalie,
I can at least give him to you this way.
Thank you for everything.

CLAIM &
PROTECT

Chapter One

Any bar owner in Dallas's Deep Ellum district would be tickled shitless with a light crowd on a dreary, October weeknight. But seeing more than half the tables of his own pub occupied and both bartenders knocking out nonstop drink orders—that was a thing of beauty.

Not too shabby for a college dropout. But then, if there was one thing Trevor Raines had learned from his brothers in the last ten years, it was that the right focus and a little ingenuity made anything attainable.

Beside him, Jace Kennedy leaned into the brotherhood's reserved table and motioned with Scotch in hand at Trevor's newest waitress across the room. "That one's a hustler."

Trevor followed his gaze in time to witness said hustler sidle up to one of the oversized corner booths with a drink-laden tray balanced on one palm. She was a little thing, five-foot-one at best and couldn't weigh more than a buck-twenty sopping wet, but she had a smokin' curvy body to go with her girl-next-door charm, a combination he'd known right away would be a hit with the men. Normally, that kind of combo would've made hiring her a no-brainer—even with her lack of experience. But for some reason, the idea of men hitting on Natalie Jordan nonstop had tweaked him hard enough he'd damned near turned her down.

"Just hired her a few weeks ago," he said. "Basically told me she'd be the best waitress I ever had if I gave her a chance." It had been the desperation behind her vow that had tipped the scales and made him offer the position. So far, she'd made good on her claim. In fact, for a woman who'd never taken a drink order in her life, she'd acclimated to her new job a whole lot better than he'd anticipated.

"Gotta love a woman with spunk," Jace said.

Another of their Haven brothers, Zeke Dugan, nursed his Bohemia Weiss and studied Natalie over the rim. "She looks familiar."

"Wouldn't surprise me," Trevor said. "Since I was just hiring for a waitress, Knox only ran a cursory background check. He still turned up an expired RN license she hadn't put on her application. Was a long time ago though."

Zeke nodded. "Yeah, that's gotta be it. But she didn't work down in trauma with me. I'd remember that swagger."

Zeke's fiancée, Gabe, looked up from the wedding magazine anchored between her and Jace's wife, Viv, and smacked him on the shoulder. "You're weeks away from being a married man. You're not supposed to appreciate another woman's swagger anymore."

"Didn't say I appreciated it, *gatinha*. I said I'd have remembered it." He snatched her hand before Viv could drag her back into all things wedding dresses and cakes, kissed her knuckles, and grinned. "I'll take your leisurely strut to a power walk any day."

Trevor reclined against his seat back and considered

his newest hire while she worked, an act he'd caught himself doing a little more often than he'd like to admit with her being an employee. Defining the way Natalie moved as a power walk was a little harsh. Yeah, she got from point A to point B without a whole lot of dillydallying, but it didn't diminish the subtle sway of her hips or the way her body flowed from one task to another. Fluid and smooth like a full river after a heavy rain.

Done with handing out drinks, Natalie wove through her section, eyes sharp and checking for needed refills. The soft mini lights strung across the ceiling cast her pixie features in an easy glow, and the standard-issue tank top with The Den's logo showcased one helluva rack. One he'd already caught a whole host of men eyeballing, and that made him seriously consider outfitting her in an oversized T-shirt.

She'd just about made it back to the arched opening that led to the main bar when she slid her phone out of her back pocket, checked the screen, and hurried out of sight.

"Damn it," he murmured before he knocked back the last of his beer.

"There a problem?" Jace asked.

Probably. Despite how good she'd worked out on the floor and the pure joy of watching her move, there were some bad habits he couldn't overlook. "Fucking cell phones. I told her they're off-limits while she's working and I've busted her with the thing twice tonight."

"Could just be checking the time," Zeke said. "And if she's taking care of her people, what's the harm?"

"If you were with a patient, would you text?"

Zeke chuckled. "Point taken. But then I don't have

time to text when someone's bleeding out all over the ER's floor."

"With your attention span, you'd probably try." Jace spun the toothpick anchored at the corner of his mouth with his tongue and focused on Trevor. "Don't jump the gun on your new girl too quick. Could've been a misunderstanding on her part. If she's doin' all right otherwise, talk to her first. Unless you're in a big hurry to start interviewing again?"

"Hell no." The last round had taken him three weeks to hire two girls. Natalie had ended up being the only one worth the effort.

Viv straightened from the mini wedding huddle at the end of the table and slid the two-inch-thick bridal magazine right in front of Gabe. "Really? You don't like that one? It'd look great on you."

Gabe dipped her chin and aimed a you've-got-to-be-kidding-me glare back at her. "I fix cars for a living and wear jeans three hundred and sixty-two days out of the year. The only thing a train is going to do for me is make sure I face-plant in front of everyone."

"I don't get it," Trev said to Zeke. "If you're not doing a big shindig, why go through all the cake and dress nonsense? Just let me fly you to Vegas like we did for Viv and Jace."

Viv scowled good-naturedly across the table. "Cake and dresses are *not* nonsense. No matter where they get hitched, every woman gets to feel pretty on her wedding day." Seemingly satisfied she'd gotten her point across, she licked her finger, flipped to the next page, and hunched closer to Gabe.

Zeke lowered his voice, obviously intent on skirting any more dirty looks from the women. "Gabe doesn't

know what she wants yet. Whatever we do will be just
family, but if she opts for someplace quick and fun,
we'll take you up on the ride."

Trevor shrugged. He still didn't get why everyone
made such a big deal out of one day when what really
mattered came after. "Whatever works."

"Spoken like a man who's not yet surrendered. One
of these days though…" Jace grinned and sipped his
Scotch.

Trevor held up both hands. "Don't turn your matchmaking sights on me. I'm not a qualified candidate for
marriage."

"Don't know why you're so against it," Zeke said.
"Out of all of us, you're the one who had the best relationship role models."

"I'd hardly call my dad a role model."

Zeke's expression blanked hard and fast. "I meant
Frank. You're nothing like your biological father, flesh
and blood or not."

Right. Because Trevor had done so well reining in
his fists growing up. Didn't mean he didn't wish Zeke
was right.

Deftly dodging a chatty group of girls who weren't
looking where they were going, Natalie hustled to a
twelve-top full of rowdy college guys and started dol-
ing out pints. If she had any clue half of them were eyeing her sweet ass, she didn't show it. He, on the other
hand, was having to fight grinding his molars to dust.

One of Natalie's customers reached out as she
rounded the table and tried to wrap his arm around
her waist.

Trevor tensed, braced to intervene, but Natalie
shifted just in time, patted the guy good-naturedly on

the arm, and hurried back to the bar. Then she slid her phone free and checked the screen without breaking stride.

Strike three.

"I gotta go deal with this." He stood, snatched his empty beer bottle, and motioned to everyone's drinks. "Anyone need a refill?"

"Nah," Zeke said. "We're good."

"Zeke and Gabe are heading out to Haven with me and Viv," Jace added. "The moms keep begging for a chance to weigh in on the dress."

Trevor shook his head. "Women." He chin-lifted toward Zeke. "You wanna tie the knot someplace outside of Texas, the offer stands. You takin' Gabe out in my Cessna might have made her giggle, but my G6 will make her purr."

"Got a rock on her finger, brother. Stop trying to sweet-talk my woman."

Winking at Gabe as he rounded the table, he squeezed Viv's shoulder. "Thought you knew. The ones you can't have are the best ones to chase."

Not that he'd ever chased a woman. Between his genes and long-term relationships being a pipe dream too dangerous to pursue, there'd never been a need. He ambled through the room, eyeballing the handsy bastard who'd tried to corral Natalie. Which was stupid, really. She'd handled it fine, and his manager, Ivan, wouldn't have tolerated it for more than a nanosecond, but for some reason it pissed him off.

Inside the main room, the gleaming honey-stained bar he'd flown in from Dublin was packed with everything from Goths to post-workday businessmen. The rock and movie memorabilia he'd paid a small fortune for hung from every wall, but gave the rest of the old-world pub décor a trendy edge. Two of the other waitresses were stationed at tables near the front but Natalie was nowhere in sight.

He sidled up to Vicky behind the bar. "Where's Natalie?"

Frowning, his top-notch bartender scanned the room and tucked her bottle opener in her back pocket.

A dark-headed guy with full sleeves and gauge earrings big enough to shoot a .44 through swiveled from his wingman. "You lookin' for the perky little waitress with the powerhouse stride?"

Great. Another one to keep an eye on. "Yep, that's the one."

The guy nodded toward the employee entrance at the back of the bar. "She ducked out there a few minutes ago."

So much for Zeke's time-checking theory. As rules went, Trevor didn't spout a long list, and he damned sure couldn't go bending the ones he had no matter how efficient an employee was. "Appreciate it."

The crowd's rumble and the bass from some new alternative rock song on the sound system faded as he strolled down the back hall. A woman leaned against the far wall with arms crossed waiting on whoever was hogging the bathroom, but otherwise the space was deserted. Maybe Jace was right and he was jumping to conclusions. Although, how the hell he could misread her palming that damned device all night he couldn't fathom.

Slowly, he eased the door latch open. The employee parking lot's lights buzzed overhead and the thick humidity walloped hard before he'd so much as put one boot heel on the asphalt.

Natalie's voice cut from the shadows on the far side of the lot. "I know you're scared, but you can't call the cops."

Stepping free of the door, Trevor found her perched on one of the more private picnic table benches his employees used for smoke breaks. Her back was to the entrance and she fisted a good chunk of her mink-colored hair on top of her head like she might pull it out in another half a second.

Oddly, seeing her so tense knocked his plans for a come-to-Jesus talk down a notch and made him want to find out what was wrong and fix it instead.

"Mom, if you call the cops, he's just going to haul us back to court. I can't afford any more attorney fees." She paused and sat up straighter, letting her dark hair fall free around her shoulders. "I know he's the one not following the rules, but it won't matter with the kind of friends he's got. Just keep the lights off, keep Levi quiet, and don't answer. I'll be home after the bar closes."

His instincts bristled, the potent fear in her voice and the fact that anyone would have to hide in their own home putting all his senses on high alert.

She glanced over her shoulder, and her eyes popped wide. Her voice dropped, but not enough to cover her words. "I gotta go, Mom. You'll be fine. Wyatt's an idiot, but not enough to break down the door."

Break the door down? Who was this asshole and, more importantly, what the fuck was he doing harassing Natalie?

She clicked off the phone and stood, slipping the device in her back pocket with the same practiced ease she'd shown all night.

Trevor forced his fingers to release their death grip and let the door swing shut. "There a problem?"

"Nope. All good." Striding his direction, she pasted a fake smile on her face and motioned toward the picnic tables. "Just needed a quick break to settle something at home."

A lie. Not one her body language indicated she was comfortable giving him, but a lie all the same. Keeping his place in front of the door, he crossed his arms and cocked his head. There were two ways his could play this—call her on what he'd overheard, or see if she'd pony up the info on her own. Considering he hated anyone poking into his own business, he opted for door number two. "Pretty sure we talked about my policy on phones during work."

She stopped just out of reach and squared her shoulders. Despite her proud stance, her gaze didn't quite reach his, focusing on his collarbone instead. "Yes, sir."

"So are you going to tell me why you'd risk your new job breaking that policy?"

"I'd rather not." The same gumption she'd shown the day she'd interviewed fired bright behind her eyes, but there was something else there tonight. A worry she couldn't quite hide beneath her sass.

He didn't know this woman. Not really. Not her backstory or what was going on at home, but everything in him fought to scoop her up, tuck her and whoever was on the phone someplace safe, and make her spill everything so he could fix whatever was wrong. Though, given the stubborn look on her face right now, that probably wasn't the most efficient path forward. Better to tackle it from a more professional angle to start. "Not gonna lie to you, Nat. You're good with the customers. Reliable. Fast. Friendly. I have a hard time finding one of those qualities in a waitress, let alone all three. I'd rather not have to cast my net for a replacement, but you're not giving me much help."

She swallowed big and pinched her lips together like it was all she could do not to rip him a new one. "My son's seven, and my mom's scared to death of my ex. I keep my phone with me so they can reach me if they need to. I promise you, I'm not letting it interfere with my service, but if that's a deal breaker for you, then I understand. I can either finish out the night, or cut bait now."

Oh, yeah. Total attitude *and* sass wrapped up with the kind of lingo he could appreciate. And she'd given him exactly the in he'd needed to dig deeper. "Your mom got a reason to be afraid of this guy?"

She held her tongue, but her face blanched a shade or two.

"Not asking for you to tell me the sordid details," Trevor said. Though calling Knox and getting every scrap available had shot to the top of his to-do list about three minutes ago. "I'm asking so I can gauge if I'm gonna have a rowdy asshole show up at my bar. I also need to know if this is going to be something you juggle on a daily basis."

She huffed out a tired exhale and her shoulders slumped. "I'd say her fears aren't unfounded, but it's not something you'd have to deal with here. Wyatt saves his tantrums for smaller audiences."

Reflexes born at a young age flared hard and fast. Trevor knew exactly the type of tantrum she meant. Had lived under his father's tyrannical fists for seven years before fate and his mother's death had turned his whole world upside down. "Get your stuff and get home."

"You're firing me?"

"No, I'm telling you to quit jacking around here and get home to your son." He forced himself to take a solid breath and unclench his fists. "From here on, if you need to keep the phone with you, that's fine, but use it in private. I don't need other employees claiming I play favorites. And next time, don't try to handle two issues at once. Tell me or whoever's managing the club you've got an issue then get your butt home and deal with it right."

For the first time since he'd met her, the careful mask she kept in place slipped. A stunning smile replaced it, so beautiful and potent it whispered through him with an almost divine absolution.

"Thank you," she said. It was barely more than a whisper, but thick with enough emotion it almost knocked him over. She reached out as though to touch his arm, but tucked her elbow back against her side just as fast. "I promise. You won't regret this."

Before he could respond, she slipped around him, yanked opened the door, and hurried down the dark hall.

He caught the door in one hand before it could close and stared after her, dangerous ideas he had zero intent of halting taking root in his head. Not only was making a concession for Natalie where phones were concerned a foregone conclusion, her ex had just stepped front and center into Trevor's crosshairs.

Chapter Two

No human being should be allowed to drive on a cocktail of frayed nerves, fear, and adrenaline. Especially not a mother trying to get home to her kid before her narcissistic ex scared him to death banging on the door.

Barely slowing to check oncoming traffic, Natalie whipped a right-on-red and gunned her Lexus SUV the last block to her apartment complex. Thank God her new boss was a decent human being. She'd been panicked reading her mother's texts all night, but had been equally terrified of losing her job. Once upon a time, her salary as even a starting RN would have made being the sole provider for her mom and Levi a doable proposition, but that was years and a bad decision ago, and processing health insurance claims didn't rake in the big bucks. Her tips working one of Dallas's trendiest bars definitely helped take the edge off.

Bypassing the main parking lot, she paralleled farther down the street and killed the engine. Trying to hide the gleaming white and chrome vehicle from Wyatt was probably a wasted effort. It stood out almost as strong as a neon sign on a clear night, but it was less than a year old, reliable, and paid for. Aside from the clothes she and Levi had managed to pack, it was the only asset she'd asked for in the divorce. Plus, it made for one heck of a reminder. A reflection of how much of herself she'd given up before Wyatt had literally knocked her back to her senses.

The car's locks engaged with a subtle click, but the automatic headlights stayed illuminated, painting a bold path between her and the staircase across the parking lot. Not exactly the stealthiest approach, but definitely safer in this part of town. Besides, if Wyatt was waiting for her, there'd be no getting around a confrontation.

Halfway up the staircase, she scanned the cars below. No lights glowed other than the old street lamp and no movement registered, but her heart hammered as though the hounds of hell were queued to pop out of the shadows at any moment. Fucking Wyatt. Just once she'd like to feel safe again. To actually believe she could call the cops and expect some kind of help.

She worked the old but solid dead bolt until it clunked open and forced the door open with her shoulder. Soft, white light glowed from the galley kitchen's stove, just enough to let her mom and Levi get around the two-bedroom apartment if they needed to, but not enough to clue Wyatt in to anyone being home. Her mom lay stretched out on the couch with Levi tucked up in the crook of her arm. His dirty-blond hair was tousled and had grown so long it nearly reached his eyes, but cutting it wasn't a battle she was ready to fight yet. For Levi, a haircut meant looking more like his dad than he already did, which meant he'd fight tooth and nail to avoid it.

She placed her purse onto the end table, eased to her knees beside him, and whispered, "Hey, sweetheart."

Her mom jolted awake, simultaneously squeezing Levi closer and shifting to protect him. Only when she realized it was Natalie crouched beside them, did she let out a shaky breath and relax into the cushions. Once upon a time her hair had been a lustrous dark brown, but now it was nearly all gray. While she never went out of the house without minimal makeup and her simple bob styled just so, tonight it was frazzled. She pressed the heel of her hand against her heart. "Warn an old woman next time, would you?"

"Sorry. I was in a hurry." Natalie picked up Levi's hand and squeezed it, loving the warmth and comfort the simple contact provided. One touch and her heart settled. At the first hint of his little boy scent, her lungs drew their first decent breath in hours.

Careful not to jar Levi, her mom pushed upright and squinted toward the cable box perched on top of the old box television set. In neon blue, 9:08 p.m. beamed back at them. "I thought you wouldn't be home until after close?"

"Yeah, well it turns out my new boss isn't just hot enough to seduce half of Texas's female population, but has a heart of gold, too." When she'd first walked into Trevor's office for her interview, his looks had literally knocked her for a loop, leaving her as coordinated as a drunken sailor wearing clown shoes. Thick blond hair tied back in a ponytail, sigh-worthy blue eyes, and a square jaw that made her think of Vikings—he was 100 percent, Grade-A visual goodness.

Apparently, she wasn't the only one who thought so. Every woman who walked in the bar rubbernecked the laid-back cowboy in blatant appreciation. For that reason alone, she'd vowed never to ogle him or his jean-clad ass again, even if it meant keeping her gaze locked on his chin through all their conversations.

She smoothed Levi's bangs off his forehead. "How long's he been out?"

"Since Wyatt quit banging on the door about forty-five minutes ago." Her mom frowned and double-checked to make sure Levi wasn't feigning sleep. "He's terrified of him, Nat. It took a full hour after Wyatt started knocking for him to believe me when I said I wouldn't let Wyatt have him."

And her mom wouldn't either. Maureen Dubois might be petite and almost seventy, but she'd protect Levi with her last breath. The same way she'd tried to protect Natalie by begging her not to marry a highfalu-tin plastic surgeon. "You know Wyatt. He only wants what he can't have. Sooner or later, he's bound to get tired and find something shiny and new."

At least that was what she hoped happened. It was a heck of a better plan than following through with her fantasies of running the bastard over with the high-priced SUV he'd bought her.

She squeezed Levi's shoulder and kissed his cheek. "Come on, kiddo. Let's get you in bed."

Levi stirred, wrinkled his little nose, and rubbed the back of his hand across his eyes. God, he deserved so much more than the father who'd sired him. Hell, he'd deserved a justice system that wouldn't turn a blind eye to an abusive man too, but in the end, Wyatt's good-old-boy network had proven stronger leverage than human decency.

Finally waking up enough to realize his mom was home, Levi's eyes sharpened and his whole body went tense. He lurched forward and wrapped his arms around her neck. "He tried to take me. It's not his turn. He can't make me go when it's not his turn."

"I know, baby." Taking him with her as she stood, she hugged him close and paced toward the room he shared with her mom, smoothing her hand down his back. "He's not going to take you yet. I promise."

A heavy knock rapped against the door.

Natalie whipped around and froze, eyes locked on her mother.

Inside her arms, Levi's once-languid body went rigid, and he whimpered.

She palmed the back of his head and whispered in his ear. "Shhh. Don't say anything. He'll go away and it'll be okay."

At least if they were lucky, he would. But then the one thing she'd learned in the most painful way possible the last eight years was that Wyatt didn't let something go once he'd set his mind on it. Ever. Once the court granted her divorce decree, what he'd decided he wanted was his wife and son back—even if he hated them both.

The knocks came harder and faster, followed by Wyatt's bellowing voice. "Open the goddamned door, Nat. I know you're home. You really think that Lexus blends with this piece of shit neighborhood?"

She kissed Levi's cheek and peeled one arm from around her neck. If she didn't defuse Wyatt quick, he'd shout the whole damned complex down. "Baby, I've gotta deal with him, but I promise you, he's not getting in, okay? Not so much as one step in the house. I'll just tell him it's not time for his visit and he'll go away." It wasn't a complete lie. More like a fervent wish that had a snowball's chance in hell of coming true, but she'd give it her best. At this point, she'd call the cops to make it happen if she had to.

Levi grappled to regain his hold, but didn't make a

noise. And how sad was that? Seven years old and already versed on how best to avoid his father's wrath.

Crouching next to the couch, she sat Levi next to her mother. "It's just for a minute or two, sweetheart. You'll see." She focused on her mother. "I'll lock the door behind me. Take Levi to your room. No matter what, don't open it. I'll tell him I'm headed out and that you two are gone to a movie. If I have to, I'll take him out for coffee until he's mollified."

"Call the police, Natalie. It's safer."

Wyatt banged on the door. "I want to see my son, Nat. Open the door. Not going to play this game all night."

"Sorry, Wyatt!" she called out as chipper and innocent as she could. "I'm coming. Just give me a minute." She frowned at her mom and squeezed her knee. "No police. We tried that once, remember?" All she'd got was a shrug from the police and extra lawyer bills when Wyatt accused her of breaking custody arrangements. Funny how the onus was on her to prove she'd abided by the decree instead of the other way around.

She cupped Levi's face and smiled as big as she could manage. "Soon as this is over we'll read a book. You wanna sleep with me tonight?"

He nodded, barely appeased by the bribe.

"Deal." She stood, struggling to keep her smile in place while Levi and her mother hustled to their room.

She could do this. For Levi, she'd relocate the damned Sierra mountain range with her bare hands. Snatching her purse off the floor, she sucked in a bracing breath and coiled her hand around the knob. *It won't last forever.* In the last nine months those words had been her mantra. The one hope that kept her sane. But tonight was here and now, and whether she liked it or not, she had an asshole to face.

As bad ideas went, snooping around Natalie's apartment with a bully ex-husband on the loose had to be damned close to the top of the list. Outside Trevor's driver-side window, a run-down 7-Eleven had a mini congregation of thugs huddled off to one corner. They couldn't be more than thirteen at most and were huddled into oversized hoodies to fight off the incoming cold front.

The quiet strains of Chris Stapleton's latest release disappeared, replaced with the automated feminine voice from the GPS. *"In a quarter mile, make a right turn on Mount Auburn Avenue."*

Shaking his head, Trevor gauged the distance on the onscreen map and fought the urge to cancel the program. He rarely stooped to using the feature that had come with his newest truck, but tonight speed seemed more important than feeding his pride.

He took the turn indicated and coasted another half a block, checking out both side windows for numbers on mailboxes.

"Your destination is ahead on the right."

As soon as the guidance trailed off and the music kicked back into play, Trevor pulled up to a smallish parking lot. The building behind it wasn't the worst apartment complex he'd ever seen, but it wasn't the best either. No gates or signs of security, and probably older than the ranch he'd grown up on, but the grounds were well kept and a few antiquated streetlights cast a moderate glow.

He snatched the Post-it he'd jotted Natalie's address on and compared it to what he'd punched in on the nav.

Yep. Definitely the right place. For some reason, seeing her Lexus in the employee lot and appreciating the simple but quality clothes she'd worn for work every night, he'd expected something completely different. Then again, all he'd really had time to learn about her was that she seemed undaunted when it came to tackling new tasks and looked damned fine doing it, which made him seriously reconsider only doing cursory background checks on entry-level employees.

This whole thing between her and her ex wasn't his business. With his past and penchant for violence, he was twenty shades of stupid for being here, but he just couldn't shake the instincts urging him to intervene. To step in and protect her no matter what the cost.

Wyatt's an idiot, but not enough to break down the door.

How many times had he heard his mother with that same fear in her voice? That same dread? No one had helped her, and look how that had ended up.

He swung his Silverado Dually into a wide spot at the back of the parking lot and killed the engine. Being here might be stupid, but he would *not* abandon Natalie the way everyone had his mom.

He'd barely put one boot on the cracked asphalt when voices sounded in the distance, one woman and one man. They weren't exactly shouting, but it wasn't a private affair either. More like a heated debate with the potential for a full-blown toe-to-toe.

Ahead, a sidewalk ran between two long buildings that faced each other. He followed it. Natalie's light Texas drawl grew clearer with each step, but with the way the voices ricocheted through the tight space he couldn't judge which apartment was hers. He'd just about neared the staircase when she and her ex came into view on the top floor standing just outside the corner unit. He ducked under the landing right beneath them.

Despite the calm delivery behind Natalie's words, her voice shook with impatience. "He was just with you four days ago, Wyatt. The court said we switch every week. This is my week."

"I don't give a fuck about the courts," Wyatt said. "He's my boy, and I'm gonna see him when I want."

"Well, you can't see him now. He's not here."

"After nine o'clock on a school night, and he's not here? Don't shit me, Nat. You keep that boy so locked to his schedule, he wipes his ass by the clock."

"Well, he's not. Mom took him to a movie."

Not a bad tactic, but not one that would work long-term. Not with a dick like her ex.

"Then maybe I need to file a case for sole custody seeing as how my boy's mother doesn't have enough common sense to have her kid home on a school night." He scoffed. "Hell, looking at this place, I'm thinking I ought to file regardless."

"It's safe, and it's clean."

Movement sounded above Trevor, and Wyatt's voice dropped low and menacing. "He's in there, and I know it. Now, open the goddamned door, Natalie."

Trevor was in motion and jogging up the stairs before his mind could reassess the action. Adrenaline surged fast and furious, but he reined it in tight. No matter how much he might want to blame his response on his past, his gut told him otherwise. That no matter how odd the idea felt inching beneath his skin, nothing else mattered except protecting Natalie and her kid. He rounded the top landing and forced his steps into an easy amble.

Nat's eyes got bigger than a July full moon.

Wyatt, on the other hand, sneered like he'd just watched a vagrant take a shit in plain sight, and damned if that didn't give Trevor exactly the plan he needed to knock that son of a bitch off his high horse. It may not be as satisfying as pounding the fucker into next week, but he'd be damned if he let some arrogant, polo-wearing bastard get the better of him. "Hey, darlin'," he said to Natalie, still twenty feet away. "What's goin' on?"

"Um." She glanced back and forth between him and Wyatt and wiped her palms on her thighs. "My ex stopped by for a chat."

So far so good. Hopefully, she'd clue in to what he was up to as fast as she'd learned how to wait tables. He slid up next to her, wrapped one arm around her waist, and pulled her tight to his side.

One second.

A mere step and the touch of her body against him, and his world clicked into place. "Yeah?" he said, a little surprised at how casual his voice came out. "You sounded upset." He kissed her temple and the scent of wildflowers surrounded him. Peaceful. Grounding him even as the fury fanned higher. He glared at Wyatt. "There a reason my woman's upset?"

Wyatt's gaze shot from Trevor's possessive grip on Nat's waist to Trevor's face. "Your what?"

"My woman." Fuck, but that sounded good. A little too good, actually. "Been seein' Natalie for about a month now and don't enjoy stopping by to make sure she got home from work all right to find her trading heated words with her ex."

Wyatt scowled at Natalie. "You're fucking someone else?"

She might have been stunned stupid up until that

point, but the crass comment kicked that stubborn streak he'd glimpsed earlier into high gear. Mirroring Trevor's action and wrapping her arm around his waist, she lifted her chin a fraction. "We're divorced, Wyatt. The day the judge signed the paper was the day it stopped mattering who I see or what I do with them."

"Not with my boy in there."

She fisted Trevor's shirt just above his jeans, and Trevor gave her hip a reassuring squeeze. "Trevor never stays when Levi's here," she said. "He only stops by to make sure I make it home. Those are the rules in the divorce decree, and I keep them."

"Those are the rules today." Wyatt scanned Trevor head to toe and cast an evil smile at Natalie. "We'll see how quick you are to jump in bed with someone else when I take your boy." He huffed and spun for the stairwell.

Muscles bunched tighter than a guy-wire in straight-line winds, Trevor fought the need to stride after the uppity jackass and throw a few threats of his own. Hell, he'd be content just to land a handful of punches. Though, God only knew what trouble that would cause Natalie after it was over.

Together, they waited, both of them eyeing Wyatt's progress through the parking lot to his shiny black Mercedes without saying a word.

When the door slammed shut and the engine revved, Trevor spoke. "He really gonna follow through on that claim?"

Nat sighed, and her shoulders sagged. "With him, there's no telling. He doesn't want Levi around. Hasn't since I got pregnant a year into our marriage, but he does want me. Or thinks he does." Only after Wyatt sped out of the parking lot did she drop her arm from his waist and hang her head. "Levi makes good leverage."

The loss of contact threw him for a loop, and for three or four heartbeats he grappled for what to do next. Part of him wanted to give in, chase Wyatt down, and end Natalie's problems for good, but most of him was fixated on how to get her next to him again. Without her body next to his he felt unbalanced. Awkward, like someone had forced his feet into new boots that fit all wrong.

Behind them, a metallic clink rattled from the window.

Trevor shifted in time to see the window blinds swing. "That your apartment, or a neighbor's?"

Nat closed her eyes and frowned. "That's mine." She dug in her purse and pulled out her keys, but the door swung open before she could use the lock.

An older woman about Natalie's height and build beamed at him from the threshold. Her hair was full gray, but there was no mistaking the resemblance between her and Natalie. Clinging to the woman's thigh and staring up at him with big eyes was the most adorable kid he'd ever seen. Sandy blond hair that was long enough it hung close to his hazel eyes. Definitely his daddy's genes, but on him they were pure goodness.

"Natalie, are you going to invite your friend in?" Her mother stepped forward as best she could with a kid glued to her leg. "I'm Maureen Dubois, Natalie's mom. This is her son, Levi." She patted the boy on the back. "Say hi to the man, sweetheart."

Levi swallowed big enough his head bobbed, but he released his hold on his grandmother, straightened, and stuck out one hand. "Hi."

Careful not to scare the kid, Trevor stepped forward and clasped his little palm. "Hey, bud. I'm Trevor. I work with your mom."

Levi's eyes got big like the sum of two plus two had just clicked in his head. "You're my mom's boss. I know 'cause she talked about you a lot for like three days."

"Did she?" Interesting. Especially since she seldom met his gaze when they talked. He'd assumed it was because he intimidated her somehow or she just kept things cool at work, but maybe there was another reason for the evasive technique. Definitely another puzzle he'd have to piece together. Trevor grinned at Natalie beside him and offered his hand to Maureen. "Nice to meet you, ma'am. Sorry if I woke you up. I just wanted to make sure Natalie made it home."

"Nonsense." She stepped back and waved him through the door, not the least bit upset to be talking to a stranger in her pink-and-gray pajama set. Come to think of it, the outfit looked a lot like the sets his adopted mom, Bonnie, had worn around at night, only Bonnie always favored blue. "Why don't you come in and visit a bit?"

Well, this was awkward. Coming home with a woman was one thing. Chitchatting with a woman, her mom and kid took things to a whole different level. "I appreciate the invitation, but—"

"He might come back," Levi blurted. "He's already been by four times tonight, and Mom says he's per-sastant."

Natalie moved in quick and cupped her son's shoulder. "It's *persistent*, Levi. And Mr. Raines has already done more than I can thank him for."

Reevaluating, Trevor wasn't too sure he'd done anything but stir up trouble. Yeah, he'd stalled the dickhead for tonight, but men like Wyatt seldom gave up without some kind of grenade tossed over their shoulder. Nothing pissed a man off more than another one marking their old territory.

He nodded to Maureen. "Levi probably needs to get his sleep."

"Oh, Levi's got another thirty minutes at least." Maureen grinned huge, a happily scheming momma if he'd ever seen one. "And Levi's right. Wouldn't hurt to have you here for a little while at least."

Trevor coughed and rubbed his chin, too chicken to make eye contact with any of them. Staying was a bad idea on so many levels he couldn't even count them all.

Nat smiled at him, the expression soft and mixed with gratefulness and resignation. "It's okay, Trevor. I appreciate what you did. We'll be okay."

Translation: *You staved things off for one night, but this won't be the last time we deal with it.*

Well, fuck that. She might have to deal with it on another night, but for this one at least, he could make sure the monkey stayed the hell off her back. He winked at Levi and planted his hands on his hips. "I reckon I can stay a little while."

Chapter Three

Nothing made a woman realize how tiny and run-down her place was until a six-foot-three hunk of a man ambled in and took his sweet time scanning every detail. A really good-looking, Adonis hunk of man that had scrambled her wits with nothing more than an arm around her waist. As powerful as his touch had been, it would take a week before her body stopped tingling.

Tucking her hands in her back pockets, Natalie cleared her throat and nodded toward the kitchen. "I'm not much of a drinker, but I was thinking I'd make some coffee if you're up for some."

"Oh, that's a great idea." Maureen ushered Levi toward the kitchen with one hand and waved Trevor toward the kitchen table. "Trevor, why don't you and Natalie take a load off, and Levi and I will get a pot going."

Trevor dipped his head in that polite way Natalie had come to appreciate. "Thank you, ma'am."

"You see, Levi?" Maureen said as they rounded into the galley kitchen. "I told you nice men always use good manners."

"But you said men should keep their hair cut too,

and his is long. If I say *yes, ma'am*, can I grow my hair long like his?"

Trevor grinned, ducked his chin, and scratched his jaw like he wasn't sure what to say. When he spoke, his voice was low enough Levi couldn't hear from the kitchen. "Sorry about that."

"Don't be," Natalie said. "Long hair I can deal with, but we've really been struggling with manners. If he takes a cue from you on that score, I'll be grateful." Realizing she was just standing there like a clueless teen, she hurried toward the kitchen and pulled out a chair. At least her mom had been smart enough to steer things toward the kitchen. With only a couch and an old club chair available in the living room, any kind of seating arrangement would have been awkward. "Have a seat."

Instead of following her straight away, Trevor glanced back at the window beside the front door, made quick work of opening the blinds, then strolled to the table. If he'd seemed big in comparison to her apartment before, seeing him rounding the ancient dinette put him on par with a giant. He settled in the chair beside hers with his back to the wall and a straight-on view of the window.

"Are you a real cowboy, or do you just dress like one?" Levi asked from behind her.

Natalie spun in her chair. "Levi, that's a rude question."

"No, it's not," he argued back, innocent as ever. "Bobby says lots of people dress like cowboys, but they're really not." He focused on Trevor, animated and warming up for the details that always followed with stories of his best friend. "Bobby's dad works on a ranch, so he's a real cowboy, but says most people who wear boots just wear 'em to look good. Since you have a bar instead of a ranch, I figured you wear 'em 'cause they're awesome."

"Levi!" Natalie shot to her feet. More than anything, she loved the guileless way her son's mind worked, but not everyone took his comments as lightly as he intended them. "How Mr. Raines dresses and why is none of your business."

"Why do you call him Mr. Raines if he's your boyfriend?" Levi glanced back up at his grandmother. "He told Dad that Mom was his woman, so doesn't that mean he's her boyfriend?"

Her mom patted Levi's shoulder and cast the same patient smile she always used on him. "I think it's rude to eavesdrop and bad form to ignore your momma when she says to still your tongue."

"But—"

"No buts." She lifted her gaze to Natalie and Trevor. "Coffee's brewing. I think Levi and I will call it a night and let the two of you talk." She held out her hand to Trevor. "Mr. Raines, it was nice to meet you."

Trevor stood and shook her hand, but it was a more polite and gentle touch than Natalie had seen him use with men at work. "Call me Trevor, ma'am. And thanks for making the coffee."

"I'm happy to do it." She herded Levi down the hall, a not so simple task considering how Levi kept craning his head around to watch Trevor with those big, adoring eyes. And damn it if that didn't break her heart a little more. That was the way a boy should look at a man. Not constantly ducking his chin and avoiding eye contact the way he did with Wyatt.

The door to their bedroom clicked shut.

"Your mom's a real nice lady," Trevor said, still standing.

Shit. Of course, he wouldn't sit until she did. Which probably explained why her son didn't have a clue on manners. Hard to teach them if she didn't follow them. She eased back into her seat, and Trevor followed suit. "I think she likes you, too." Probably more than Trevor would be comfortable with if he had any inkling what the gleam in her mom's eyes meant. On the plus side, Maureen Dubois's stamp of approval said a lot about a man. Neither her mom nor her dad had cared for Wyatt, and look what ignoring their warnings had gotten her.

Angling his chair for a better angle on Natalie, Trevor reclined in his seat and rested one arm on the table. "Your ex always pull stunts like tonight?"

And there was the rub. The reason why she kept herself so isolated as far as friends or relationships went. Being reminded every day of how stupid she'd been marrying Wyatt nine years ago was bad enough. Having to own it with others was mortifying. She studied the dinette's old cherry veneer and tried to come up with some answer that wouldn't sound as bad as reality.

"You don't have to tell me anything you don't want to," he said, "but it might help me better understand what I jumped in the middle of."

He had a point. And considering he'd bought her and Levi a little wiggle room, he deserved at least the basics. "He wasn't always this way."

Trevor kept his gaze trained on her, his focus utterly undivided. Now that she thought about it, he was always like that. Focused on one thing or person at time, always giving them his full attention. But while his expression stayed neutral, there was something more behind his eyes tonight than she'd seen before. An intensity and a promise that silently encouraged her for more.

She swallowed, hating the truth as it fought its way out. "I got pregnant with Levi right after our one-year anniversary. Things changed after that." She shrugged and smoothed one palm along her thigh. "I tried to fix it, but nothing worked."

"Tried to fix it how?"

God, he was quick. Sharp and always focused on the smallest nuances. She'd need to remember that going forward. "To be the wife he wanted. Social events, lots of friends that weren't really friends, a housekeeper. A plastic surgeon's trophy wife." She met his stare and smiled the best she could. "That just wasn't me."

"How long have you two been split up?"

Not long enough. Every day she prayed Wyatt would find some new focus for his life, and yet the one time he'd backhanded her still felt like it happened yesterday. Like the bruise still pulsed beneath her skin. "About a year. I tried to save up before I walked out with Levi, but time ran out, and I had to make do with what I had. Mom helped. She sold her house and we used the money to cover legal bills and get set up here."

Trevor frowned. "What do you mean, time ran out?"

Oh yeah. Nothing got past Trevor Raines. She scrambled for something to say, anything to put him off course.

He tensed and narrowed his eyes. "He hit you?"

"Uh…"

"Or was it Levi?"

She clamped her lips together hard, fighting the need to run and hide away in her room like she'd always done with Wyatt.

But this wasn't Wyatt. This was Trevor. A man whose employees respected him and who ran a tight ship at work. Who'd calmly walked up beside her and taken a stand against her ex. Although, the way that he studied her now, she was beginning to think her new boss wasn't quite as laid-back as she'd thought underneath.

Trevor's gaze shot to the front door, then back to Natalie. "He got any way of getting in your apartment?"

"No. I told the people who manage the place there's history I'm trying to get away from, so they know better than to let him in. I've told Levi and my mom never to answer the door for anyone."

"So he *did* hit you."

In that second, Natalie half expected Trevor to launch out of his seat and track Wyatt all the way to his fancy Grapevine home. The idea should have terrified her. Or at least have spurred her to defuse Trevor's growing anger. Instead, all she could process was relief. A much-appreciated sense of protection after months of feeling alone, no matter if the sensation was real or not.

"Should have decked the fucker like I wanted." Trevor scanned her tight posture, let out a slow breath through his nose, and unclenched his hand on the table. "Sorry. Abuse is a trigger for me."

It was? The unexpected scrap of information hit her so hard out of left field, she nearly asked him as much, but caught herself before she could let the question air. She'd already shared more with her boss than she should. Asking him personal questions would only clear the path for him to dig deeper in return. "It's okay. I understand."

Behind her, the coffee maker gurgled and hissed as the last of the hot water emptied the reservoir. She stood and motioned for Trevor to keep his seat when he started to do the same. "Relax. I appreciate the manners in front of Levi, but it's not necessary with me. How do you take your coffee?"

"Black's fine."

Natalie shuddered and pulled out a few of her mother's oversized clay mugs. The yellow cups had been in her mother's kitchen as long as she could remember and would probably work as self-defense weapons given how heavy they were, but they brought good memories. "I don't know how anyone can drink the stuff straight. I need almost as much milk and sugar in mine as I do coffee."

"Got a sweet tooth, huh?"

She poured the coffee and slid the carafe back on the burner. "Guilty. Pastries, cakes, or candy, it doesn't matter. I'm a glutton." Pouring milk in one cup, she huffed out a chuckle. "Makes keeping my booty a reasonable size a bit of a challenge the older I get, but if I have to choose between dessert or a small behind, then I'll take dessert, thank you very much."

She finished off stirring in her sugar, turned with both mugs in hand, and nearly stumbled mid-stride back to the table.

Trevor's smile was gone and his smoldering gaze took a long, leisurely trip up her body. "If sweets are what give you those curves, I'd say it'd be a damn shame for anything healthy to pass your lips."

Dear Lord in heaven. How any woman alive could keep from melting into a puddle of goo beneath that expression, she'd never know. It'd been years since a man had looked at her like that, and wowza, did it do a number on her girly parts.

"Thank you." It was a lame retort, but what else was she supposed to say? No matter how good the attention felt, he was still her boss. Even if he wasn't, she wasn't sure she'd ever be up for tangling with another man. Clearly, her judgment wasn't sound enough to pick healthy partners.

She set his coffee in front of him and carefully took her seat, blowing across the top of her mug and studiously avoiding his gaze.

"Your kid's a hoot." One simple, easy statement and he had them back on track.

Part of her was reluctant to let the moment go, but it was probably for the best. "He's the spitting image of his dad at that age, but they couldn't be more different in personality. Levi's got a huge heart. And he's smart. Never misses anything." Some of the moment's light-heartedness dimmed. "Especially not the struggles I was having with Wyatt. Even as a toddler, he steered clear of his dad or found creative ways to keep us apart."

"How the hell did an abusive dad end up with joint custody?"

For a moment, she thought about deflecting and keeping them in safe conversational territory, but having someone to talk to, someone willing to simply listen for once, was too tempting to pass up. "Because Wyatt is nothing if not connected. Aside from the car and our clothes, I didn't ask for anything in the divorce except for custody of Levi. So naturally, that's the one thing he wanted."

"But he hit his own kid. The judge didn't factor that in?"

She shook her head and cupped both hands around her mug on the table. "It only happened once to Levi, and once to me before that. When he hit me, it woke me up. I started planning and saving. But when it escalated to Levi, I knew I couldn't wait any longer. I got us out as soon as Wyatt left for work the next day. Only problem was, the mark Wyatt left on Levi's cheek wasn't enough to convince the police Levi had done anything except fall off a bike. Wyatt played me up as a vengeful wife, and the judge bought it."

On the surface, Trevor seemed to keep his cool, but the air around him changed. Whatever it was that somehow tied him with abuse, it was entrenched deep.

She laid one hand on his wrist and squeezed. "Let it go. God knows that's what I'm trying to do."

Trevor's gaze dropped to the place where her hand rested. Almost as quickly, he circled his wrist, bringing her hand so it rested inside his palm, and smoothed his thumb against her knuckles. "Hard to let it go when he's knocking on your door."

"True." Much as it killed her to do so, she pulled her hand away and sipped her coffee, the warmth of his casual but oh-so-delicious touch heating her from head to toe. He was her boss. Nothing else. "Eventually, Wyatt will fixate on something or someone else, and he'll accept I'm not coming back. That's my hope anyway."

"That's what he wants? You two to reconcile?"

"No, he made it quite clear what a disappointment I was as a wife. According to him, my getting pregnant ruined our marriage. He wanted someone to attend events and travel with him when it suited, not the responsibility of a parent. Though, if you ask me, what really pissed him off was that he wasn't the center of attention anymore."

"Then why's he coming around?"

"Because he can't have me, and Wyatt always wants what he can't have." She winced. "That sounds really pompous doesn't it?"

"Not if it's the truth. And he wouldn't be the first man who didn't know how to take no for an answer."

"What about you?"

He cocked his head and crossed one foot over his knee. It'd been forever since she'd owned a pair of boots. Well over a decade, in fact, but she'd bet good money his black boots were top-dollar Luccheses. "What about me?"

"I've spilled my guts since you got here, and all I know about you is you've got the patience of a saint and are Deep Ellum's reigning pub king."

"Pub king?"

She shrugged. "That's what Ivan calls you. He says most bar owners don't hold a following in that part of town as long as you've been able to."

He smiled and rubbed his knuckles along his chin. He didn't quite have a five-o'clock shadow yet, but she'd bet he'd have an irresistible one first thing in the morning. Clean shaven, he was dreamy, but with some stubble he'd be every daddy's worst nightmare. "I got lucky with The Den. Though my brothers know bars like a native language. They guided me into it. My real love is flying."

She raised her eyebrows, silently encouraging him for more.

"Been flying since I was eighteen. Once I met my brothers, I set out to make it my profession. Now I've got a private charter service."

"What do you mean you 'met your brothers'?"

His expression blanked. It wasn't a complete shut-down, but more of a topic he didn't quite seem ready to share. "Long story." Picking up his mug, he uncrossed his leg and stood. "It's late, and according to your application, you've got a day job tomorrow."

She nodded and stood as well, torn between begging him to sit back down, and welcoming the chance to be alone and gather her wits. Funny, looking back at the time since he'd arrived it was more than just the physical contact that had shaken her. It was the connection, too. The ease of talking to him and the way he made her feel safe just by being here.

She took his mug and carried it to the sink. "Thank you again for what you did. I know you didn't have to, but I'm hoping it'll get Wyatt to back off for a little while." Not to mention her baby boy would be chattering nonstop about manners and cowboy boots for days.

"You're my employee, Natalie. You don't have to thank me."

See? That's all his action had been grounded on. A good man looking out for someone he felt responsible for. Still, lightening the mood with a little playfulness couldn't hurt. She planted a hand on one hip and leaned into the counter. "You're telling me you spend a lot of time checking up on all your waitresses after hours?"

"Nope. I'm saying I've got a vested interest in you having your head in the game at work. If that means helping you not worry about your boy by stepping in, it's a no-brainer." He grinned. "Plus, it satisfies the shit out of me for a man like Wyatt to get a little of his own medicine."

With that little quip, he winked and sauntered to the door.

Natalie followed, shamelessly enjoying the way his

faded jeans molded to his very nice ass. Funny, she couldn't remember the last time she'd ogled a man, but Trevor was a prime candidate for brushing up on long-dead skills.

He opened the door, studied the parking lot beyond, and motioned at the blinds he'd opened. "You close those up, and lock up tight, all right?"

"Yep. Got it."

For a handful of heartbeats, he just stood there, studying her. "Want you to promise me something."

She tilted her head. "What kind of promise?"

He narrowed his eyes and stepped close. The same woodsy cologne that had coiled around her when he'd tucked her tight to his side assailed her senses and sent her heart kicking in a happy rhythm. "I appreciate you've told your mom and Levi not to answer the door, but if your ex comes back, I want your promise you won't answer the door either. And I don't give a fuck what kind of beef the cops gave you in the past. He shows, you call 'em anyway."

"That's two promises."

God, he had an amazing smile. Gorgeous white teeth and a roguishness that made her insides tingle. "Yeah, it is. Now tell me you'll do what I asked."

She nodded, too muddled by his presence to do anything else.

"Good." He cupped the side of her face and brushed his thumb along her cheekbone, the simple touch alighting flutters in places she really shouldn't feel for her boss. If she could have frozen the moment, she would have done it in a second. Savored every heightened sensation and clung to it on the nights when loneliness and fear crept in.

"If the cops don't treat you the way they should, you let me know." He dropped his hand and the loss resonated through every part of her, a chill that had nothing to do with the open door licking beneath her skin. He strolled out the door, but there was no missing the dark promise in his parting words. "Wyatt's not the only man with connections."

Chapter Four

Texas might be the closest thing to hell on earth in the summer, but in late October there was no place better. Seventy-two degrees and not one cloud in the sky. If it weren't for the twenty-plus errands still left to tackle before sunset, Trevor would ditch reality and get a bird in the air. As it was though, The Den's first Halloween bash was only four days away and he was nowhere near ready.

He pulled his truck up outside Beck and Knox's security office and punched the gearshift into park. Aside from the badass brushed steel sign that read Citadel Security above tinted, double glass doors, the single-story building had zero personality. Just sterile gray concrete that stretched a good fifty feet in either direction and some shrubbery hardy enough it could live through three droughts and still not die.

He was still five feet away from the entrance when the security latch clicked open. Trevor swung the door wide and found Knox's newest employee perched behind her pristine desk, smiling ear-to-ear. On first blush, she didn't seem the intellectual type. More like a woman who'd choose a trip to the spa or a shopping trip over networks and hardware. But the second anyone got past general introductions and steered toward technical jargon, the pretty little blonde bowled people over with her smarts.

"Good to see you again, Mr. Raines."

"Good to see you too, Katy, but if you don't quit calling me by my last name, I'm gonna make Knox give you nothing but outdated computers to work with."

"He'd have to pry my babies out of my cold dead fingers first." She smirked and waved him toward Knox's office on the right. "Go on back. He's waiting for you."

Of course he was. Knox was nothing if not plugged in, especially where his brothers were concerned. The first thing he'd done when Trevor had bought his newest truck was install a tracking device. Ever since, Trevor'd been a little afraid to drink too much around the guy for fear he'd pass out and wake up with a tracker installed at the base of his skull.

He strolled down the long hallway, the glass walls on both sides showcasing a whole lot of technical muscle. Tidy wires ran in neat rows up the backs of each server stack then disappeared in iron grids above, but it was the soft blue glow emanating from overhead and behind the equipment that gave the rooms a space-age edge. He rapped two quick knocks on the ebony door at the end and pushed it open without waiting for an answer.

A blast of air to rival a January cold snap hit him hard. "Damn, brother. It's October, not August. What's with the overdone AC?"

Knox's fingers worked fast and furious on the keyboard, his eyes locked on one of four oversized monitors arranged in a semicircle around him. "Your horses like working hard in the heat?"

"Not if they can help it."

"Well, neither do mine. Mine just run on wires and electricity instead of flesh and blood." He hit the enter button a few times and spun in his uber-sleek office chair. Mounted high on the wall behind him were at least fifteen smaller monitors with feeds from all kinds of businesses that relied on his and Beckett's watchful eye. "What brings you to my electronic empire?"

Trevor dropped into one of the cushioned chairs in the sitting area to one side of Knox's command central. It was way more contemporary than anything he'd ever want to be surrounded by, but it was comfortable and fit Knox's super-spy vibe. "Want to have you take another look at Ivan Bower."

"Your new manager?"

"Yep. I invited him out for Thanksgiving, but I'm thinking it's time to dig deeper in his past."

Knox raised both eyebrows. "You're putting him up for the brotherhood?"

"Maybe." God knew, he'd never met a man more willing to put himself out there. Ivan might have first been hired as a bouncer, but he'd worked his way up to his new position by taking on any task needed. Hauling trash, dealing with puking drunks, and calming down irate customers—he dealt with them all with the same care and attention he put on each night's bank deposit. And while Ivan had never shared much about his past, Trevor had a hunch it was ugly. It said something about a man who went through hard times and still came out whole on the other side. "Thought you guys could talk him up and see what your instincts say."

"Kinda early for a deep dive then, isn't it?"

"Not gonna bring it up at rally unless I'm sure he's good for us."

Knox shrugged and anchored one leg over the other. "Easy enough."

In one of the monitors, a feed from The Den caught his eye. This early in the day there weren't much in the way of customers, just a few businessmen who'd ditched work early for a drink and some hipsters hanging at the bar. For about the twentieth time that day, his mind shuttled back to Natalie. How she'd looked at him before he'd left last night. Those brown eyes of hers had been big enough a man could drown and lose himself in a heartbeat if he wasn't careful. And those lips? Yeah, he'd do well to keep a safe distance between him and his curvy employee.

"Something else on your mind, or did someone kick your dog?"

Trevor frowned and refocused on Knox. "Need you to do some digging on a guy named Wyatt Jordan. He's a plastic surgeon. Lives in Grapevine."

Knox spun to his keyboard and started typing. "Why does that name sound familiar?"

How the guy got his fingers to move that fast and not come out with a whole lot of gobbledygook, Trevor would never know. Heck, he did good to use his two pointy fingers and not fuck up whatever he was typing. "You did a base-level background check on my new waitress a few weeks back. Natalie Jordan. Wyatt's her ex."

"Little brunette? Has a young kid?"

"That's the one."

Knox stopped typing and faced him, his focus about five times sharper than seconds before. "What's she to you?"

"Besides an employee, nothing, but I broke up a

shouting match between her and Wyatt last night, and I wanna know what kind of blowback it might earn me."

"What kind of shouting match?"

"The kind that made it crystal clear he's a narcissistic jackass with a hot head. I gotta assume he knows where she works, and I'm certain I pissed him off, so I wanna know what kind of history he's got."

Knox's office door opened just as Knox asked, "Pissed him off, how?"

Beckett back-and-forthed a look between the two of them. "Pissed off who?"

Knox nodded at Trevor. "Trev butted in between an employee and her ex."

Beckett winced, shut the door behind him, and sauntered to the chair next to Trevor. "Not a good move. Thought you were the level-headed one of us."

"I am until a man threatens a woman. Then I tend to lose my shit." The scary part was the level of fury he'd felt staring down Natalie's ex was about ten times what he should have felt for a woman he barely knew. No way in hell was he sharing that tidbit with his brothers, though.

Beckett's relaxed posture went on-point in a second. "What kind of threats?"

"Standing outside her apartment late at night and demanding she get her boy out of bed so he could see him. Threatening to take her to court for full custody when what he really wants is to fuck with Natalie."

"That a common pattern?" Knox asked.

"He hit her place up four times last night before she finally came out to deal with it," Trevor said. "Nat says he's kept his hands off her so far, but he's got a history of violence prior to the divorce, both with Nat and the kid."

Knox frowned, his gaze distant for a second, before

he swiveled back to his computers. "Could have sworn the divorce decree said irreconcilable differences."

Trevor scoffed. "Yeah, what she couldn't reconcile was getting backhanded anymore. The judge is apparently a friend of Wyatt's and ignored her abuse claims. He actually granted joint custody."

"Hold up." Beckett sat up and planted his elbows on his knees. "You said this went down at her place?"

Knox glanced back at Trevor and waggled his eyebrows. "Excellent point. Share more about that."

Trevor shook his head and scowled at Beck. "It's not what you think. I overheard her talking to her ex before she left work and followed a hunch."

Beckett grinned.

Knox chuckled. "A hunch? Is that what they're calling sassy brunettes these days?" He looked to Beckett. "You should see her, brother. Posts all kinds of shots of her and her kid on Facebook. A mix of homemade apple pie and pixie all rolled up into one."

Boy, he'd hit that one on the head. Though, he'd failed to mention her sweet curves. Ever since Trevor had pulled her next to him and palmed her hip, his mind had been more than happy to remind him how good she'd felt.

His phone let out a sharp ring. He slid it out of his back pocket, intent on punching the silence button until he saw the name on the screen. "Sorry, guys. I gotta get this."

Knox shrugged and spun back to his computer.

Beckett kicked his feet up on the ottoman. "Take your time. I'm not going anywhere until I hear more about Miss Homemade Apple Pie."

Trevor huffed out a chuckle and swiped the screen. "Been a while, Doc," he said into the phone.

That perked Beck and Knox's attention, both of their gazes homing in Trevor.

Doc Stinson had sounded terminally exhausted ever since Zeke had introduced him to Trevor over a year ago. Though, when you spent your days trying to save people with next to no chance at living, it probably took its toll on even the hardiest person. "Yeah, well. My preference would be you never had to hear from me."

"I take it that means you've got another one?"

"Stomach cancer," Doc said. "We've tried everything we can get our hands on, but he's not responding. There's a new experimental drug being manufactured in Germany. Was hoping you could work your magic again."

Magic was a bit of a stretch. More like illegal importing with a hope and a prayer his international passengers covered what he was doing. "Who's the patient?"

"A man in his early forties. Family guy. Has a wife who's as nice as can be and two daughters, one thirteen and one nine." Doc let out a sigh and got quiet. "I want 'em all to make it, but this guy's worth going the extra step for the win. I wouldn't ask if he wasn't."

"I know you wouldn't." And Trevor didn't even consider the risk unless Doc vouched for them. He scratched his jaw and mentally rifled through his upcoming trips. "Let me see what I can work out. If I can swing something, I'll call you for the details."

"Appreciate it. Tell Zeke I said hello."

"You got it." Trevor killed the call and tossed his phone next to Beckett's boot-shod feet. "Damned if I know how I'm gonna pull this one off."

"Zeke's friend needs another run?" Beckett asked.

"Some drug out of Germany. One of his patients has stomach cancer and is out of options." Trevor dropped his head back on the cushioned chair back and studied the ceiling. If he took the job, it'd be his fourth gamble, but it could also be the fourth life he'd helped save. Knowing three people were still breathing because of his actions made it awful compelling to make the run happen.

"You worried about the risk?" Knox asked.

Trevor shook his head. "Not the risk so much as the logistics. I've got no overseas hauls in the next month, and if I'm gonna cover the expenses, I'll have to add a load of those cosmetic meds again."

Knox snagged a pen up off his desk and twirled it between his fingers. The poor guy had more problems sitting still than Zeke ever had, and the only way he managed to sleep at night was the release he earned via the never-ending stream of women who graced his bed. "I keep telling you. Keep to the booze runs. They're easier."

"They're easier, but they take up a ton of space in the plane and don't make nearly as much," Trevor said.

"Then have the patients cover the difference," Beckett said.

"No way in hell I'd go that route." Trevor sat up straighter and snagged his phone. "By the time they've done all these treatments, Doc says their money's usually maxed out. What I make on the injectables covers the cost of the flight as well as the drugs."

"Brother, you're pushing it," Knox said. "You forget I'm the one who dropped all the extra cash you cleared from the last haul into that sick lady's bank account. You could cover the cost with the booze."

Maybe. But if people wanted to spend their hard-earned money shooting their faces up with drugs that were admittedly beyond the FDA's approval, then he had no problem passing on the profit to people who just wanted to live. He checked his watch and stood. "I gotta get back to The Den. Ivan can only cover for a few more hours."

Beckett stood as well and gave him a stern look. "Knox is right. Think about it. Penalties on alcohol aren't gonna be near as hard on you if you get caught."

Trevor nodded and strolled to the door. "You gonna run that check on Natalie's ex?" he said to Knox.

"Yep. How fast you need it?"

"When you can. Odds are it'll be a wasted drill, but if he's a nutcase with a history, I want to be prepared."

Trevor hated it when Knox was right. Considering the brainpower generated between Knox's ears, this particular I-told-you-so was just one of many.

He stared at the numbers on his screen and tapped his pen on his desk. If he could get a high-end client for an overseas trip, he could take the G6 and squeak by with enough liquor to cover the price of the meds.

Then again, not just any passenger could swing the price tag that came with his Gulfstreams, and a smaller plane meant less space to haul with. Injectables took next to nothing in storage, and if this patient was like the last three, their bank account was likely in the red.

"Fuck it." He snatched his burner phone out of his bottom desk drawer and dialed up the faceless middleman he'd used for the last two trips. Zeke had indirectly turned Trevor on to his contact months ago, but no one had ever met him. The mystery man just paid for and accepted delivery of the goods wherever Trevor left them, then peddled the merchandise for God only knew what kind of markup.

By the fourth ring, Trevor was just about to hit the end button when a familiar but groggy voice answered. "Hello?"

"Kind of late for a working man to be asleep, ain't it?"

Apparently, Trevor's voice was enough to shake the sleep off, because the next time Middleman spoke, he seemed wide awake. "Was wondering when I'd hear from you again."

Which was why Trev switched phones after every transaction. The faceless/nameless routine worked both ways. "There a market for any more of the shipment I brought in this summer?"

"Enough I could sell your last shipment twice over. Everyone wants to be young these days. You give me a date and I'll be ready."

It was almost too easy. Although, he'd still have to find a passenger. Without it, the trip would be too risky. "No date yet, but I'll let you know when I've got one."

"Make it before Christmas, would ya? My kids are on me for some new game system."

Trevor grunted and ended the call before he could volley back with something nasty. Talking with the guy never sat well with his instincts, and he couldn't care less about what the guy's kids got for Christmas. The only thing that mattered in this scenario was someone actually living through the holiday and the ones that came after.

He popped the battery out of the phone and dropped it back in his drawer.

Before he'd closed it, two short raps sounded on his office door. "Yeah."

It opened a second later and Ivan towered in the entry. Bulk-wise, he gave Beckett a run for his money, and between his dark skin, muscles, and long dreads, the guy could stop a belligerent drunk with little more than a glare. He could also cock a smile, crook his fingers and have any number of women jumping in his lap. "Inventory's done, and Vicky's running the bar," he said. "You need anything before I head out?"

Yeah, he did. Preferably, taking over running his bar and keeping it in the black so he could get back to flying full-time. Of course, then he'd probably get some wild-ass idea and start another business. Flying made for the best brainstorming, second only to working with his horses. "Nope. We're all good. You got Mary tonight?"

Ivan smiled huge at the mention of his four-year-old. He and his baby momma hadn't been an item long enough to do more than procreate and barely tolerated each other for more than ten minutes at a time, but mention of his little girl never failed to bring out a full set of pearly whites. "Got her the whole weekend. Gonna take her out trick-or-treating before the Big Bash kicks into full gear on Monday. You cool with that?"

"Only thing I'd be pissed at is if you missed taking her." He started to wave Ivan off, but caught a glimpse of the curvy woman his mind had been fixated on since last night in one of the security monitors. In less time than it took him to blink, all the rest of the day's hustle and bullshit disintegrated, replaced with the same heated buzz he'd walked away from her with last night. "Thought Nat had the night off?"

Ivan scanned the screens on the wall and latched on to the one with Natalie. "Sarah called in sick. Nat said she'd take whatever extra days I could swing her, so I called."

A good thing for extra cash in Natalie's bank account, especially on a Thursday since half the downtown crowd was ready to blow off a whole lot of stress by then. Not so good when she had a kick-ass kid at home she could be spending time with.

"Something wrong with callin' her in?" Ivan asked.

Trevor shook his head, but kept his focus on the monitor. Hard to do anything else when she was bent over a recently vacated table with her ass on prime display. "Not a problem." *Not one fucking problem at all.* "Just surprised to see her here." He slid his attention to Ivan, a little of the fury he'd felt the night before wiggling its way free. "You ever see a guy in here bugging her since she started? Five-foot-eight, looks like Malibu Ken, and still thinks polos are the shit?"

"Nope. Should I?"

Trevor reclined in his chair and crossed his arms. With anyone else, he'd have to mind what he shared, but this was Ivan. If he couldn't lay shit out there without worrying, Trevor had no business putting him up for the brotherhood. "Not necessarily, but keep your eyes sharp. Him or anyone else gives her shit, I want 'em out. Especially the handsy ones. Had one last night clamoring for her ass."

Ivan's eyes narrowed, enough shrewdness firing behind his gaze to show he was all-too-easily reading between the lines. Between the two of them, every waitress had more than enough protection, but not once had Trevor ever singled one out before.

"I'll talk to Ben and the rest of the guys watching the door," Ivan said. "We'll make sure she's covered."

"Appreciated." Trevor motioned toward the door with a chin lift. "Have a good night with your girl."

"You know it." Ivan grinned and shut the door behind him.

In the monitor, Natalie sauntered up to a four-top and laid a sweet smile on a pair of khaki-wearing businessmen.

The men smiled back and Trevor fisted the hand on his desk. Man, he hoped like hell Ivan kept an eye on her. With the way his mind had been churning through thoughts of last night and the way her body had felt close to his, he'd likely pulverize any poor bastard who hurt her on his watch.

Chapter Five

The closer Natalie got to Elm Street, the sweatier her palms got. It was the second drive-by she'd made past The Den's employee parking lot, once after she'd escaped the monotonous grind of the health care office she worked in and now after her trip to the grocery store. Ever since she'd come up with her cockamamy idea, her body had buzzed on a constant flow of adrenaline. Which, considering the seven-to-four shift she'd just pulled glued to a desk and a telephone, counted as an official form of torture.

She pulled into the lot and circled toward the far end.

Backed into the over-sized slot reserved just for her boss sat Trevor's behemoth truck, the metallic sheen of the silver paint glowing beneath the street lights.

Natalie let out a shaky breath and stared at it, her heart thumping twice as fast as the pop tune playing low on the radio. This was nuts. Absolutely, certifiably insane. But if it meant keeping Wyatt off Levi's back and making her boy's last night at home brilliant, she'd run naked through Times Square.

She parked her SUV and hopped down to the asphalt. The temps had dropped to the upper fifties shortly after the sunset, but it hadn't damped any of Deep Ellum's weekend enthusiasm. Already, the soft chatter of patrons strolling up and down the streets and the muted thump of live music filled the air.

With one hand pressed to her stomach to combat the incessant flutters, she marched inside and scanned for any sign of Trevor. It was barely after seven o'clock and the place was already close to full, which meant everyone on staff would be headed home with a nice chunk of change in their pockets. They'd also have throbbing feet, but Natalie had actually liked that part of her shifts. It reminded her of the days she'd spent in the hospital and the career that would be hers again—just as soon as she earned enough time and money to get her license back.

"Hey, sweet girl. What are you doin' in on your night off?"

Natalie jolted at the sound of Ivan's voice behind her and spun so fast she nearly lost her balance. "Ivan. You startled me."

"I see that." The light smile he'd had on his face slipped, replaced with a sharpened scrutiny. "There a reason my girl's so jumpy?"

"Me?" She tried to play her startled response off with a laugh, but it came out more of an awkward snort. "Not at all." *Liar.* "You just snuck up on me, that's all."

He nodded, but his expression said he wasn't buying it. "So why are you here instead of chillin' with your boy?"

Damn. Time to put her crazy idea into motion. And sooner rather than later, because no way was all this pussy-footing around doing her heart any good. "I needed to talk to Trevor. I saw his truck outside. You think he'd have a minute to talk to me?"

Something flared behind Ivan's gaze. Not a gleam

exactly. More like comprehension. Though what pieces he'd clicked together, she couldn't fathom. "Yeah, I 'spect he'd be glad to give you a minute." He waved her toward the more eclectic half of the bar where the women liked to hang out and the hallway beyond. "He's in his office. Just got in about thirty minutes ago and is running through last night's numbers. Head on back."

Well, that was a plus. At least in his office the noise wasn't so loud, and if she crashed and burned with her request, she wouldn't have a ton of witnesses. "Thanks, Ivan."

"You bet, sweet girl." He grinned and sauntered off, sliding behind the bar and chatting up those seated on the other side like they were his long-lost friends.

Before she could chicken out, Natalie wove between those milling around tables and worked her way toward the office. Trevor was a nice man. Fair and reasonable. He'd proven that more than once in the last few weeks. Best case, he'd graciously accept her offer and keep things as platonic as she meant them. Worst case, he'd draw the line and politely tell her it was a bad idea. Even if he thought her idea was stupid, he wouldn't laugh in her face. At least she hoped he wouldn't.

She paused outside his office door, hands fisted at her sides while her stomach did a Cirque du Soleil routine. *Right. Okay.* She could do this.

She knocked on the door and held her breath.

It took a few seconds before Trevor responded. "It's open, Natalie."

Well, of course he knew it was her. He had those damned monitors mounted up on the wall with a clear view of every inch of his pub. He'd probably tracked her every step from the parking lot.

She opened the door and pasted a smile on her face. He was already on his feet before she'd fully stepped across the threshold, a tall, blond Adonis with sky-blue eyes and a mouth made for sin. "Hey, Trevor. You got a second?"

"Got whatever time you need, darlin'." He rounded the desk, headed for the same leather chair he'd interviewed her from, and motioned her toward the sofa. "Take a load off, and tell me what's on your mind."

Moving away from the door took every ounce of courage she hadn't yet spent. If it was up to her, she'd stay standing for a quick retreat, but no way would Trevor sit if she kept her feet. She perched on the edge the couch, knees squeezed tight together and hands folded in her lap the same as when she'd interviewed. She was tempted to focus on his chin the way she had those first few days at work so she wouldn't stammer like an idiot, but what kind of person asked another for a favor without eye contact? "Well, first I wanted to thank you again for the other night."

"You already gave your thanks Wednesday night. No need for you to keep giving it when I was happy to step in." He cocked his head in that playful way that always set people at ease. "Now tell me what's got you so uptight I could bounce a quarter off you."

She swallowed hard and the pulse at her throat pounded hard enough to rival the bass reverberating from the sound system outside.

Trevor frowned. "Your ex come back?"

"No!" The word came out so hard, she nearly stood with the force of it. "Nothing like that. I mean, if anything, Wyatt was nice yesterday. He actually called and asked to chat with Levi on the phone. Which was kind of weird because he never wants to talk to Levi one-on-one like that, but since he was being nice I let him."

Anchoring one elbow on the heavily padded chair, Trevor rubbed his knuckles along his jawline. "How'd that go?"

"Good at first."

Trevor got tense. "And then?"

And then her boy had gone from light and breezy to twitchy and uncomfortable. "And then Wyatt started asking him things about my new boyfriend."

Trevor dropped his hand and his face got scary.

"I didn't know what was going on at first," she added quickly. "The conversation was light enough, Levi got into it and was his usual happy self. I left the room for a few minutes to put up the laundry and when I came back everything had changed."

"Levi tell you what Wyatt asked?"

"How long we'd been seeing each other. Why Levi hadn't mentioned you before. What your name was, and what you did for a living."

"But Levi didn't know anything except my name and that you work for me."

"Exactly." She let out a relieved sigh, so grateful Trevor had cottoned on to the problem she was half-way tempted to cry.

"So how do we fix that?"

She smoothed her hands over her knees, the well-worn denim both soft and rough beneath her palms. "He goes back to Wyatt's house Sunday morning. I thought, if you're not too busy and wouldn't mind, I could have you over for dinner tomorrow night?"

Trevor nodded, a quick decisive dip that made her head snap back. "Done."

"It doesn't have to be anything fancy," she said. "Just a little time so Levi could have some answers if his dad prods him anymore."

"Nat—"

"Plus, it'd give us a chance to give you a proper thank-you for what you did."

"Natalie, I—"

"And Levi hasn't stopped asking questions about you since he woke up Thursday morning. He's said *please, ma'am*, and *thank you* so many times in the last few days, my mom's on top of the world. If you came, it would really make his week. Heck, his whole month."

Trevor sat forward, his elbows on his knees and his hands clasped loosely between them. He smiled the same easy grin that left most of the women who strolled into The Den dim-witted and goofy. "I said yes, Nat."

"Oh."

His grin got bigger. "Oh."

She ducked her chin and threaded her fingers together in her lap. "Thank you."

"I keep telling you, thanks aren't necessary. If anyone's a winner in this deal, it's me. Only home-cooked meals I get are when my moms get me out to Haven on the weekends."

She snapped her head up. "You have more than one mom?"

His face softened. "Had two mothers before I was ten, one blood and one adopted. Earned two more when I found my brothers ten years ago. So yeah, I've got more than one."

That was nice. Though with the mother God had given her, she had more than enough. Even in the face of her stupid decisions, Maureen Dubois had stood beside her and fought to bring her back to the light. "I'm glad."

Silence settled between them, a comfortable pause that settled her nerves more than words ever could.

His gaze dropped to her mouth and for a second she half expected him to lean forward and put those wicked lips of his against hers. "What time do you want me there?" he said instead.

She swallowed hard, her mind scrambling up from the mental roadblock the mere idea of his kiss had created. Saturday nights at The Den were always the busiest, so he'd likely want to be back here before things got into full swing. Which was fine considering how early they always sat down for dinner. "Would six o'clock be too early for you?"

"Six o'clock's fine."

"Great. That's perfect." She stood, suddenly eager to get someplace private so she could suck in a steady breath. God knew she'd need a little time to rebuild her defenses before now and tomorrow night. "Thank—"

He cut her off with an upheld hand and moved in close enough his woodsy scent and body heat robbed the rest of her words. "Don't say it again. Already told you I'm looking forward to it." He lifted his chin toward the door, the look on his face saying if she didn't skedaddle quick she might get that kiss after all. "Now get home to Levi, and tell him I'm looking forward to seeing him tomorrow night."

"Yes, sir. I'll do that."

She'd barely got the door opened when he added, "Think you'd better drop the *sir* going forward. Only one scenario where a woman of mine would use that word, and since we're just pretending, I don't expect I'll get to hear it from your lips."

Her eyes popped wide, and her cheeks flamed blow-torch hot in an instant. She couldn't be 100 percent sure he'd meant the comment the way she'd processed it, but Lord, did it conjure up a whole feast of visuals for her already taxed brain.

He winked, clearly tickled with the fact that he'd knocked her for a loop and not the least bit repentant. "See you tomorrow, darlin'."

Chapter Six

Fifty-dollar bottle of merlot in hand, Trevor marched up the steps outside Natalie's house at six o'clock sharp. The gesture was probably overkill, and frankly, he'd rather have brought a stout single malt, but Bonnie would have leapt out of her grave and rained fire and damnation on him if he showed without something in hand. Even more surprising was the fact that he'd *wanted* to make a good impression. The last time he'd had an honest-to-God date with parents even remotely involved, he'd been seventeen and had barely done more than a grab and carry bundle of flowers at the local grocery store. For Natalie, he'd spent the better part of forty-five minutes wandering the aisles of a high-priced liquor store and still wasn't sure going the moderate route was the right pick.

It was just dinner. A chance to perk up her kid and give him some fodder to use with his old man. Nothing else. Though, that didn't mean his mind had failed to offer up a ton of wicked other ideas. Especially after she'd blushed clear to her hairline after his totally inappropriate, but hot as fuck, innuendo.

He knocked on the door and tried to blank his dirty thoughts. Going there was definitely dangerous territory.

Levi's excited little boy voice rang behind the thick door. "I'll get it!"

"Levi." The terse reprimand was all he caught of Natalie's voice before it dropped to little more than muffled words.

A second later, the door swung open and Natalie stood in front of him, cheeks pink and eyes bright. "Hi!"

Maybe it was just him, but the simple phrase came out with a Marilyn Monroe huskiness that turned the crisp October night July-sultry. The way her soft pink sweater and jeans clung to her tits and hips only made it worse. He cleared his throat and wished like hell Levi and Maureen weren't rooted less than ten feet away and watching his every move.

Then again, he had an image to portray. No man worth his salt would let a prime opportunity like this one slide. He stepped through the entry, slid his hand around the back of her neck and pulled Natalie tight against him. The top of her head barely reached his collarbone, but her face was tipped up to hold his gaze, her full, raspberry-pink lips parted on a near-silent gasp. Fuck if he wasn't tempted to see if they tasted as good as they looked.

"Hey, darlin'." He kissed her forehead instead, letting his fingers tangle in her hair just above her nape. The strands were as soft as they looked, the easy waves that made her look like she'd spent her day at the beach tickling his knuckles. He closed his eyes and let his mouth linger a second longer than he should have, soaking up her wildflower scent. Only when her palms gently pressed against his pecs did he ease back. He kept his hold on her nape. "Know you're not a big drinker, but figured if you're cooking, the least I could do is bring wine."

"That's lovely." Maureen pressed her hands together above her heart and hustled forward. With the gleam in her eye, Trevor wasn't sure if she was talking about the wine, or the way he'd barely avoided locking lips with her little girl. She took the bottle Trevor offered and hurried to the kitchen. "It's been forever since I had a good wine. It's so nice of you to make the gesture."

"Happy to do it, ma'am," he said as she disappeared around the corner.

Against his chest, Natalie's hands fluttered as though she couldn't quite figure out what to do with them. He had a few ideas he was tempted to share, but none of them fell into the appropriate-for-company category. She settled for loosely fisting one above his sternum and burying the other in her back pocket. "Levi, can you finish setting the table, please?"

"Sure!" He spun, stopped and looked back. "I mean, yes, ma'am." And then he was off again, scooping up the big stack of utensils laid out on the table with both hands and working his way around the place settings.

Natalie twisted, cocked one eyebrow and lowered her voice. "Laying it on a little thick, aren't you?"

He tried to stave off a grin, but she was just too damned cute to hold it all back. "When a woman asks a man to do a job, the least he can do is aim to knock it out of the park."

Behind them, Levi fumbled a fork that clattered against the wood dinette. Not surprising since he was having a heck of a time doing his job and ogling Trevor and his mom at the same time.

"How about I go help your boy, and you make sure

your mom's not ordering our wedding invitations on the sly?" he said.

"You caught the enthusiasm, huh?"

"I can spot an eager momma at twenty paces." He slid his hand down her spine, more than a little tempted to palm her pert ass. "I don't mind. Havin' you next to me is worth whatever ideas she comes up with. Plus, she's sweet. I like knowin' you've got someone looking out for you."

Natalie bit her lip, her dark brown eyes filling with so much gratitude he decided then and there, Maureen Dubois wouldn't be the only one looking out for her going forward. "Thank you."

"We covered the need for thanks already." This time he gave in and playfully swatted her butt, wishing like hell he could follow it up with a good squeeze. "Now go help your mom. Levi's only got one place setting done, and I'm hungry."

From there the dinner prep went from comical to off-the-charts cute, mostly because Levi chattered Trevor's ear off. In the space of five minutes, the kid had covered every event of consequence at school for the last two days and what he and his buddy had planned for the week ahead.

Just as Natalie and Maureen made for the table with both hands full of platters and bowls, Levi placed the last of the napkins and slid into his chair. "Bobby's mom wanted us to go trick-or-treating at the mall on Monday 'cause she said it was safer and we'd get more candy, but Mr. Randolph said anything but door-to-door was just wrong. So, he's gonna drop us off at one of the big neighborhoods and follow us in his truck."

Trevor stayed standing beside his own chair while the

women loaded up the table with food. "Hey, bud." He dipped his chin toward where Levi was sitting. "How about you hop up and wait till the ladies are done with their table before you settle in?"

Maureen and Natalie both froze for a second, their mouths open and eyes wide.

Levi's gaze darted back and forth between the women and Trevor. "How come?"

"'Cause they made you a nice dinner and you can show 'em how much you appreciate it by not sitting down before they do."

Maureen folded her lips inward as though fighting back a chuckle, and that awestruck gratitude Natalie had given him at the front door blasted back to life.

Levi scrambled to his feet faster than a girl with a June bug stuck in her shorts. "Sorry, Mom. Want me to get anything else?"

"No, Levi. You're good."

"So nice having a man set a good example for Levi," Maureen crooned. "What can I get you to drink, Trevor? Wine, water, or tea?"

"If it's sweet, I'll take tea. Otherwise, water's fine."

"Tea it is then." She bustled back to the kitchen counter and the two glass tumblers filled to the rim with ice. "In our family, there's no such thing as tea without sugar."

"Anything without sugar is wrong in Mom's book," Natalie added. "The first thing she taught me to make were cookies." She motioned Trevor and Levi into their seats and eased into her own.

Following Trevor's lead, Levi slid back into his chair. "Mom made chocolate and peanut butter cookies for dessert. They're my favorite."

"You only get them if you eat your meatloaf and all of your veggies," Natalie said.

Levi wrinkled his nose and lowered his voice just for Trevor. "The meatloaf's awesome, but I have to hold my nose for the Brussels sprouts. They're gross."

Well, he wasn't gonna fight the kid on that one. He'd probably have to do the same, but if it helped Nat get decent food down her kid's gullet, he'd suck it up.

Maureen took her seat and handed Trevor a heaping bowl of mashed potatoes. From there, everything settled into an easy rhythm. Not at all the awkward yet polite conversation he'd expected, but a light, welcome banter more on par with his meals at Haven. What's more, Natalie and her mom could cook. Outside of Bonnie's kitchen, he didn't know many people who could do meatloaf justice, but these two women knew how to do it up right, complete with some kind of sauce that packed a serious kick.

"Levi," Natalie said, "Mr. Raines owns the pub I work at, but he flies airplanes for a living, too."

"Nuh-uh." Levi stuffed a whole sprout in his mouth and talked around it. "That's so cool! Like little planes or great big ones?"

Trevor wiped his mouth and set his napkin back in his lap. "Depends on where I'm going and who I'm taking. But if it's got wings, I'll fly it."

"And they're yours?"

"Yep. My dad took me flying when I was eighteen, and I started learning to fly right after. First one I flew solo in was a single-prop Cessna 152. Now I've got four turboprops, two Citations, a Falcon, and two Gulfstreams."

"I have no idea what that means, but it sounds impressive." Maureen slid her plate back an inch or two and reached for her tea. "Are they for cargo? Or do you charter for people?"

"What's charter mean?" Levi asked.

"It means he flies people where they need to go," Natalie answered before Trevor could.

Levi's head whipped to Trevor. "So you're like a commercial pilot."

"Just like that," Trevor said. "Only I don't have to wear a stuffy outfit, and I'm my own boss."

Levi crossed his arms on the table, his sole focus on Trevor. "Where do you take 'em?"

"Anywhere they want to go."

"New York?"

"Yep."

"France?"

"There too, in one of my bigger jets."

"India?"

"Levi," Natalie cut in. "When he said *anywhere*, that means any place you can think of." She stood, taking her plate with her. "Everybody stay put. I'm just going to get us some more tea. Levi, why don't you get the cookies?"

"Cool!" He spun and darted to the far end of the kitchen where a foil-covered plate sat on the plain gray countertop.

"You're a very busy man, Trevor," Maureen said. "Two businesses can't leave you much time to relax."

Trevor shrugged. Since he'd met Axel and Jace and got his head screwed back on right, it'd seemed he had more than enough time to tackle whatever he wanted and still had some left over. Only in the last six months had he really itched for something different. "Hard to call either of my jobs work. I love flying, and The Den made for challenge and diversity. Plus, Ivan's nearly trained up to handle the bar solo."

Natalie sidled up beside him with a pitcher of tea. "Mom's right though. Don't you ever want to just unwind?"

"Says the mom who works two jobs." Trevor splayed his hand on the small of her back, only realizing what he'd done when Natalie gasped and damned near missed his glass mid-pour.

"Sorry." Actually, he wasn't. Although it was weird as shit he'd taken the action without thinking on it first. Somewhere between the front door and now, touching her had shifted from purposeful to reflex. Which was some seriously scary shit considering their combined pasts. After her history with Wyatt, Natalie deserved a guy who could give her long-term and stable. Not a man born into an abusive family. Eager to dodge any deeper analysis, he focused on Maureen. "When I'm not working, I'm at my ranch."

"I knew it!" Levi hurried up beside him and dropped the now foil-free plate on the table. "Bobby said your boots were probably for show, but I knew better. I bet you've got lots of horses."

Trevor chuckled. Hard not to when the kid got all riled up and animated. Especially when the topic was something that got him fired up, too. "Only five. It's not a working ranch. More like a retirement home for geldings who've put in a hard life. They get a reward for the job they've done, and I get a place where I can ride and relax when I want."

"But you know how to take care of them?"

"'Course I do. I grew up on a working ranch about

an hour north of Houston. I've got a guy who helps me out and makes sure they're taken care of when I'm not there."

Natalie handed out small dessert plates and snatched two cookies off the top of the pile before she strolled to her seat. "How big is your ranch?"

"About seven hundred acres." Trevor took a cookie for himself and handed the plate to Maureen.

She gaped at him for at least three seconds before she shook herself out of her stupor and took the cookies. "That's pretty big for a man who's already busy. How do you take care of it?"

"It's not that big. Not really. My parents' place was five times that. And remember, I've got a crew to take care of things when I need it." He bit into the cookie, the chocolate and peanut butter goodness guaranteeing he'd give Levi a run for his money on scarfing back dessert. "You ever ride a horse, Levi?"

"Nope. I only got to pet one at the fair last year. It was huuuge."

"I'll take you out to my place someday and let you ride one of mine."

Natalie perked up in her chair, her eyes wide with one of those oh-no-you-didn't looks. "I'm not so sure that's a good idea."

"Sure it is," Trevor said, a whole new round of tempting ideas taking root. Long-term might not be his strong suit, but short-term he could handle just fine. "Every kid should get to ride a horse. You can come, too."

"Oh no." She shook her head and wiped her fingertips on her napkin. "I do good with dogs and goldfish. Horses are out of my league."

"You'd be great." To his mind, his horses didn't get

near enough attention. And Deuce was a complete sucker when it came to women. He subtly inclined his head Levi's direction. "It couldn't hurt."

Yeah it was a shit tactic, but the more he thought about it, the less he cared. If even half the reality Natalie had shared was true, Levi was due for goodness. Not to mention, he'd give a lot for some time away from work with Natalie.

"I think it's a fantastic idea," Maureen added before Natalie could argue. "Trevor's right. You've been working so hard to save up for your classes, you could use a break."

"What classes?" Trevor said.

"Mom's saving to get her nursing license again," Levi said around a mouthful of cookie. "She used to work with kids all the time, but then she had me and she couldn't. Now she's gonna do it again."

"I didn't give up my job because of you, Levi. I gave it up because your father asked me to."

"I thought you processed health insurance claims during the day." Sure, Knox had already uncovered the history she left off her application, but background checks seldom offered the nuances of innocent conversation.

"That's a temporary arrangement." Nat's lips pressed together for a second, a tiny flare of the stubborn determination she'd shown so many times at work moving across her face before she banked it and took another bite of her cookie. "I'm not sure I could stomach it for the long run, but my experience at the hospital helped me land it."

"What hospital did you work at?" he asked.

"At Baylor. I was in pediatrics for about a year."

"You ever hear of Zeke Dugan?"

"The trauma doc? Yeah, I've heard of him. He's got a great reputation." Her mouth quirked to one side. "Particularly with the nurses."

"Yeah, well his popularity's probably not as high these days. He's engaged to a pretty little mechanic from Rockwall."

"A mechanic?"

"Yep. A damned good one, too. Sweet." He sipped his tea. "So the classes are for your license?"

"As soon as I get the money saved up, yes. I've got a long way to go, though. Continuing ed. Refresher courses. State exams and licensing fees. It's a lot."

Maureen leaned in and squeezed her daughter's shoulder. "You did it once. You'll do it again."

Of that, Trevor was 100 percent certain. He'd sensed an underlying strength in Natalie the first day he'd met her, but rebooting her life with next to no support from a vengeful ex and a kid and mom to feed took grit most men didn't have.

Levi dusted his hands off over his plate. "Are you gonna stay and watch *X-Men* with us? It's on cable so we'll have icky commercials, but the movie's still awesome."

"Levi, I told you earlier," Natalie said. "Trevor has to work tonight."

"Your mom's right, bud." Though he had to agree about the movie. *X-Men* was the shit even with commercials. "I gotta relieve my guy at the club so he can go spend tonight with his little girl."

Scrunching up his face with the same determination Natalie favored, Levi cocked his head to one side. "You really gonna let me ride a horse?"

"Soon as I talk your momma into it." He held out his hand. "Deal?"

That got Levi's smile back in place, a blinding one full of teeth. He shook Trevor's hand. "Deal!"

"All right then." Trevor stood and nodded to Maureen. "I appreciate you taking the effort with the food, ma'am."

"No effort at all." She stood and picked up the plate of cookies. "Levi, why don't you help me finish cleaning while your mom walks Mr. Raines out?"

"Walks him where?"

Natalie chuckled and handed Levi two fistfuls of dirty napkins and silverware. "To the parking lot, silly."

Levi tracked Trevor rounding the table, locked eyes with him, and grinned huge. "What she means is, she's gonna walk you outside so you can kiss her."

Natalie cleared her throat and tried to downplay the blush setting her cheeks on fire. So much for a low-key, no-pressure end to the night. "Levi, remember how we talked about thinking before you speak?"

Trevor's hand curled around one of Natalie's shoulders a split second before he stepped in behind her, his big, deliciously firm torso tight against her back as he grinned down at Levi. "Kisses aren't a given, bud. Ever. You gotta earn 'em first."

"Well, I think you earned one," Levi said. "You helped set the table and everything."

Good grief, could this moment get any more awkward? "Levi, maybe you should mind your business and leave the grown-up things to us."

Her mother abandoned the dishwasher and the plates still stacked on the counter and wiped her hands on a dishtowel. "Change of plans. I'll help Natalie with the dishes later and get Levi ready for bed now so the two of you can actually talk."

Thank God.

Her body must have echoed her internal relief, because Trevor's body shook with barely retained laughter.

She faced him and crossed her arms, the loss of his heat against her back a downright shame. "I'd apologize, but I love the things that come out of his mouth. Even when they embarrass the heck out of me."

"He says what he thinks, and he's cute as hell. I'd be tickled to have a kid like that."

An entirely different warmth unfurled beneath her sternum, ideas she'd be foolish to let take root painting happily ever afters in her head. Levi deserved someone like Trevor in his life. Someone solid who saw the good in him instead of cataloging every annoyance that came with parenthood.

But Trevor was her boss. A boss that definitely didn't qualify as the happily ever after type. No one had come right out and said it, but every one of the waitresses had commented on his lack of steady relationships. She smiled to cover her melancholy thoughts, uncoiled her arms and headed toward the door. "Come on. I doubt a big guy like you needs an escort to the parking lot, but I can at least see you to the stairs."

"And here I thought you were a date who'd give me the full treatment. I'm a little wounded."

Giggling low, she shut the door behind them and ambled slowly beside him. Even in an awkward moment he made things easy. Like the world moved at a different pace in his presence, unhurried and light. "Thank you for doing this. I know this couldn't have been the most enjoyable way for a man like to you to spend a Saturday night."

He stopped and faced her. Cocking his head, he leaned against the balcony rail, propped his elbows along the top and crossed his ankles. "Kinda curious what *a man like me* means in your book."

She shrugged and stuffed her hands in her back pockets. "I don't know. Someone with an exciting social life, I guess. Definitely not sitting around a tiny kitchen table in a dingy apartment eating meatloaf."

"I ate meatloaf damn near once a week for eleven years of my life. Seein' as how tonight brought back good memories, I'm not complaining." He waggled his fingers between them. "Keep 'em coming. What other preconceived ideas have you got up in that hamster-wheel head of yours?"

She grinned, all too easily sliding into the playful moment. "Probably out flying your fancy planes and meeting important people. Oh, wait!" She held up one hand. "It's Saturday night, so according to the girls at work, you'd be out with some leggy blonde."

"Ah, employee gossip." He ran the back of his hand against his chin and hung his head, one of those classic poses her son used when he knew he was busted, but was having a hard time not laughing in her face. When he looked up, the mischief in his eyes nearly knocked her back a step. He leaned forward and lowered his voice. "At the risk of spoiling my apparent reputation, I really don't date that much."

No. Way. A man with Trevor's swagger and good looks never went without female company for long. "Why not?"

He shrugged and crossed his arms. His answer came

out light, but his gaze didn't quite meet hers. "Just not convinced I'm the best kind of man to settle down."

Metal clinked against the window behind them.

Natalie twisted just in time to watch the blinds Levi had pried open with both hands snap shut.

"I think your boy's chomping to see his momma get kissed," Trevor said. It was a lighthearted comment. A simple yet fond acknowledgement of her son's eager and wide-eyed approach to life. But the tenor of it vibrated through her, low and rumbling like an approaching storm.

She sighed and faced him. "I'm really sorry. He doesn't mean anything by it."

"You got a habit of apologizing for things that don't need it." He pushed away from the rail and prowled the few steps between them. "Been a good night. Great food, good conversation, and killer cookies." He coiled his fingers around her wrist and tugged.

Caught off guard, she lost her balance and splayed both hands against his rock-solid chest. God, he felt good. Warm, strong, and all man, his woodsy scent wrapping her up tight. She swallowed and smoothed her fingers against his button-down, the starched cotton doing little to disguise the muscles underneath. "What are you doing?"

Banding his arms around her, he anchored one hand at her nape and the other low on her back, the heat from his palms seeping clear to her bones. "A man like me gets a chance to round out a night like this with a kiss, he takes it."

Her heart kicked and her stomach did that funny dipidy-doo reserved for roller coasters and teenage heartthrobs. "You don't have to do this," she whispered.

His gaze lingered on her lips then lifted to her eyes. "You gonna stop me?"

She should. He was her boss. A man who could lure any woman into swan diving off a break-neck cliff with a single look. But it wasn't just any woman right now. It was her. And after eight years of nothing but cold and empty and another year beyond that of nothing at all, she couldn't have stepped away from him if she'd tried. "No."

"Good." He cupped the side of her face and lowered his head. His voice vibrated through her, gruff and thick. "'Cause I enjoyed your cookies, but I want a taste of your mouth more."

He claimed it, swallowing her gasp and scattering what was left of her fragile logic in one heart-stealing swoop. Holy smokes, Trevor Raines didn't just kiss. He devoured. Commanded. Possessed and plundered.

And she liked it. The taste of him and the way he demanded her response. The slick, wet glide of his tongue against hers and his effortless control. She rolled up on her toes and wound her arms around his neck.

He groaned into her mouth and palmed the back of her head, holding her in place as he feasted from her lips.

The blinds behind them rattled and Levi's happy squeal echoed behind the glass.

Jolting inside Trevor's arms, Natalie pushed against his shoulders and wiggled free, her heart clamoring as if desperate to escape her torso. God, she was an idiot. Tonight was supposed to be about giving Levi enough to cover if his dad asked more questions, not set him up for long-term disappointment. Heck, in another minute or two she'd have clawed her way up Trevor's torso and wrapped her legs around his waist. She pressed her fingers to her still-tingling lips, too flustered for eye contact. "I'm sorry."

"I'm not."

She lifted her head and her lungs hitched. On the surface, the words might have sounded flippant, but something deep and uncertain moved behind his gaze. Like a man who'd just stumbled onto something unexpected and wasn't quite sure how to process it.

Although, more likely, she was reading too much into the moment. Hard not to with her body still humming from a single kiss. A single, very delicious and heated kiss. "I should head back in."

"You probably should."

Probably should because the awkward factor had gone off-the-charts high? Or *probably should* because he wouldn't be held accountable for what came next? Logic assured it was the former, but the way he kept his body angled toward her made her wonder if maybe he hadn't minded locking lips with a single, sex-starved mother.

Before her mind could add any more fuel to the concept, his gaze slid to the window and his mouth quirked in an almost smile. "Do me a favor and tell your mom and Levi goodnight for me." With that, he tipped his head and turned for the stairs.

She should let him go. Just go inside and not say another blessed word. God knew the next time she saw him at work was going to be weird enough.

"Trevor," she said instead.

He stalled at the top of the stairs with one hand on the iron rail beside him and cocked an eyebrow.

"Thank you," she said. "For everything."

The smile he gave her was pure trouble and promise all rolled up into one. "Darlin', that was entirely my pleasure."

Chapter Seven

She wouldn't get away from him this time. Every other time, something had come between Trevor and Natalie, but this time they were all alone. No mother. No Levi. No one from work. Just him and Natalie alone on his front porch.

She leaned one hip into the porch rail and sipped a cup of coffee, her gaze aimed at the blazing sunset. A soft wind ruffled her glossy dark hair around her shoulders. He knew how it felt in his hands now. Craved the silky feel of it as much as he craved her taste.

Careful not to startle her, he swept it aside and kissed her neck.

Gripping the rail in front of her, she sighed, tipped her head, and gave him room to work. "You don't have to do this."

Yes, he did. Needed to feel her body against his and hear those sweet little sounds she made when he kissed her deep. He slid his hands around her waist, her pink sweater soft against his palms. He should go slow. Knew she deserved slow and steady, but couldn't stop his hands from gliding up and cupping her breasts.

She moaned and let her head drop against his shoul-

*der, covering his hands with her own and arching into
the touch.*

*Fuck, she was perfect. One hundred percent natural,
full breasts more than filling his hands. He plumped
them, grinding his dick against her pert little ass and
teasing her nipples with his thumbs. He wanted them
in his mouth. To toy with and suck on them while she
rode him hard.*

The bed shook, shattering Trevor's dream and jolting him straight into reality.

Lady jumped and spun in an insistent circle at the
foot of the bed, oblivious of the out-fucking-standing
dream she'd just blown to smithereens. She stopped and
dropped back to her haunches, ready to play. Most days
it was cute. A perfect way to start the day. But with his
cock hard and heavy on his belly and no relief in sight,
he had to bite back a curse.

"Yeah, Lady. I'll get you breakfast." He palmed his
dick beneath the covers and squeezed. Almost nothing
kept him from getting up at the crack of dawn, no matter how late he'd been up the night before. Today all he
wanted was to linger where he was. Damn, that dream
had been hot. So vivid his mind had no problem picking
up right where his subconscious had left off.

Lady barked and waggled her tail.

He chuckled and released his cock. He might be
willing to laze in bed with thoughts of his sweet little
waitress, but his border collie never deviated from her
routine if Trevor was home. Fighting it would only drive
them both nuts. Besides, the real-life kiss he'd scored
from Natalie last night was a one-time deal. Stoking
the fire any hotter was a bad idea all around. For him
and for her.

He tossed the sheets aside and padded bare-ass naked across the hand-carved wood floors, his cock bobbing a reminder of his indulgent dream. He tugged some loose pajama bottoms on and headed for the kitchen, Lady close on his heels. The clock over the mantel showed 6:15 a.m., which was actually a little late for Lady's routine, and only a hint of morning lit the skies outside. In another few weeks, the time would shift backward and every room would be bathed in that sweet pre-sunrise glow he'd grown to love as a kid. The only requirements he'd insisted on from his architect after he'd bought his land was to keep the layout simple and give him views from every room. Nothing kept him more centered and balanced than nature, not even his planes. With the design he'd ended up with, he'd come as close to outdoor living as a man could get and still have a roof and walls around him.

Lady bounced beside the back door and circled again, her boundless energy eager to have free rein. He'd barely opened the door before she snaked her limber body through the opening and took off full-steam for the acreage behind his home. In another thirty minutes or so she'd circle back for chow then spend the rest of her morning pestering Thomas while he tended the horses.

Yawning, he snagged one of the handy little single-serve coffee pods Vivienne had turned him on to and popped it in the brewer. Bonnie would have loved the contraption. The first thing she'd done for Frank and Trevor every morning growing up was get coffee brewing and fire up a full breakfast. Didn't matter what time of year it was or how she was feeling, she loved taking care of her crew and always pried herself out of bed to do it.

Almost two years she'd been gone now and the melancholy that came with thoughts of her was still thick. How Frank had adjusted as well as he seemed to on the surface still amazed Trevor. He and Bonnie had been a perfect match. An ideal couple in every sense of the word. For months when Trevor had first moved into their home, he'd had been fascinated by them. How easily they interacted and how open they were with affection. A complete opposite to the shouting and violence that had constantly shaken the home he'd been born into.

The coffee machine gurgled and sputtered out the last of his brew, the rich, nutty scent that came with it filling his open kitchen.

He'd bet Natalie was up already like Bonnie would have been. Heck, the way Levi had knocked back his meatloaf last night, she probably had to feed the kid five meals a day to keep him sated. She'd do it though. He hadn't learned much about her in the last few weeks, but he'd seen enough to discern she had the same quiet strength as the woman who'd raised him. That she didn't just go through the motions of raising her son because she had to, but because she loved being a mom and taking care of her family. Exactly the kind of woman he wanted for himself.

Except that kind of woman deserved a man like Frank. Calm. Solid and patient. For years, Trevor tried to emulate him. To keep the fire that burned inside him banked and far away from the people he loved.

You're nothing like your biological father.

He wished Zeke was right. More so since he'd actually met a woman worth wishing for. He grabbed his phone off the charger and sipped his coffee on the way to the kitchen table. Almost on reflex, he pulled up his favorites and punched Frank's number as he settled at the head of the table.

Frank answered on the second ring, his hardy voice already sharp and focused. "'Bout time you got around to calling your old man."

"Sorry. Had my hands full with a lot of charters the last few weeks. Every businessman in Dallas wanted to get their trips in before the holidays kicked in." Trevor set his mug on the table and kicked one foot up on the chair next to him. "I catch you at a bad time?"

"Got a cup of coffee and pretty blue skyline out my kitchen window. Can't think of a better time to sit and talk to my boy."

Trevor cleared his throat, the same swell of emotion that had billowed up the first time Frank had called him that years ago still overpowering him twenty-seven years later. Back then, it'd taken him a good five minutes to be able to talk without tearing up and embarrassing himself. Now, he just appreciated the burn behind his sternum and let it fill up all the empty space inside. "You still coming up for Thanksgiving?"

"Wouldn't miss it. Though I'm hoping Axel's momma's got a man to keep her occupied this year. Never met a woman so forward in my life."

Frank wasn't wrong on that score. For about thirty minutes during last year's dessert, everyone had half expected Sylvie to crawl in Frank's lap and spoon-feed him her chocolate silk pie. "If you think she's direct, you ought to see Axel's approach with ladies."

"Apple didn't fall far, I take it?"

"More like the apple got bigger, bolder, and stuck true to its roots. Though with that brogue of his, the women practically volunteer for whatever he wants."

Which, with Axel's proclivities for all things kink, was quite the offering.

Trevor sipped his coffee. "You good driving up, or you want me to come down and get you?"

Frank's voice dropped low and stern. "I'm old, not blind. Besides, driving's my best time to think. Hell, I'd drive myself to my own funeral if I could figure out how to pull it off."

That was certainly true. More than once, Frank had pulled an overnight run hauling new cattle or horses and never batted an eye. "How you liking the new truck?"

"New truck's fine, son, but we're gonna have to talk about you buyin' me things I don't need."

"It's got all the latest gadgets, though. You can talk on the phone without using your hands."

"Don't talk on the phone while I drive. Takes my focus off where it should be. And there was nothin' wrong with the truck you bought me two years ago." He paused, the silence between them growing thick in seconds. "I know you're still upset about Bonnie being gone, but I ain't going anywhere. Not anytime soon, God willing. And I know you love me, but I'd rather see your face than tool around in shiny new toys."

Trevor grunted and took another drink of his coffee. Arguing with his dad wouldn't do any good. When Frank Raines talked, a person listened, nodded, and took it in.

Outside the picture window across from him, deep blue skies slowly lightened and backlit the south pasture, smatterings of trees barely visible in the morning glow. The details might be different than the view outside Frank's kitchen, but in that second, even with more than two hundred miles between them and silence buzzing through the phone line, he felt like he was home.

"What's rattling in that head of yours?" Frank said.

"What makes you think I'm gnawing on anything?"

Frank barked a short laugh. "Known you damn near all your life, Trevor. Even those first few days at the ranch, you'd brood when something got in your craw. Told you then and I'll tell you now, best way to tackle something is to get it out."

Yeah, he had. Over and over again until Trevor had finally opened up.

He hurt her. A lot.

The simple words hadn't been much, but for a young kid who'd lost both his parents and fought his way through countless foster homes after, it had felt like an hour-long dissertation.

But it had also felt great.

Frank had listened, always patient, yet never prodding too far. Just like he was now.

"I want what you had." The admission burned Trevor's throat on the way out, as short as the first time he'd spill his guts, but just as potent.

"From where I'm sitting, I'd say you've built a fine life of your own."

Trevor loved his life. Loved how he spent his time and the people in it. Between his ranch, his businesses, and his brothers, his life was exceptionally grounded. A far sight different than the way things had been when Axel found him. "It's not that. Got everything I could ever need and most of what I want."

"But?"

Dragging one finger along the handle of his coffee mug, Trevor dug for the right words. A way to string his fears together that wouldn't come off half-cocked. Then again, this was Frank he was talking to. The man who'd stood beside him for years and helped him untangle his fucked-up past. It wouldn't matter what he said so long as he got it out. "You know what I've got inside me. Where I come from. How can I bring a decent woman into what I've built and ever feel confident it won't spill over?"

The scratch of wood on wood sounded in the background, and Trevor could easily picture Frank leaning into the long trestle table and resting his elbows on the honey-stained surface. "Because of that right there. You know yourself. You know what's inside you and keep yourself grounded with goodness. What you've got to understand, son, is that a good woman by your side isn't a liability or a weakness. It's the best damned blessing there is, and the sweetest, most reliable anchor you'll ever have, because you'll use that fire to keep her shielded."

The memory of Natalie leaning over the table and refilling his glass blazed bright. Touching her had felt right. Even that first time with her ex raining his nasty sneer on both of them, she'd tucked up next to his side just right. He wanted more of it. A lot more.

Frank's mischievous voice rattled him out of his thoughts. "So, when do I get to meet her?"

"Meet who?" Trevor flinched as soon as the response popped out of his mouth. No lie ever got past his dad, even it was innocently uttered.

"The woman who's got my boy thinkin' about hearth and home."

The table in front of him blurred, old fears and new hopes tangling up in a messy knot. "Not sure it's a good idea to pursue her. Got a few hurdles between the two of us that could get messy."

"You meet a woman you think about before you go to sleep and first thing when you wake up, she's worth chasing no matter how messy it is." He paused a minute and sighed the way he always did when he finished off his coffee. "Now quit lollygagging and figure out how to clear those hurdles. I want a grandkid to spoil before I'm too old to enjoy doin' it."

"Kinda rushing things, don't you think?"

"You wake up thinking about her?"

Thinking about her and dying to sink his cock inside her, not that he was gonna tack that little tidbit into the conversation.

Before he could answer, Frank softly chuckled and said, "That's what I thought." Movement sounded through the line followed by the clink of dishes. "Gotta get to work, son, but you wanna call me and keep me updated on how things move along with your woman, I'll be here."

"You're gettin' ahead of yourself."

"Doubt that," Frank muttered, "but have fun feedin' yourself that line while you still can. See you at Thanksgiving."

"Yeah, see you then." Trevor ended the call and set the phone on the kitchen table. He wasn't feeding himself a line. He was being reasonable. Recognizing his limitations and accepting them for what they were.

He stood and carried his mug to the sink, remnants of his dream and the very real memory of how Natalie had felt against him during their kiss the night before flaring bold and brilliant. Reasonable or not, it didn't mean he couldn't enjoy the fantasy while it lasted.

Chapter Eight

Someone needed to rein Trevor's ass in the next time he placed a marketing order. Ten boxes of T-shirts would take forever to sell and took up too much space in his storage closet. What he really needed were the damned coasters.

He shifted the last box he'd checked over with the others, putting them in order by size on the storeroom's middle shelf. The laughter and shouts from his better-than-average Friday night crowd were mostly muted by the thick storeroom walls, but the bass from the sound system surrounded the ten-by-twenty space like a heart-beat. He nabbed a smaller box off the top shelf and sliced open the packaging tape with his pocket knife. Nestled inside was a mother lode of cardboard coasters with The Den's logo imprinted in the center. "Finally."

Behind him, the storeroom door swung open and the chatter and music from the main bar swelled to full roar.

Box in hand, he spun, expecting to find Vicky ready to read him the riot act for taking his sweet-ass time in delivering her goods, but found Natalie frozen in the doorway.

Her gaze darted from the box in his hands, to his face, then down to her navy-blue Keds. "Sorry, I didn't know you were in here."

"Last I checked, the storeroom's not off-limits for employees."

She shifted her feet and tightened her grip on the door, still not meeting his eyes. She'd been doing that a lot around him the last few shifts, always giving him a wide berth, but watching him when she thought he wasn't looking.

But he'd always been looking. Hell, his whole body went on point the second she walked into the bar and his brain got very single-threaded anytime she got within twenty feet of him. It was like his body had fashioned an inner radar calibrated just for tracking her. "Relax, Nat. I was looking for coasters, not committing a crime."

She blushed a pretty pink and waved her hand toward the syrup boxes lined up on the wall closest to the bar. "Vicky told me to switch out the Coke syrup."

God, if she blushed that pretty finding him with just a box in his hand, she'd have fainted busting him in the shower the last five days. With all the dirty scenarios his subconscious had offered up since their kiss, it was either take his dick in hand and find release, or walk around with constant wood.

"Don't have to explain why you're here, darlin'. Do what you need to." He set the box of coasters aside and forced himself back on task. The last thing she needed was him breathing down her neck and making her even more nervous than she already was. Although, the idea of being close enough to make her jittery appealed on a whole lot of levels.

The door snicked shut, dousing the crowd's rumble.

He slid a few more boxes around, but damned if any others matched the first one. Planting both hands on his hips, he scanned the shelves one last time.

All at once, the lack of sound behind him registered.

He twisted and found Natalie staring motionless at the mess of hoses leading out of all the boxes. "Vicky bother to tell you how to switch 'em out?"

"I can figure it out."

"No doubt in my mind you can, but someone showing you once wouldn't hurt." Plus, there was the added bonus of proximity, a feat he'd had a hard time pulling off with her lately without drawing attention from the rest of his staff.

She inched closer to the boxes, angling her head to one side like the change in view might hold some clue on how to start.

God, she was cute. "You always this stubborn learning new things?"

She popped upright and frowned. "I'm not stubborn."

Oh, yeah. Totally cute. Especially when she got her back up. He bit back a chuckle and ambled toward her. "Says the woman with a determined scowl on her face." He turned her by her shoulders, parked himself as close behind her as he could without completely spooking her and pointed to the box on the bottom shelf with the Coke logo. "Grab the connector and release the latch."

Bracing a hand on the shelf above it, Natalie leaned over and wrapped her hand around the hose. "Release it how?"

Trevor couldn't think. Couldn't process anything except Natalie's sweet ass on prime display right in front of him. He fisted his hands at his sides, fighting the impulse to grip her hips and fit himself against her. He let out a slow breath instead and leaned over her, his chest mere inches from her back, and pointed to the latch beneath the connector. When he spoke, his voice rumbled with the same depth as the bass reverberating around them. "Squeeze right there."

Fingers trembling, she wrapped her hand around the latch. "Here?"

Fuck no. Wrapped around his rapidly hardening cock would be way better. Or hanging on for dear life while he drove himself inside her. He inhaled deep and her wildflower scent filled him. More than anything, he wanted to slide his hands around her rib cage and see if her tits filled his palms in real life as good as they had in his dreams. "Yeah, you've got it."

She fumbled the first time, then tried again, bearing down harder until the latch popped free.

"Now just switch out the box with the one beside it and plug the hose back in to the new connector." The more she moved, the more her glossy hair slipped forward and hid her face. From here he could easily move it aside and explore the line of her neck. He'd bet anything she had a sweet spot there, one that made her eyes all heavy and heated like last weekend.

He straightened and stepped away, his blood pumping even faster than his dangerous thoughts. Five days he'd kept his distance. Five nights he'd fallen asleep with her in his head and woken up to thoughts of her first thing in the morning. For the life of him, he couldn't figure out why. He'd always gone for statuesque blondes, but watching Nat's curvy ass wiggle while she fit the new nozzle in place, he couldn't envision anyone else but her. Not even when he tried. Being around her did weird shit to his head.

She levered herself upright and spun, a huge smile on her face. "I did it."

"'Course you did." He motioned to the empty box

and fought the need to adjust his throbbing dick. He tried to keep his voice normal, but it came out gruff. "Drop that by the back door, and I'll toss it in the dumpster on the way out. I gotta run some errands as soon as Ivan's back."

Her smile slipped a notch. "Everything okay?"

"Right as rain." Or it would be as soon as she wasn't within grabbing distance. As it was, if she so much as inched a toe his direction, he'd have the storeroom door locked, her back to a wall and his mouth on hers faster than she could say *yes*. "Tell Vicky I'll be up with the coasters in a bit."

"Okay." She cocked her head like she thought about saying something else, then shrugged, grabbed the empty syrup box, and headed for the door.

You meet a woman you think about before you go to sleep and first thing when you wake up, she's worth chasing no matter how messy it is.

"Nat."

She froze with one hand holding the door open and glanced back at him.

"You got Levi this weekend?"

She shook her head, and a little of the lightness behind her eyes dimmed. "He's not back until Sunday."

Great. Here he'd gone and reminded her how her kid was spending the week with his dickhead dad. "So next weekend he's back at your place?"

"Yeah, why? You need me to work?"

He could say yes. Completely play shit off and act like that was all he wanted. Damned if that was the route he was going to take though. "Was actually thinking you and Levi might want to come out to my place. The weather's supposed to be nice the next few weeks.

Thought I'd make good on my promise to Levi for a horse ride. Your day job's only Monday through Friday, right?"

A mix of emotions moved across her face, the wave too fast to discern which one held more sway. "My company's closed on the weekends, but I'm not so sure Levi and I coming to your place is a good idea. Levi's over the moon with the idea I'm seeing someone, particularly when he can brag about that someone with his best friend."

"Not sure I'm seeing how that's a problem."

She bit her lip and tucked her free hand in her back pocket. "Because at some point I'm either going to have to tell him the truth, or pretend we've parted ways. He's already going to be crushed. I can't risk hurting my son."

He prowled closer, the pain and worry in her gaze tugging him to her more thoroughly than any lasso. She was right, though. Common sense said they'd be smart to let things fizzle on their own, but damned if his gut could get with the program. "There's another option."

Her brow knitted up tight and her head jerked back an inch. "What option?"

"We keep doing what we're doing and ease him into the idea we've decided to stick to a just-friends relationship. No kisses. No hugs. Just friends who look out for one another." Of course, as soon as he said it, his head screamed *bullshit foul*. Now that he'd felt her against him—tasted her mouth and heard those sweet sighs she made—the concept of friends didn't appeal at all.

She swallowed and slid her hand from her back pocket to rest on her belly. "What about people at work? I don't want them to get the wrong impression."

"Do I look like a man who gives a rat's ass about impressions?"

"You're the boss. You don't have to care, but I do."

He leaned in close, halfway tempted to coil his hand around her nape and take what he craved. "Anyone on my staff so much as gives you the hairy eyeball, they won't make it another second on my payroll." He held his place long enough to let his vow sink in, then straightened and gripped the edge of the door. "Now are you gonna help me keep the promise I made your kid, or do I have to get creative on how I talk you into it?"

Her eyes flared wide, and the same dazed hunger he'd seen in them after their first kiss blazed bright. "I'm not sure what to say."

"Easy. Say yes."

A shy smile tipped her lips. "You're bossy."

"And we've established you're stubborn, but I'm also persistent." He inched closer.

She licked her lip, the innocent swipe making his cock strain a little farther. "You're sure about this? Levi's a handful."

"Levi's got nothing on me. I was a seven-year-old boy once too, remember?"

Her gaze roamed his face, and her smile softened in a way that soothed everything inside him. "I can only imagine." As soon as she said it, her focus sharpened and she took a discreet step back. She nodded. "All right. Just this once. Levi's been through a lot, and I'd like to see him have a special day. Just remember, we're working our way toward friends. I can't risk hurting him more in the long run."

Friends. It was the smart move. Definitely safer for

Nat, but it still didn't sit right in his gut. For her, though, he'd give it a shot.

For now.

Next Saturday? Maybe not.

He winked and dropped his hand from the door. "Next Saturday it is. I'll pick you up at eight."

Chapter Nine

Natalie twisted in front of the full-length mirror and reconsidered the chambray shirt she'd pulled on over her white tank top. From the front it gave her an easy, casual vibe, but from the back she had zero figure.

She shouldn't care. Trevor was just a friend, which meant it didn't matter what her booty looked like.

Scowling, she gathered up the tail of her shirt and tied it around her waist. Friend or not, there was no way she was sauntering into today looking like a sack of potatoes. She checked the effect over her shoulder, let out a satisfied harrumph, and cocked her hip in a sassy pose. Wyatt may not have appreciated her backside while they were married—had even gone so far as to suggest she needed to lose a few pounds in their last few years—but Natalie liked it. Especially in her favorite jeans with the pretty silver stitching on the pockets.

Levi's voice ricocheted from the living room. "Mom, he's here!"

Great, now both of her neighbors were probably sitting upright in their beds contemplating murder. Very few tenants were up and about in her apartment complex before ten o'clock on the weekends. Before eight o'clock was an absolute ghost town.

Steady footsteps sounded on the concrete walkway outside her window.

"Mom, did you hear me?"

"Yes, Levi. So did the people next door. Now, settle down." She snagged her purse off the dresser and hurried into the living room. It felt weird not having her mom there, but she'd suspiciously come up with breakfast plans with some of her friends the night before. While she'd come clean with her mom about her and Trevor's pretend relationship, Natalie had a feeling Maureen was still secretly planning their wedding.

Trevor's sharp knock sounded on the door, and Natalie's heart kicked in answer.

You're just friends. That's all. Over a week, she'd chanted that mantra, but those stupid flutters that came with the merest thought of Trevor refused to buy into the idea. She opened the door and caught her breath, the brilliant sunrise backlighting Trevor's broad shoulders and narrow hips like something out of a movie. She stepped aside and waved him in. "Good morning."

"It is now." His smile matched his playful tone, but the deep appreciation as he ambled inside and gave her a thorough head to toe left her flushed and out of sorts. His gaze shifted to Levi and he hooked his thumbs in his pockets. "Nice boots, bud."

Levi beamed and puffed out his chest. "Thanks! I told Mom if we were ridin' horses we'd need some, so we went shoppin'."

"Did you, now?" Trevor twisted toward Natalie, nodded toward her simple white Keds and cocked a lopsided grin. "I see mom didn't splurge for her own pair."

"Do you know what it costs to keep a growing boy in clothes? I promise you, answering endless questions about insurance claims all day doesn't generate the pay-check you'd expect. I did good to get Levi a pair." She slung her purse on her shoulder and feigned a casual-ness she absolutely didn't feel. "Besides, I'm just along for the ride. I'll take air-conditioning to the great out-doors any day."

"Darlin', if that's the case, you haven't been doing things right." He waved Levi toward the door. "Come on, bud. Time to get your momma up on a horse."

Natalie locked the front door and trailed the two of them down the stairs to the parking lot. The pair made for a sight almost as glorious as the early November sun creeping up the horizon. Trevor's easy saunter was a beautiful thing to behold any day, but with her son beside him, chatting up a storm and watching Trevor's every move, the moment was perfect.

When Trevor guided them to his huge silver truck parked in the back row, Levi's strides quickened. "Whoa! You've got a dually!" He stopped and studied the long body with big eyes. "Mom, look! He's got a Sil-verado Duramax Diesel Dually." He turned to Trevor, all levity replaced with a sincerity reserved for conver-sation between men. "Bobby's dad has a Ford, but your Chevy's way better."

Natalie stepped closer to Trevor and lowered her voice. "What's a dually?"

Grinning, Trevor splayed his hand at the small of her back and steered her to the passenger side. "More tires in the back. I like to take my horses out on trail rides and the dually makes a better hauler when I'm pulling a trailer."

"I bet it guzzles a lot of gas, too."

"Well, it's not gonna win any efficiency awards, that's for sure." He opened her door and held out a hand.

"Ain't you gonna drive?" Levi said from beside her.

"*Aren't* you going to drive," Natalie said.

"Yeah, bud, I'm gonna drive," Trevor said, "but I'm gonna get your momma settled first."

Levi shrugged and strode forward, ready to climb in.

Trevor gently snagged him by the shoulder and pulled him back against his legs. "Ladies first, bud. We'll get you settled in the back."

Natalie hesitated and braced to smooth over Trevor's gentle guidance, but Levi just nodded, cataloged the information away, and waited for her to get on with business.

She climbed in and swallowed around the knot blossoming in her throat. This was the kind of life she'd wished for Levi. For her son to have a coach and a role model he could rely on instead of a man who viewed him as a nuisance or a means to an end.

The forty-five-minute drive to Trevor's ranch felt more like fifteen, and not one second of it lagged for conversation. Of course, most of it ping-ponged between Trevor and Levi, but with her son's rampant curiosity, the topics kept her highly entertained. Planes, ranches, bars, and sports, Levi covered it all.

Several miles down a less-traveled country road, Trevor slowed in front of an open black iron gate. A rustic four-rung fence stretched on either side for what had to be at least a mile, and the winding driveway led to a dark wood home with a green tiled roof. While she'd never traveled to the mountains, the home's design was exactly what she'd have expected to find at such a locale. "Is this your place?"

"Yep."

The click of Levi's seat belt coming unhitched sounded and his little hands curled around her seat back a second before his head popped up between them. "Wow! Cool house!"

"Thanks, bud."

Levi pointed to a tan metal building off to one side. "Is that where you keep your planes?"

"Just a little Cessna 310," Trevor said. "It's the prop plane I told you about. I keep all my commercial planes at an airport south of downtown."

Practically bouncing on the seat, Levi's hands tightened on the seat back. "Can we fly it?"

Trevor drove them around the back of his house and parked outside the garage. Another truck like Trevor's was parked off to one side, though it was black and splattered with mud. About fifty feet away was a miniature version of Trevor's home, and a little beyond that was a barn that looked nicer than some high-end homes.

"I'll make you a deal," Trevor said to Levi. "You pay attention and earn those boots your mom bought, and I'll take you out on the next trip. That work for you?"

"Yeah!" Scrambling to his door, Levi yanked the handle and hopped out.

Before Trevor could do the same, Natalie gripped his forearm and squeezed. "I appreciate this. Really I do. But I don't think it's smart to make Levi any more promises. We're supposed to be winding down this farce to just friends, and he'll be crushed enough by that alone."

For several seconds, Trevor just stared at her, a mood she couldn't quite pinpoint moving behind his pale blue eyes. "One thing you need to learn about me, darlin'.

If I say I'll do something, I mean it. I don't give empty promises. Damn sure not to a seven-year-old boy who can charm the spots off a ladybug." He twisted and cupped side of her face, the contact both comforting and possessive. "And the friends thing won't be an act. That's a promise I'm making you."

Friends. He'd said *friends.* She was sure of it. But the tone behind the word caressed her in a far more intimate stroke. Charm the spots off a ladybug, indeed. God help her if Levi grew up to be as alluring of a man as Trevor. She'd have more love-struck girls sniffing around her house than she'd ever be able to deal with.

When she found her voice, it came out soft and shaky. "Okay."

He grinned, clearly pleased he'd earned the answer he wanted. "Good." His gaze dropped to her mouth and his smile slipped, a sexual focus slipping into place that set her whole body on fire.

Levi's delighted voice rang across the clearing. "Mom, look! He's got a dog!"

The mood broken, Trevor exited the truck and helped her out. By the time she stepped clear of the door, Levi was kneeling in the grass just outside the barn, his arms wrapped around a border collie who seemed determined to lick Levi's entire face.

Trevor shut the passenger door and whistled sharp. "Lady, settle."

On cue, Lady dropped to her butt, but her tail kept moving ninety miles an hour.

Levi took full advantage, moving in closer and rubbing both hands behind her ears. "Isn't she cool, Mom? We need a dog like this. We could train her and everything."

"Gee, thanks," Natalie said low to Trevor.

He chuckled and urged her forward, that same claiming touch he'd given her a few times before settling low on her back. "Sorry. Wouldn't be the full ranch experience without a dog though, now would it?"

A stocky man in seriously faded Wranglers, a white-and-blue-striped button-down and cowboy hat that had probably been white about ten years ago, strolled out of the barn and waved to Trevor. "Good timing, boss. Just got your boys rounded up and fed."

Trevor held out his hand. "Appreciate it, Thomas."

Thomas shook it, pounded Trevor on the back hard enough it had to have hurt, then turned his attention to her. "You must be Natalie?"

"I am." She motioned toward Levi now running and dodging Lady, who seemed to think it was her sole mission in life to herd him their direction. "That's my son, Levi."

Tipping his hat just a fraction, he grinned enough to make his eyes crinkle at each side. Black hair peeked beneath the edges of his hat and curled a little at his shirt collar. The way he moved, he seemed as young and spry as Trevor, but his deeply tanned skin gave him an older appearance up close. "Nice to meet you, ma'am."

"Thomas and his boys manage the ranch and take care of the horses for me," Trevor said. "Known him since before I moved to Dallas."

"Fifteen years, at least," Thomas tacked on with a smirk. "First time he's ever brought a pretty lady out to his place, though."

Trevor slid his arm around Natalie's shoulders and tucked her tight against him, but the smile on his face said the good-natured ribbing was a frequent occurrence between the two of them. "You keep flirting, I'll rat you out with your wife, and you'll have to sleep in the bunkhouse for a week."

"Man, you're lucky it's only me bustin' your chops. Tessa heard you were havin' company and damn near came out herself to lay eyes on the woman who'd scored the invite." Thomas winked at Natalie before shifting his focus back to Trevor. "Don't worry, I'll be out of your hair directly. Workin' on the fence in the north section this morning, then headin' out. The boys are running errands with their momma."

"Works for us." Trevor tipped his head down to her. "You and Levi want a tour of the house first, or would you rather get right after the horses?"

Even if the place didn't look like a mountain resort, she'd have jumped at a chance to see what kind of place a man like Trevor called home. "Considering I'm still not convinced I've got any business on a horse, I'll start with the tour."

Trevor's eyes lit, a devilish glint that made her insides smolder even with chilled wind licking her cheeks. "You're gettin' on a horse, Nat. Only choice you're getting is riding solo, or mounted up in front of me."

Holy smokes.

The smolder flashed to a raging blaze, her all-too-vivid imagination conjuring up the feel of his hips pressed against hers and his muscled chest tight against her back. She cleared her throat and shifted her attention to Levi to hide the heat climbing up her face. "I can do solo."

He gently squeezed her shoulder and leaned in close, his voice low and only for her, but just as potent as his woodsy scent. "Chicken." Straightening, he spoke to

Thomas. "I'll handle Titan when we're done, but do you mind gettin' Deuce and Peso saddled up while I show them around?"

"Don't mind a bit." Thomas pinched the rim of his hat and tipped his head to Natalie. "Nice meeting you, ma'am. You and your kiddo come back this way, I'll bring Tessa and the boys around for an intro."

"I'd like that," she said. Not that there would be another time around. Clearly, Trevor was the type who appreciated his privacy and had already gone out of his way to share it with her son. Letting herself think anything else was akin to riding an elephant across a barely iced-over pond.

Trevor's sharp whistle pierced the quiet morning. "Let's go, Lady."

Snapping to attention, the collie darted toward Trevor, stopped, circled back to Levi to make sure he was headed in too, then raced right along beside him.

"I'm ready to ride!" Levi said, his lungs heaving from all the exercise.

"Got all day, bud." Relinquishing his hold on Natalie, he waved Levi toward the house. "Gonna show your mom around and let you hit the head first. Then you can help me saddle up Titan."

Moving in tight to Trevor's side, Levi grabbed his hand and doubled his strides to keep up with Trevor's longer ones.

Natalie's own steps nearly faltered, the simple gesture from her son and the easy way Trevor accepted the connection drawing tears to her eyes. She swallowed to combat the burn crawling up her throat and dropped her gaze, pushing the emotion as deep as she could bury it. Later she could wallow in it. Could remember the image and savor it when Levi headed back to Wyatt. Right now was for making her boy happy and making sure he had enough memories to carry him through until he got home.

Two thickly padded loungers and at least ten different kinds of potted plants and flowers adorned the covered back porch. Trevor opened the back door and stepped aside.

Levi almost waltzed right through, but stopped two steps away, shuffled back and waited for her to go first.

She ruffled his head on the way past. "Such a gentleman. You do that for your nanna and you'll end up with double desserts for a month."

Trevor's hushed voice sounded behind her. "Good job, bud."

Letting out a shaky breath, she stopped in the open kitchen and let the homey space around her settle her rioting emotions. A wide trestle table with benches on each side and big, hand-carved chairs at each end sat in front of the huge picture window. On the opposite side of the room was a rock fireplace nearly big enough for Levi to stand in, fronted by a well-worn leather couch and two club chairs covered in an evergreen chenille. Perfect for cozying up on a cold night.

Heck, the whole place was perfect for anything cozy. And didn't that just give her mind more fuel for her already out-of-control thoughts. She eyed the exposed wood beams stretching up the vaulted ceiling then shifted to the pictures situated on each end of the mantel. An older man and woman sat side by side on a porch swing in one, both with gray hair, but their smiles full of youth and love. At the other end was a candid picture of six men, each of them seated at the table Trevor kept reserved for him and his friends at The Den. You couldn't have picked a more motley crew. On first blush, none of them looked the type to hang out with the other, but the familiarity and comfort in the way they sat together spoke of a deep, unflinching bond.

Trevor's voice drew her attention. "Those are my brothers." He tapped Levi's arm and pointed toward the opening on the far side of the fireplace. "Bathroom's back that way on the right, bud. How about you take care of business before we head out?"

Levi nodded and strutted down the hall, his quick steps telegraphing how hard he was trying to rein in his excitement.

She motioned to the picture. "They don't look anything like you."

"Some families you get by blood. Some you take by choice." He nodded to the picture. "Everyone on that mantel is the latter."

She spun back to the picture of the man and woman, questions poised on the tip of her tongue.

You're just friends.

Swallowing her curiosity, she turned and tucked her hands in her back pockets. "Your home is lovely."

He grinned and leaned back against the kitchen counter. "You expect something different?"

"I think you threw all my expectations out the window a few weeks ago." She scanned the tidy space, looking for something, anything to knock him off his too-perfect pedestal. "Do you really keep this place all to yourself, or was your friend just giving you a hard time?"

"My dad comes out off and on, and my brothers stop

by from time to time, but other than that, it's pretty quiet."

"That's a shame." Outside the picture window, unspoiled land stretched in soft rolling planes, intermittent clusters of trees rustling in a soft breeze. "A place like this is meant to be shared."

"Maybe I'm just waiting on the right person to share it with."

His retort stretched taut between them, the tenor of his voice laced with something between playful challenge and need. The dare she understood, his lighthearted flirtations with customers seemingly as second-nature as his swagger. But the need...that part was unexpected. A tiny crack in his otherwise unruffled veneer.

Before she could come up with a response to his odd statement, Trevor pushed off the counter and strolled her direction. "Come on. I'll show you the rest of the place."

The layout was simplistic, but made the most of the exceptional views with every oversized room boasting huge picture windows. Three guest rooms decorated in rich, yet welcoming colors of sage, cornflower blue, and gold took up one end of the house, none of them appearing to have ever been used. The rustic décor of Trevor's office matched the kitchen and the rest of the living areas, but was offset by a multitude of model planes emblazoned with his company's phoenix logo on the sides.

Natalie glanced up the stairs outside his office. "Your room is upstairs?"

"Nope. That's the rec room. Pool tables, video games, and all the other stuff that proves I'm still a kid at heart." He steered her around with one hand at her shoulder and motioned her ahead of him. "My room's down there."

A shadowed hallway with dark woodwork on either side stretched fifteen feet in front of her. The door at the end was closed, a perfect reminder of the very real line neither of them could afford to cross. She spun back around and clasped her hands in front of her. "I'm sure it's lovely."

He cocked one eyebrow. "Not curious?"

Oh, she was curious, all right. More so than she'd ever admit. But the last thing her brain needed was any more late-night fantasy fodder to work with. "More like I don't want to intrude on your privacy."

Grinning, he loosely coiled his fingers around her wrist and led her forward. "Not intruding if there's an invitation, is it?"

She followed, her pulse thrumming stronger with every step and her skin tingling beneath his touch. Her mind scrambled for a polite reason to bail.

He opened the door and pulled her through behind him, only releasing his hold once he'd guided her to the center of the room.

A shiver snaked its way down her spine, the sensual awareness she'd tried to ignore since that first kiss blossoming to full bright. The rest of his home fit his lifestyle, but his bedroom fit the man. Rugged and edgy. A taste of refinement wrapped in rural trappings. A thick pale gray rug silenced her footsteps, and brilliant morning sunshine slanted from the massive picture window. Opposite the glass, an entire wall finished in raw, dark wood served as the backdrop for an opulent king-size bed covered in a chambray-covered down comforter.

She'd bet anything it was as soft as it looked. As decadent as the ideas just looking at it conjured.

Down the hall, a door clicked open.

"I'm ready!" Levi called. His quick footsteps sounded on the hardwoods. "Where are you guys?"

"Back here, bud," Trevor answered, though his voice sounded as distracted as her thoughts.

Natalie shifted her focus to the rolling green vista beyond and tried to calm her heart's haggard rhythm.

Trevor moved in tight behind her before she'd so much as drawn a steady breath. His voice rumbled deep and decadent beside one ear. "How about you, Momma? Are you ready?"

Her eyes slid shut, and her core clenched. God, was she ready. Though what she wanted wasn't something he'd likely be willing to give. At this rate, she'd never make it through the day. Watching Levi, eyes bright with undiluted hero worship and eager for every scrap of knowledge Trevor had to offer, was hard enough. Being this close, this intimate even without physical touch, would have her in a quivering puddle of mush before noon.

"I'm ready," she said, hating the needy rasp of her voice when it came out and praying he'd chalk it up to her inexperience with horses.

You're just friends.

Charade or not, it was all he had to offer. Entertaining any other ideas would only leave her with a welling hole of disappointment. A chasm ten times deeper than anything she'd felt running away from her marriage. She turned just as Levi rounded the entry, stepped away from the temptation of Trevor's towering body, and forced a bright smile for her son. "What's say we get this show on the road, huh?"

"Yeah!" Levi spun on his heel and strode down the hallway with the excited gait of a kid hopped up on too much sugar and adrenaline.

Natalie hustled right behind him, the heady press of desire Trevor had created and the unhurried clip of his boots behind her a seductively challenging presence.

Distance was good. Downright necessary if she wanted to make it through the hours ahead, but damned if a part of her wasn't tempted to pause at the porch door and give Trevor the opportunity to pull her back inside.

Outside, brilliant sunshine blanketed the sweeping acreage, and the crisp November air rustled trees thick with deepening gold and russet leaves. A comforting silence as only nature could provide it whispered on the wind and whipped her hair across her face. She slowed her pace and drew the sweet scent of hay into her lungs.

Not the least bit interested in the beauty around him, Levi marched closer to the barn's open sliding doors while Lady pranced dutifully at his side.

Trevor's voice cut from behind her. "Hold up, bud. Time and a place to get yourself in high gear, but horses aren't one of 'em. You get me?"

Levi stopped and his shoulders snapped back to match his sharp "Yes, sir." The overall response would have come off like a little soldier in training if he hadn't promptly pinned his hands on his hips and practically bounced with impatience.

Ambling up beside her, Trevor matched his strides to hers and slipped his hand in hers as though he'd done it a thousand times before.

And God, it felt good. So good it was all she could

do not to stop walking altogether, close her eyes and savor the contact.

The stretch of land between them and the barn was far enough he didn't have to lower his voice, but he did it all the same. "You all right?"

No. Not really. More like on top of the world and terrified all in one breath. "I don't know how to answer that."

"How about just saying what's on your mind?"

Boy, wasn't that a scary proposition? She wasn't sure she was ready to handle the ideas scampering around in her head, let alone share them with anyone else. "You're easy to be with. Sometimes too easy."

"Not sure there's such a thing as too easy, and if there is, I can't see how it's a bad thing."

She huffed out a short chuckle. "It's bad if it makes me forget what we've agreed to or the consequences that go with it."

His quick smile rivaled the sun and held zero remorse. "Then darlin', *too easy* is exactly what I'm countin' on." He winked, released her hand and gave her a playful swat on her butt. "Now stow all that shit clouding your thoughts and get your head in the game. Time for you to cowgirl up."

Before her thoughts could rewind and translate the underlying meaning behind his words, he'd upped his pace, covered the distance to Levi, and steered him into the stable's center aisle. Inside the shadowed confines, the temperature was at least five degrees cooler and the air thick with the scent of hay, horses and leather. It took two or three blinks for her eyes to adjust, but once they did, her lungs hitched.

Five spacious stalls lined each side of the barn, but

at the far end of the long corridor, two gorgeous horses were saddled and tethered. One was a rich gray that bordered on silver, and another a deep brown with a black mane and shiny black points at his ears and feet.

Levi stood in front of the gray one, his head tipped back and eyes rounded with awe. His usual boisterous voice was couched with a gentle reverence. "Aren't they pretty, Mom?"

Pretty didn't cover it. All by themselves, the animals were proud and gorgeous creatures, patiently—or more like lovingly—waiting for Levi to take in the moment. Watching Trevor standing beside him, the sunlight haloing them both as Trevor taught him how to stroke the horse's muzzle—that was priceless.

As quietly as she could, Natalie inched closer. "Will they bite?"

"Peso? Are you kidding?" Trevor chuckled and patted the horse's neck. "It'd take a whole lot of prodding and maybe Armageddon for either of these guys to bite anyone. Consider them the equivalent of two seasoned soldiers who've done and seen it all. You'll never be safer."

Well, that was good. Especially since one of them alone outweighed her by God only knew how much. Heck, the top of her head barely reached the top of their backs. "Well, he's very handsome."

Levi twisted enough to grin over his shoulder, but never stopped petting Peso. "Trevor said Peso's a blue roan." He glanced up at Trevor. "He's mine, right?"

"Yep." Trevor motioned to the saddle on Peso's back. "Thomas brought one of his boy's saddles over for you, so you're good to go."

The dark-brown-and-black horse behind Trevor

shifted enough to nuzzle the back of Trevor's neck and snorted as though giving him a gentle reminder.

Completely unfazed or startled by the touch, Trevor turned and gave the horse his undivided attention.

Fascinated by the easy way Trevor interacted with the creature, Natalie sidled closer. "What's his name?"

"This is Deuce. And you may as well get yourself within touching distance, because he's a sucker for ladies and will pester me until you properly introduce yourself."

Okay. Right. It was just a horse, and a friendly acting one at that. Surely if her seven-year-old could get nose-to-nose with one, she could, too. She inched closer, hands fisted close to her waist. "So, what do I do?"

Before Trevor could answer, Deuce stretched forward and nudged her hand with his nose.

Trevor's laugher was as warm and velvety as the horse's touch. "Whatever Deuce tells you to do, apparently." He stroked one big hand down the center of Deuce's forehead. "Pretty much anything with this guy works so long as you're touching."

Emboldened by the animal's reaction, Natalie mimicked the way Levi had petted Peso and tentatively caressed his muzzle.

Deuce gently lifted his head as if to guide her hand higher and huffed out a hot breath.

Natalie giggled like a little girl, pure joy blossoming behind her chest. "He is a little bossy."

Trevor grinned and opened his mouth to say something but was cut off by a commotion in a stall behind them.

Natalie spun just as a big black horse popped his head above one of the gates. He shook his head hard enough to toss his mane and whinnied in a way that said he wasn't at all pleased.

"Deuce isn't bossy," Trevor said. "But that one is." He strolled around her and up to the agitated animal like he didn't have the least of concerns. "Pal, you're gonna have to cool your jets for a few more while I get our friends settled." Settling one hand on the horse's neck, Trevor lowered his voice and mumbled something else Natalie couldn't hear in his ear.

Whatever he said, the animal settled and actually greeted Trevor with a brush of his head against his shoulder.

Still gushing over Peso, Levi turned enough to ask, "Is that Titan?"

"Yep." Trevor scratched Titan's forelock and glanced back at Levi. "You wanna help me get him saddled up?"

"Yeah!" Despite Levi's sudden and very loud enthusiasm, none of the horses seemed bothered.

"Um." Natalie stepped away from Deuce, ready to put herself between Levi and Trevor. "I'm not so sure that's a good idea. Titan seemed upset."

To his credit, Trevor at least tried to fight back his smile. "Nat, been workin' with horses since I was nine. Titan was just jealous he wasn't getting attention. He's a little more high-strung, but I'm more than capable of handling him." He paused long enough to make solid eye contact. "Calming the skittish ones is the best part."

Her belly did a swoop and barrel roll to rival the hairiest thrill ride. "You're sure?"

The gleam in his eyes added a heat wave to her already rioting reactions. "Oh, yeah. Absolutely sure." Not taking his gaze off her, he motioned Levi closer.

"Come on, bud. We'll get Titan ready to go and then we'll get you up on Peso."

The next twenty minutes passed too quickly, the indescribable joy of watching Trevor work with Levi mingling with the soothing presence of Deuce and Peso beside her. She'd thought she'd found her balance and had just decided she'd be able to keep an even keel through the rest of the day when Trevor sauntered over, untied Peso's reins, and led the big horse and her son out into the big corral.

With a distracted pat to Deuce's neck, Natalie hurried after them. "What are you doing?"

This time Trevor didn't even try to fight the smile. "Well, the goal of the day was to ride horses, so it seems a quick lesson on how Levi can get Peso from point A to point B might be in order." He paused long enough to cast her a wink. "Best keep your ears open while we're at it so you can do the same with Deuce."

"But—"

All three heads turned calmly back at her—Trevor, Levi, and the blasted horse—as if to say, *"Woman, please."*

Natalie stopped and forced her arms to relax at her sides. "Sorry. They're just really big and Levi's... well..."

Levi groaned and offered a long-suffering "Moom."

Trevor patiently motioned her closer. "Come on, Momma. You can listen and be close at the same time."

As soon as she was within distance, Trevor handed her the reins and focused on Levi. "You ready, bud?"

Levi quickly bobbed his head.

Not waiting for any further encouragement, Trevor lifted Levi up and onto the saddle and set about adjusting his stirrups. Once done, he helped Levi guide his boots into place, took the reins from Natalie, and knotted them at the end. "You remember how I said Peso's been around a while?" he said to Levi.

"Yep."

"Well, that means he knows his job and a little goes a long way. You want to start moving, you nudge him with your heels. You want to go right, you lay the reins to your right. You want to go left, you lay them left."

"What if I want to stop?"

"You ease back and tell him to *whoa*. Peso's a light touch, and I'll be close if you need me."

Levi gave a quick, sharp nod. "Got it."

"All right, bud." Trevor stroked the side of Peso's neck and shifted a few steps in front of the horse. "Give him your heels and let's see how you do."

Natalie held her breath and crossed her arms across her chest, her fists as white-knuckled as they could get.

Eyebrows pinched into a sharp V and mouth pressed into a concentrated line, Levi bounced his heels off Peso's sides.

Lo and behold, the horse rambled forward nice and easy. Left. Right. Stop. Forward. Over and over, Trevor put Levi and Peso through their paces, always close by in case either of them needed him. In fact, the whole routine went so smooth and easy, it was if they'd been born to be together. Two males happily bonding over a shared joy despite their difference in age. Or maybe it was age span that made it so beautiful. One man handing down knowledge to another with care and reverence.

Trying not to call too much attention to herself, she snaked her phone from her back pocket, waited until Trevor stepped in for more coaching, and snapped a handful of shots. She zoomed on the last one and her breath caught.

Her boy beamed down from his horse while Trevor watched him with open pride. Two absolute peas in a pod surrounded by brilliant sunshine and genuinely grounded in the moment.

Trevor's voice cut through her quiet appreciation of the image. "All right, bud. You practice while I get your mom in the saddle."

Oh. Shit.

If she'd had a half a second more before Trevor turned around and pinned her with a knowing smirk, she'd have hauled ass back to the house. Instead, her stubborn streak kicked. She tucked her phone back in her pocket and forced her chin up a notch.

"You get all that?" he said, headed toward Deuce still tied up at the end of the barn's center alley.

"Nudge with your heels, ease back on the reins to stop, left and right to turn." Simple. Easy enough her kid could do it. At least that was the line she was going to feed herself while she prayed Deuce was as obliging as Peso.

"Paying attention in class. I like it." Trevor ambled closer with Deuce close at his side, the horse's reins dangling from his easy grip and a wicked smile on his face. Once they were close enough, Trevor guided her up to Deuce's side facing the saddle and moved in close to her back. His breath ghosted warm against her cheek. "Gotta admit though. Was kind of hopin' you'd need me to mount up behind you to get started."

Before she could overcome the shiver that danced down her spine, he handed her the reins and guided her hands to the saddle horn. "Put your hands right here.

I'm going give you a leg up and you swing your right leg over Deuce, all right?"

No. She wasn't all right. Wasn't even sure her lungs had found a way to function after that last visual he'd given her mind to chew on. She didn't dare tear her gaze away from the saddle for fear he'd know exactly where her thoughts had gone.

"I can still saddle up behind you if you want," he murmured.

Bad idea. A deliciously tempting and perfect idea, but still a bad one in the long run. "No, I can do it. I just... I was picturing it in my head."

He chuckled so low and dirty it resonated straight between her thighs. "Believe me, darlin'. I was picturing it, too." He bent and picked her left leg up so he gripped her around her ankle and shin. "Ready?"

She let out a long, slow breath and nodded.

In a whoosh so powerful it knocked her senses for a loop, she was up, astride Deuce's back, and gripping the saddle horn for all she was worth.

Trevor covered her hand with his and gave a gentle squeeze. "Easy. Just take a deep breath."

Easy. Yeah, right. He wasn't the one teetering on top of a powerful animal and completely out of control. On the tail of that thought, her gaze shot to Levi across the corral.

Unlike her, he was happily owning his place in the saddle and dutifully practicing his commands with the reins.

Trevor's voice drifted through her fear, soft and patient. "Give me your hand, Nat."

She forced her attention back to the task at hand, though it took a handful of blinks and a good headshake to get her mind back on topic. "Sorry, it's just really, really high up here."

"Yep. Another thirty minutes and you'll love it, trust me." He urged her hand off the saddle horn and guided it toward Deuce's neck. "Lean over, give him a pat, and let him know you're all right. He already knows you're nervous, and it'll make you both feel better."

Well, that made sense. Nursing 101 was to connect with the patient wherever possible. Although, in this scenario she wasn't even remotely in control. At least not yet.

Patient as always, Trevor gave her time to get her bearings then put her through the same routine he had with Levi. Surprisingly, it was as simple as it had looked, even if her heart had bucked and threatened to gallop right out of her chest through the first ten minutes.

After she'd circled the corral a few times and demonstrated a tolerable ability to direct Deuce one way or the other, Trevor murmured something low in Deuce's ear and moseyed toward the barn.

Natalie straightened from the comfortable position she'd finally adopted in the saddle. "Where are you going?"

He laughed and shook his head in that way men reserved for perplexing women. "Gonna need my horse if we're going to actually ride somewhere outside the fence, darlin'." With that, he disappeared into the shadows.

"You're doin' really good, Mom." Like he'd been doing it his whole life, Levi guided Peso her direction. "This is gonna be awesome."

It would be. Maybe not for her butt, which was already questioning the soundness of agreeing to this whole affair, but if the glow on her son's face was any gauge, the day was on target to be stellar. "You just promise me you'll do what Trevor says. And don't do anything to spook your horse."

"Peso won't spook. Trevor said he's a vateran."

"A *veteran*," she corrected, trying not to focus on the fact that way too many veterans suffered from PTSD. "But you still need to follow Trevor's rules, and don't let yourself get too cocky."

Levi's gaze slid past her shoulder and his eyes got huge.

Natalie twisted in the saddle to see what had grabbed her son's attention and barely stifled an appreciative *whoa* to match Levi's dumbfounded look. Day-to-day Trevor was a walking, talking thing of beauty, but Trevor astride a big black quarter horse complete with a worn straw cowboy hat was an image to strike ninety percent of the female population stupid. God, he was handsome. One hundred percent man, in his element, and totally in control.

He steered Titan their direction. While his body appeared at ease, there was also a focus behind his expression and movements she hadn't seen as he worked with Deuce and Peso. Which, considering the bristling energy that emanated from Titan, made a whole lot of sense. "Okay, Levi. Want to see you put Peso through the routine one more time before we head out."

Levi nodded his agreement without so much as a beat of hesitation and gave Peso a nudge with his heels.

For a kid who'd only seen a horse at the fair, he really was doing exceptionally well. Though, she wasn't sure how much of that was due to Levi, the horse, or the man who'd done the teaching.

A quiet sigh slipped free, a mix of appreciation and

concern releasing with it. This whole charade was dangerous. Not just to Levi, but to her as well. Being around Trevor—the person he was and the genuine life he led—it was all too easy to fall off track.

She felt more than saw Trevor and Titan move alongside her. "You doin' okay?"

She shook her head, the truth coming out as soft as the gentle breeze against her cheeks. "I'm not sure this is a good idea."

He stopped studying Levi's progression and turned his assessing gaze on her. "Not sure if we're talking about riding horses or the fact that we're both still thinkin' about giving my sheets a good tussle."

She swallowed, her throat as dry as the dirt beneath their horses' feet. "Maybe it's both."

His lips quirked in a devilish grin, and he did something that made Titan sidle closer to Deuce. Curling his hand around her nape, he captured her mouth with his.

Worry, questions and details winged straight to the brilliant blue skies overhead, chased into nothingness by the potent and oh-so toe-curling brush of his firm lips. In that second, she was free. Grounded and happy with so much lightness in her soul the sun seemed dim in comparison.

He lifted his head only enough to whisper against her mouth. "You gonna let all that chatter in your head go now? Or do you need another dose to tide you over?"

Oh, she could go with another dose. Several of them actually. And preferably in a location where she could do a better job of adding her hands into the mix. "I'm good," she said instead.

Straightening in his saddle, he turned his attention back on Levi and let out a sharp whistle. "All right,

Levi. Time to go. Bring Peso over here and I'll open the gate." As soon as he'd finished his instruction, he leaned over and lowered his voice. "As for both of your worries, I'd say your horse is out of the stall and your ass is in the saddle. Might as well hang on and enjoy the ride."

Chapter Ten

This friends business was for shit. All damned day long,
Trevor had fought to keep a respectable distance from
Natalie, but the woman was fucking built for his touch.
Hell, he'd shot past wanting his hands on her to needing it the second she'd laid eyes on his bed and got that
heavy-lidded, hungry look on her face. How he'd made
it through a whole day of horseback riding, fishing,
grilling out, and marshmallow roasting without tossing
her over his shoulder and carting her off to his room
had to put him up next for sainthood.

The drone of his tires against the highway filled the
cab of his truck, and the soft strains of a Dierks Bent-
ley ballad matched the easy tenor of the outstanding
day they'd left behind on the ranch. Levi was passed
out cold in the back seat, the reflection of him slumped
down and head cocked to one side in Trevor's rearview
mirror one of the cutest things he'd ever seen. The kid
had been up for everything and anything all day long,
sticking to Trevor's side for every second. Especially
the fishing. Who'd have thought teaching a kid to put a
worm on a hook would have been so much fun?

Beside him, Natalie stared out the window, her body
relaxed and a soft smile on her face.

"Admit it," he said, keeping his voice low so as not to wake up Levi. "You're more of an outdoor gal than you thought."

Her smile grew, mirroring the same delight she'd shown the first time she'd laid eyes on Deuce. The big bay's rich, glossy brown body and ebony points always captured people's attention first, but it was his sweet demeanor that snagged their appreciation long-term. Apparently, Natalie was no exception. "I might have been a little short-sighted in my earlier assessments." She swiveled her head toward him. "Though, I can promise you I'd never agree to a day like today in July or August."

"And the horses?"

She shifted a little in her seat, which only reminded him of how cute she'd been walking—or trying to walk, as it was—when she'd hopped down after an hour in the saddle. He'd been more than a little tempted to offer to rub her sweet ass and make it all better. "It wasn't like I thought it would be. It wasn't scary so much as it was powerful. Natural, maybe."

Yeah, it was. The best stress reliever in the world as far as he was concerned, especially when he and Titan could disappear for a day and do nothing but enjoy quiet trail rides. Maybe he should arrange one of those for Levi and Natalie, too. They'd both settled into the feel of riding quick and took good direction.

And that right there proved why friends wasn't going to work. Never in his life had he thought about taking anyone on his trail rides with him. Not once. Not even with Frank.

"You fell in love with Deuce," he said. "Admit it."

The expression on Nat's face shifted, not sad exactly so much as wistful and distant. "There was a lot in today to love. Thank you."

Well, damn. The last thing he'd wanted to do was put a damper on her happy glow. Unlike the usual hustle and hurry behind her actions, today she'd let go and shown a different, more easygoing side of herself. And it was a good thing she'd opened up to the idea of being outside, because if anyone belonged there it was her. Especially with the wind tossing her dark hair around so it teased the sides of her face. At least ten times he had to stop himself from tucking the silky stuff behind her ear or just sliding his fingers through it. But then he'd have caved and kissed her, and she'd have gone tense on him again. "You're awful quiet."

She pulled in a deep slow breath and let it out through her mouth. "Wyatt's week starts tomorrow. He'll be by around three to pick up Levi." Her mouth tightened and she shuttled her gaze to his. "I hate Sundays."

Fuck, the way she looked, he hated them, too. Yeah, he'd comprehended how jacked the idea of her ex having any kind of custody was, but until that moment, he'd never really considered the torture she dealt with. No parent worth their salt could easily send their kid into the lion's den once let alone every other week.

Checking to make sure Levi was still asleep through the rearview mirror, Trevor lowered his voice. "You said he only hurt Levi once. You think he'd ever do it again?"

Nat shifted enough to glance over her shoulder at Levi then shook her head. "So long as things stay like they are? No. According to Levi, Wyatt spends most of his time at work and once he comes home, Levi steers clear of him. Most of his time outside of school is spent with the nanny Wyatt hired after he got joint custody."

She fisted the hand in her lap and glared out the windshield. Her voice cracked when she spoke. "I hate the time he's away from me. Makes it hard to think about anything except if he's okay."

Trevor shifted in his seat, subtle whispers from his conscience stealing along the perimeters of his mind. He could help her. Wade in beyond the precautionary steps he'd taken with Knox and Beckett and see what options the brotherhood might have at their disposal. Maybe sniff around and see what skeletons Wyatt had to rattle and arm her with an attorney who didn't mind playing dirty.

But taking those kinds of actions meant staking a claim with his brothers. A claim he had no business making for a woman he barely knew. Hell, he could barely get within five feet of her without her locking up tight and stepping away.

Except it wasn't fear that had her keeping her distance. A skittish woman didn't watch a man the way Natalie watched him when she thought he wasn't looking. A few times the heat behind her gaze had sent his cock swelling in painful seconds, the need to sate the hunger radiating out of her curvy body nearly overpowering common sense.

He parked in the back row of her parking lot and killed the engine.

Natalie pried her purse from between her leg and the center console and twisted toward the back seat. "Levi? We're here. Wake up, baby."

Levi didn't budge, and given how much he'd put into his day, Trevor didn't imagine he would until bright and early tomorrow morning.

Trevor unfastened his seat belt. "Let him sleep. I'll get him."

It should have been weird. Awkward or at least foreign, but Levi settled into his arms like he'd done it a hundred times before, easily trusting that he was where he needed to be. In truth, the whole day had been this way. Not just between him and Levi, but with the three of them as a whole.

The space behind Trevor's sternum tightened, a not altogether uncomfortable cramp squeezing down on his heart the same as it had when Levi had offered Trevor his first s'more. Carrying Levi in with Natalie beside him after a full day together felt right. A conventional feeling he'd never thought in a million years he'd experience. Just like the days he'd spent with Frank and Bonnie except that now he was the adult. The one giving and caring.

Natalie finagled the lock and leaned her shoulder into the heavy front door. "Give me a head start to get his bed pulled down." She hurried toward the hall, tossing her purse on the coffee table before she disappeared.

The room was mostly dark, only a light from the kitchen stove spilling into the small living room. As always, the space was tidy and, not surprisingly, minus one sweet, but meddlesome mother. Through the day, Natalie had finally opened up more about how little she'd walked away with. How her mom had sold her small home in Forney, used her furniture and furnishings to outfit their two-bedroom apartment and the proceeds of the sale to fund legal bills and give them a base. Aside from Natalie's tricked-out Lexus and clothes, she hadn't asked for a thing, and that dickhead ex of hers hadn't offered. Which just made Trevor wish he'd given in and pummeled the pompous fuck all over again.

Natalie stepped out of the bedroom. "Okay, bring him on back."

Trevor hitched Levi higher against his chest and ambled toward her.

Levi's steady breaths puffed against Trevor's neck, the memorable scent of a little boy who'd put in a full day slingshotting Trevor back to his own youth. He could give Levi more days like this if he wanted to. Give Natalie and her little family all the things Wyatt was too stupid and stubborn to provide.

But then what? Natalie and Levi had been through enough with Wyatt's abuse. The last thing she needed was another round with a man with a history like his own. Hell, some of his historic outbursts made Wyatt look like a fucking saint.

He laid Levi down on the twin bed. The black-and-white *Star Wars* comforter was neatly pulled back, and the small bedside lamp casted a soft glow on Levi's tousled blond head.

With well-practiced moves, Natalie tugged off his boots and clothes and wiggled his sleep-weighted body into pajamas.

Trevor leaned a shoulder into the doorjamb and soaked it in. How efficient she was, but still sweet and careful so she didn't wake her kiddo. Man, she was a great mom. Just like Bonnie had been with him.

And she was going to send him off tomorrow.

He pushed upright and stalked to the living room, the burning violence surging beneath his skin too hot to stay in one place. The muscles along his shoulders and forearms bunched tight, needing release as much as he needed to breathe.

"Hey." Natalie padded up from behind him and touched his arm. "You okay?"

Hell no, he wasn't okay. He wanted to physically punish Wyatt Jordan in a way he'd never forget. Wanted to fuck his entire world up the way he'd upended Natalie and Levi's. But mostly, with her standing so close and looking up at him with those big dark brown eyes, he wanted to bury his hands in her hair, yank her against him, and kiss her until nothing else existed.

"I'm good." He forced a smile and took a step back, adding much-needed distance between them before he could act on impulse. She already had a nasty day ahead of her. The last thing he needed to do was heap more for her mind to juggle on top of it all. "Anytime you two want a repeat of today, you let me know."

"Don't let Levi hear you say that. He'll have you out there every week."

Not exactly the worst proposition. Better if he could supplement it with time alone with Natalie. "You forget, time spent on a horse or outside's my way of winding down. Wouldn't be a hardship having more days like today."

She ducked her head and buried her hands in her back pockets, the pretty blue shirt she'd left unbuttoned peeling back with the movement and putting her perfect tits on prime display.

Fuck, but he needed to get his head straight. What kind of asshat considered coming on to a woman when he knew she was scared shitless about how her kid was going to spend the next week? "You scheduled at The Den tomorrow?"

"No." She shrugged and tried to smile, but it came off a little crooked and empty. "It usually takes me a day or two after Levi leaves to be decent company, let alone be a friendly waitress. I'm not in until Tuesday night after work."

"Then I'll see you Tuesday." Not giving himself time to do anything stupid, he strode to the door and pulled it open, but hesitated at the threshold. "Listen, you change your mind and decide you want to get out of the house, or just want someone to rail at, you give me a call."

She padded closer, crossing her arms to fight off the chilled air driving through the open entry. "I appreciate the offer, but I'll be okay."

Which meant she'd be stubborn, hole up in her house, and worry about her kid all alone until she found some balance. "Nothing wrong with letting someone help you, Nat. Life goes a whole lot easier when you don't carry the load all by yourself."

She met his gaze, such stark honesty and openness in her expression it knocked him even farther off center. "I'm not afraid of sharing my load, Trevor. I'm afraid of crossing a line I'd have a hard time coming back from."

The nagging need he'd had all day to lay hands on her flared blowtorch bright. He swallowed down a hungry growl and fisted his hands at his sides to keep them off her. "Who said there had to be a line?"

"We both did. Friends. Remember?"

"That what you want? Friends?"

"It's what's smart. You don't need an employee causing you problems at work, and I've got to be careful what impression I set for my son. Especially with someone he adores."

To hell with that. To hell with being smart and with

him worrying about his past and his penchant for violence. As far as he was concerned, the neighborly, no-touching bullshit was over. "I'll give you that tonight. Maybe even tomorrow." He leaned in close enough she gasped and took a hesitant step backward. "But you should brace, darlin'. One way or another, we're resetting those lines to a place where I don't have to walk away from you without taking your sweet mouth in a long hard kiss."

Barely fighting back the urge to taste the surprise on her lips, he spun and headed for the stairs. Warning her which direction his thoughts were headed probably hadn't been his smartest move. With her recent past, she might pack and high-tail it for Timbuktu, but even if she did, he'd find her. He might not be long-term material for a quality woman like Natalie Jordan, but he was by God going to make her right now a whole lot better. He was also going to curl her fucking toes in bed and give them both some much-needed relief while he did it.

Chapter Eleven

Something wasn't right. Wyatt was never nice when she dropped Levi off at his father's place, and he sure didn't dote on his son, but today he'd been a modern version of *Father Knows Best*.

She uncrossed her feet off the simple wood coffee table her parents had bought ages ago and anchored her heels on the couch, wrapping her arms around her shins and resting her chin on her knees. Maybe stirring a reaction was what Wyatt was after. Given the way he'd behaved in their marriage, any ploy to get a rise out of her made sense. What better way to poke at her confidence than to send her away wondering if he might somehow manage to lure her son away from her?

Nestled in the corner of the couch with her feet tucked under her legs, her mother muted the rerun crime program and set the remote aside. "You could always call Wyatt and ask him to let you check in with Levi."

God, she wished it was that simple. True, hearing Levi's voice would go a long way toward easing the clawing anxiety in her stomach, but it also played right into Wyatt's games. Worse, it put Levi smack-dab in the middle of them. "He's better off staying close to his nanny. Me calling only makes it so he's forced to spend more time with his dad."

The opening video for the ten o'clock news filled the otherwise dark living room with a blast of color. Natalie blinked against the brightness and tried to focus on the program instead of dress-rehearsing every worst-case scenario her mind dished up. Two hours she'd sat in this same spot, eyes glued to the television without taking in one bit of the programming. It was the same routine as every other handoff night. Clean the apartment top to bottom until there was nothing left to scrub, force down food, pretend to watch whatever program her mom picked, then head to bed and stare at her ceiling until she fell asleep. Not that anyone could call what she did until sunrise *sleep*. More like a light doze with lots of tossing and turning. Working wasn't much better. Even with the endless phone calls and usual irritated customers, her worry for Levi nipped at the back of her conscience.

A heavy knock rapped against the front door, jolting Natalie upright. "Levi." She shot to the door and yanked it open, eyes trained where Levi's little blond head would be, but got an eyeful of jean-clad hips instead. Her gaze shot upward, a shocking amount of relief settling her nerves once her mind registered her unexpected guest. "Trevor?"

"Hey." The easy smile he'd paired with the greeting slipped as he scanned her head to toe. "I get you out of bed?"

Only once he'd said it did the cool November air slipping through the open door push past her surprise. The soft cotton pajama set she'd donned after dinner with its clingy lines and simple spaghetti straps wasn't exactly revealing, but it didn't make for comfortable front-door conversation either. She stepped back and waved him in. "No, we were just watching TV."

Trevor ambled in and surveyed the room. "Who's we?"

Natalie stepped out from behind Trevor and found only a dent in the cushions where her mother had been. "Well, Mom was here a second ago. She must not have wanted you to see her without her makeup on." At least that was the excuse she was sticking with. More likely her mother had sensed another prime opportunity to set her daughter up with what she'd deemed an ideal catch. God knew, her mother had pointed out enough of Trevor's virtues the last two weeks.

For a second, she considered ducking into the bedroom for a robe, but her jammies covered as much as her tank and jeans combination at The Den and were a whole lot more comfortable so she blew it off. "Can I get you something to drink? Coffee maybe?"

"Nope." Trevor settled on the couch, taking her mother's previous spot and snatching the remote like he'd visited a hundred times. Like usual, his blond hair was pulled back in a ponytail, but a tiny chunk of it had slipped free, dancing around one side of his strong jawline. His button-down was pale blue to match his eyes, and his shirtsleeves were rolled up, showcasing strong, tanned forearms. He stretched one arm along the back of the couch and nodded at the space on the couch beside him. "Have a seat. I'll hang until you're ready to go to bed."

He would?

More than a little stymied by his casual attitude, Natalie padded around the coffee table. For a second, she thought about switching on the lamp, but remembered her lack of makeup and settled for the television's forgiving glow. She eased onto the couch's opposite corner, leaving a whole cushion between them.

Trevor sucked in a long, steady breath, set the remote on the end table, and swiveled his head toward her. "You get two choices. You can either scoot over here, or I can crowd next to you and make it so you've got less wiggle room. Which one do you want?"

Natalie swallowed, his statement from last night about resetting lines fighting its way out of the dungeon she'd buried it in the second she'd closed the door behind him. Men like Trevor didn't go for women like her. They went for the model-types with Barbie doll hair and Crossfit bodies. Even if he *was* interested in her, she wasn't so sure she was ready to give her own judgment a run for its money, not with Wyatt still offering a daily reminder of how ill-equipped she was to pick men.

When she found her courage and spoke, it came out raspy. "Why are you here?"

His lips curved in a subtle but cocky smile. "Told you I'm persistent."

"Trevor, I can't…" Shit, what the hell was she supposed to say? Surely he didn't think she'd be capable of conversation tonight, let alone anything intimate. "About what you said yesterday… I can't go there. I can't even think about it with where my head's at right now."

His smile slipped and the same intensity she'd glimpsed the first night he'd visited pulsed around him. "Not here to push you on that score. We'll cross that bridge soon enough." He leaned over and gently coiled his strong hand around her wrist. "I'm here because I knew you weren't looking forward to tonight. You're strong, and I know you've got your mom to lean on, but now you've got me, too. So are you scootin' your ass over here, or am I going to have to pick you up and move you myself, 'cause I've decided I like this corner."

A sledgehammer to her solar plexus couldn't have knocked her off balance any better. "I've got you, too?"

"I'm here. I'd say that's a pretty clear message." He cocked one eyebrow. "Though one of us is still sitting in the wrong place."

Her heart punched and kicked in an awkward rhythm, the stubbornness he'd accused her of time and again digging in even as another far more vulnerable side of herself encouraged her to scramble close like he'd asked. "I'm not sure I'm ready to make decisions where you're concerned."

"Right." He leaned her direction so quick she barely had time to gasp before he gripped her around her rib cage, lifted her up and across the cushions and into his lap. With her back to the armrest, he tucked her torso up close to his chest, snagged the remote and changed the channel. "Good call. I think this arrangement works out better anyway."

She levered herself away enough to see his face, uncontrollable flutters and dangerous adrenaline pumping through her system. "Have I told you, you're bossy?"

He shifted his attention from the television to her, let his gaze rest on her lips for all of two seconds, then met her stare. "I can take a lot, Natalie. Can give you space if you need it. Can go as slow as you need me to go when it comes to what's burning between us. But one thing I don't have it in me to give is to watch you scared and fidgety as a rabbit in a cougar's sights without touching you. On that one, you'll have to suck it up, lean in and let me hold you."

Whoa.

For the first time since she pulled up into Wyatt's driveway this afternoon, the muscles in her stomach unclenched and her body lightened. She pressed her palm against his sternum, the steady beat of his heart beneath her palm anchoring her in a way she'd never experienced before. "I think that's the nicest thing anyone's ever said to me."

"That mean you'll sit there, try to take your mind off things, and relax a little?"

Relax? On his lap? With her kid in God only knew what kind of situation thirty miles away? "I doubt I'll qualify as relaxed until next Sunday, but I'll accept the comfort."

He squeezed the arm wrapped around her shoulders and rubbed his hand up and down her arm. "Appreciate it."

She nestled closer, resting her cheek against his chest and breathing in his woodsy scent. Beneath her ear, his heart *kathumped* a steady, soothing rhythm. "Trevor?"

"Mmm hmmm?"

"You're still bossy."

His chest shook on a quiet chuckle. "Darlin', you haven't seen bossy yet." He lifted his arm off the back of the couch, slid his hand up her thigh to her hip, and squeezed. "Not yet, but you will."

Her belly contracted, the mere hint of Trevor taking control in a more intimate setting lighting an entirely different tension. One that warmed her from the inside out and made her feel more alive than she'd felt in years.

As if sensing the direction of her thoughts, he

slouched deeper into the couch and kissed the top of her head. "Easy, Natalie. I've got no expectations."

He might not have, but curled up against him, it was awfully hard not to start building her own. To envision what something more than friendship with him might be like.

She smoothed her hand across one pectoral, savoring the crisp feel of his button-down and the hot skin and firm muscle underneath. Bit by bit, her pulse slowed and her muscles unwound. This was intimacy. Maybe not the steamy erotic stuff that so many people associated with the word, but real closeness. Emotional depth without a single word spoken. Two people connected in a simple yet comforting fashion.

One news story bled into another, the words and video clips no more than meaningless chatter while her mind shuffled every worst-case scenario it could come up with.

"You want to talk about it?" His simple question vibrated through her, warm and filled with a sincerity that surprised her.

He'd think she was nuts if she told him. Even her mother's first reaction to her suspicions this afternoon was closer to relief than fear, and Maureen had seen some of Wyatt's outlandish behaviors firsthand. Then again, he was a man and might be able to offer a different perspective. Maybe a viewpoint she hadn't considered that might let her actually sleep tonight.

She gently cleared her throat, but stayed cuddled next to him. "I think Wyatt's up to something."

Trevor tensed beneath her. "You think Levi's in danger?"

She shook her head and smoothed her hand against

his chest. "No, nothing like that. More like he's scheming. Planning some surprise that's guaranteed to send our world spinning." She shrugged. "Maybe another lawsuit. With Wyatt, you never know."

He lifted the hand at her hip, cupped the back of her neck and worked his fingers in slow, comforting circles. "He do something to tip you off?"

And here it was. The moment when he'd likely write her up as paranoid and tell her to relax. "You know how he was the other night? Arrogant and judgmental?"

"I'd label him more of a general jackass, but yeah, I get your point." He hesitated a beat. "He do something worse? Threaten you?"

"More like he was a perfect gentleman. Was polite to me and acted like having Levi back at his house was the best thing to ever happen to him. He even had his housekeeper make all of Levi's favorite foods for dinner." She waited, braced for his response.

His fingers slid higher until his palm cradled the back of her head. He hugged her tight against him, and he inhaled deep. "Whatever he throws at you, you'll be ready."

Her mind tripped and immediately rewound his response. She pushed against his chest and met his gaze. "You don't think I'm being melodramatic?"

He frowned back at her. "You married to the guy for eight years?"

"Well, yes."

"You got a pretty good bead on the way he operates?"

"Um, usually."

"Then I'd say you're smart to go with your instincts, keep an eye out and be ready for whatever he throws down."

A scratchy knot worked its way up the back of her throat and her heart squeezed. "But what if he wins Levi away from me? He can give him things I can't. Can use gadgets and toys to make his life with me seem dull."

Trevor smiled softly and cupped the side of her face. "Darlin', your ex could throw every penny he's got at Levi, and he'd still come up on the short end. Your kid loves you. There's not enough money or trash talk in the world to change how a boy feels for his momma, especially when the mom in question is you." His smile dimmed and his eyes narrowed as though to add more emphasis to his words. "And I'll repeat. Whatever Wyatt brings, you'll be ready."

Tears welled in her eyes and blurred his image until they spilled down her cheeks. Her bottom lip trembled as she spoke, the surge of emotion behind her words nearly too powerful to contain. "You believe me."

His fingers tightened. "Yeah, babe. I believe you."

A sob ripped free, the force behind it so strong her shoulders shook with embarrassing ferocity. In the space of a second, it was as if every beleaguered feeling she'd stuffed for countless years surged front and center, purged by Trevor's simple testament.

Before she could dampen her outburst or escape to her room, Trevor banded his arms around her and pulled her close, tucking her face in the crook of his neck. He didn't shush or try to calm her, only smoothed one hand up and down her spine while the other kept a steady hold at the back of her neck.

A part of her insisted she push away. That she wrap her pride around her and keep the blistering pain private, but another far more vulnerable part of her burrowed closer, instinctively accepting what he offered as though he'd been born to give it. The tears fell faster, his comforting presence and his unyielding strength creating a silent haven for her release. A refuge to unleash all the terror and fear she acknowledged only in the darkest hours of too many sleepless nights.

Countless whimpers and hitched breaths passed, his manly scent permeating her lungs while his heat thawed her from the inside out. When was the last time she'd felt this safe? This protected and cherished? For God only knew how long, he simply held her and silently offered one of the greatest gifts she'd ever received.

She hiccuped and eased away from his neck. Wet splotches from her tears dotted his shirt and the once-crisp fabric was wrinkled from the way she'd curled against him. She smoothed one particularly nasty crease and sniffled. "I ruined your shirt."

"Darlin', if it means I get you curled up next to me, you can ruin all my shirts." He grinned and tucked her hair behind one ear, seemingly nonplussed by her crying jag. "Feel better?"

Ducking her chin a bit, she nodded. "Embarrassed though." She sniffed again and brushed the last of her tears off her cheeks. "I never break down like that."

"Then I'd say you were overdue." He nudged her face upward with gentle fingers beneath her chin and leaned in close. The chunk of hair that had escaped his ponytail fell forward to his jawline. "Nothing for you to be embarrassed about. If anything, I'm honored you trusted me to hold you through it."

Such a simple claim, but it rattled her whole world, righting all the misshapen ideals she'd let Wyatt warp and destroy. Holding her was an honor. Not a burden.

Not a disappointment or a task to be endured. "Thank you," she whispered.

"No need to thank me when I was where I wanted to be." His warm minty breath ghosted against her face, his lips achingly close and flooding her with the memory of how firm and talented they'd felt against her own.

Without conscious thought, she traced the lower one.

His arms flexed around her. "Careful, Nat."

The barely contained growl behind his broken voice dragged her attention from his lips to his heated blue eyes. She gasped and snatched her hand away, clenching it against her chest. "I'm sorry. I just—"

"Don't." He shifted just enough so his hold on her went from one of comfort to domination, and he palmed the back of her head so she couldn't look away. "Whatever you do, you don't apologize for touching me. Ever." He scanned her face and his inhalations deepened, so much intensity radiating from his body her own tingled in response. "I don't want you to mistake why I'm here. That line you're dancing close to right now is one you and I are definitely going to cross, but not at the expense of you doubting my motives tonight."

So honest and open. Completely transparent. In fact, the more time she spent around Trevor, the more she realized her mother was right. He wasn't Wyatt. Not even close. There was honor in the way he operated. A stability and confidence that grounded his life, even to the point of clearly stating his intent. Now if she could just figure out how much she was willing to risk from a man who'd openly stated he wasn't the relationship type. "I believe you."

Holding his gaze, she softly traced the line of buttons on his shirt, letting her fingertips dip below the starched placket where the buttons parted and splaying her palm against his hot skin. His heart thrummed strong and steady, a strong and sexy lure that sent her own pulse racing.

"Nat?"

She swallowed, need and desperation warring with safety and common sense. She could either walk away, or lean in and press her mouth to his. She licked her lip instead.

A sexy rumble vibrated from his chest, and he dipped close, running his nose along the side of hers. "This what you want?"

His scent and touch filled her. Intoxicated her until her body hummed on sensation alone, all reason cast aside in favor of the here and now. She mustered what was left of her courage. "One night."

"Not going to agree to that." He teased his lips against hers, touching only enough to build a desperate ache before he pulled away. "I've had your mouth. Felt the way you moved against me." He pulled away only enough to meet her eyes head-on. "No way I'll get enough of you in one night."

Her sex clenched, and a sweet, decadent flutter swirled low in her belly. "I'm not sure I'm cut out for more than one. Not without screwing things up."

"We'll keep it light." He dragged his thumb along her cheekbone, his gaze roving her every feature as though mapping details to explore. "Only what feels good for as long as both of us are into it. No one else but the two of us so long as we're exploring."

Light. No strings beyond exclusivity, and no expectations. It sounded so simple, and her body practically begged her to accept. "If I want to stop?"

"Then we stop. No questions." Mimicking the touch she'd given him before, he slid the pad of his finger along her lower lip.

On instinct, her mouth parted and her tongue flicked against it.

"Fuck, that's hot." His hips flexed against her and he exhaled rough and ragged. "Say yes. Tell me you want this." A command and a question all rolled up into one.

She could do this. It might hurt like hell in the end, but for one small slice of time she could feel and luxuriate in the moment. Live and revel in the simplicity of white-hot passion. She slid her hands up around his neck and speared her fingers into his thick hair, slightly loosening the tie that held it in place. She dragged in a solidifying breath and whispered, "Yes."

Chapter Twelve

Best. Fucking. Answer. Ever.

Trevor straightened on the couch, lifting Natalie along with him, and guiding her legs around his hips. Before she could get her bearings or settle in, he slipped one hand beneath her ass and stood, hugging her lush body tight to his with the other.

"Trevor," she whisper-scolded as she glanced toward her mother's room. "What are you doing?"

"Not gonna play with you on the couch like a sixteen-year-old boy when I can lay you out and take my time on a bed not twenty feet away." He hefted her higher and gave her butt a meaningful squeeze. "Wrap me up, darlin'. Gonna make sure you sleep so hard tonight, you won't even know your first name when you wake up."

She gasped, studied his face for all of a second, then giggled as she locked her ankles at the small of his back.

Damn, but he liked the sound of her laugh. Light-hearted and sweet like the rest of her, but a sound she didn't make nearly enough. He'd give her that too, if she let him. Right after he made her moan and scream loud enough to make her mother blush.

He shut the door behind them and pressed her back against it, resting his forehead on hers and savoring the press of her body against his. He'd been with beautiful women. Fit, shapely women who turned heads even when they strolled out of the house in sweats and T-shirts, but none of them felt like Natalie. Everywhere he was solid, she was soft, molding against him in the most welcoming grasp of his life. Christ, he hadn't even kissed her yet and his cock was hard enough to be a skyscraper's cornerstone.

"Trevor?" She tightened her arms around his neck and her fingers tangled in the band that kept his hair back. "You okay?"

Perfect. Outstanding on a scale he didn't dare pause to evaluate. "Left *okay* way behind when you opened your front door in your pajamas." Just the idea of her tooling around without a bra on had given him a semi and all kinds of sly ideas on how to cop a feel. Feeling her natural and unbound next to him on the couch had been a sick but delicious torture.

Sliding his hands out from under her ass, he gripped her hips and eased her feet to the floor. "Only get once to have you the first time. Not gonna screw it up by rushing through it." Keeping his body close to hers so she couldn't slip away, he smoothed his hands up her arms and let out a slow breath. Only the barest glow from the parking lot lights trickled through the dark room, leaving her tiny form mostly in shadows. "I want to see you."

Her muscles tightened, and her breath caught. "I'm not so sure that's a good idea to start with."

Like hell it wasn't. He toyed with the thin, soft straps holding her top in place, sorely tempted to tug them down and fill his palms with her breasts. "Imagined you, Nat." He skimmed his fingertips beneath the straps and down along the edge that covered her chest. "Felt you against me that night and filled in the blanks with so damned many dirty scenarios you'd blush for weeks if you ever saw them."

She hesitated and her fingertips dug into his shoulders. "I've had a kid. It does things to a woman. I doubt I'm anywhere near what you're used to."

"You trust me?"

Another pause, this one ending with a cautious "Yes."

"I want to build on that. Want you to see with your own eyes what your body does to me. Kinda hard for you to mark my appreciation in the dark." He cupped the back of her neck and let his fingers tangle in her hair. Fuck if it wasn't as soft and slick as the sexy pajamas she had on. "It make you feel better if I go first?"

A shiver moved through her, and her voice came out thick and raspy. "Okay."

Damn, but he liked that sound almost as much as he liked her acquiescence. Come to think of it, the only words he'd like hearing more were *yes, sir* and *harder*.

He forced himself back a step, circled her wrist with his fingers, and pulled her against him the same as he would for a casual two-step. "Then relax. We're just going to play and have fun. Only what feels good, remember?"

She splayed her hands high on his chest and angled her face to his, easily following his lead as he slow-danced her toward the bed. "Easy for you to say. You've done this in the last few years."

Meaning she hadn't, and fuck if that knowledge didn't make him want to knock tonight out of the park even more. The backs of her knees hit the mattress, and he lifted her onto the bed. "Sweetheart, you might think you're rusty, but the way you kiss, you were born for this." With one hand holding him propped above her and his knees caging her on each side, he dipped low and teased her lips with his. "Now give me your mouth, darlin'. Time to get you back in the saddle."

"You're bad," she muttered, a little playful but a whole lot breathy.

He palmed the back of her head. "Not yet, but I'm working on it." He slanted his mouth over hers, swallowing her gasp and savoring the press of her plump lips against his. God, he loved the taste of her—honey-sweet yet unique to her alone. Loved the way she opened for him and tangled her tongue with his, as easy and natural as breathing.

She whimpered and dug her fingers into his shoulders, urging him to close the distance he kept between them.

"Easy," he murmured against her jaw, licking and kissing his way down the line of her neck. "Got all night to give you what you need."

She angled her neck for better access and fisted his shirt. "How about if we do a quick run the first time and explore later?"

He chuckled and nuzzled the sweet spot behind her ear. "The only thing quick happening tonight is me getting my mouth on your pussy."

Rolling her hips, she moaned and speared her fingers in his hair. "Trevor."

Fuuuck. The only thing better than a sexy firecracker like Natalie when it came to fooling around was a sexy firecracker who got off on dirty talk. Damned if her response didn't leave him cranked and ready to muddy the waters. He grinned against the delicate skin of her neck, slid his hand down her spine and gave her butt a quick squeeze. "Now slide higher up the bed and let me shuck my clothes. I've got work to do."

"Ugh." She dropped her hands to the bed with a melodramatic flair. "You ever heard the term cruel and unusual punishment?"

Oh, yeah. Playful Natalie was going to be a whole lot of fun. He rolled away from her, perched on the edge of the bed and toed off his boots. "I'm not much into pain, but if that's a sly way of you asking me to spank your sweet ass, I'm game."

Her soft giggle sounded behind him and the bed shifted, but instead of scooting back toward the pillows like he'd asked, she moved in behind him, snagged his ponytail holder and pulled it free.

He smiled into the darkness and tugged his socks off. Outside of the tentative touch she'd started their little dance with on the couch, it was the most aggressive move she'd ever made with him. He liked it. A hell of a lot. He stood, tossed his billfold on the nightstand and switched on the bedside lamp. "Feelin' frisky, are you?"

For a second, she blinked against the sudden light, then zeroed in on his hands working the buttons on his shirt. She bit her lower lip. "Maybe."

Maybe his ass. More like way past go and ready to pounce if the gleam in her eyes was any indication. He peeled his shirt free, tossed it aside, and crawled onto the bed. Stretching out beside her, he tucked his hands behind his head and crossed his ankles. "You want to play, then do your worst."

Her lips parted and her eyes got huge, their focus rooted to his left side. "You've got a tattoo."

"That surprise you?"

"Yes." She frowned and studied the richly detailed phoenix spanning his ribs. "I mean, no. I mean...it looks right on you. I just never imagined..." Her gaze shot to his and she snapped her mouth shut. "Sorry, that sounds bad."

He grinned. "Darlin', if you've been trying to imagine what I look like naked, that is anything but bad. Now are you gonna put your creativity to work, or make us both suffer longer?"

She cocked her head to one side. "I can do anything?"

"Make me hurt. Whatever moves you. Just remember, what's good for the goose is good for the gander."

Slow as molasses in winter, her gaze slid down his torso. Rolling to her knees beside him, she lifted the dog tags he'd worn damn near every day of his life for the last ten years away from his chest and cradled them in her palm. Unlike standard-issue military tags, they were heavy platinum and etched in black with the Haven symbol Jace had designed eons ago. "What are these?"

"A gift from my brothers."

She ran her thumb along the image and shifted her gaze back to his tattoo. "You worked them into the design." Releasing the tags, she traced her fingertip along the subtle Haven details he'd incorporated in the bird's belly. "You're the phoenix and they're a part of you."

His stomach clenched, the simple torture of her touch and the piercing accuracy of her assessment knocking him off center. Less than five minutes since she'd seen the reminder he'd had inked on his skin, and she'd zeroed in on its meaning. The only people who'd understood before had been his brothers. "Something like that."

Emboldened, she rose higher and straddled his hips. "You don't want to talk about it?"

He fisted his hands to keep them behind his head and swallowed hard. "Don't mind sharing. Just having a hard time focusing on anything except you getting your hands and mouth on my body." It wasn't a complete lie. He truly craved the contact as much as he needed air, but in one simple observation she'd cut so close to the heart of him it was hard to breathe. If he didn't get them back on a lighthearted track, shit was going to get way more explosive than was good for either of them.

Her mouth quirked to one side, a mix of a smile and a cute mew that spelled all kinds of inspired trouble. "I seem to remember wanting you to get on with business not five minutes ago, and you turned me down."

"Wasn't turning you down, darlin'. Was seeing to logistics." He uncrossed his ankles and bent his knees.

The movement shifted her off balance and she caught herself with hands on his pecs.

"The sooner you get my jeans off," he grumbled low, "the sooner I can get *you* off."

"Oh." Her eyes slid shut and she wiggled her hips, grinding her sex over his engorged cock. "Hard to argue with logistics."

He growled and gripped her hips. "Baby, you don't take control and get us going, I'm taking over and paying you back times twenty."

"Okay, okay, okay." She mock pouted and shimmied backward, forcing his legs straight so she had room to work. Leaning in close, she pulled in a low, sexy breath and pressed her lips to his sternum. Her words came out husky and hot against skin. "Have I mentioned you're bossy?"

"Once or twice," he croaked, his thoughts too tangled up by the press of her mouth and the way she licked a path down his belly to come up with any witty retorts.

With nimble fingers, she worked his button and zipper. The denim parted, giving his brief-covered dick much-needed breathing room, but before he could appreciate the relief, she cupped him through the cotton and squeezed.

"Fuck." He flexed against her palm and fisted his hands at his sides, the mix of her bold grip and the open wonder on her face drawing his nuts up tight. "Remind me never to piss you off. You play this dirty when we're on good terms, I'll never live through makeup sex."

She lifted her innocent gaze to his and licked her lower lip. "Was that bad?"

"Oh no. Not bad at all. Only one thing that would make it better."

"Yeah?"

"Yeah." He covered her hand on his cock, guided it up and then under his briefs. "Now it's perfect."

Undiluted hunger flashed behind her near-black eyes, and her tiny fingers wrapped around his shaft, the heat of her palm scalding his skin in the abso-fucking-lutely best torture known to man.

Lifting his butt, he shoved his briefs and jeans past his hips. Only when he'd worked them to his thighs did she snap out of her stupor and help him finish the job, tugging the denim free. The heavy fabric had barely hit the floor before she resumed her place, one knee on either side of his legs. She traced a bulging vein along the top side of his cock in a barely there touch. The light contact shouldn't have been so shocking after her firm grasp of seconds before, but it powered through him like a lightning bolt.

"I think you're right." She reached the end of him and circled the pre-come pooled there. When she swiped her slick finger beneath the sensitive ridge, it was all he could do not to buck her off him. "Lights are a great idea."

"Glad to hear it, darlin', 'cause now it's my turn." Before she could protest, he knifed up, gripped her hips, and dragged her so she straddled his cock. He toyed with one of the tiny straps, running his finger beneath it and teasing the sensitive flesh along the top swell of her breast.

Bracing herself with hands on his shoulders, she circled her hips. "I didn't get to enjoy my turn very long."

Trevor tugged the strap down and let it hang loose around her bicep. "You want me to stretch out and let you explore, I'll give you carte blanche later." Much later. As in after he'd felt her come around his cock and they were too boneless to think, let alone talk.

He lifted his gaze to hers and guided the other strap over her shoulder. The loose top slithered down her torso and pooled in a featherlight circle around her waist.

"Perfect." It came out as reverent as he meant it, his heart urging him to step shit up and add some tactile appreciation to the mix. Since the first time he and his buds from school had pilfered a dirty magazine, he'd known he was a tit man. Big, little, it didn't matter. He loved them all. But Nat's rack was a thing of beauty. The gold standard that would forever make every other woman's breasts pale in comparison—natural and full with dark nipples that practically begged for his mouth. He skimmed his fingertips up her rib cage and dragged his thumbs along the skin beneath them.

A shiver worked through her torso and the already tight points hardened further. Her eyes slid shut and she rolled her shoulders back, silently urging him for more. "Trevor."

"Yeah, babe, I got you." He trailed a path up the center of each breast and circled her areolas, keeping the contact light. He pinched each tip, not enough to hurt but enough to gauge her response.

She groaned and let her head drop back.

"More?"

"Yes."

Thank fuck, because the way his body was thrumming he wasn't sure he could maintain gentle for long. He rolled her nipples between his fingers and increased the pressure, gently tugging her toward him. "Lean over here, sweetheart. Need these sweet nipples in my mouth."

She moved quickly, a breathy but schoolgirl-cute "Okay" whispering past her lips as she tilted forward and gave him what he wanted. He loved that about her, too. No games. No sexual posturing and trying and put herself in the best light possible. Just adorable, sexy Natalie eager to dive in and enjoy.

Filling his palms with her heavy breasts, he pushed them together and got to work, licking and sucking to his heart's content.

Her hips rolled with each draw, and her nails bit into his shoulders. When he scraped his teeth along one peak, her head dropped forward and her dark hair spilled around them. Christ, it was like he'd died and gone to heaven, her flowery scent and the taste of her skin rocketing his need off the charts. At this rate he wouldn't get his cock inside her without coming, and no way in hell was that happening until he got a taste of her pussy.

Not giving her time to brace, he rolled them to her back, hooked his fingers in her pajamas as he sat back on his heels and peeled them down her legs in one unbroken motion.

It was a bad move, one he should have known better than to make given how the sight of her tits alone had thrown him into outer-orbit, but fuck if he could do anything about it now. He was too shell-shocked. Too utterly undone to force his slack jaw shut and ease her into the slow appreciation she deserved.

Uncertainty quavered in her voice. "Trevor?"

He couldn't find the right words. Wanted to desperately, but he doubted any language had words ample to cover how gorgeous she was. He forced his gaze to hers, taking time to soak in every generous curve and her creamy skin along the way. "We are never, *ever* doing this with the lights off."

She smiled, relief and that innocent goodness that made her who she was flickering back to life.

He centered himself between her knees, smoothed his hands up her outer thighs, and squeezed the voluptuous slope between her waist and hips. A faint scar arched low on her abdomen, one that some men might have considered a flaw on an otherwise perfect canvas, but all he could do was marvel at how she made it look sexy. He dipped low and traced it with his lips. "No words, Natalie. Not one that does you justice."

"You don't have to say that. I know having a kid changed me."

"Got no idea how you looked before and don't really care," he murmured against her skin. He licked lower, painting a wicked path toward her sex. "My guess though, it just made a great thing even better. Remind me to give your kid a pat on the back the next time I see him."

She propped up on her elbows, but her body shook with the effort. Even her voice held a subtle tremor. "You can't be serious."

"Oh, darlin', I've never been more serious about anything in my life." Poised right over her mound, he slid his hands under her ass, angled her sex for his mouth and lifted his gaze. "Now lay back and let me work."

He wasn't sure which of them moaned louder, him when her taste exploded in his mouth, or her from the way he speared his tongue deep, but one thing was for damned sure—he wasn't coming up for air anytime soon.

Natalie speared her fingers in his hair and held on tight, grinding her honey-coated sex against him. "Trevor!"

He smiled against her flesh and circled her clit with his tongue. He was probably going to hell for making her shout with her momma not thirty feet away, but for right now she was mindless and he fucking loved it. He slid a finger inside her and nearly came when her walls clamped down and fluttered around them.

Oh, yeah. Totally ready. Primed and ready to fly. He tongued her clit and added another finger, building a rhythm to match his pounding heart. "Grab my billfold, Nat. Need a condom."

She rolled her head on the pillow and fumbled for the nightstand.

The second her hand closed around his wallet, he surrounded her clit with his lips and suckled deep.

She fumbled the billfold to the bed and her torso bowed, riding the none-too-gentle tug of his mouth and the pleasure that went with it. Beautiful. Utterly open and guileless.

"Don't you dare come," he growled, grappling for his billfold where she'd dropped it by her side and pumping his fingers inside her with the other. He flipped it open, pried out a condom, and tore it open with his teeth. "When you go over, I'm going with you."

She pried her eyes open and the dazed pleasure behind her gaze nearly forced his release. Sliding her hand down her belly, she dipped her fingers between her thighs and toyed with her clit, still slick from his mouth. "Hurry."

The profoundly erotic act locked him up tight. His cock pulsed with the need to slide inside her wet heat and claim her in the most fundamental way possible. With shaking hands, he gloved up faster than was wise, braced above her and slicked his throbbing glans through her drenched folds. His voice came out broken and deep, his lungs barely able to function from the tension gripping his chest. "This what you want? My cock inside you?"

She moaned and arched, widening her legs and baring the pretty pink folds of her sex as her fingers speared downward and grazed either side of his cock. "I don't want it. I need it."

Christ, what a sound. A plea and a demand all rolled

up into one. He notched the tip of his shaft inside her and hitched her leg high against his hip. "Hang on."

He powered forward, filling her in one bold thrust he felt clear to his toes. In the space of a second, his whole reality shifted. All that mattered was the velvet heat surrounding him and Nat's ragged, needy mewls. The slap of their hips and the hedonistic tap of his balls against her perineum. This wasn't just casual sex. This was a no-holds-barred earth-shattering thing of beauty. The kind of carnal thunderbolt teenage boys fantasized about and grown men dreamed of. He couldn't get close enough. Couldn't drive deep enough to mark her the way he wanted.

Dropping back to his heels, he palmed her hips, angled upward, and drove his cockhead against the sweet spot inside her.

She dug her heels into his flanks and squeezed her ripe tits, every thrust making them jiggle inside her grip. Christ, he could come just from looking at her. The heavy weight of her stare, how she watched them move together, and the sight of his shaft pistoning in and out of her pretty pink sex.

He licked his thumb and teased her swollen clit. "That's it, sweetheart. Take my cock. Come for me and milk it dry."

"Trevor!" Her hips jerked in time with her startled cry and her pussy clenched hard, pulsing around his shaft so hard he couldn't breathe.

He drove to the hilt and let go, rolling his hips against hers while his release jetted free. With every throb, the silky heat of her and her sweet whimpers marked him, branded a part of him he hadn't known existed.

Slow and easy, he rode the waves, shifting his torso

forward and savoring the soft press of her breasts against his chest. The feel of her hands along his back and her legs banded around his waist. He buried his face in her neck and inhaled her wildflower scent, the rapid thump of her pulse wild against his lips.

Her fingertips trailed up his spine then tangled in his hair. "You okay?" Her voice was breathy and shook to match the subtle tremors in her thighs.

Hell no, he wasn't okay, but damned if he'd tell her that. He'd promised her light and by God, that's what he'd give her, because no way in hell was he letting her get away. Not until they'd both had ample opportunity to work this need out of their systems.

"A lot of words to pick from, darlin', but *okay* isn't one of them." He forced himself up on his elbows and kissed her swollen lips. "Think I could settle on out-standing or fan-fucking-tastic, though."

She grinned, her cheeks flushed and her eyes bright and pretty as they'd been at the ranch. "Me too."

Oh he was fucked. Well and truly screwed twenty different ways where this woman was concerned, because he'd been wrong. Natalie Jordan wasn't born for sex. She was born for *him*.

Chapter Thirteen

A faint, warm draft tickled Natalie's shoulder, gently lifting her from deep, delicious sleep. A part of her insisted she scratch it before her mind could kick into scrambling-mother mode, but the rest of her was content to relax. To burrow deeper into the snug cocoon around her and enjoy the quiet moments before her alarm went off. She hummed and smiled, wiggling against the firm heat blanketing her back.

Her eyes snapped open and her heart lurched. That wasn't a blanket. That was 100 percent man spooned tight against her, complete with arms banded around her waist and legs tangled with hers. And they were both naked.

Every high-definition detail from the night before blazed bold and bright. How beautiful he'd made her feel. How thoroughly he'd seen to her pleasure, and how playful and easy he'd made every moment.

Well, not every moment had been playful. A few times she'd sensed them dancing awfully close to a line he wasn't willing to cross, while others had shaken her clear to her soul. The whole night had been a revelation. A decadent temptation to toss caution to the wind and drown in the picture-perfect fantasies he'd created.

But she couldn't do that. They'd agreed to light and easy, not happily ever after. The only chance she stood of keeping her heart from being shredded was to keep that reminder foremost in her thoughts.

The soft-blue readout on her alarm flicked from 5:57 to 5:58 a.m.

Thirty more minutes to savor and enjoy the feel of him next to her before her alarm went off. A whole half hour of indulgence before she faced reality without him there to distract her from all her worst-case-scenario mind games. But he'd given her last night. Helped her through her fears and given her something amazing to hold on to. Calmed her thoughts in the most toe-curling way possible.

His chest rose and fell in a deep, steady rhythm, and his breath ghosted across her bare shoulder. God, he felt good. Not once in her life had she woken with a man like this. Wyatt hated cuddling after sex beyond what he felt was obligatory, and she'd never actually spent the night with a man before him.

What was the protocol for a morning-after moment like this anyway? Should she be sweet and attentive like she would on a date? Or was she supposed to act like having him there was no big deal?

His arm around her waist tightened and he nuzzled the sweet spot behind one ear. The deep rumble of his voice moved through her like a caress, a sexy, sleepy rasp that stroked in all the right places. "Turn that mind of yours off and relax."

"I can't," she whispered. "I have to get up and go to work."

"Bet I can find a way to make you forget about work." He inhaled slowly, kissed the back of her neck, and ground his hips against her ass, making it abundantly clear that one particular part of him was wide awake and raring to go.

So, was she supposed to let him sleep, or roll over and initiate them kicking off their day with a quick and dirty version of last night?

"You're overthinking it, darlin'." He pushed up on one elbow and rolled her to her back. His thick blond hair fell forward as he cupped the side of her face and swooped in for a kiss.

For a split second, she froze, panicked by the one-two reminder punch of morning breath and bed head, but then his lips touched hers and switched her worries into neutral. How he did it, she couldn't figure out, but the second he got his mouth on hers, all her common sense went out the window.

This morning's kiss was no exception, though it was still a new experience. While the others they'd shared had been quick to flare and deeply heated, this one was light and languid. A lazy feast of lips and tongues reserved for quiet Saturday mornings.

Slowly, he lifted his head. "Promised you I'd keep this light and I meant it. You gonna let whatever worries were scampering around in your head go now?"

Light and easy. No happily ever afters.

She rolled toward him and snuggled against his chest. "I wasn't worried so much as I was trying to figure out morning-after protocol. I don't think I've ever woken up with a man wrapped around me."

He grinned, the languorous weight of his heavy-lidded stare making it alluringly potent. "It feel good?"

The best. Completely safe and protected in a way she'd never felt before. "Yeah."

His grin spread to a full-on smile full of teeth and dimples. Though, before she could fully appreciate it, he rolled to his back and pulled her with him so her torso lay half on and half off his chest. He combed his fingers through her hair like he'd done it a thousand times before. "What time do you get up?"

"Six-thirty. My title might say I'm a processing agent, but it's really more of a glorified call center role. So long as I'm at my desk by seven-thirty, appearance isn't high on the importance scale."

"Good, then you've got time to talk."

All the lighthearted easiness of the morning *whooshed* out of the room, leaving her muscles locked up tight.

He chuckled low and hugged her tighter. "Just reminded you I plan to keep things light. Not going to follow that up with the *It's been fun* speech. Now, relax." He traced her bare spine with his fingertips and goose bumps lifted in their wake. "Don't know much about pregnancies and deliveries, but I'm thinking that scar isn't because of Levi."

She huffed out an ironic laugh and smoothed her hand above his sternum. His heartbeat thrummed strong and steady, and the faint dusting of hair between his pecs tickled her palm. "Oh, it's because of Levi all right, but not his delivery."

The hand coasting up and down her spine stilled. "Was it Wyatt?"

"Not like you're probably thinking. He only struck me once, and it was after I'd goaded him pretty hard."

"No excuse for hitting a woman. I don't care if you went after him with a baseball bat."

"Maybe not for a man like you, but Wyatt's got a

sizable ego to go with his MD. It's bad enough when a wife questions his judgment, but when I called him out on something as a nurse, he flipped."

"Called him out on what?"

She shrugged, hating the topic now as much as she had back then. "I found some bootleg pharmaceuticals in his office. Designer injectables from God only knows where. I pushed him to fess up and he hit me."

The loose hold of his hand on her shoulder tightened and the mood in the room shifted to something dangerous.

She propped herself up beside him.

His mouth was tight and his gaze lasered onto the ceiling.

God, how stupid could she be? He'd told her abuse was a trigger for him, but she'd gone and red-flagged it all over the place. "The scar is from a tummy tuck," she added, hoping the distraction would take his mind off wherever his thoughts had gone.

He shifted his attention to her and frowned. "A what?"

"A tummy tuck. Women get them when they've got loose skin around their middle and want to get rid of it. Levi did a number on my belly and Wyatt didn't like it. I didn't want the procedure, but I was so damned eager to earn back even a little of the man I'd married, I finally agreed."

He smoothed her hair away from her face and cupped the back of her head. "You were smart to run when you did. Someday Levi will thank you for it."

"I should've gone sooner. I just got too lost. Too hung up on trying to get back what I thought we'd had, but the more I tried, the worse it got. By the time he hit me, I'd lost so much of myself it was hard to function."

"But you found your way."

Her voice dropped to a whisper, the reality of how far she'd sunk before she ran a weight she couldn't shake. "Not before he hit Levi."

"No, but you took action as soon as he did. That's something to be proud of." His voice hitched. "Trust me."

There it was again. That hint of something raw and vulnerable he kept tightly guarded. More than anything, she wanted to take it from him. To ease the burden if only for a moment the same way he'd done for her. "You say that like a man who's got his own secrets."

"Not secrets. Regrets maybe, but not secrets." He toyed with her hair, winding one strand around his finger while he studied her face. "Not all women get out. Some of them live it their whole life. Worse, some of them die young never knowing they could have had better."

"Anyone in particular?"

He hesitated, pain flashing behind his beautiful blue eyes for one defenseless second. "My mom."

The room's quiet roared and her heart squeezed. No wonder he'd reacted like he did. Why he'd been so willing to step in and help her. She laid her head on the pillow and cuddled beside him. "Is it too much if I ask what happened?"

"The same thing that happened almost every day in some form or fashion. Dad was in a mood and he took it out on Mom. The only difference that day was he took it too far and killed her. He used his pistol and took his own life when he'd realized what he'd done. Fucker was too much of a coward to face the consequences, I guess."

"Where were you?"

"At school." His expression hardened. "I found them when I got home."

Desperate to comfort him, she ran her fingers along his strong jawline. His morning stubble rasped against her fingers. "I'm sorry."

He rolled to his side and faced her, a little of his tension eking back to wherever it was he kept it hidden as he studied her face. "Don't be. It sucked watching my mom go through that, but their deaths brought me Frank and Bonnie. It took six foster homes and more trouble than my social worker could handle to get there, but I made it. Frank helped me get my shit straight. Gave me a home and taught me what a family's supposed to look like."

"They adopted you?"

"Yep. Best day of my life when my last name changed to Raines."

"Smooth sailing after that, huh?"

He grinned and rolled to his back, some of his playfulness rebounding. "Uh, no. Up until I graduated maybe, but I took sowing my wild oats after high school to a whole new level. Damn near threw away all the upbringing they gave me before Axel found me."

"Axel?"

"One of my brothers."

She frowned at that. "One of the men in the picture?"

"Yep." He knifed up and prowled over her, pressing his hard body against hers in a way that promised all kinds of decadent distractions. "But that's a different story, and you've gotta get to work."

"I can be late."

He cupped the side of her face and gave her more of his weight. "Got plenty of time to learn all my dirty laundry. This week's about us having fun and me keeping your nights distracted. Now are you good with me crashing here with your mom on the other side of the living room, or are you packing a bag and staying at my place?"

Her mind hitched and scrambled to reprocess. "I'm sorry, what?"

"Distraction, darlin'." As if to remind her what his special brand of distraction was, he rolled his still very erect cock against the core of her. "I'm keeping your nights busy until Levi's back. I promised I'd keep it light, but that doesn't mean it'll be boring."

"You can't be serious. You've got two different companies to run."

"Yeah, and feeling your heels digging into my ass while I'm driving my cock deep is fan-fucking-tastic stress relief. Now what's it going to be? Your place or mine?"

She opened her mouth.

"A word to the wise," he said before she could speak. "You're loud when you come."

"I am not!"

"Are too." He smiled and nipped her lower lip. "Fucking love it, too."

Her cheeks burned and it was all she could do not to duck under the covers. Still, it had been forever since she'd had even the slightest inclination to do something so spontaneous and fun. To throw her schedule out the window and live like she didn't have a thousand responsibilities hanging around her neck. "Okay you win. I'll pack a bag. But if I do, you'd better give me something spectacular to scream about."

He chuckled low and bit his lower lip. His eyes smoldered with wanton promise. "Darlin', you won't just scream. You'll beg."

Chapter Fourteen

What a fucking day. Not bad so much as chock-full of unexpected curveballs and challenges—starting with the shock of how much he'd liked waking up next to Natalie. That alone had been enough to rattle Trevor's cage and keep him off balance for days, but learning that Wyatt was using non-FDA-approved drugs? That had shaken parts of his reality he hadn't cared for, enough so he'd perked right the hell up and decided it was time to take action.

Trevor turned into Haven's long driveway and killed his headlights as soon as he got close to the house. At one o'clock in the morning, the guys might be up and waiting on him, but Sylvie and Ninette rarely stayed up past the ten o'clock news. If either of them had an inkling their boys were gathered for a late-night rally, they'd pry their butts out of bed no matter how tired they were and make sure there was an endless supply of coffee and food.

Aside from the porch light and the pendulum fixtures above the massive kitchen island, the house was dark, but a sweet, buttery scent lingered in the air that said Sylvie had concocted one of her wicked desserts before she'd turned in for the night.

He kept his footsteps as light as his boots would allow on the dark wood floors and stalked through the kitchen to the basement door. The second he opened it, light and his brothers' voices rumbled up in greeting. He closed the door behind him and jogged down the steps. "Sorry I'm late."

Jace and Beckett jerked their chins up in silent greeting.

"Yo."

"Hey, brother, what's up?"

"You want a beer?"

This from the rest of the crew already in their seats and waiting.

From his place at one end of the table, Axel rounded out the chorus with a grin. "'Bout time you got here." Unlike the rest of the guys who favored jeans and T-shirts, he was gussied up in his fancy slacks and a cashmere sweater that probably cost as much as Trevor's Lucche-ses. While he normally kept his wild russet hair knotted up and out of the way, tonight it was loose, blending with his full beard to make him look like a Scottish warlord who'd battled and conquered the entire *GQ* staff.

"Sorry. The Den was packed when I left. Never seen a Tuesday night like this one." Trevor snagged a bottle of Bud from the full-size stainless steel fridge in the corner and popped the top. Thank God, Natalie was on the closing crew or he'd have felt like shit for planning the late-night rendezvous at his place later. "I knew shit would get busy before the holidays, but I didn't factor it would ramp up a full week early."

"Weather's been good and people are ready to blow off steam," Jace said from the opposite end of the table. "Crossroads has been up a good fifteen percent over last year. I say take it and run while you can. Come January, everyone'll be moaning over their holiday credit card statements."

"Can't remember you ever calling rally," Knox said to Trevor. It was rare to see his brother without some kind of electronic device within reaching distance, but around this table Knox gave his brothers his undivided attention. "Something wrong with Frank?"

Trevor pulled his chair out from its place to the left of Axel's. Rather than trick the basement out in high décor the way Jace had with the rest of the house, the basement was raw and filled with memories of where they'd each come from. Every man picked their own chair, something that stood for a piece of their past or a hope for their future. Compared to the rest of the guys, his was simple, a ladder-back chair in green enamel paint that had come from Bonnie's kitchen when she'd bought a new dining room set, but it grounded him. Reminded him of the sacrifice his biological mother had made and the good life she'd given him, even if it had taken her death to do it.

"You didn't tell 'em?" Trevor said to Axel.

Axel shook his head and sipped his Scotch. Outside of Frank, the wily brother had been Trevor's biggest champion and go-to confidant, including this morning when he'd strolled out of Natalie's apartment with an uneasy edge he couldn't shake. "Your instincts. Your story. I just told the guys you'd run across a complication."

Meaning he suspected there was more to Trevor's concern than just protecting his business interests, but Trevor wasn't going there. This thing he'd started with Natalie wasn't safe for either of them long-term. They'd scratch their itch, have fun, and move on.

Trevor swiveled toward Jace and Zeke. "You two remember the waitress with the cell phone problem about three weeks ago? Natalie Jordan?"

Both nodded.

"Well, turns out the reason she was running the thing ragged was she was fielding panicked calls from her mom. Her ex is a piece of work. Keeps badgering Nat and using her kid to get her back. Nat doesn't want to go because he hit her and her kid. She bailed without anything more than a car and their clothes. I had a hunch and followed her home that night. Ended up jumping into the middle of an altercation that was brewing its way up to ugly."

Jace spun the toothpick perched at one side of his mouth with his finger and thumb. Being the one who'd helped Axel cover Trevor's tracks after the bloody altercation that had put him on the road to being a brother, Jace knew the extent of Trevor's penchant for fists firsthand. "Jumped in the middle how?"

"Not like you're thinking," Trevor answered. "The last thing I wanted was to cause problems for Natalie, so I stalked up and pretended like she and I were an item. Told her ex I didn't like coming to check on my woman and findin' her trading insults with him outside her front door."

Beckett chuckled low and leaned into the table, crossing his huge forearms in front of him. "Now there's a little detail you left out before."

"No shit," Knox said, grinning huge.

Danny planted his beer bottle on the table and scowled at Knox and Beckett. "You knew about this shit and didn't fill me in?"

Zeke cocked an eyebrow. "Didn't share with me either."

"It wasn't a big deal," Trevor cut in before Jace and Axel could chime in too. "I went to Knox and asked him for more info on the ex. Just a precaution in case the guy decided he wanted to start a pissing contest at The Den. Natalie had on her work clothes, so there's no way he'd have missed the logo."

Axel zeroed in on Knox. "You find anything?"

"Not much beyond what I got the first go-round digging into Natalie. His practice makes bank, he dabbles in a shit-ton of side investments and he likes to gamble, but never more than he can afford to lose. Everything Trevor said about the divorce was spot-on. She got a Lexus SUV, their personal effects, and nothing else. Bastard got joint custody even though Natalie's lawyer claimed abuse."

"How the bloody hell does that happen?" Axel said, the growl in his voice reminding Trevor of a nasty bull-dog.

"Connections," Knox answered before Trevor could. "The judge on the case is a member of Wyatt's country club."

Jace leaned to one side of his battered banker's chair and anchored his elbow on the arm. "So that was three weeks ago. He make a move?"

"Not yet." He hesitated a second and glanced at Axel.

Axel dipped his chin, a barely perceptible nod of encouragement. "Tell 'em, brother."

Slouching a little in his chair, he splayed his knees wide and let out a heavy breath. Now was when the real razzing started. "Ever since the altercation, Wyatt's been quiet. Not what you'd expect with the narcissistic type. I should have caught it earlier, but my gut says he's spent that time up to something."

"Up to something how?" Jace said.

"I don't know. But Natalie's been antsy since she dropped her kid off for his week at Wyatt's. Said he was acting shifty in a way that usually spelled problems for her."

"Probably another legal claim," Knox said. "He's used the system to keep her hopping for the last year."

"That's what I thought too," Trevor said. "But then she said something this morning that tweaked me. It's probably nothing, but if it is, I need to watch my back."

Beckett smirked and rocked back on his chair's hind legs. "Why do I get the impression this conversation went down while you were curled next to her in bed? Or has your spunky waitress left her insurance claims job for a full-time gig at The Den?"

Trevor scowled and kept going. With a little luck he could gloss over the timing and they'd let shit drop. "What's got me tweaked is she was telling me about how things went down the first time Wyatt hit her. She mentioned something about him using non-approved drugs on patients."

The room got quiet, two and two adding up just as quick for them as it had for him this morning.

"Same kind of product you've been hauling?" Danny asked.

"It sounded like it."

Jace's eyes narrowed in a way that didn't bode well for Wyatt Jordan. "You think he might be one of your buyers?"

"Maybe. If his practice is doing as good as Knox

says, it's possible he's luring them in with cutting-edge product."

"Can your middleman give us buyer names?" Knox asked.

Zeke shook his head. "He won't do it. I've never met the guy. At the time, I figured that was in our best interest and let it ride."

Beckett shrugged his shoulders and scanned the rest of the guys. "Then we need to give him a reason to change his mind."

"You'd have to find him first," Trevor said. "All Zeke and I have is a contact number, and I'd bet good money it's a burner with no GPS."

Axel reclined back in his tattered club chair and anchored one Hugo Boss-clad foot on his knee. His usual laid-back tone came out grated and dangerous. "Then we ferret out the scunner another way."

Trevor fought back a chuckle. It usually took a lot of Scotch or a particularly challenging woman to get Axel's more colorful words to come out and play. "Are we talking about Wyatt or my middleman?"

"Your woman's ex," Axel fired back quickly. "You've got another haul you're workin' on now, right?"

Trevor dipped his chin, purposefully ignoring the part about Nat being his woman. The last thing anyone needed was more encouragement.

"Then see if he bites this time around." Axel's gaze shifted to Beck. "Your team can run a tail once word gets out and see if he's a purchaser."

Beckett frowned. "I'd like it better if we had someone on the inside."

"No way we'd pull that off on this short of notice,"

Knox said. "It'd take at least a month to get someone on his payroll."

"Not as an employee," Beckett said. "As a patient. You said he does big business, right? People talk. Word of mouth is everything, especially in that line of work. We're better off getting someone to go in and say they're after the latest and greatest."

Danny snickered. "Not thinking anyone would buy one of us shoppin' for some bootleg Botox."

Jace huffed out a sharp chuckle and lifted his Scotch toward Axel. "I don't know. Our dapper Don Juan might need to look into those wrinkles setting up shop on his forehead."

"You're just jealous you can't carry my style."

Before Jace could kick in with their usual back and forth banter, Beckett dropped his front chair legs to the floor. "Hold up. I didn't mean one of us."

All heads twisted to Beckett.

"There's a bodyguard I met on a job in LA about a year back," he said. "Gia Sinclair. She relocated here about six months ago. Total badass when shit gets real, but you'd never think it by looking surface deep. Comes off as a curvy Southern belle when she wants to. She'd work this Wyatt asshole no problem."

Trevor leaned into the table. "You think she'd go for it?"

"To bring down a dude who'd slapped his wife and kid around?" Beck scoffed. "You'll be lucky if she doesn't wipe the floor with the dick before the job gets started."

Man, he'd pay to see that. Wyatt getting his ass handed to him by a man would do serious damage to his ego, but having a woman dish it out? Yeah, someone might as well store his nuts in a Mason jar. "So let's say Wyatt bites. Then what?"

Jace pulled his toothpick free and tossed it to the table in front of him. "That's really up to you, brother."

The room got quiet. An itchy uncomfortable quiet.

"What's that supposed to mean?" Trevor said.

"It means are we just protecting your business interests, or are we using this haul to set this fucker up so he doesn't jack your woman around anymore?"

Fuck. He needed to shut this shit down once and for all. "She's not my woman."

Jace grinned, a quick and dirty one that said he wasn't even close to buying it.

Across the table, Knox and Beckett suppressed a laugh, and Danny avoided eye contact. Trevor didn't dare look at Axel.

Zeke, at least, managed to keep a straight face. "Give it a rest, guys. Trev knows his own mind." His voiced lightened, a hint of laughter trickling through. "At least we can let him think he knows his own mind. For a few weeks at least."

Beckett shook his head. "Sad, man. I thought you were gonna be the holdout with me and Knox."

"I'm solid with you two," Danny said. "Got no interest in a woman for a long damn time."

Jace peered at Danny over the rim of his crystal tumbler. "Careful. You say that shit too loud and fate'll trip you up faster than you can say *I didn't mean it*." He sipped his Scotch and shifted his focus to Trevor. "You sure there's not more here that you wanna share?"

Trevor forced himself not to shift in his chair and kept his expression bland. "If you're asking if she's more than my employee, then yeah. She's in my bed and I plan to have her there for a while. But am I claiming her? No."

For the longest time, Jace just stared at him, the same intense gaze that made most people take at least three steps back on instinct.

"No shame in finding a good woman," Axel said. "The way I hear it, she's a pretty thing."

"Spunky too," Zeke added.

"Not ashamed of Nat," he grumbled. Hell, if anything, Natalie was the kind of woman a smart man staked a claim on the first chance they got. At least any man who could be trusted in a long-term relationship. "Just don't think we're suited long-term."

"Don't think you're suited, or don't trust yourself?"

"What difference does it make?"

"Because one's being wise to the future. The other's livin' in the past." Axel kicked one foot up on the edge of the table then crossed the other over it. "You figure out which one's driving you, and you'll have your answer."

Chapter Fifteen

This was what a Thanksgiving get-together was supposed to be like. Lots of people, loads of laughter, and endless food. Not the over-planned and rigid affairs Wyatt had hosted the eight years they were married. Curled up close to Trevor on an outdoor chaise with a fleece blanket tucked around her shoulders, she watched the flames dance in the outdoor fireplace and savored the snap and pop of the burning wood. Trevor and his family might refer to the palatial estate in one of Dallas's most elite and established neighborhoods as *the compound*, but the rest of the world would have called it gorgeous. It couldn't have been more than ten years old, but the Italian Villa design and homey décor created a warm and welcoming presence with a historic feel.

Trevor set his beer bottle on the slate-covered end table beside him, tugged her tighter to him and kissed her forehead. "Told you you'd have a good time."

She had. The best holiday since before she'd met Wyatt. Leaning forward enough to peek around Trevor's chest through the kitchen window, she spied her mom still chatting Frank's ear off at the dinette. Like always, her mom had made herself right at home and made fast friends with everyone, Ninette and Sylvie in particular.

But she and Frank had hit things off on an entirely different level. Like two people born into similar worlds and comfortable with each other's language.

And Levi? Well, he'd stolen the show from the minute he'd stepped foot through the front door—or at least he had until Ivan had shown up with his little girl, Mary. After that, the two of them had been inseparable buddies, running around the house and getting into everyone's business like they played here every day.

And Trevor's family had welcomed every bit of it with open arms.

"Okay, I admit it. You were right." She eased back into the cushions and rested her head against Trevor's chest. She'd fought him on the idea of mingling their families for the holiday, for fear of setting Levi up for too big of a fall once things dimmed between her and Trevor, but like always, he'd brought an entirely different perspective to the table.

"I'm not a random hookup, Nat. I'm the man who's spending considerable time with Levi's mom. You ever consider that you showing Levi what a healthy dating life looks like might be a valuable lesson for him to draw from in the future?"

The viewpoint had knocked her for an unexpected loop. Yes, it was her job to protect Levi from the ugliness of life, but Trevor had been nothing but a positive influence on her son. No matter how things ended between her and Trevor, she had every confidence Trevor would handle it with the utmost honor and compassion. And wouldn't that be a powerful lesson to teach her son?

She smoothed her hand against his chest, loving the mix of his cologne, the night, and the wood smoke from the fire. She doubted she'd ever get enough of touching him. Exploring him. For nearly a week and a half now they'd had more than ample intimate time together, including a few late-night rendezvous when she'd snuck him in the apartment after everyone else had gone to bed. Both of them had laughed themselves silly at how it made them feel like a couple of under-sexed teenagers—right up until Trevor had found a few inventive ways to make sure she didn't get too loud.

"Your brothers are pretty colorful characters." She drew back enough to see his face and cocked her head. "You never did tell me how you met them."

Trevor stared into the fire, his fingers idly working through her unbound hair the same way he always did before they fell asleep tangled in each other. "I was in a rough patch. They found me and helped me out of it."

"Ah…" She grinned at him and waggled her eyebrows. "The wild oats you mentioned sowing."

He chuckled, anchored his elbow on the chaise's arm and propped his head on his hand. "Sowing my wild oats might have put too pretty of a gloss on it. More like an eruption of male testosterone. I was eighteen and thought I needed to prove myself to the world. I set out for Dallas and proceeded to fuck things up right and left. Flunked out of my first year of college. Made a living doing things you'd never believe if I told you today. Drank three times my weight on a regular basis."

"And this is different from most young men how?"

The lightheartedness in his expression dimmed. "I fought a lot."

Something in his tone snagged her attention. Before thinking better of it, she shifted from her place beside him and straddled his lap. "What do you mean?"

Trevor shrugged, and for the first time since they'd

pulled into the compound's circular drive, he seemed unsettled. Distant and a little edgy.

"It couldn't have been that bad." She smoothed her hand against his cheek and waited until he met her eyes. "Everyone gets mad. Men in their late teens and early twenties have a lot of biological stuff going on."

"Not like me." He frowned and for a minute she thought he'd clam up completely. Instead, he cupped her hips and pulled her closer. "Being with Frank growing up was exactly what I'd needed. I was angry. Lost. Frank taught me how to restrain my anger and find other outlets for it, but without him there to balance me after I left, I lost it. I didn't go around picking fights, but I sure didn't walk away from them either."

"And?"

He stared up at her, thoughtful. "The night I met Axel, I almost killed a man."

She waited, her senses so zeroed in on the steady thump of his pulse beneath her palm where it rested above his sternum, her own heart matched its rhythm.

"There was a woman I was friends with," he said. "I knew her from the year I'd gone to school. She came over to the apartment I was sharing with a friend, tears streaming down her face, and said her boyfriend had hit her. I didn't think. Just went after the bastard." He huffed out an ironic laugh and shook his head. "I was so bent out of shape, so heated to make a point, I attacked the guy just outside a bar." He shifted and met her stare. "Axel's the one who pulled me off him. I'm lucky the guy lived."

"Surely you don't think anyone would think less of you for what you did. I mean, yes, you almost went too far, but Axel was there, and you acted because you cared about your friend. Not because you set out to hurt someone."

Trevor shook his head. "The girl lied to me. I didn't pause and think about it. I just acted. Turns out the guy had ended things with her and she just wanted revenge." He huffed out an ironic laugh. "Hell of a way she went about it."

Before she could say anything or try to offer any comfort, Levi's voice rang out across the backyard. "Mom!" He hurried around the pool, both hands gripping thick paper plates and his boots ringing on the concrete. Gabe, Zeke, and Axel trailed him, each with plates of their own in hand.

She pried herself off Trevor's lap just as Levi scampered up beside the chaise, out of breath and smiling ear to ear. He handed her a plate of chocolate silk pie. "Miss Sylvie and Miss Ninette said it's time for second dessert."

"You hang around Ma long enough, lad, and you'll learn it's *always* time for dessert." Axel handed off a fresh beer to Trevor along with a slice of pie, then settled onto the big chair next to him. "You two lovebirds missed the big announcement, so we brought the news to you."

"What announcement?" Natalie said.

Gabe and Zeke snuggled into the love seat closest to the fire, but it was Zeke who spoke. "Gabe finally found the dress she wants and decided she wants to fly to Tahoe for the wedding. We're thinking the week before Christmas if you can swing it," he said to Trevor.

Trevor grinned huge and lifted his beer in salute. "Now *that's* the kind of wedding I'm talking about." He leaned toward Levi perched on the edge of the chaise and shoveling back his pie, and nudged his shoulder. "You hear that, bud? We're going on a trip."

Natalie perked up, a fresh wave of panic surging to full bright. "Trevor!"

"What?"

"You can't just invite us to their wedding."

He paused, looked at Zeke and Gabe, then over to Axel who shrugged like he didn't have a clue what she was talking about, then rounded back to her. "Pretty sure I just did."

"But it's their wedding."

Gabe giggled and hugged her fiancé a little tighter. "Relax. You'll get used to it."

Natalie studied Gabe and Zeke's amused faces then redirected to Axel. "Used to what?"

Axel winked and grinned at Trevor. "Sounds like you've got more approving votes. The rate you're goin', you'll be the last one to the party."

Pushing upright, Natalie twisted for a better angle on Trevor's face. "What's he talking about?"

Trevor scowled at Axel, shook his head, and tucked her tight against his side. "Just ignore them. They like to meddle." He glanced at Levi, who'd nearly polished off his whole slice, oblivious to the banter going on around him. "But you're still going. I promised Levi a ride on the plane. Right, bud?"

"Yep," Levi said around a mouthful of pie.

Axel forked a bite of dessert that even Levi would've struggled to finish. "Wait'll you see Trevor's Gulfstreams, lad. They're a thing of beauty."

"I already got to see some last week, but not close-up." Levi twisted and aimed his commentary to Trevor. "They were huge, just like a commercial jetliner. One of 'em even had one of those bird pictures on the back tail like your models in the house. Cool, huh?"

Trevor's body got tight and his gaze shifted to Axel. "*Just* like the ones inside? The same logo?"

Levi bobbed his head, oblivious to the rapt attention aimed his direction.

Axel set his plate aside, but beneath his careful movement was a tightly coiled tension.

Something wasn't right. Levi had been a lot of places and done a lot of things, but he'd never flown anywhere, let alone hung around an airport. Especially not the private one Trevor flew out of. "What were you doing looking at planes?"

Levi scooped up the last of his pie, stuffed it in his mouth, and shrugged. "I dunno. Dad just said he had to run an errand and drove around an airport."

"He didn't stop?" Trevor asked. "Just drove around."

"Yep." Levi looked up from his plate and focused on Trevor. "When I see yours, will I get to sit in the cockpit?"

Trevor nodded, but his voice came out a little distracted. "Absolutely."

Zeke stood and tapped Levi on the arm. "You know Miss Sylvie gives extras when you bring your plates back to the kitchen, and I saw about three different kinds of cookies hidden in the pantry."

"Really?"

Gabe gathered up Axel's plate and Trevor's empty beer bottle. "Snickerdoodles and sugar cookies for sure. Not sure what the other dozen were."

Levi twisted back to Natalie. "Can I get more?"

Geez, he was going to be wired on sugar for hours. Though after learning her ex had been tooling around

Trevor's business with no apparent purpose for being there, she probably would be, too. Damn Wyatt and his meddling. He just couldn't leave well enough alone. "Sure, why not? But tomorrow you have to eat good all day."

"Cool!" Levi gathered up his plate and hurried off as fast as he'd arrived, Gabe and Zeke ambling slowly behind him.

She swallowed and looked up at Trevor. "You don't think Wyatt's out to cause problems for you, do you?"

Just like the night she'd cried in his arms, he cupped one side of her face and gave her a smile that said the world could end tomorrow and he wouldn't care so long as he had right now. His vivid blue eyes burned with promise, the same unshakable fortitude she'd seen in him from day one. "Doesn't matter what he tries, darlin'. Wyatt can throw what he wants at me all day long." He lifted his head toward Axel and his expression shifted, the careful protector he'd shown her slipping just enough to show the warrior underneath. "Me and my brothers don't go down easy."

Chapter Sixteen

At night, Jace and Axel's mega-club, Crossroads, was a wonderland of colorful laser lights and patrons dressed up in their party best, but pre-opening on a post-Thanksgiving Saturday night with the fluorescents buzzing overhead it was kind of depressing. Trevor ambled toward the main staircase that led to the VIP balconies and the private stairwell to the main offices one more floor up. From their third-story view, Jace and Axel's offices offered an unfettered view of the dance floor below. What they couldn't see of the other, more unique sections of the bar through their one-way mirrored glass, they watched via the vast number of security monitors mounted opposite their desks.

Despite the West Coast edge of the bars and dance floor in the middle, it was the specialty areas orbiting the perimeter that gave Crossroads its cool factor. The difference that kept people coming back long after the grand opening curiosity had worn off. The club was exactly what it was named for—top to bottom opulence with a place to blow off steam for everyone. A pub complete with rich dark wood furnishings for the older crowd and businessmen. A chrome and mirrored hangout for the more technically inclined. A coffee shop corner with all the trendy quirks you'd expect to find in a Seattle hole-in-the-wall, and a dive bar for the bikers. Everyone was included.

And Jace and Axel ruled it all.

Splaying his hand against the biometric palm scanner, Trevor waited for Knox's digital security wonder to do its thing and flip the locks. Only a handful of people had access to Jace and Axel's inner sanctum, and Trevor could count on one hand how many times they'd met there for Haven business, but given its central location and the fact that Knox had upended everyone's Saturday schedule with urgent business, today it was the Haven hubbub.

The lock disengaged just as Knox, Danny, and Beckett's low voices sounded at the top of the VIP stairs.

Trevor held the door open and waited. Knox and Beck both had matching scowls on their faces, which wasn't much of a surprise for Knox. He practically always sported a frown while untangling whatever his cyber challenge of the day was, but Beckett seldom let any emotion show. Danny strolled beside them, not nearly as tense as his counterparts, but wary all the same.

"Who crawled up your ass sideways?" Trevor said once they stalked into talking distance.

Beckett motioned Trevor through the door with a jerk of his chin. "No one you're gonna like. Everyone else here?"

Well, fuck. And it'd been a damned good day so far too, even if he'd had to sneak out of Natalie's apartment at the ass crack of dawn before her kid could bust in her room and find him wrapped up tight with his momma. Trevor took the black carpeted stairs two at a time. "Just got here, but I saw Zeke's ride out front and Jace and Axel's out back."

Sure enough, Axel's gruff voice sounded from the conference room that bridged his and Jace's private offices. The second Trevor stepped into view, whatever story he'd been sharing with Jace and Zeke died on his tongue. He sat up taller in his chair at one end of the table, eyes rooted on Trevor while Beckett, Knox, and Danny filtered in behind him.

Definitely not good. "Starting to get the feeling I'm the only brother who doesn't know what's got us all in one room."

"That was my call," Axel said. "Couldn't risk you goin' off half-cocked before we had a plan."

"Half-cocked about what?"

Knox slid into one of the oversized leather chairs on the far side of the twelve-foot conference table and braced his elbows on top of it. "We've got a problem."

Sensing he was about ten seconds from needing to pace, Trevor kept his feet and wrapped his hands around the back of one chair. "I gathered that looking at Beckett's face. You wanna get to the point?"

"I got a contact early this morning from a skip tracer friend of mine. She's good. New to this area, but good. She got a lead on a guy willing to pay big money for a deep dive into your background. And by deep dive, I mean the client's after dirt."

That no-good bullying son of a bitch. No wonder Axel had waited to tell him until he'd gotten here. "Wyatt Jordan."

"Yep," Knox said.

At the opposite end of the table, Jace anchored one boot-shod foot on his knee. "She take the gig?"

"Not yet. She stalled and told him she'd think about it, then ran it past me. Frankly, we're damned lucky she gave us the courtesy. I only know her through online contacts, but she's got a rep for being thorough."

"You got a way you think we should play it?" Axel said.

"I think we want to keep control," Knox said. "Offer to double Wyatt's payment in exchange for feeding him what we want him to know."

Danny slouched lower in his chair beside Zeke and splayed his knees wide. "Yeah, but will she play along? Who's to say she won't play both sides?"

Knox grinned. "She can't play both sides if I get dirt on her. Trust me, if we go this route, I'll find what we need to keep her neutralized."

It was a smart move. Anyone with a mind to digging into brotherhood business was worth knowing more about, but right now Trevor needed something more immediate. Namely something that kept Natalie's ex out of their hair and left Natalie the fuck alone. "So what do we do about Wyatt?"

"I say we keep moving forward with our plan," Axel said. "Draw the bawbag out. If he's a past buyer, odds are good he'll want in again. When he does, we'll set him up to take a fall and get him out of everyone's hair once and for all. Trevor's woman included."

"So long as we don't expose Trevor in the process." Zeke focused on Trevor. "If he's digging like it sounds he is, you need to keep your tracks covered. Hell, we need to keep Doc Stinson covered. If this shit blows back on him, a lot of sick people are gonna lose options they wouldn't have otherwise."

"I'll get a tail on him," Beckett said. "See if we can't

get a bead on his mobile while we're at it. I wanna track this middleman down, too. Any chance he'd spill info to his clients?"

"Not sure what he'd spill," Trevor said. "I'm a ghost to him as much as he is to me. All he knows is the product's flown in."

"If he's shared that info to his clients, the leap for Wyatt to tie things to your business isn't a huge one. Only a handful of full-service charter companies in Dallas."

Knox huffed out a haggard breath and dragged one hand through his hair. "I'll dig deeper and look for ties between his bank accounts and your earlier hauls."

"What about the latest run?" Danny sat up taller in his chair and looked dead-on at Trevor. "You get a date set?"

"Not yet. I need overseas passengers and there's no one on the books. If I go without bodies on board, I won't have the right alibi."

"It can't just be anyone on board," Zeke said. "Not for this trip. You already put the word out product's coming, right?"

"Yeah, about a month ago."

Zeke narrowed his eyes. "Now Wyatt's getting nosy and driving Levi past the same airfield your planes are stored at. You gotta assume that means he's looking for a way to set you up. Best way to counter that is with clients on board with serious clout. Hard to dig too deep if the questions being asked build a political shit storm."

Trevor scoffed and straightened from where he'd leaned his elbows into the chair back. "Clout's not gonna cover things if the DEA's waiting when I touch down."

"That's nothing. We just offload the product before you land." Beckett turned his attention to Jace. "You've got connections through your investments and the charity groups. Any heavy hitters who might need a trip for the holidays? Maybe someone we could snag with an incentive and an interim stop on the East Coast?"

Jace frowned and scratched his chin. "I'll dig around. Viv's gotten tight with Evelyn Frank, and Evelyn's tied to everyone. If any socialites are planning overseas vacations, she'd know about it."

"What about your inside gal?" Zeke said. "Gia game for helping us get in with the good doctor?"

Beckett's chuckle was coated with pure deviant pleasure. "She's all over it. Said she's got a few government contacts she can leverage if he bites and we want to stage a sting to take him down. Wouldn't have a single tie to us if we work through her."

Jace sat up on the edge of his chair and tucked a fresh toothpick in his mouth. "So, Gia's in, Knox handles his skip tracer, and I get Viv scrounging for passengers with big bank accounts and heavy stroke. Sounds like we've got a solid plan, assuming everyone's on board."

Axel was the first to speak, his voice on par with a growl. "The bloody bastard sealed his fate the second he started nosin' in our business. I vote we take him down."

"Agreed," Jace fired back.

Danny and Beckett answered at the same time.

"Yep."

"Me too."

Knox grinned in a way that said he couldn't wait to get back to his computer and dig in. "It's a no-brainer in my book."

"You know I'm in," Zeke said. "Gets a double win for us. Wyatt out of our hair and Natalie something tangible to sue for full custody."

Yeah, it did. And seeing how frazzled she was this morning, keeping her chin up even though she struggled with the fact that her kid was headed to that asshole for another week, only made him twice as eager for leverage.

Jace nailed Trevor with a pointed stare, the intensity behind his dark eyes shaking loose another chunk of the resistance he'd fought so hard to keep in place. "Think it's down to you, brother. We've got your back, but it's your ass hangin' in the wind, so you make the call."

It was more than just his ass. It was Natalie's, Levi's, and their whole damned future. He might not be worthy of happily ever afters with a woman like Natalie, but she was his right now, and he'd be damned if he didn't take the chance to make her life better while he had it. "I say we take the bastard down."

Chapter Seventeen

Stomach weighted with yet another sinful meal, Natalie swallowed the last of her burger, nudged her red plastic tray out of the way, and propped her elbows on the Formica tabletop. One thing about Trevor and Levi, they could eat. A lot. As in her ass was going to be bigger than the metroplex if she kept trying to keep up with them.

Just outside the restaurant's front window, Levi stood motionless beside the big yellow slide, his head down and eyes focused on his newest "toy." Normally, a playground meant a requisite thirty minutes of Levi giving every piece of equipment a thorough workup, but today he'd spent most of the time fiddling with the overpriced cell phone Wyatt had sent him home with that morning.

She frowned and snagged a fry off Trevor's tray. "He won't put the stupid thing down."

Trevor moved her abandoned tray out of the way and slid his between them so she'd have easier access to the double order of fries he'd yet to make a dent in. "You put rules around it when you're with him, he'll figure it out. Plus, the upside to a kid his age is they've got the attention span of a gnat. Get him busy with something else and he'll move on."

Well, that was true. Keeping up with Levi was a challenge on even her best days. If she taught him decent habits with the device right out of the gate, maybe he wouldn't end up nose-to-screen twenty-four/seven like some other kids she saw. Although, having a phone on hand also meant she'd have a harder time monitoring conversations between Levi and Wyatt. "It just feels like the phone's a ploy. A trick to get Levi's attention on top of Wyatt's father of the year impersonation."

"Is it working?"

Horrible as it probably was, Natalie had to fight back a triumphant smile. "Not really. He grumbled less when I dropped him off last weekend, but he was still reserved. Plus, I'd barely put my car in park this morning before he shot out of the front door with his backpack slung over his shoulder." Her thoughts drifted back to the years living with Wyatt. "Even when he was little, he avoided Wyatt. Unless we were fighting, then he'd get creative with ways to get me away. I lost count of how many times he faked an injury to get me away from one of Wyatt's lectures."

"So, there you go. He's not buying it."

"Trevor, it's a top-of-the-line smartphone."

"And you're a top-of-the-line mom. No comparison." Trevor snagged a fry and dragged it through the mound of ketchup. "Seriously, darlin'. You're not giving Levi or your relationship with him enough credit. No way he'd choose fancy gadgets or any other scheme Wyatt comes up with over you."

Maybe. Maybe not. Once upon a time she'd thought she was pretty smart and look where she'd ended up.

Trevor wiped his fingers on a paper napkin and wadded it up in one hand. "You're forgetting the upside, too."

She froze with her hand halfway to the mound of French fries and cocked one eyebrow in silent question.

"Wyatt can call Levi whenever he wants now. No going through you, right?"

"Yes."

"So turnabout is fair play. Now you can call Levi whenever you want. If you get antsy on drop-off night, then call him. If Levi avoids his dad as much as you think he does, Wyatt will never know." He grinned, snagged her loosely clasped fist off the table and kissed her knuckles. "It works both ways."

True. Although, with Wyatt's improved attitude and Trevor's creative diversion techniques while Levi was away from home, she'd been a lot less antsy on her weeks alone. "I suppose."

He stood and picked up their trays. "Don't let it get to you. You spend your days worrying, then Wyatt wins. Now, you ready to go pick out a tree?"

Absolutely. Though it was taking every ounce of mental fortitude not to read too much into the highly domesticated act. Guys like Trevor weren't supposed to like spending Saturday afternoons with a kid in tow, let alone shopping for a Christmas tree. The fact that he'd been the one to insist on today's agenda had left her teetering on the edge of varied, imaginative fairy-tale endings.

Across the street, the Christmas tree lot was bustling with customers eager to pick out their holiday center-piece. Mini-lights were zigzagged above the trees on display and a weathered wooden shack sat off to one side where a line of people waited to buy hot choco-late. The way they all stomped around with their hands stuffed in their pockets, you'd have thought it was near freezing out, but the temperature had barely dipped below fifty degrees. For a Texan, that first cold snap was a bear.

Ushering her out the door to the playground with a possessive hand splayed low on her back, Trevor whistled for Levi. "Let's go, bud."

Not bothering to put the phone away, Levi hustled to them as fast his boots could carry him without breaking into a full jog. "This is gonna be cool! We've never had a real tree before."

Trevor crouched in front of Levi and put them eye to eye. "It'll be cool, 'cause picking out a real tree is a treat, but it ain't gonna be special if your nose is in that phone the whole time we do it."

Levi frowned big enough the insides of his eyebrows formed a sharp V and his bottom lip bordered on a pout. "Everyone's got phones. They're fun."

"They can be," Trevor said, clearly not as impacted by Levi's boo-boo lip as she was. "But life's fun, too. There's a time and a place for phones, but when you're out with your mom and me isn't one of 'em."

"Except for pictures," Levi added. "Those are okay, right? So you can look at 'em later."

"Yep, pictures are good. You keep your phone in your back pocket until we're done and I'll take a shot of you next to the one we pick out before they bag it up." Trevor held out his hand to Levi. "Deal?"

Levi shoved his phone in his back pocket as fast as he could and clasped his little hand against Trevor's. "Deal!"

A quick jaunt across the street later they were surrounded by everything from balsams to Frasers, the sharp, fresh scent of evergreen eradicating any trace of the city outside their Christmassy bubble. "I had no idea this many people still did real trees."

"At the Raines household it's real or nothing." Trevor wrapped his arm around her waist and pulled her in tight, ambling slowly behind Levi while he studied every tree one at a time. "From the weekend after Thanksgiving to the day after New Year's our whole house smelled like this. And it wasn't just the tree either. Bonnie got fresh garlands for the mantels and wreaths, too."

"She sounds nice."

Trevor stopped, cupped the back of her neck, and smiled down at her with a touch of melancholy. "She'd have liked you." For a second, an emotion she couldn't quite identify moved across his face. Pensiveness maybe, but with an unsettled edge. "She'd have liked you a lot."

She ducked her head, too knocked off-kilter by the solemn statement to hold his gaze. In that moment, it could have been twenty below zero and she'd have been toasty enough to dance around naked, the smoldering warmth of his words enough to fight back the deepest chill.

Levi's voice rang out from behind her. "What about this one!"

Twisting, Natalie found him standing next to a tree barely taller than him and missing a huge chunk of limbs on the right side.

Trevor paused in front of it, scratched his chin with his knuckles, and braced the other on his hip. "You know, if you were gonna tackle that one on your own, it'd be a pretty good choice, but at my place the ceilings are kind of high. How about we look for one a little taller? Say, something about a foot taller than me."

Levi's eyes got huge, a mix of wonder and purpose firing behind his hazel gaze. "Bigger." He spun on his heel, scanned the rest of the lot and took off in that determined stride she loved. "I see some."

"Smooth," Natalie said. "I don't know whether to appreciate your charm, or worry you'll teach my kid all your tricks to use on me later. He's already a handful now. Can you imagine the hijinks I'll have to deal with when he's a teenager?"

"If he stays out of half the things I did, you'll be home free."

He wrapped one arm around her shoulder and her own slid easy around his waist. In fact, everything was easy with Trevor. Walking side-by-side. Talking. Putzing around in the kitchen. Sex.

No, scratch that. Sex with Trevor wasn't easy. Natural maybe, but not easy. More like cataclysmic and addictive with an extra punch of dirty thrown in for fun.

"Natalie?" Wyatt's voice resonated from somewhere behind them, the same tight and oh-so-polished delivery he used on clients and those he wanted to impress.

Unlike her, Trevor didn't so much as flinch, only squeezed her shoulder in encouragement before he let her go and turned with her to face her ex.

"Dad?" Levi marched around Natalie and craned his head up at her, the expression on his face one of utter confusion and a pinch of disappointment. "Is he helping us pick out a tree?"

Trevor moved in tight behind her and braced both hands on her shoulders. Not just a proprietorial move, but an outright challenge.

As ashamed as she was to admit it, she absolutely loved it. "I don't know what he's doing, sweetheart." Though whatever it was couldn't possibly end up good. Wyatt seeing her out with Trevor was one thing, but seeing their son happy and out on the town with any kind of competition would only spur her ex's creative backlash. "Maybe your dad's changing things up at home this year, too."

Wyatt's expression blanked and he scanned the trees around them as though he'd forgotten where he was or why he was here. As quick as the dumbfounded look had come, it disappeared, replaced with his smooth clinical smile. "Oh, no. Not for the house. You know I find it more efficient to have the florists handle the décor." He tucked his hands in his high-dollar chinos and zeroed in on Levi. "I was just picking up some wreaths for your grandmother's house. She likes the natural ones and said she wouldn't have time to drive over."

Levi frowned and inched closer to Natalie.

She couldn't blame him. Wyatt's mother was about as nurturing as an angry python, particularly when a blustering, messy child set about placing their sticky fingers on her priceless furnishings.

Wyatt snapped to attention and offered his hand as though he'd just realized Trevor even existed. "Good to meet you again. Travis, wasn't it?"

Trevor moved only enough to grip Wyatt's hand. His grin said he knew damned well what Wyatt's game was and wasn't the least bit put off by the slight. If anything, it was Wyatt who flinched from what she imagined was Trevor's unyielding grip. "Trevor."

"Ah, right," Wyatt said. "Sorry. I get so many names

coming through the office, I have a hard time keeping them straight."

Which was another load of crap. Wyatt Jordan never forgot a name, especially when he thought the connection might glean something for him in the long run.

Natalie motioned to the trees behind them. "I don't mean to be rude, but we promised to help Trevor pick out a tree and we don't have a lot of time if we want to get it unloaded and decorated before Levi's bedtime." Okay, maybe the part about being in a hurry was pushing it, but the tiny fib was worth it to see the irritation flash across Wyatt's face.

"Oh, absolutely. Yes." He cast a doting smile down on Levi then nodded at her and Trevor. "I didn't mean to intrude. I was just surprised to see you here and didn't want to leave without saying hello."

Right. More like snatching a chance to interfere in her life while he had the chance. Some things never changed. She nudged Levi's shoulder. "Why don't you give your dad a hug, kiddo, and we'll get back to finding the right tree."

Levi jerked an uncomfortable-looking nod and made quick work of the request, being as nice to his dad as he could while obviously impatient to get back to his tree selection.

As Wyatt strolled to the weathered shack on the side of the lot, where wreaths hung on hooks along the outside wall, Trevor steered them back to the taller trees. He leaned in close enough Levi couldn't hear his voice. "You really think him showing here's a coincidence?"

Natalie slowed her steps and pulled away enough she could gauge Trevor's expression. Not one hint of humor or sarcasm marked his face. "What else could it be?"

Ahead of them, Levi wound between the trees, study-ing each one carefully before he moved on to the next.

"He ever visit a live tree lot when you were married?"

She frowned. "No, not that I know of."

"His mom ever have real wreaths when you visited?"

Beneath her feet, the thick mulch that covered the lot was damp but still crisp from setting up for the holiday season. Wyatt's mother never had a living *anything* in her house, and any shrubs or flowers outside were main-tained by a service company. Dirt and disorder sent the woman into outer orbit. "I don't remember any." She snapped her gaze back to Trevor's. "You think he's fol-lowing us?"

Trevor shook his head and chin lifted toward Levi, who'd paused in front of a nine-foot tree in the back row. "He doesn't have to. That phone's got location services on it and I'd be willing to bet it's active."

"He wouldn't." She swallowed and glanced back at the shack.

Wyatt strode toward his car with two smaller-sized wreaths looped over one arm. Small wreaths. Not some-thing fitting for the grand entrance of his mother's es-tate, and definitely not something he'd put in his pristine car if he didn't have to.

"On second thought," she said, "he absolutely would." She checked to make sure Levi wasn't listen-ing and lowered her voice. "So what do I do?"

His gaze roamed her face, the intensity behind his eyes snapping with a protective glint. "Nothing for you to do. You've got nothing to hide." He cupped the side of her neck and his lips lifted in a devious grin. "That said, I'm not too fond of his surprise visits jackin' with your head. You got any problem with me teaching you how to deactivate the locator in the phone?"

"You can do that?"

"Just a flip of a switch and he won't have a clue where to find you, not unless he's got serious connections with the government."

Hard to tell with Wyatt. He collected favors with influential people the way young girls fan-girled over teenage heartthrobs, but most of the people he rubbed shoulders with were politicians and businessmen. "So we'd just disappear?"

"Yep."

Which, if he were really trying to track them would totally piss Wyatt off. Her cheeks strained on a huge smile. "I'm totally in. Show me how it works."

Chapter Eighteen

Over two weeks Trevor had waited for this moment. Nineteen days biding his time while Knox, Beckett, and his friend Gia worked their magic and prepped for today's setup. He'd been more than willing to cast his vote when Wyatt had dared to dig into his life, but the second he'd dragged an innocent boy and Natalie into his games, Wyatt had sealed his fate. Whether the plans Trevor had made with the brotherhood to take him out via the drug sting panned out or not, Wyatt Jordan was fucked.

Arms crossed against his chest and boots planted shoulder-width apart, Trevor glared at the row of un-eventful video feeds they'd hacked via Wyatt's security company as if that might somehow hurry along the action. Knox was kicked back behind his desk with three different keyboards laid out in an arc in front of him and his combat boot-shod feet propped up on the ledge. Axel, Jace, and Danny were sprawled on the sofa and oversized club chairs on one side of the room, and Beckett was camped out in the good doctor's parking lot with a live eye on the scene in case anything went south. Zeke hadn't been able to shake his trauma shift, but he'd texted for updates almost as much as a teen-age girl.

Trevor uncoiled his arms and braced his hands on the back of the empty chair in front of him. The only sounds that registered through the high-end speakers mounted in each corner of the room were the subtle pings and the chatter of background office noise. "What the hell's takin' them so long?"

Knox waggled a pen between his fingers. "Patience, brother. It's a doctor's office. You're used to rapid access with Zeke, but the old-fashioned wait-your-turn bullshit takes forever."

Forever as in thirty minutes past Gia's scheduled appointment time. His phone vibrated in his back pocket, no doubt another request for an update from Zeke. As strung out as Trevor was from waiting, he'd be smart to ignore it, but then Zeke would just think something had gone wrong. He tugged it out, let the fingerprint reader do its thing, and punched the text app.

Instead of Zeke, a message came in from his secretary.

Can you swing an overseas trip the day after you're back from Tahoe? Just had a booking request from Quinn Dixon for a four-passenger trip to London. They mentioned something about a Broadway Tickets holiday package?

Trevor grinned and met Jace's stare across the room. "Your woman scored the booking." And not just any booking either. As influential people went, you couldn't get much better than Dallas's former mayor, Quinn Dixon, but paired with the Chief of Police, Randy

Trammel, and both of their wives, he'd have some serious character witnesses at his back if things went bad. "Looks like they fell for the holiday promotion package, too."

Danny lifted his head off the back of the chair. "What holiday package?"

Jace smirked and gave his toothpick a twirl. "Viv caught wind that Dixon and his buddies were planning a quick run to London for Christmas shopping, so she mentioned how Trevor's company was offering a free layover in New York City complete with Broadway tickets to all overseas customers booked and chartered in the month of December."

"Niiice," Knox said. "They get a free show and a night on the town while Trev unloads his product."

"The lass is a fucking genius." Axel slid his gaze to Jace. "You're a bloody lucky bastard."

Trevor tapped out a response.

Book it. I'm flying. Jerry's copilot. The tickets are a perk. Ask Dixon what show his crew wants to see and pass it on to me. Book two suites at The Plaza for layover night.

He hit send, tucked the device back into his pocket, and nudged Knox's shoulder. "Hope your fancy hacks can work a few wonders on Broadway. I got a feeling scoring the kind of tickets Quinn Dixon will want won't be easy."

"If he can't, I can." Axel kicked his feet up on the coffee table and laced his hands behind his head. "I may not have nimble fingers that get me in all the cyber nooks and crannies of the world, but I know a pretty little lass I can call in New York."

Jace chuckled. "Worked your nimble fingers on her, did you?"

"My fingers, my cock, and a good number of toys." He smirked. "No Scot worth his salt leaves a lass anything but happy and sated."

The sound of a door opening pinged through the speakers followed by a woman's distracted voice. "Mrs. Jones?"

Knox dropped his feet and sat up straight. "That's us."

Sure enough, Beckett's petite friend stood, hooked her purse over one shoulder, and sashayed toward the woman in pink scrubs standing in the open doorway.

Axel, who'd missed Gia's arrival at Wyatt's office, sat up on the couch and twisted for a better look. "Christ, but she's a looker." He stood and paced closer, his eyes locked on her prominent curves. Her dark brown hair was loose and styled to compete with Dallas's most elite women. "Tell me Beckett's not sleepin' with her."

Knox shifted enough to give Axel a warning look. "I wouldn't go there if I were you."

Axel's shoulders dropped. "Fuck, he's already on it."

"Not hardly." Knox swiveled back to the screen. "More like treats her somewhere between his best friend and his little sister. You even think of doing the kinky shit you do with your women, Beckett will gut you with a plastic knife."

Frowning, Axel pulled one hand from the pocket of his tailored slacks and ran his fingers along his bearded jaw. He cocked his head to one side just as Gia disappeared through the door. "It might be worth it."

Danny and Jace snickered from their seats while Gia

and the nurse shared idle chitchat about the weather and her weight on the way to the patient rooms.

"The DEA is getting this too?" Trevor said.

Knox nodded and punched some keys on the keyboard. "Gia leveraged her contacts. She's got two bugs attached to her purse, one for us and one for them."

The nurse guided Gia into a room and shut the door behind her, leaving them with only audio. Paper crinkled and something sounded against the industrial tile floor. Likely one of those rolling office chairs given how muted it was.

"So, what are we seeing you for today, Mrs. Jones?" the nurse said.

Gia's voice was as smooth and tempting as her curves with a thick Georgia drawl. "I was rather hoping Dr. Jordan could help me with some stubborn wrinkles. I know loads of people who've had success with fillers, but my body seems immune. I'm just not ready to try surgery yet."

The soft click of the keyboard registered before the nurse spoke. "I don't blame you at all. And don't worry, Dr. Jordan is known for his advanced techniques. I'm sure he'll be able to find something to help you reach the results you're after."

The back and forth continued, the nurse reviewing Gia's medical history and medication list and confirming insurance information. By the time the nurse finished up and left the room, they'd killed another ten minutes.

Knox put on his headset, pulled up a map with Beckett's coordinates near Wyatt's office, and punched a button on the keyboard. "Any movement from our Feds, Beck?"

Beckett's voice squawked through the speakers. "Not a thing. Two agents in a silver Corolla in the next to the last row. One woman, one man, both too damned obvious if you ask me."

The blue dot indicating Beckett's location pulsed in a slow, hypnotic rhythm.

Trevor grinned, remembering how judicious and downright gleeful Natalie had been with Levi's location settings the last week. "I tell you about Wyatt's latest ploy?"

Knox spun enough to make eye contact with Trevor and raised an eyebrow.

"Fucker bought Levi a smartphone. Top-of-the-line."

"Christ," Axel said. "When I was seven, all I had was a stick and an old bike to play with."

Jace chuckled and stretched one arm along the back of the couch. "We were also learning how to pick locks and could pocket just about anything out of a convenience store. With or without electronics, Natalie's kid's a saint compared to us."

"Yeah, well, I don't think Wyatt got it for him to play with," Trevor said. "I think he got it to keep dibs on me and Natalie. He showed up at a live Christmas tree lot we were shopping at a little over a week ago with some bullshit line about picking up wreaths for his mom. Problem is, Wyatt's never dabbled in Christmas decorations. If he had the sense God gave a goose, he wouldn't have tipped his hand and shown at all."

"Too big of a temptation," Jace said. "A guy like Wyatt thinks he's invincible and wants the world to know it."

"You turn the location services off on the phone?" Knox said to Trevor.

"Before we even left the lot. Taught Natalie how to set 'em, too."

Knox nodded, started to spin back to his computers, but frowned and froze. "Levi got your number programmed in his phone?"

Trevor shook his head. "Not yet. I'd planned to until Wyatt showed up, but then thought better of it. Kind of sucks 'cause if he's gonna have the damned phone, I'd like knowing there's a way for Levi to reach me if he needs to."

A fresh screen popped up on one of Knox's monitors. "Not a problem," Knox said. "We'll get you a VoIP number and forward it to your mobile. Program the interim number into Levi's phone and you're set."

"Hate to mention this, brother," Axel said. "But if our goal's to make sure Wyatt suspects there's a new load of pharmaceuticals coming in, it might be wise to mention your trip over the pond to Levi the next time you see him. As much as Wyatt's likely pumpin' the lad for information, it's bound to come out you're takin' a trip overseas."

"No." The second the sharp response came out, Trevor regretted it. Axel was one hell of a strategist and was likely right about the info getting back to Wyatt, but he'd be damned if he used Levi to make it happen. "Nat and Levi are in the middle of this because I caught that asshole's notice. I'm not drawing them in any farther than they already are."

Danny leaned forward and braced his elbows on his knees. "Wouldn't matter if you drew his notice or not. So long as Doc Jordan is in their life, they'll be wrestling one shit storm or another. Only difference this time is you're the lightning rod instead of them. And don't forget, if this works, they won't ever have to deal with his shit again."

The truth of Danny's statement weighted the room, yet another powerful reminder of the biggest reason why Wyatt needed to go down.

As if on cue, the asshole in question strolled down the hall toward the room where Gia waited. He rapped twice on the door and eased the door open. "Mrs. Jones?"

The same high-level back and forth ensued. Medical history, why she was there, and what issues she'd encountered in the past. From Botox to Juvéderm, Gia listed every injectable on the market along with a healthy dose of desperation.

"I just don't understand it," she said. "Lots of my friends have seen great results, but I've seen no difference at all." She paused for a moment, the light crinkle of the paper liner covering the exam table filling the pregnant silence. When she spoke again her tone was lower, hushed, and conspiratorial. "I hope it's okay to share this, but a friend of mine told me she'd had problems like mine. She said you were able to help her." Another hesitation. "She said you were able to access more advanced medicines. I was hoping you could help me, too."

Wyatt cleared his throat. "Mrs. Jones, I pride myself on always providing the best care possible. Perhaps if you could provide me the name of the client who steered you my direction, I might have a better idea of the treatment you're referring to."

Knox sat up taller in his chair.

Trevor couldn't blame him. He'd have been tense too if he'd been the one tasked with hacking into Wy-

att's medical records and siphoning out the most likely
candidates who'd paid for Trevor's bootleg products.
It'd taken Knox the better part of a week to compare
delivery dates, treatment types, and price structures,
but he'd finally zeroed in on a list of ten very high-
paying women.

"Roxie Royce," Gia nearly whispered.

Silence buzzed through the audio feed, and Knox
waggled the pen balanced between his fingers double
time.

Wyatt couldn't quite hide the surprise behind his
voice when he spoke. "How do you know Ms. Royce?"

Not too surprising of a question considering Roxie
was the star entertainer at one of Dallas's most popular
gentlemen's clubs. Thankfully, Roxie had been on the
top ten list, and Jace had all kinds of naughty connections in the local entertainment biz. She'd been more
than open to sharing her success with Dr. Jordan and
his cutting-edge treatments.

"We were friends back in high school," Gia said.
"Our lives took different paths, but we still stay in
touch. She told me you were the best." She hesitated.
"So will you help me?"

"Mrs. Jones," Wyatt said. "I feel compelled to tell
you that Ms. Royce's treatment was very…aggressive.
Those procedures come with risks I can't guarantee,
and your friend signed releases acknowledging that in
advance."

"I understand," Gia said. "Whatever I need to do, I
will. This is important to me…" Her voice quavered.
"It's important to my marriage. Whatever the cost or
risk, it won't be an issue."

"Oh, she's good," Jace muttered. "A desperate housewife with unlimited funds. No way he'll turn that down."

Movement sounded through the speakers, a shift of fabric against leather and the rattle of plastic wheels against the tile.

"You're willing to sign off on the risks?" Wyatt asked.

"Yes. Whatever you need."

More silence.

Knox stopped waggling his pen and clenched it tight.

"All right," Wyatt finally said. "It might take me a while to locate the medicine we need, but we'll get you taken care of."

Trevor let out the breath he'd been holding, and Danny dropped back in his chair as though equally relieved.

Knox spun in his chair and grinned from ear to ear. "That, my brothers, is how you snare a dirty doc."

"He's not snared yet," Jace warned. "Baited yes, but not snared. And we've still got to get the goods in to set him up with."

"We'll get him." Trevor forced his fingers to release the fine leather he'd put a death grip on and met Axel's stare. "One way or another, Wyatt Jordan's days jacking Natalie and Levi are numbered."

Chapter Nineteen

Natalie slowed her SUV near the turn Trevor's directions indicated and swallowed huge. A ten-foot high chain-link fence with razor wire coiled around the top stretched down the empty side street, and wide metal buildings painted in varied earth tones were lined up beyond it, but the huge aircraft parked on the tarmac in the distance was nothing short of magnificent.

Behind her mother's seat, Levi's nose was practically flat against the side window. "I told you they were huge."

Her mother motioned to the sliding gate directly ahead. The handwritten instructions she'd navigated from wiggled between her pinched fingers. "It says to pull up to the intercom, punch the button, and give them your name."

Easy for her to say. As sweaty as her palms were right now, she'd do good to keep a decent grip on the steering wheel. In the nine years she'd been married to Wyatt, she'd grown pretty accustomed to money, but never *this* kind of money. Trevor might look like an average-income cowboy with his jeans, boots, and button-downs, but no way could he finance a plane like the one parked and waiting for them without a bank account that would make Wyatt weep. And he didn't just have one of them. He'd said he had two, plus all kinds of smaller ones.

Maureen leaned over enough to study Natalie's face. "Sweetheart? Is something wrong? You've been acting funny since this morning."

Natalie shook her head and eased the car forward. "Sorry. Just a little surprised, that's all." And scared to death. Where the fear had come from she wasn't sure, but somewhere between Trevor's sweet and sexy goodnight phone call and the none-too-kind blare of her alarm clock, she'd developed a boatload of relationship anxiety.

Punching the white button on the intercom, Natalie let out a slow breath and focused on the crisp wind outside her window. This wasn't a fairy tale. It was just some hard-earned vacation time away from her boring desk job and a fun weekend away with a wonderful man. An experience for her son, and a treat for her mom in a beautiful place. Nothing more. Nothing less.

A chipper feminine voice through the speaker shook her from her inner pep talk. "Ms. Jordan, we've been expecting you."

Natalie whipped her head to her mother. "How'd they know it was me?"

The woman's delighted chuckle resonated through the speaker. "There's a camera mounted on the gate. Trevor told us what you'd be driving and told us to keep an eye out. Just pull ahead when the gate opens, and drive your car to the aircraft straight ahead."

Hard to miss which plane she was talking about. Like Levi had said time and again, it was as tall as a commercial jet, and nearly as long. The door was open, and a red rectangular carpet lay at the bottom of the stairs. "Just drive up to it?"

"Yes, ma'am," the woman said. "Tony's on his way out to help you with your bags and will park your car."

"Oh." More than a little dumbfounded, she snapped her mouth shut and shrugged. "Well, okay then. Thank you."

"Thank you, Ms. Jordan. We've been looking forward to meeting you."

Natalie frowned at that, but remembering the cameras, quickly smoothed it away. She punched the up button on her window and stole a glance at her mom while the gate trundled open. "What do you think she meant by that?"

Her mom's canary-eating grin was entirely too smug. "What it means is Trevor's not bashful about making sure everyone knows who you are and what you are to him."

"Mom." Natalie subtly jerked her head toward the back seat and navigated her SUV through the gate. "Trevor and I are just casual. We're two responsible adults enjoying each other's time. It's nothing serious." No matter how much she wanted to fantasize otherwise.

Levi snickered from the back seat. "Yeah, whatever."

Maureen lifted both eyebrows as if to say, "See?"

"Levi, I'm serious," Natalie said. "I don't want you getting big ideas about Trevor and me. We're just dating. That's what grownups do. Sometimes things work out for the long haul, but more often than not they move on to meet other people."

"Yep, I remember." He swiveled his head and hit her with his happy hazel gaze. "But Trevor likes you. Like *a lot*. And you like him, so what's the big deal?"

"Yes, dear," her mother added. "What's the big deal?"

Natalie shoved the gearshift in park and opened her mouth to answer, but before she could, her door swung open.

Standing with one hand on the door frame and wearing blue coveralls was an early twenty-something man with sun-streaked brown hair and a pearly white smile. "Hey there, Ms. Jordan! I'm Tony. Hop on out, and we'll get you settled on board."

Before she could fully gather her thoughts or muster any more worries, the eager man had ushered her around the car and helped her mother out as well. A whirring sound droned from the jet's engines, and December's chilled wind whipped her hair across her face as she climbed the steps behind her mom and Levi.

Not the least bit intimidated, Levi disappeared through the open door first and let out a delighted "Whoa!"

She rounded the entrance behind her mom and nearly echoed her son's sentiment, her jaw slack enough it was likely comical to the cluster of men grinning at her from their plush seats. Where the outside was impressive on sheer size, the interior was pure opulence. Creamy leather upholstery and rich cherrywood paneling lined either side of the cabin, and thick taupe carpets so pristine she was tempted to take off her shoes lined the floor.

Standing in the center of what she guessed was a galley kitchen, Knox pulled a mini-bottle of Sprite out of a small fridge, twisted off the lid, and handed it over to Levi. "Here you go, cowboy. If you can hold out till we're leveled off, we've got snacks from Miss Sylvie tucked away."

"Snickerdoodles?" Levi asked.

"And oatmeal raisin and sugar cookies," Zeke fired back. Like Danny, Beckett, Jace, and Axel, he was kicked back in a chair with a casualness that said he'd long ago grown accustomed to the luxury of private flight, but Trevor was nowhere in sight.

Axel grinned and sipped from a crystal tumbler full of what appeared to be Scotch. "Don't let the fancy digs get to you, lass. If it were up to your man, he'd have this place done up like some cabin in the woods."

An awkward laugh gurgled past her lips, the truth of Axel's statement mingling with her shell-shocked senses and lingering anxiety. Even more surprising was how open and welcoming they were with her and her family. Like she and Trevor were more of a thing than what they were in reality.

But we're not.

Strolling through the galley, Levi scanned the miniature appliances mounted on either side, then opened the door at the end of the cabin without a beat of hesitation. "Wow! Mom, come check it out! There's a bathroom and everything."

A chorus of rich, masculine laughter filled the plane's interior, but it was Jace who spoke. "Nothin' says high livin' to a kid more than a mile-high bathroom."

Maureen settled on the empty couch next to where Natalie stood rooted in place and scanned up and down the aisle as though trying to figure out what to do next.

Boy, could she relate. True, she'd spent more than her share of time Thanksgiving Day chatting up Trevor's family, but without him there to act as a buffer, the testosterone flooding the cabin was off the charts. She shifted her purse strap higher on her shoulder and smoothed one sweaty palm against her jean-clad hip. "So, where's Trevor?"

"Doin' his pre-flight thing," Danny said. His head was down and his focus concentrated on the sketch pad in front of him while he outlined a design in short, quick strokes. "Said he needed about ten minutes, fifteen minutes ago."

She shifted her focus to Zeke. "What about Gabe and the rest of the women?"

"They bolted yesterday. One of Trevor's other pilots flew them and the moms up early to do some pre-wedding stuff." Zeke frowned and rubbed the back of his head. "I'm not sure if that bodes good or bad for me and my checking account."

"I doubt even my mother could strain your checking account with only a day's head start." Jace pushed to his feet and set his beer in one of the drink holders built into his chair's armrest. "Come on, sugar. Let's get you situated before your man comes in and sees you all jittery."

Natalie trailed him to the closet just inside the front entrance. "I'm not jittery," she whispered.

He opened the door and cocked a know-it-all eyebrow. "No?" He motioned for the thick duster-length cardigan she'd pulled over her button-down and grinned around the toothpick at the corner of his mouth. "'Cause from my point of view, it looks like you'd bolt down those stairs and hotdog it all the way home if your car was still parked outside."

Masculine voices sounded from the tarmac, and heavy footsteps worked their way up the steps.

"Okay, maybe I'm a little nervous," she hedged. If

she was lucky, Jace would just chalk it up to a fear of flying instead of the emotions jangling her insides.

Done with his perusal of the bathroom, Levi closed the door behind him and ambled down the aisle. "Hey, Mom. Do you think Trevor will let me fly?"

Before she could answer, Trevor ducked through the opening, his smile huge and blue eyes bright with pure joy. He pulled her flush to his torso and gave her a quick kiss, settling his arms low on her back as he looked to Levi. "Not sure about flying, bud, but after we get in the air and get settled, I'll let you have a turn in the jump seat. That work for you?"

"Cool!" As soon as he said it, his expression shifted from delight to confusion, and his gaze slid to Maureen. "What's a jump seat?"

"I have no idea, sweetheart, but if we want to find out, I'd guess you need to find a seat so we can take off."

Trevor's chest shook against hers, and his familiar forest scent worked like a balm on her frazzled nerves. Not thinking better of it, she laid her cheek on Trevor's chest, closing her eyes long enough to let his heartbeat thrum against her palm.

"Hey." Trevor cupped her nape and angled her face to his. He studied her then shifted his gaze to Jace behind her, a frown pushing his eyebrows into a tight V. "Something wrong?"

For a second, the two of them shared an intense stare she wasn't sure how to interpret, but Jace broke it with a quick nod in her direction. "Nothin' a quick pre-flight tour of the cockpit won't fix, I'll bet." He winked and sauntered back to his seat.

Grasping her hand, Trevor stalked to the cockpit.

A dark-haired man who had to have at least ten years

and twenty pounds on Trevor sat at the controls, flipping levers and checking gauges.

"Jerry, do me a favor and get the doors locked up," Trevor said. "I need a minute with Natalie."

Jerry twisted, laid eyes on her and aimed a knowing smirk at Trevor. "Sure thing, boss." He crawled out of his seat and hustled through the opening, dipping his head as he passed. "Nice to meet you, ma'am."

She opened her mouth to answer, but before any words could come out, Trevor tugged her forward, shut the cockpit door and backed her against it. "Talk to me."

No way was she spilling the thoughts that had been percolating in her head all morning. Especially with a plane full of people not twenty feet away. "Talk about what?"

He scowled and crowded closer. "Don't play with me, Nat. I've spent the better part of almost two months around you, half of that with us in each other's beds. I know that doe-eyed look for what it is."

She raised her eyebrows higher. "Confusion? Innocence?"

"Bullshit. The kind you slap on those grabby bastards at the pub when you slip past their hands and act like you don't know they were trying to cop a feel." He searched her face. "Wyatt do something to hurt you?"

God, getting him riled up about Wyatt was the last thing they needed right now. Him flying a plane in a bad mood had to be a horrible idea, not to mention she'd likely spoil the atmosphere for everyone else. "No, nothing like that."

"So what's bugging you?"

"You're making something out of nothing." More like he was too sharp for his own good and digging up topics he'd do well to steer clear of. "I'm just a little off today. Edgy, I guess."

"About flying? I thought you'd flown before."

"I have. I just…" Crap. What the heck was she supposed to say that wouldn't upend their trip before they even got off the ground? "I'm just a little nervous, I guess. It's a big weekend, and I'm with your family. It's… I don't know. Intimate."

The tension eked out of him and his eyes got a curious, speculative look to them. "You didn't mind them at Thanksgiving."

Of course, she hadn't. Thanksgiving had been casual. A social endeavor she could navigate without putting too much imagination behind it and accept it for what it was. A wedding was something entirely different. An event that planted all kinds of wistful ideas in her lonely head. The last time she'd dared to imagine fairy-tale endings, she'd ended up married to Wyatt. "It's not your family, Trevor."

Obliterating what was left of the distance between them, he pressed his body against hers, framed either side of her face with his strong hands, and dipped his head so his lips whispered against hers. "We can do this one of two ways. Either you tell me now and I kiss you for being brave enough to share, or you keep that shit to yourself for now and I spank it out of you later."

A delicious jolt speared low in her belly and her sex clenched. She barely stifled the need to roll her hips against his, but couldn't stop from digging her fingers into his shoulders.

His low chuckle resonated through the cockpit, the rich, rumbling tenor of it dancing across her skin in a decadent caress. "Think I need to amend. You tell me, and I'll kiss you for being brave now then I'll up the reward with my hand on your ass when we get to the hotel."

Her eyes slipped shut, need and the sheer power of him blanking out all her fears and reason. What difference would it make if she told him? A healthy relationship meant being open and honest about how you felt, even if it was a short-lived one. Then again, sharing might be the one thing guaranteed to bring their agreement to an end.

He ran his nose alongside hers and wound his fingers through her hair, holding her firm for his sweet assault. "Got lots of patience and no timeline, darlin'. I can keep this plane on the tarmac all damned day long if that's what it takes."

Forcing her eyes open, she sucked in a shaky breath. "I'm scared."

"Think I got that already. Of what?"

"Of us. Of where we're going." She swallowed and fisted one hand in his shirt. "Or maybe where we're not going."

He studied her face, taking time to let his gaze whisper over her every feature. "It make you feel any better if I told you I was scared shitless, too?"

Trevor? Afraid? Cautious or practical, she'd buy. Even jaded, given the home he'd been born into, but afraid? "Why?"

His expression softened and, for a single heartbeat, a vulnerability she'd never thought to see on such a proud and confident man radiated as open as the summer sun. "Because you're everything I've ever wanted in a woman. For a man who never believed he'd find, let alone deserve, such a treasure, doing anything to lose you is a terrifying proposition."

Oh. My. God.

Her knees trembled, and if he hadn't had her pressed against the cockpit door, she suspected the endorphins bubbling through her bloodstream would float her into the stratosphere like an untethered balloon. "You think I'm a treasure?"

He grinned, pressing his lips to hers in a lingering yet simple kiss before he answered. "A diamond. One of those rare ones only the luckiest bastards stumble on and everyone tries to steal." He kissed her again, longer and teasing his tongue along her lower lip until she opened to him and wrapped her arms around his neck. Whether he kissed her for five minutes or an hour, she couldn't say, but by the time he eased away, what was left of her morning jitters was gone.

"Feel better?" he asked, still not giving her room to escape.

A gentle heat stung her cheeks, but she held his gaze. "Much. Thank you."

"Don't thank me yet, darlin'." He tugged her away from the door, spun her toward the entrance and guided her through the opening. His sinful voice rumbled low behind her. "Gotta get you buckled up and get this bird in the air so I can tan that sweet ass of yours later. *Then* you can decide if you got a fair deal."

Chapter Twenty

The door to Trevor's hotel room clicked shut behind him, the harsh metal-on-metal sound ricocheting up and down the empty hallway like the hammer of an empty gun. He strode toward Natalie's suite just a few rooms down and huffed out an ironic chuckle. Fuck if that wasn't the most appropriate analogy for where his head was at right now. Natalie might not have cottoned to it yet, but he'd dodged one helluva bullet this morning, diverting her question about where they were headed and distracting her from her fears the best way he knew how.

The funny thing was, he'd been juggling the same idea of something more with enough frequency it scared him shitless. Was she really interested in more than the light-and-easy arrangement they'd agreed on? Or maybe he'd misunderstood her carefully veiled confession and she was trying to find a polite way to get him to back the hell off.

He stopped outside Natalie's door and bit back a frustrated grumble. Whatever was going on between them, he didn't have to figure it out right now. Right now was for relaxing and supporting Zeke and Gabe. The rest could come later. Preferably after all the shit with Wyatt was behind him. He knocked and stuffed his hands in his slacks pockets.

Levi's voice sounded through the thick wood. "I'll get it!"

Trevor grinned, and a little of his tangled emotions loosened. One thing about Levi—it was impossible to be in a bad mood around him. Ninety percent of the time he was as innocent and playful as a curious puppy with a new toy. The other ten percent Trevor would swear a wise old man was hidden inside Levi's little boy body.

The door swung open and Levi scanned him from the top of his unbound hair, down his charcoal-gray suit, to his shiny dress shoes. When he finally looked up, his face was pinched in a hard frown. "I don't like suits."

Well, that tidbit didn't take a rocket scientist to figure out. Levi might have his pants and shoes on right, but Trevor'd seen scarecrows wear a shirt and jacket better. His red tie hung unknotted, dangling around his neck.

"They're not all bad," Trevor said. "Rumor has it, chicks love 'em. You just have to get 'em situated right." He chin-lifted toward the room behind Levi. "How about you let me in and I'll help get you sorted."

Levi's scowl shifted more toward resigned acceptance, and he stepped back and let Trevor in.

As suites went, the one he'd secured for Nat, her mom, and Levi was completely tricked out. Rich cherry-wood furniture, a fancy green couch, and saddle-colored leather chairs gave the front sitting room an old English study feel, and a huge picture window offered a sweeping view of the lake and the snow-capped mountains in the distance. Tucked into one corner of the room was a wet bar, a mini fridge, and a ransacked basket of snacks. "Where's your mom?"

"Getting ready." Levi slunk toward the open bedroom door on the left. "She said she'd help me with my tie when she's done with her hair, but that was forever ago."

The room Levi led him to was pure class. Unlike the entry, it was light and airy with most of the colors trending toward ivory and gold, but the main feature was the king-size bed. Tall posts reached nearly to the ceiling and some kind of girly, sheer fabric was draped over the top and tied at each corner. A mound of silk pillows to match the taupe comforter were artfully centered in the middle.

Even without recognizing some of the clothes strewn across the couch in the corner, he'd have known Natalie had chosen this room by the wildflower scent lingering on the air, and damned if his body didn't get tight in response. "Gotta give women their time, bud. Besides, we're the ones who get to appreciate 'em when they're done, right?"

"I guess." Levi glared at his image in the armoire's full-length mirror and wrestled with his jacket.

"Relax." Trevor perched on the foot of the bed directly behind Levi and motioned him over with a crook of his fingers. "How about we start with you losin' the jacket so we can get your shirt buttoned up right and your tie lined out?"

To his credit, Levi bit back any further complaints and complied, even going so far as to trade out his pout for focused attention while Trevor realigned his buttons.

Trevor picked up Levi's tie where he'd tossed it on the bed. "You learn how to tie a knot yet?"

Levi shook his head. "I'd rather not have to wear one at all. They're too tight."

Chuckling, Trevor turned Levi by his shoulders so he faced the mirror and flipped up Levi's collar. "Can't blame you on that one, but every man's gotta know how to do it. Might as well start now. Besides, it's not as hard as it looks."

"That's easy for you to say. Mom does it fast."

Out of nowhere, an image of Natalie helping him with his own tie crashed front and center in his thoughts. Bonnie used to do that for Frank, too. She'd fuss and straighten every tie Frank ever knotted on his own, even when they'd been perfect, and Frank had always taken advantage of the closeness by finishing off her preening by pulling her close and stealing a quick kiss. Fuck, but he wanted that. Not just for a little while, but…

Nope. He wasn't thinking about that. Not right now. He cleared his throat and adjusted the tie so the wider end hung a little lower. If Levi noticed anything wrong with the rough edge to Trevor's voice when he spoke, he didn't show it. "The trick is remembering three loops— one on the left, one on the right, and one on the center."

Levi watched his every move, his faced etched with concentration.

Twenty-plus years melted away, leaving the first time Frank had taught Trevor how to do this very thing super-imposing itself over the here and now. The memory was as fresh and clean as it had been all those years ago. The importance of it. The patience Frank had shown in every second, and how only hours later, a judge had declared Trevor officially Frank and Bonnie's son. And now he was sharing it with Levi.

He made the knot's final loop and guided it up and

over the back. He could have more times like this. Share the same kind of love and care with Levi that Frank and Bonnie had shown him if he wanted. If he dared.

The bathroom door opened behind them, shaking Trevor from his thoughts.

Still facing the mirror, Levi's gaze shot from Trevor to Natalie and he smiled huge. "Mom, look! Trevor fixed my tie."

Natalie faltered mid-exit from the bathroom and smoothed her hand down the front of her bold blue dress. The fabric was sinful enough to remind him of silk sheets, and the wrap design accented her curves in a way that ensured he'd spend the rest of his afternoon fighting a hard-on. Likely all the other men would too, which meant he'd also spend the day fighting the urge to punch half of his brothers.

"Sorry." She glanced toward the main room then to Trevor. "I didn't hear you come in or I'd have hurried faster. Are we late?"

"Nope. Not late." Though if Levi weren't right next to him, he'd be tempted to make them late. Very, very, unforgivably late. "Wouldn't matter if you were though if it meant I got to see you in that dress."

Her cheeks fired a pretty pink, but her smile was bright enough to rival the late-afternoon sun sparking off the lake through the window. "Thank you."

"Think the gratitude's all on my end." He squeezed Levi's shoulder. "Besides, we took the extra time to learn how to work a Windsor knot."

"You did?" Her gaze shot to Levi and she smiled as she hustled forward, the sexy sway of her hips not doing one little bit to fight back his seriously developing wood. Getting a load of her strappy matching heels only made things worse. Eventually, he'd get to peel her out of that dress, but no way in hell were those coming off. "It looks great, Levi."

"Trevor showed me a trick," Levi said as Natalie crouched in front of him and smoothed his collar into place. "All you gotta do is three loops and it turns out perfect."

"I see that." She stood and snatched Levi's jacket off the end of the bed. "How about we get your jacket on and get going?"

Maureen was already waiting on them in the sitting room, a Cheshire smile on her face that said she'd heard the lion's share of conversation between him and Natalie and had wisely kept her distance. The second they emerged from Natalie's bedroom, she swept into grandmother mode and kept Levi tight to her side, conveniently allowing Trevor to keep Natalie tight to his.

The next hour went by in a rush. Natalie disappeared with the rest of the women to wherever Gabe was hiding, and the men plied Zeke with good-natured barbs about the demise of his bachelorhood. Only when Viv, Natalie, and the mothers emerged, did Danny peel off from the rest of them, and the minister guided everyone to the short pier that jutted over the lake's glassy surface.

If he ever did tie the knot, this was the kind of place he'd want to do it. Natural and easy. Unlike standard hotels or the busy hubbub of Jace and Viv's Vegas wedding, the resort Gabe and Zeke had picked had more of an oversized lodge feel. The sun was only a few hours from dipping beneath the horizon, and the temperature couldn't be much more than mid-forties, but inside the perimeter of towering space heaters, it felt more like an early fall afternoon.

The second Zeke saw Gabe emerge from the lodge, his shoulders pushed back and he smiled big enough to show a full set of pearly whites. No fear. No hint of worry, just pure pride and excitement.

Natalie shifted closer to Trevor, giving him some of her weight as Gabe's brother, Danny, led her down the aisle. The minister's words were little more than background noise, the mix of how Gabe and Zeke looked at each other mingling with Natalie's presence beside him and doing wonky things with his thoughts. Would Natalie like a place like this to get married? Or a place like his ranch? He'd bet his Gulfstreams she'd had the big enchilada when she married Wyatt, so maybe she wouldn't want another one. If she did, she'd get a bigger one than her first. No way he'd let Wyatt Jordan outdo him with Natalie.

The muscles in his torso locked up tight, the realization of where his thoughts had gone jolting him out of his languid haze. They weren't getting married. He *couldn't* get married. It was too soon. Too dangerous for her and for Levi.

Natalie snuggled closer, her front pressed along his side and her palm just below his heart.

Trevor pulled her in tight and wrapped his arm around her shoulder. All the women gazed at Gabe and Zeke with a mixture of sappy and romantic expressions, but Natalie's was different. Almost wistful.

A strong, unyielding squeeze took root behind his sternum, and a pleasant weight settled in his gut. Like his heart had grown two sizes in the space of seconds, and his body had found gravity after years of floating adrift. Maybe that was the anchor his dad had talked about.

You're nothing like your biological father.

Zeke had repeated the same line for years. So had Axel and the rest of his brothers. Frank insisted his anger was a good thing, a tool to keep those he loved shielded instead of a threat. Maybe they were right. Maybe he *could* dare to think about something like what Frank and Bonnie had.

Trevor's arm tightened around Natalie's shoulder, the force of his thoughts plowing through him and rearranging his future in one merciless blast. Natalie could be his. Where his brothers and Frank had tethered him to some degree over the years, she and Levi could be the cornerstone he'd craved. Could bring more goodness into his life than he'd ever dared dream. Frank and his brothers wouldn't steer him wrong. Not in this. And if Nat was even remotely entertaining the same thoughts he was, he'd be a fool not to take a chance. All he had to do was nut up and make it happen.

Chapter Twenty-One

One thing about country bars, they made for great people watching. Granted, none of the crew Natalie was with blended with the rest of the crowd, but being only three blocks from their lodge and packed with friendly people, it had proven to be the perfect place for the brothers, their mothers, and Viv to unwind and relax.

Of course, Gabe and Zeke weren't there. The groom had swung his bride up about a nanosecond after the photographer deemed his work done and carted Gabe away amidst a flurry of jibes and well wishes. Natalie's mom was missing in action too, having lured Levi into staying at the hotel with the promise of all the room service he could eat. Trevor had jumped all over that idea and volunteered to pony up for the bill.

Not that he'd let her or her mom pay for anything so far on this trip. She'd tried at dinner and had earned an affronted male glare not just from Trevor, but every one of his brothers.

Beside her, Viv recounted a debacle from one of her recent events, a tale that involved the chairman of the board, a socialite housewife, and the unfortunate discovery of the two in a compromising situation between dinner and dessert—by their spouses. The moms, Syl-

vie and Ninette, listened and laughed throughout the
sordid tale, while Jace sat beside Viv, seemingly content just to hear her voice.

The rest of the men took turns at the pool table behind them, their rich voices mingling seamlessly with
the music. Well, all of them except Trevor. He'd stayed
close to her, rarely leaving her side except to take his
turn with a cue or to get the next round of drinks.

As it had since they'd commandeered the big table at
the back of the bar, Natalie found herself watching the
couples shuffle past on the dance floor. Some kept their
steps simple, while others spun and twisted in intricate
moves that left her astounded. More than that, she found
herself enjoying the music. She'd gone through a country music phase in her senior year of high school, but
none of the songs she remembered sounded like these.

Trevor's strong hand cupped the back of her neck
and his sexy voice purred beside one ear. "You want
to give it a go?"

She craned her neck to take in his handsome face.
She'd thought by now the simple act of looking at him
wouldn't still tangle her tongue, but she was as stunned
speechless now as she was the day of her interview.
"Give what a go?"

He tilted the pool cue he'd anchored butt end on the
ground toward the dance floor. "You want to dance?"

"Me?" She shuttled her gaze between the dance floor
and Trevor. "Oh, no. That's waaay beyond my skill
level. My dancing is limited to house cleaning and im-
promptu moments with a good song in the car."

His lips twitched like he was trying awfully hard not
to smile. "I think I'd pay to see either one of those." His
hand on her neck tightened and his expression shifted to

something she couldn't quite name. Contemplative maybe, but smoldering with a possessive glint that terrified and thrilled her. It wasn't the first time she'd seen that look tonight either. Ever since the wedding, he'd vacillated between his usual indulgent self and a sexy stalking puma.

Axel straightened from the pool table and frowned at the eight ball nestled at the corner of the red felt-covered top. "Damn it all, I thought I had this one." His gaze shifted to Trevor. "You're up, brother."

Trevor's thumb skated back and forth along the pool cue's lacquered surface, his focus never straying from her face.

The upbeat song came to an end and a slower one took its place. Twice the number of couples hurried to the dance floor.

Wedging his pool cue behind Natalie's chair, he grinned down at her, clasped her hand and tugged her off her stool. He glanced back at Axel. "How about I pass and we agree you won this one?"

"Gonna show the lass your smooth moves, are ya?" Axel chuckled, pulled the rack out from beneath the table and waggled his eyebrows at Natalie. "Doubt he'd show you all his tricks here, but if you're nice, maybe he'll give you the full show later."

"Tricks?" Her mind was still trying to puzzle out Axel's meaning before it registered they were headed toward the dance floor. She dug in her heels and tried to pull her hand from Trevor's. "Trevor, really. I can't do this. I mean, look at me."

Unlike her efforts to stop him physically, her words stopped him on a dime. He turned, scanned her head to toe and smiled. "Been looking all day and still can't decide if I like the blue dress or the ass-hugging jeans better. Don't see what that's got to do with dancing though."

"I've got on Keds, for crying out loud." A tactical error she'd made when Trevor had shown up at her door in a tight-fitting navy-blue T-shirt, jeans, and black Lucchesses. She'd assumed his casual attire meant they'd hang out at the lodge's bar and head right back to their room. Not head out for a local club.

Trevor moved in close, his confidence engulfing her as strongly as his arms around her waist. "Trust me when I tell you, it wouldn't matter if you were barefoot and wearing a tutu. If you can count to two, I can not only get you around this dance floor, but you'll have a good time, come back out of breath and smiling."

Oh, boy. Clearly, Trevor had never seen her moves, or more like the lack thereof. "Um, you've never seen me dance."

"I've seen you dance plenty. You were naked every time and close enough I didn't miss a second. No doubt about it, you'll be fine." He cupped the side of her face and lowered his voice. "Trust me, darlin'. It's just a slow dance."

She peeked around his shoulder, a mix of terror and curiosity banging around in her chest. Yeah, she'd probably look like an out-of-place dork, but she was over fifteen hundred miles from home, for crying out loud. "Just a slow dance?"

"To start. If you're done after that, we'll call it quits."

"You have to swear you won't laugh."

His mouth twitched again.

"I mean it, Trevor. I really suck at this. No laughing, or no deal."

He pried her hand off his bicep, placed it over his heart, and laid his own over the top. "I'd cut out my own tongue before I'd laugh at you, and I'd throttle anyone else who did."

He'd said it a little tongue in cheek, but the sincerity behind his sky-blue gaze buzzed through her like a live current.

"Now are you gonna come dance with me," he asked, "or do I have to skulk back to our table like a loser who struck out?"

This time it was her who had to fight back a smile. "Okay. One song, but then we reevaluate."

True to his word, he really was an excellent teacher, starting them off to one side so he could ease her into the rhythm before he steered her into the main flow. By the end of song, she wasn't even counting anymore, just following his lead and enjoying the feel of his body close to hers.

"Dare to go one more?" he said close to her ear.

The new song's tempo was just a little faster than the last, nothing nearly as quick as some of the others she'd heard. She'd made it this far and hadn't stumbled. Surely she could make it through another one. "Okay."

His answering smile alone was enough to make the gamble worth it. Pure pleasure coursed through her blood and mingled with the flood of adrenaline in her system. In the end, she didn't just make it one more song, but two, and had even made it through a few spins without falling flat on her face. As he'd promised, she traipsed back to the table by his side, out of breath and smiling so big her cheeks ached.

She climbed up on her stool. "That was fun!"

He chuckled and maneuvered himself between her thighs, the stool's height lining her hips up perfectly with his. And didn't that just make her think of an entirely different dance? "Never doubt me on a dance floor, darlin'." He nodded toward her beer bottle. "You want a fresh one?"

More like two if she was ever going to come back down from her surprise thrill ride. "Please."

That intense, brooding look flashed across his face, and her sex clenched at the promise behind it. He palmed the back of her head and skimmed his lips against hers. "You're gonna say that a lot later. I suggest you start practicing in your head now, along with *yes, sir* and *no, sir.*"

She gasped against his mouth, and he captured it with a long, leisurely kiss. When he lifted his head, it was all she could do to uncurl her hands from around his neck and let him go. No man had ever affected her the way he did. Never left her wet and aching from nothing more than a kiss.

Heck, who was she kidding? Trevor didn't even need to kiss her. She'd been primed and ready to take him with just a look. She watched him walk away, his sexy, confident stride and the way his T-shirt and jeans clung to his muscular body drawing feminine appreciation along the way. But he was hers. Maybe not long-term, but for now she'd soak up every second.

Vivienne's teasing voice barely registered over her rioting thoughts. "I do believe our girl is well and truly smitten."

Trevor disappeared into the crowd.

Natalie sighed and swiveled back to the table. "He's a really good dancer. I mean, I guess I should have assumed. He does everything else perfect."

Vivienne rolled her lips inward as though biting back a comment.

Ninette snorted and Sylvie guffawed loud enough to make the guys playing pool drop their conversation and take notice.

Jace's mouth twitched a second before he looked away.

Natalie studied each of the women. In less than one

sentence, she felt like she'd gone from heaven to dancing through a land mine. "What?"

Vivienne raised both eyebrows. "He hasn't told you?"

"Told me what?"

Viv eyeballed Ninette and Sylvie.

Both shrugged in a *Don't look at me* motion.

"Jace?" Vivienne said.

Jace sucked in a slow breath and shifted his gaze to
Natalie. "You care about my brother?"

All at once, the noise and music dropped to nothing.
The air around her sparked with a potency reserved for
thrill rides and life-changing moments. She swallowed
as well as her suddenly parched mouth would allow.
"More than I think he's comfortable knowing."

He studied her with a fierceness she felt all the way
to her soul and took his sweet time doing it. He twirled
the toothpick at the corner of his mouth. "You accept
the parts of his past he's not proud of, you won't have
to tell him you care. You'll show him."

His gaze slid to Viv, and he nodded.

Viv grinned huge. "Is that the royal go-ahead?"

Jace gave his wife a smoldering look that said she'd
pay for her jab in the most delightful way possible.
"More like a little nudge to get these two going."

"Oh, fer Pete's sake," Sylvie blurted. "What they're
tryin' ta tell ye is that Trevor spinnin' ya round the dance
floor is tame compared ta the dancin' he used ta do."

Ninette covered her mouth and Jace chuckled.

How the heck could dancing have anything to do
with Trevor having a past he wasn't proud of? "You
mean, like professional dancing?"

This time it was Vivienne who giggled. "Oh, it was
professional all right. As in a male stripper."

Chapter Twenty-Two

This had to be what a rabbit in a predator's sights felt like. Ever since Trevor had leaned in, nuzzled Natalie's neck and murmured, *"Need you in my bed and my cock inside you,"* the air between them had sparked with a delicious yet dangerous current.

Trevor held open the door to his room and waited for her to step through. Why she was so damned jumpy and didn't just waltz on through she hadn't a clue. True, Vivienne's little info-bomb had surprised her a little, had even sent her mind off on all kinds of interesting tangents, but there was something else going on between them. A shift she couldn't quite put her finger on.

She stepped through the entry and wandered deeper into the room. Unlike her suite, his space was more in line with a standard hotel layout, but the décor suited him perfectly. All the furniture was huge, made of rich mahogany and accented by rich upholstery in chocolate and soft taupe. One look at the bed and she nearly swallowed her tongue. Logically, she knew it couldn't be bigger than king-size, but with the thick wood posts stretching toward the ceiling at each corner and the decadent silk comforter, it looked like a sinful playground for a giant.

Trevor coiled one arm around her waist, swept her hair away from her neck, and pressed a lingering kiss to the sweet spot behind her ear. "Wanted you in that bed since the second I walked through the door this morning. Posts like that make it damned handy to tie a woman up and have his way with her."

A shiver too potent to hide waterfalled from her shoulders to her knees, and she gripped his forearm at her waist just to be sure she didn't crumble to the floor.

He nipped her earlobe and ground his hips against her ass, making it vibrantly clear he was already primed and ready to go. "You open to that kind of play?"

Was she? Sure, she'd had fantasies. More so since Trevor had sauntered into her life, but the real deal was a whole different matter. She couldn't just imagine away the parts of her post-baby body that sucker punched her confidence, and if things didn't go well or had a lackluster impact, he could easily lose interest.

The people-pleasing thought doused her as thoroughly as a frigid plunge through an icy lake. She wasn't that woman anymore, and Trevor wasn't Wyatt. He didn't lie or point out her defects. He encouraged her. Pointed out all the things about her he found beautiful and sexy instead of every place she was lacking. "I've never done anything like that."

His big hands skimmed up her rib cage and cupped her breasts through her thin white sweater. He plumped them and teased her rapidly hardening nipples with his thumbs. "Didn't ask if you'd done it. I asked if you wanted to."

Yes. The answer rang loud and clear in her head, but didn't quite slip past her lips.

"It's okay, darlin'." He kissed a path down her neck,

his lips and tongue warm against her skin, lulling her deeper and deeper. "Won't ever ask you to do anything you don't want to."

"I want to." The second she said it, her heart kicked into double time and her belly clenched. She might be scared to death, but she'd be pissed at herself if she didn't take the chance. Worse if she let any doubt about her interest pile up in Trevor's head. "I don't have a clue what to do, and I'm a little worried I'll do something wrong, but I want to."

"Not tonight." He scraped his teeth along the tender spot where her neck and shoulder met, not quite a bite, but not tender either. "Soon, and only when we've got plenty of time to explore. Right now I'm too hungry. Want to strip you down and bury myself inside you."

His phrasing brought to mind Vivienne's surprising revelation, and all the curious questions and images she'd entertained on the way home bubbled back to the surface. "Can I talk to you about something?"

Trevor froze, his hot breath buffeting against her kiss-slick skin and his arms tightening around her. "Something wrong?"

"No." She turned in his arms, the edge in his voice triggering an instinctive need to soothe and calm whatever anxiousness she'd created. "Nothing's wrong. I just…" She smoothed one hand along his sternum and focused on the navy-blue cotton stretched tight against his pecs. "Vivienne told me something tonight, and I was curious."

"Told you I wouldn't keep secrets from you. Something you want to know, just ask."

She swallowed and bit her lip. "I told her how good of a teacher you were. You know…when we danced."

Forcing herself to look up, she sucked in a deep breath. "She mentioned that you used to…um…"

Before she could find the right word, his body went rigid and his eyes flared. "You mean that I stripped."

Oh, shit. Clearly she'd gone and stepped somewhere she shouldn't have.

His harsh voice scraped as hard as stone against stone. He dropped his arms and edged a cautious step back. "That change things for you? About me? About us?"

Change things? How on earth could something so small change anything?

You accept the parts of his past he's not proud of, you won't have to tell him you care. You'll show him.

God, she was an idiot. Jace had tried to tell her, and she'd utterly bungled things. She closed the distance between them, frantic to fix the hurt she'd caused. "It doesn't change anything. Not how I view you, or how I view us. I asked because I was curious." Her cheeks flamed hot as August asphalt in Texas, but she forced herself to keep going. "I asked because after she told me, I couldn't stop thinking about what you'd look like. How that was something I'd like to see."

A little of his tension left him, and he frowned hard enough his eyebrows made a sharp V. "You're not freaked out?"

"Freaked out?" She huffed out a short laugh at the absurdity of it. "Not in the least. I mean, surprised, yes. Jealous, absolutely. But not even close to freaked out." She ran her fingertips along his jawline, so strong and proud, exactly like the man. "Why would you think I wouldn't accept you and all the past that goes with you? I let a man bully and dictate my life for eight years.

Gave up my career because he said I should, but you didn't think less of me."

"That's different. You had a kid to look out for."

She smiled big enough her cheeks strained. "And you were a young man out on his own for the first time. You're gorgeous now. I can only imagine what you looked like then. If I were you and had the skills, I bet I'd have done the same. What man wouldn't want to drive women nuts and make money doing it if they had the chance?"

He ducked his head. Not the polite way he usually did when he was trying not to let her see him smile at something goofy she'd done, but one that spoke of unease. The same discomfort she battled every time their clothes came off.

"Trevor, look at me." She waited until he complied and nearly staggered beneath the raw vulnerability in his eyes.

"It was stupid," he bit out. "All I saw was the money and the women, and I jumped in. I was good at it, so the money only got better."

Her smile hopped back in place. She couldn't have stopped it if she'd tried. "I bet you were."

The playful approach seemed to work, because his frown turned into a sheepish shrug.

"I think you're amazing," she said. "You're honorable. You're disciplined. You take care of the people you love. It's everything you've done that makes you who you are today, and I'm absolutely crazy about you."

That got his attention, a hint of the predator who'd ushered her across the threshold perking up and taking note. "Crazy, huh?"

She nodded. "Crazy and curious." She untucked his

T-shirt and splayed her hands above his rippled abs. "You can't blame a girl for learning such a juicy thing about the man she's sleeping with and wondering what it would take to get a private show."

"Not sure I'm up for that."

She cocked her head and smoothed her hands higher up his chest. "I think I understand. Somewhere along the way, you got it screwed up in your head that what you did was something to be ashamed of. I'm the same way with my body. You keep telling me I'm beautiful and that having a baby didn't make me less desirable, but my brain hasn't quite caught up." She wrapped her arms around him and held him tight. "I'm just telling you, I think the mere idea of you doing that is sexy."

He tangled his fingers in her hair and studied her face. For a moment, it was like they were back out on the dance floor, the two of them connected by something more than physicality even without the music or movement. "We're a pair aren't we? I'm embarrassed about flaunting my body, and you're gun-shy about showing yours."

She laughed, a surprised body-shaking chuckle that echoed throughout the room. "You have a point."

A roguish grin tilted his lips and he walked her backward toward the bed. "Maybe we should work on that."

"Work on what?"

"Our hang-ups."

The backs of her knees hit the bed. "I thought that's what we were doing."

Instead of guiding her to the mattress like she'd expected, Trevor spun them around, perched on the edge of the bed and pulled her astride his thighs. "Dad always says action's more powerful than words, so I'll make you a deal. You dance for me, I'll dance for you."

"Yeah, that's not going to happen. You proved you're an exceptional dancer and teacher tonight, but I think we both know I'd have face-planted with anyone else. A lap dance would take my embarrassment to a whole new level."

"Darlin', you are many things, but rhythmically challenged isn't one of them." Gripping her hip with one hand and palming the back of her head, he guided her mouth to his and ground his cock against her sex. "Every time I've had you against me, you followed my rhythm just fine."

As if to prove his point, he slanted his lips against hers and led them in an entirely different kind of dance. She followed as easy as he'd claimed she would, tangling her tongue with his and circling her hips so the seam of her jeans and his iron shaft pressed just right against her clit.

She gripped the hem of his T and tried to pull it up.

He caught her wrists and eased them away. "Oh, no." He nipped her lower lip. "I think I'm on to something and we're not getting distracted."

He tugged his billfold out of his back pocket and tossed it toward the head of the bed. "Don't need that yet." As in the condom, or as it was these days, condoms. The way they'd gone through them, she was a bit surprised he didn't start carrying around a man purse to haul their supply.

"What are you doing?" she said.

From his other pocket, he pulled out his smartphone. "Just getting the right music. Hard to get into the mood if you don't have something to work with."

"Oh my God. You're serious."

"Hell, yes, I'm serious." He eased her off his lap, stood, and rounded toward the nightstand, thumbing through something on his screen along the way. "You think I'd pass up a chance to see you peel your clothes off and swing your pretty hips? I might be slow sometimes, but I am far from stupid."

He plugged the device into the alarm clock's cradle and punched a few more buttons. Music filled the room, a slow, sultry song she'd heard a thousand times on the radio and the absolute last selection she'd have expected Trevor to have on his phone.

"Ariana Grande?"

He shrugged and settled on the bed. "I favor country, but I work in a pub and shit grows on me." He stretched his legs out in front of him, crossed them at the ankles and laced his hands on his stomach. She might have been ready to bolt for the door, but he looked as at-ease as he'd be watching Sunday afternoon golf. "'Dangerous Woman' seemed fitting." He paused long enough to cock one eyebrow in a silent dare. "Unless you're not up for owning it."

Every muscle from her thighs to her shoulders trembled and her heart chugged in a ragged, uneven beat. "Trevor, I can't do this."

"You told me once there wasn't anything in this world you couldn't do if you set your mind to it. I want you to see how beautiful you are. Want you to see how hard and ready you make me."

"That's not fair. I don't have a clue what I'm doing."

He paused for a single heartbeat, but it was enough to punctuate his words with the utmost sincerity. "I'm scared too, Nat."

The stark confession obliterated all the arguments piling up on her tongue. "Why?"

"I told you. I view that part of my life as a stupid move. People find out what I did and they look at me different. Like I'm a joke. I can stand up to a hell of a lot, but if you looked at me that way, I'm not sure how well I'd rebound. So, yeah. I'm scared, too. But if it helps you come to grips with the fact that you're fucking sexy as hell just like you are, I'll happily put myself at risk."

Her heart hitched on an awkward beat, and goose bumps spread across her shoulders and down her arms. "You would?"

"Absolutely."

It was a huge offer. His pride in exchange for her self-confidence. Maybe he was right. Maybe actions spoke louder than words. If it meant bringing the two of them closer together and her slaying a few of her own demons, it couldn't hurt. "You won't laugh?"

He uncrossed his legs, crooked one knee, and gripped his obviously erect cock through his jeans. "Darlin', my dick's about to punch out of my jeans, and you haven't done a damn thing yet. I might fuck you silly, but you're absolutely guaranteed I will not laugh."

She shifted her feet and looked around the room. The windows were drawn tight, so no chance of anyone else but Trevor catching her highly inexperienced show. Not that the knowledge did much to help her nerves. "What do I do?"

He wagged his fingers. "Come closer."

She frowned. "I thought there was supposed to be a no-touching rule."

He grinned at that. "Gonna be hard to coach you if I

can't help you out when you need it. Now get your pretty ass over here and take off those shoes."

Not the least bit interested in being sexy, she flounced to his side of the bed, plopped down next to him and popped off her Keds.

"For the record," he said eyeballing her shoes on the thick carpet, "we may need a repeat performance with those heels you wore this afternoon."

"Let's get through my debut before we schedule any encores." She stood next to him and fisted her hands at her sides. "Now what?"

He cupped her hip and grazed his thumb along her hip bone. "For starters, I'd say relax. Close your eyes, and forget I'm here."

She scowled down at him. "Fat chance of that." She closed her eyes anyway and let out a slow breath.

"Just listen to the music," he said. "Don't worry about anything. Just sway to it. Think about when we were on the dance floor. Put yourself there again."

That, at least, wasn't too hard. The moment had been seared on her brain, the sheer joy of moving with him a thrill she'd treasure for the rest of her life. Slowly, she began to move. More of a sway than anything erotic or sexy, but it didn't feel bad for a start.

"Pretty," he murmured. "Imagine me touching you."

The way he'd teased his lips along her neck came to mind and she tilted her head, offering up access for his imaginary kiss.

"Just like that."

Bit by bit, he walked her through it, his voice growing deeper and rougher with each moment and one song blending into another. Every second drew her deeper. The soft brush of her sweater whispering over her head and the silky caress of her hair against her bare shoulders. The rasp of denim and lace against her hips. Before she knew it she was naked, slick with arousal, and aching in a way she hadn't thought possible. She opened her eyes and her knees nearly buckled.

Tension and an animalistic hunger marked his every feature, from the blazing fire behind his blue eyes to the vicious grip on his cock. "Crawl up here."

"But I—"

"Need you up here, Nat. Need it now."

Oh, to hell with it. If it meant easing the pulse between her legs, she'd happily take a rain check on his performance. She scrambled toward the bed. The second she got into grabbing distance, he snagged her around the waist and wrangled her so she straddled his thighs.

He caught her hand and pressed it against his cock. "You feel that? You think I could make that up? Think I could get this hard for just anyone?" He rocked into her touch. "That's all you, darlin'. You. Your pretty smile. The way you move. Your perfect tits and outstanding hips."

"Okay, I get it," she rasped. At least she thought she did. Though, it was awfully hard to concentrate with his knuckles skimming slowly down her abdomen.

He teased her trimmed curls and licked his lower lip, his eyes trained on her sex. "About damned time, 'cause now you're about to get something else." He slicked his fingers through her folds. No teasing or easy caresses, just blatant, carnal touch. Back and forth, he guided her wetness up and around her clit, never lingering on the swollen bundle of nerves long enough to give her release.

Her moan filled the room, pure pleasure amplifying the sound and reverberating through the vast space. She braced her hands on his shoulders and widened her knees, angling her hips in a silent plea for more. "Don't tease. Not right now. Later maybe, but not right now."

"Who said anything about teasing?" He plunged two fingers deep, angling his wrist so they stimulated the sweet spot along her front wall. "You want to come, then take it. Roll those hips and ride my fingers."

God, yes. She threw her head back and followed his lead as easy as she had on the dance floor, grinding and circling her pelvis in a perfect, escalating rhythm. His jeans chafed the insides of her thighs, and his breath ghosted against her sweat-damp skin as release crept closer and closer.

"Fuck, that's sexy." The hand at her hip tightened and his thumb grazed her clit. "Soon as I get you home, I'm getting you some pretty silk rope, tying you down, and teasing your pussy just like this."

The image he created flashed in crystal clarity in her mind, knocking her over the edge. Her sex vised around his fingers and her hips bucked. "Trevor!"

"There it is." Relinquishing the lead, he followed every undulation, pumping his fingers in time with the fierce spasms and smoothing his free hand up and down the curve of her hip. "Never get enough of seeing you come. Never."

Fresh goose bumps lifted across her skin and her heart squeezed, the sweetness of his words mingling with physical pleasure still pulsing through her body. Sex before Trevor had always been purely carnal. A series of carefully timed bodily acts—some intricate and some clumsy. But with him it was beautiful. Meaningful and profound.

With shaking legs, she leaned closer, resting her forehead against his while she tried to catch her breath. "I'm not sure that's a good thing. That one almost killed me."

"No dying yet, darlin'. We haven't made it through the main act yet. You gotta keep those eyes open long enough to get your lap dance."

She pried her eyes open, the languid comfort and power of the release he'd given her making the task a Herculean effort, but there was no way she'd force him to go through with their deal. "You don't have to dance for me."

His eyes narrowed. "What's goin' on in that head of yours?"

How could she say it in a way he'd understand? A way that wouldn't come off wrong? "You asked me to dance to build me up. I don't want to ask you for something that might tear you down. It doesn't matter to me what you did or who you used to be. All that matters is who you are now."

His expression shifted, shock and maybe a little awe leaving him tongue-tied for all of two seconds. Then he was in motion, rolling her to her back and taking her mouth in an all-consuming kiss. Lips, teeth, tongue, he wielded them all, feasting from her mouth as though he'd been starved for days. When he finally lifted his head, they were both breathless. His gruff voice danced along every nerve ending. "You ready for more than just light and easy between us?"

Kiss-frazzled and still sluggish from her release, she wasn't sure she'd heard him right. "Are you?"

He cupped the side of her face. "Don't think I could stop wanting more even if I had to."

She traced his swollen lips, her fingertips trembling on a flood of emotion. "Me, either," she whispered.

The confession earned her a brilliant smile, one as warm and heart stopping as Levi's on Christmas morning. "Then I'm keepin' my promise. Not gonna have my past or anything else between us. You take me like I am, I'll give you anything you want." He touched his lips to hers, a simple touch in comparison to the kiss they'd shared before, then flexed his jean-clad hips against her bare core. "Think you'd better brace, though. I'm in the mood to play dirty."

Chapter Twenty-Three

Naked as the day she was born and teetering between terror and the best thrill ride of her life, Natalie lay sprawled in the middle of Trevor's king-size bed. Normally, she'd have found an excuse to crawl under the comforter the second Trevor had moved away from her, but with his mischievous, tempting words still lingering in the air, she had more important things to do. "For those of us less familiar with the more adventurous side of sex, I don't suppose you could define *playing dirty*."

Beside her on the edge of the bed, Trevor yanked off his boots and tossed them to the floor. Watching him do anything was a thing of beauty, but with his tight-fitting blue T-shirt, she got the added bonus of enjoying the flex of his lean, perfectly defined muscles beneath. He peered over one shoulder, aimed a lopsided grin at her and pulled off his socks. "You want a show, I'm gonna give it to you. Just going to play a little game along the way." He stood and snatched his phone off the dock.

Natalie rolled to her side and propped her head up on one hand. "Why do I get the feeling this game is going to be woefully one-sided where rules are concerned?"

His lips twitched and he punched something on his phone's screen. He put the device back in its cradle, crawled like a stalking cat onto the bed, and caged her with his hands and knees. "Only gonna feel one-sided until my cock's pounding inside you and you come hard enough to see stars."

Her sex spasmed and she squeezed her thighs together on reflex. "Oh."

"Yeah." His gaze trailed, slow and covetous, down her torso. "O is what you're gonna get. Though, swear to Christ, how I'm gonna dance for you as hard as my dick is remains to be seen."

She licked her lip and cupped him through his jeans. "I could fix that first. Make things easier for you."

He growled and covered her hand with his. "Darlin', you keep that up, we'll skip your dance altogether." He tugged her hand away, but kept his fingers curled around her wrist. Smoothing his thumb along her pulse point, he sat back on his heels. "Rule one, I get to touch you however I want."

She smiled and splayed her hands against the top of his muscled thigh. "I like that one."

"Yeah?" With his free hand, he tugged his pony-tail holder, shook his hair free and captured her other wrist. "Not sure you'll like this one." He leaned over her, guiding her arms up and over her head. "Rule two, your hands stay over your head."

As fast as her thrill had risen, a mood to rival a sleep-deprived two-year-old bubbled up. "Where's the fun in that?"

"Oh, it'll be fun." He pressed an easy, lingering kiss to her lips then muttered against them, "For me." He rolled off the bed in a move so fluid she'd almost thought he'd started without music.

"Seriously, you're going to dance and I can't touch?"

"Dead serious." He punched his phone's screen and the first strains of a sexy R&B song filled the room. He ran his thumbs along the inside of his waistband and smirked. "The second you touch me—hands, arms, legs, mouth—it doesn't matter. The show's over and I get to claim what's mine."

She whimpered and the muscles low in her belly fluttered.

"You like that?" He ambled closer to the bed, one strong hand moving across his pecs in a way she'd love to imitate. "Ready for me to claim your sweet pussy and make it mine?"

Her hips flexed the same as if he'd slid his fingers through her folds and she grabbed on to the pillow beneath her head for all she was worth. Her voice was little more than a hiss, but she felt it in every inch of her body. "Yes."

"That's my girl." In one molten glide, he was on the bed, his knees wedged under hers and her thighs spread wide. He rolled his hips, the rough surface of his jeans little more than a whisper against her sensitive flesh, but a perfect promise of what was to come. He bit his lower lip and reached over his head, grasping his T-shirt and pulling it off.

He took his time, blending subtle touches and liquid, sensual motion with the music's throbbing beat. She'd always sensed something beneath his country-boy surface, something untamed and blatantly carnal, but watching him move was a thing of beauty. Animalistic power and grace in its most decadent form.

Dipping low, he nipped the inside of her thigh, caught the backs of her legs with his shoulders, and glided forward so her ankles were anchored by his ears.

He pumped twice with his hips, intimating exactly what they both really wanted. The corded muscles in his abdomen flexed and released in an enticing ripple and her hands slipped from under the pillow of their own accord, eager for touch.

"Damn it," she grumbled and stuffed them back into place, clamping down twice as hard. No way was she stopping this ride before he lost his jeans. God knew, she wouldn't make it much beyond that.

"Almost." Carefully, he eased her legs from his shoulders and stood tall on his knees in front of her. "Okay, sweetheart. You want the rest of this?"

"You mean, you naked and next to me?"

He popped the button on his jeans and eased the zipper down. "Naked, next to you and buried deep."

"Then yes. Absolutely yes."

A wicked grin tilted his lips. "Good answer."

Before she could analyze what new tricks she was in for, he snatched her by both wrists, tugged her upright and spun her so she sat on the edge of the bed. The change in position amplified every sense. The depth of the music's thrumming bass. The room's chill against her bare skin. The shadows cast from the bedside lamp across Trevor's defined muscles as he shoved his jeans past his hips and kicked them to the side.

Even standing still he was a visual treat. A mouthwatering temptation few women would pass up. But clad in only black boxer briefs and undulating his hips in time with the music, with an erection so powerful the tip peeked past the waistband, he left her slack jawed and dumbfounded. "Did you get this close to women when you danced before?"

He slid to one side of her, a smooth move she'd never

expect to see outside of a breakdancing competition, let alone on a cowboy. "This close? Yeah, a few got this." He whirled and straddled her lap, his perfect ass smack-dab in front of her face, then dropped his hands to the floor and pumped his hips.

She fisted the comforter in her hands, desperate to feel his flexing ass beneath her palms. Thankfully, he twisted upright and faced her before she could give in.

He slid his fingertips beneath the waistband of his briefs. "You know what they didn't get?"

She squeezed her knees together and bit her lip. "Who?"

His shameless chuckle rippled across flesh. He dipped his hand inside his briefs, grasped his shaft, and ambled closer, bringing them knees to knees. "The women I danced for. You know what they didn't get?"

Oh, that. She forced her gaze to his. "What didn't they get?"

"This." In a move that made her disrobing look comical in comparison, he shucked his briefs and straddled her thighs. His beautiful cock was lined up square with her mouth, the shaft so swollen and marked with raised veins it looked painful. The tip glistened with pre-come. "Or this."

Just as he had seconds before, he rolled his hips, pumping his staff so close to her lips the heat of him radiated against her mouth and his musky scent filled her lungs. She couldn't have kept her hands to herself if she'd wanted to. It was too much and not enough all at once. Too much sensation and not nearly enough contact.

Smoothing her palms up his corded thighs, she pressed her lips to the base of his cock.

"Thought you'd never get around to that." He growled and gripped the back of her head. "Show's over, darlin'."

Maybe for him it was, but for her it was just getting started. Gripping him at the base, she licked along one prominent vein and hummed against his turgid flesh. "I want this."

His grip in her hair tightened, sending tiny pinpricks of pleasure and pain across her scalp and down her spine. "Not gonna say no to anything that involves your mouth and my dick." He flexed his hips, though unlike the moves he'd demonstrated before, this one was pure reflex.

She swirled her tongue around the tip and his salty taste exploded on her tongue. Palming his tight sac in her free hand, she took all of him that she could and peered up at him from beneath her lashes.

"Fuuuck." He worked his shaft between her lips, matching his rhythm to hers. "You have no idea." He gripped the other side of her head, the tension in his body so rife she couldn't tell if he was on the verge of losing control, or bolting for the door. "The things I want to do to you. The way I want to take you. Want to fuck you so hard and deep I'm all you think about. All you remember."

She suckled harder, teased his cockhead with the slightest graze of her teeth, then whispered against the tip. "Okay."

The word was barely out and the world spun around her, her body maneuvered up from her perch on the side of the bed and tossed facedown in the middle of the king-size bed. Before she could draw a breath or assimilate her situation, Trevor yanked her hips up from behind her and spanked one side of her ass. "Think you meant, 'Okay, *sir*.'"

Oh God.

Every nerve ending went from sensitized to super-charged in an instant, the power of every fantasy and desire she'd entertained for months surging to a fine point in a single second. "Trevor." It was the only word her mouth could form, desire, fear, and excitement knotted so tightly she could barely draw a decent breath.

The mattress dipped and the sound of crinkling foil sounded behind her. "You want to use my name, you do it when you come. Understand?"

"Yes."

Another whack, this one on the other cheek. "Yes, what?"

Her sex quivered, a fresh release already so close her thighs trembled with it. "Yes, sir."

He chafed the globes of her ass and squeezed, the light dusting of hair along his quads ghosting against the backs of her thighs. "Fuck, darlin', you have no idea how sweet that sounds." He slicked his fingers through her folds and pumped two fingers inside her. "Gonna make you say it a lot. Scream it before you come shouting my name." His fingers disappeared and he smacked the inside of her thighs. "Knees wide. Ass up."

Eagerly, she widened her stance and arched her hips. Two months ago, she'd have never been confident enough to offer herself like this. Would have never been so motivated to explore the edgier, darker side of sex. Sure she'd taken Wyatt on her hands and knees, but this...this was so much more than positioning. This was animalistic. A primal connection so far beyond the ho-hum experiences of her past it was as if she'd never lain with another man.

"So pretty." He slicked the head of his shaft through her drenched labia. "Swollen, pink, and all mine." Forgoing her entrance, he pushed forward and teased the side of his shaft against her clit. He blanketed her back, and the heat of his torso scorched and soothed her tension-laced muscles. His fingers speared through her hair and fisted tight, wrenching her head back and leaving her throat exposed. "Say it, Nat. Want to hear it from your mouth."

Dear God, she'd say or do anything he wanted right now. Find a way to give him the sun, moon and stars if he'd fill her up and push her over the edge. "I'm yours. Anything you want. However long you want."

He jerked her upright so hard and fast her lungs seized, the merciless grip he kept in her hair not giving an inch. "You think I'd let this go?" He released his grip and cupped her breasts, kneading her mounds just short of too rough. His lips coasted along the line of her neck in a devastatingly soft contrast. "You'll walk before I ever give up what's between us."

Like hell she would. For years with Wyatt, she'd twisted and turned herself inside out trying to be someone she wasn't. Trevor took her as she was. Accepted and championed her son, and chiseled past the surface to facets of herself she'd never known existed. Wyatt hadn't proven worth the fight, but for Trevor she'd storm the pits of hell. "Then you don't know me very well. I want this. Need this." Grinding her clit against his cock, she reached behind him, one hand tangling in his thick hair and the other sinking nails in his flanks. "Please."

His answering growl vibrated against her back and he bit her shoulder. His hips shifted, bringing his cock in line with her weeping entrance. "Anything you want. Everything. As long as you're mine."

He surged forward, filling her in one savage thrust. Claiming her in the most primitive way possible and branding her more thoroughly than any iron. Together, they fell to their hands, his powerful body pistoning against hers in a hedonistic rhythm. This was the stuff of legend. The kind of passion few women ever found but every one of them craved.

And it was hers.

His.

Theirs.

He clenched her hips and powered deep.

The sweet, powerful pulse of impending release swelled, so close her lungs burned with a barely stifled roar.

"Trevor!"

"Not yet." His fingers dug deeper in her flesh, holding on for dear life and marking her in a way she'd feel and remember until the day she died.

"Please." She dropped her head and her hair fell around one shoulder, the soft strands gliding against her hypersensitive skin like satin. Her breasts bounced and swayed with each slap of his hips, an erotic sight to be sure, but nowhere near as startling as watching his cock tunnel in and out of her eager sex. "I'm there. Now."

"A little more. Take it. Ride it."

"I can't." Reaching between her legs, she cupped his sac and gently squeezed. "You said anything."

"Fuck!" He rolled his hips the same as he had when he'd stripped, only faster and driving to the hilt. "Goddamn right, anything. Everything." One hand slipped between her legs and found her clit. "Come. Now."

He pinched the tight bundle of nerves and her pussy clenched tight, the power of her release seizing all but the haggard rhythm of her heart and the convulsing muscles at her core.

"Mine!" Trevor bucked one last time and his cock jerked inside her, the force behind his claim mingling with each flex and release of her sex and resonating clear to her toes. "Say it."

Say it? She'd sky-write it if it meant easing the vulnerability behind his demand. She covered his hand between her legs, her fingers lying atop his as they soothed and guided her back to earth. "All yours," she whispered, then gave him back his own. "Anything. Everything."

In and out, each velvet scrape of his length inside her sent tiny shock waves rippling out in all directions. Her muscles shook, but she was too languid and peaceful to care. Too content to just be in the moment. Somewhere in the fury, the music had long died out, the only beat that remained was the ragged tempo of her heart in her ears.

His palm glided soft and reverent up and down her spine, and his ragged voice drifted between their heaving gasps, so soft she doubted he even realized he spoke aloud. "Never thought I'd risk it." Splaying his hand against her pelvis, he held their connection, sat back on his heels and guided her up against his chest. His warm breath ghosted across the back of her sweat-dampened neck. "Won't let you regret it, Nat. Swear to God, I won't hurt you. Won't let myself, no matter what happens."

Something in his tone jangled her instincts, but the bone-deep lethargy and lingering aftershocks coursing through her muscles swiped all non-critical queries aside. Later she could tend to whatever wound lay beneath his cryptic promise. Right now was for savoring the moment. For comforting each other and fortifying the growing bond between them, starting with a vow of her own.

She guided his hand above her heart, rested her head against his shoulder and rolled it enough to meet his gaze. "I trust you. Everything you've done and what it took to get you here, I want you just like you are."

Chapter Twenty-Four

Sunday nights didn't get better than this. Good food, great people and simple time spent kicked back in front of the television. From his place at the end of the couch, Trevor squeezed Natalie's shoulder and tucked her tighter to him. She'd thrown on a simple cotton pajama set about fifteen minutes after they'd carted in their luggage and declared it a pizza and *Avengers* night, which was perfectly fine with him. Hell, anything would have been fine with him so long as he could touch her and reassure himself last night hadn't been a figment of his imagination. Waking her up this morning in time to sneak her back to her room before Levi woke had taken every ounce of discipline he'd had. She belonged next to him. Not slinking off like what they'd done was wrong.

The explosions from the movie's final action scene filled Natalie's tiny living room and lit up the otherwise dark space. Maureen had cleared away the empty pizza boxes halfway through the movie, refreshed everyone's drinks, and now sat dozing on the opposite end of the couch. Just like Trevor had when he was little, Levi was parked front and center of the screen, his back propped up on the coffee table. The way his eyes were glued to the set, the Hulk would have had to stomp through the front door before Levi would've looked away.

Sweeping Natalie's hair to the side, Trevor nuzzled her neck and inhaled her wildflower scent. He kissed the sensitive spot behind her ear and murmured, "Gonna have a hell of a time sleeping this week without you beside me."

Her lips curved in a satisfied smile and she twisted enough to whisper back, "It doesn't have to be the whole week. We could sneak you in when you get home Thursday night."

A little of his quiet bliss dimmed, the reminder of his overseas trip the next morning pile-driving him back to reality. If Wyatt had really managed to tie Trevor to the bootleg product winding its way through Dallas, Trevor might end up spending Thursday in a jail cell, no matter how influential the passengers on board his plane might be.

He tucked her hair behind one ear. Much as it pained him to be away from her, the last thing he needed to do was give her ex any extra ammunition. At least not until Trevor had the bastard tucked between a rock and a hard place. "Not so sure our late-night visits are a good idea right now. Wyatt might be playing nice on the surface, but he's already shown he's tracking Levi. If he's got someone watching the house too, he'd likely use me staying overnight as a reason for another lawsuit."

She toyed with the hem of his T-shirt, and the peaceful glow behind her dark eyes faded. "I don't like sleeping without you."

"I know, darlin'." He ran the backs of his knuckles along her cheek. "I don't like it either, but it won't last forever. I promise you that."

Levi glanced over his shoulder and frowned. "Mom, you're missing it."

Natalie bit back a smile and traded a *Lord, save me* expression with Trevor. "I've seen it five times already, Levi. I don't think the Hulk's temper tantrum is going to be any different this time around." Still, she squared her shoulders back to the television and nestled back in the crook of Trevor's arm.

Trevor chuckled. "My bad, bud. No more interruptions. I promise." Besides, the movie was nearly over, which meant his quiet time with Natalie was almost gone. Tomorrow, he'd be wheels up and headed for his fate.

I trust you. Everything you've done and what it took to get you here, I want you just like you are.

Over and over, he'd replayed her earnest words, torn between a euphoric high and bone-chilling terror. She'd shared them in reference to his past, but what happened if she found out about his present? She'd made no bones about how little she'd approved of Wyatt's involvement with the unapproved drugs, and the odds of her feeling any different on who was doing the peddling were slim.

For the umpteenth time that day, he considered bailing on tomorrow's run. Someone else could fly his passengers to London while he stayed put in Dallas and let the whole deal go. God knew, he'd rather take a more direct approach with warning off Wyatt. Preferably one that involved a whole lot of pain and months of healing on Wyatt's end.

But then a wife might lose her husband. Kids might lose a dad. And he'd lose a chance to get Natalie long-term leverage with Wyatt. Her ex might have connections a plenty now, but if their plan worked and the Feds caught him with a load of non-FDA-approved drugs, his highfalutin cronies wouldn't even acknowledge his existence.

No, even if he landed in jail and lost Natalie in the process, those were some pretty stout reasons to suck it up and take the chance. Risk was part of life, and a man didn't play things safe when it came to doing the right thing. Especially when the right thing made his woman's life better.

Just as the credits began to roll, Natalie's phone lit up and sent her generic ring tone blasting loud enough to jolt Maureen from her nap.

"Levi, turn it down." Natalie crawled over Trevor to the end table and snagged the device, putting her sweet ass on prime display. If Levi hadn't craned his head around at that exact moment and Maureen wasn't in direct line of sight, Trevor would have happily sampled a handful.

She checked the display, scowled, and plopped back down beside him. "Hey, Wyatt. What's up?"

The post-movie high on Levi's face slipped, replaced with a wariness Trevor recognized all too well. He'd felt it himself at the same age, and he'd be damned if Levi lived another year dreading the mention of his father's name. No way was he backing down on his plans.

Natalie did her best to blank her expression while she listened to whatever Wyatt said on the other end, but the way she clenched her hand around his wrist belied her exterior calm. Her grip eased a fraction and surprise spread across her features. "Really?"

Only a hint of Wyatt's voice registered from the device, the words unintelligible.

Her gaze shot to Trevor, then to Levi, and a sunrise-potent smile stretched ear-to-ear. "Yes, of course. I'd love that. I just…" She looked to Trevor as though he might offer the elusive words her tongue refused to form. "It's just unexpected."

Her eyes sparked with pure joy. "Yes, I'll tell him. I'll pick him up on Friday. Thank you. Really. It means a lot."

It shouldn't have pissed him off, but hearing Natalie thank that bastard for anything sliced deep. Especially knowing whatever gift he'd given would come with a price.

She ended the call and tossed her phone to the couch, her focus shifting between her mom and Levi. "Wyatt said he has a Christmas Eve function he has to go to with his parents. He offered to let Levi spend Christmas Eve and Christmas with me."

Oh, yeah. Definitely a ploy. And a damned good one, given the way both Natalie and Levi bounced with barely contained glee.

She twisted to Trevor. "You'll be with us, won't you? I mean, your dad's welcome, too. Mom and I hadn't planned much, but with Levi here, maybe we could do dinner that night and watch some Christmas movies after?"

Clad in his Iron Man pajamas to match their Sunday night movie, Levi scrambled to his feet. "You'll like it, Trevor. I promise. We open presents on Christmas morning and I bet Mom and Nanna would cook us a huge breakfast after." His eyes widened, the blaze of some grand idea firing behind his gaze. "Hey, what if we spend the night at the ranch? Then Lady and the horses wouldn't be alone, and your dad and Nanna can spend the night too!" He focused on Natalie. "Santa could still find me there, right?"

"Now, Levi," Maureen chimed in. "You can't go volunteering Trevor's home for him. It's not nice."

The hell if he couldn't. Especially when the idea went a long way to undercutting whatever favors Wyatt hoped to gain with Natalie. "I think it's a genius idea." He grinned at Natalie. "Levi's right. I've got a lot more room at my place, and everyone knows Santa knows where kids are on Christmas Eve, so we're covered there."

"And Trevor's got a real tree!" Levi added, practically jumping up and down. He aimed the biggest set of puppy dog eyes Trevor had ever seen on Natalie. "Please, Mom? We'd get to spend Christmas on a real ranch. Even Bobby can't top that one. It'd be cool."

Natalie bit her lip and did some kind of woman to woman silent communication thing with her mom. From the look on her face, Trevor couldn't decide if she was looking for moral support, or asking for permission.

Maureen grinned much as a cat would if a mouse danced in front of its nose. "Well, we would have a bigger kitchen to work with, and I imagine Frank would appreciate more time with his son."

Oh, she was good. A finagler to rival Frank's matchmaking efforts for sure. He'd have to be sure Santa left a few extra goodies for his fellow conspirator as a thank-you.

Trevor smoothed his hand up Natalie's spine and cupped the back of her neck. "See? Perfect reasoning. All you need to do is say yes."

She huffed and put on a decent show of being put

out, but she couldn't quite keep the smile from her face. "Like I can fight all three of you."

"Wahoo!" Levi bounded over to Maureen and hopped in her lap. "Wait till you see Lady, Nanna. She's pretty and fast. And the horses are *huuuge*."

Maureen laughed and corralled him in her arms, hugging him tight as she stood. "I'm sure they are, but you've still got one more week of school to get through before you can have your country Christmas. How about we get you to bed so you don't go to sleep during class?"

Trevor tried to stifle his chuckle, but it still eked out. Maureen had about as much chance of getting Levi to sleep as a bug had of surviving a windshield.

Natalie nabbed a fistful of Trevor's T-shirt and tugged him toward her. "You look mighty pleased with yourself."

Oh, he was pleased all right. Nothing beat one-upping an asshole like Wyatt, even if the idea had come from an innocent seven-year-old kid. "Well, you gotta admit. It's a genius idea. More space, lots of bedrooms…" He pulled her astride him, squeezed her ass, and lowered his voice. "And your ex can't see when I sneak you in my bed. Best Christmas present ever."

Her laughter filled the room and she lowered her head for a sweet kiss.

More than ready to indulge in her mouth and the press of her body against him while he still could, he palmed the back of her head and deepened the kiss.

Natalie dug the heels of her hands into his shoulders and pushed away, her gaze sober and searching. "You're sure you're okay with this? Mom's right. We shouldn't just intrude on your home."

But it wasn't just his home anymore. Where the certainty came from or how long it had been there, he hadn't a clue, but he wanted her there. Not just for a holiday. Not just for a night. But forever. Her and Levi. Even her mother if that's what made Natalie happy. Hell, the guest house would be perfect for Maureen.

He urged her closer and teased her lips with his. "I'm more than okay with it. I want it." He sealed his words with a kiss. One way or another, he'd make it all happen just as soon as he got Wyatt behind them. First, he had to get through the next four days without everything falling to shit.

Chapter Twenty-Five

Trevor's copilot, Jerry, switched the plane's comm radio frequency to 125.2 and activated his headset with the push-to-talk. "Regional approach, Gulfstream N152HB, level fifteen thousand."

A deadpan masculine voice crackled through their headsets all of two seconds later. "Gulfstream N152HB, regional approach, turn left heading two-one-zero, descend and maintain niner thousand."

Jerry nodded and updated the nav system accordingly. Like Trevor, he always kept his attire casual, leaning to jeans and Ts or button-downs when he flew, but in every other respect they were night and day. Dark hair cropped close to his head, rich Hispanic skin, and clipped mannerisms.

Trevor eased up on the power, eyeballing the altimeter as he snatched the satphone off the cabin wall beside him. The call he placed took all of one and a half rings before his brother answered.

"I see you just handed off to regional approach," Knox said without preamble. The distant quality of his voice and the muted click of a keyboard in the background indicated he had Trevor on speaker.

Trevor huffed out a short chuckle despite the tension knotting his gut. "Hanging out on the flight radar website again?"

"Hey, it's fascinating stuff. You never realize how many planes there are until you see 'em mapped out and moving online. What are you, thirty minutes out?"

"More like twenty." Trevor glanced at Jerry. If he was even remotely worried about how the next hour was going to go down, he didn't show it. It was one of the main reasons he'd singled Jerry out as copilot the first time he'd flown one of these runs. The other was the huge family he had to support. In exchange for keeping Trevor's side venture to himself, Jerry walked with thirty percent of the net profits. The rest went to the patient's family.

"Got any news on any visitors that might be waiting on us when we land?" he said to Knox.

Knox's hesitation told him all he needed before a word was uttered. "Four suits showed up in two unmarked units at your office about an hour ago. Your secretary checked in with me about fifteen seconds after I clocked them on the monitors. I told her it was probably just a routine check and to be her usual sweet self, but Danny's stationed in the hangar just in case we need an extra hand on-site."

"Guess that answers whether Wyatt put two and two together on his own."

"He's smart, has deep connections, and doesn't like getting one-upped by people like us. Not much better motive than that." Knox's fingers tapped on the keyboard. "You clean?"

"Sparkling." Hell, the crew that had swarmed his plane last night had left the thing nicer inside and out than it had been the day he bought it. They'd charged him a pretty penny for it, too. "The load Beckett's handling isn't so spic and tidy, though. Seems someone came up with the crafty idea of hooking our product up with tracking devices."

"Admit it," Knox said. "I'm a genius."

He absolutely was. With the trackers in place, they'd not only get a bead on their middleman but could follow the product all the way into Wyatt's office after the sale went down—assuming Wyatt took the bait and went through with a purchase. Given the huge debits Knox had found coming out of Wyatt's investment accounts around Trevor's last shipment, he was banking on the narcissistic bastard feeling too sure of himself to say no. "Brother, your dick might need to be stroked on a frequent basis, but your ego absolutely does not."

The engine's hum filled the silence, and the prickling weight of what was about to go down hit him in a rush. "If shit goes south, I need you to make sure my staff's covered. Anything that happens stays on me only."

Instead of Knox replying, it was Axel's voice that came through, his voice gruffer and more menacing than normal. "We take care of our own. You know that." He paused long enough the silence swelled. "We'll take care of your woman and her boy, too."

A denial pushed to the tip of his tongue, long years of practice and disbelief making the retort instinctive. He bit it back. "Appreciate it."

A round of chuckles rumbled in the background mingled with Jace's deep "Good to see you're comin' around."

"It's not what you think." At least not yet, it wasn't. He'd barely acknowledged where he wanted things to go, let alone tackled sharing with her what being tied to him entailed. The future he wanted with her meant full disclosure. No secrets between them. But if she'd struggled with Wyatt's shady business practices, the brotherhood's endeavors might well send her screaming. "She doesn't know about us. Not gonna claim a woman who can't back the decisions we make."

"But you're leanin' that way?" Axel said.

Leaning. Hoping. Making plans and imagining a future that thrilled and terrified him. "Yeah."

"Then she's protected," Axel said. "Whatever that looks like. Whatever it takes."

The headset squawked and the controller running their approach cut through the speakers. "Gulfstream N152HB, turn left heading one three zero. Descend and maintain five thousand. Slow to two-two-zero knots."

Jerry punched the push-to-talk and answered back, "Left to one three zero, down to five thousand, slowing to two-two-zero knots. Gulfstream N152HB."

As soon as Jerry killed communications to control, Trevor zeroed back in on his brothers. "Gotta go. Jerry needs an update and I wanna get this shit over with."

"I hear ya on that," Jace said. "Get those wheels on the ground, and we'll rally at Haven tonight."

Man he hoped that was the case. As delays in getting back to Natalie went, he'd take meeting with his brothers over a night in jail any day. "Roger that." He cut the connection and hung the satphone back in its cradle.

"I take it we've got company?" Jerry's accent was thicker than what he allowed with the tower or their clients.

For a second, Trevor thought about downplaying what Knox had shared, but nixed the idea. "DEA. Pretty sure they got a tip from a man with an ax to grind where

I'm concerned, but the plane's clean. Unless someone caught us unloading at LaGuardia, they'll have a hard time making any claims stick. No matter what they ask, you know nothing. You're clean in this. Hear me?"

Jerry turned his dark eyes to Trevor and dipped his chin in one sharp jerk. "I hear you."

The next fifteen minutes raced past, the calm, well-practiced routine as they neared the runway keeping the tension in check.

The plane banked, lining up with the runway. Blinding sunshine spotlighted the pale gray concrete and cast an afternoon haze on the horizon. Only in the last few weeks had the landscape relinquished its green luster to the faded browns of deepening winter.

For years, this had been his passion. The power of the engine at takeoff. The drone of the jets and the time to think with nothing but clouds and sky around him. The challenges nature pitted against technology from time to time, and the sense of triumph at each landing. Funny how fast his dream had changed. Two short months and now he'd happily surrender the business he'd built for a life with Natalie.

He pulled back on the power and dropped the landing gear. The back wheels thunked into position a beat before the front snapped into place, and three green lights on the panels confirmed their readiness.

He was right where he needed to be. The certainty came out of nowhere, but it grounded him as sure as Natalie's touch. He was doing what he'd deemed right. No matter the outcome, he'd live with the repercussions and be proud of the choices he'd made.

Three minutes later, the plane was on the ground. Jerry traded direction with ground control while Trevor taxied the plane toward the hangar. Two Feds were already in place when the plane stopped, one man and one woman, both in suits and loitering next to Tony like they had all the time in the world. Behind them, one unmarked gray sedan was parked at an angle on the tarmac and another ugly brown one was parked just outside the office's front door, which probably meant poor Susan was stuck entertaining their friends inside.

Jerry climbed out of his seat and stowed his headset. "How you gonna play this, boss?"

"Same way you are. Smile and act like I don't have a clue what they're doing here." He killed the jets and motioned for Jerry to go ahead. "I'll get the door. Do me a favor and work your customer satisfaction spiel on our guests. See if you can't buy me a few minutes' head start before they deplane."

"You got it." He popped the latch on the cockpit door and disappeared into the main cabin.

For too many wasted seconds, he stared at the forward door, both fists braced on either side while he centered his thoughts. He forced himself into motion, unlocked the hatch and unfolded the stairs.

The agents waiting for him were about as cliché as they could get, both of them hiding their eyes behind what he'd bet were knockoff aviators. The crisp December air whipped the bottoms of their nearly matching charcoal-colored suit jackets, but otherwise, they stood motionless beside the red carpet.

Next to the two suits, Tony kept both hands stuffed in the pockets of his navy-blue coveralls and shifted from one foot to the other like standing in one place was about to kill him. Not like he had much of a choice though. The Feds had likely warned him about hopping in the plane to do his job before they gave the go-ahead.

"Hey, Tony." Trevor stopped in front of him. "There a reason our guests don't have their car waiting?"

Tony swallowed big enough his Adam's apple bobbed. He glanced at the fancy pair next to him.

"I'm afraid that's on us," the woman said before Tony could answer. Her skin hinted of Latino heritage, but nowhere near as dark as Jerry's, and her dark hair was pulled back in a ponytail so tight it looked painful. She offered her hand to Trevor and paired the action with an empty smile. "I'm Special Agent Isabel Fuentes, with the Drug Enforcement Agency. This is my partner, Special Agent Jacob Lineman."

As if the introduction was a routine they'd done a thousand times before, Jacob whipped his identification from the inside of his jacket and flashed it for Trevor.

"DEA?" Trevor stuffed his hands in his jeans pockets, scanned the hangar behind them and the main office in the distance and grinned. "Is that a joke?"

"I'm afraid not, Mr. Raines." Jacob peeled his sunglasses off with the same overblown melodrama he'd expect in an action flick. "We received an anonymous tip on Monday indicating your involvement in shipping non-FDA-approved pharmaceuticals and an impending delivery this afternoon."

A whopping twenty-four hours after he'd shared his overseas gig with Natalie and Levi on the way home from Tahoe Sunday night. Man, but he was tired of that son of a bitch using Levi as the key tool in all his ploys. "Someone said I'm running drugs?"

"Pharmaceuticals," the woman corrected. "Professionally manufactured drugs not yet endorsed by the

FDA. Your flight plans indicate you're just arriving from London?"

"That's right. We had a layover in New York City last night for my guests to attend a Broadway show."

Stern frown in place, Jacob tucked his aviators in his breast pocket. "We'd like to take a look at your cargo before anyone disembarks."

Feigning surprise, Trevor scratched his jaw, glanced over one shoulder at the plane then back to the dynamic duo. "Got no problem with showing you whatever you want to see, but I'm gonna have a problem if my guests get any kind of harassment. I run a business that caters to wealthy people. The one thing those types don't like is hassle. Word gets out that it's anything but smooth sailing with my team, it'll cost me income."

Ms. Fuentes pursed her mouth somewhere between a smile and bitter pucker. "We completely understand. Unless we find something suspicious, we'd simply like to ask your guests a few unobtrusive questions to corroborate your flight plans. Outside some interesting charges many years ago, your record is spotless, but we can't let tips like these go unanswered."

Trevor waited a beat, pretending to consider her statement, and nodded his head. "You keep it professional, I can go with that."

Leading the way, he headed up the steep steps and moseyed through the cabin to the tiny group gathering their things. "Ms. Fuentes, Mr. Lineman, I'd like you to meet my guests, former Dallas mayor Quinn Dixon, Dallas Chief of Police Randy Trammel, and their wives, Rayanne and Gloria."

The agents' blasé expressions slipped and they shared an uncertain look.

Quinn offered his hand to Ms. Fuentes. "Pleasure to meet you both. I wasn't aware Trevor had clients booked back-to-back or we'd have wrapped up our goodbyes sooner."

"We're not clients, Mr. Dixon. We're special agents for the Drug Enforcement Agency. We received a tip earlier this week that a shipment of non-FDA-approved pharmaceutical products was being smuggled in on this flight."

"DEA?" Quinn said. He stared at Trevor. "This some kind of joke?"

He might have had to fake his surprise before, but his laugh this time couldn't have been more genuine. "That's what I said. Seems someone thought it would be fun to call in a pre-holiday prank and waste good government dollars."

Randy let out a long-suffering sigh and cast a commiserating glance at his wife. "More like someone scrambling for a headline." He frowned and focused on the two agents. "You're welcome to look at whatever you want, but we've seen nothing to support the tip you got. Trevor's team has been nothing but professional. I'm afraid your office has gotten caught up in some political maneuvering. Our crackdown on drugs since I took office has caused a lot of these kinds of tactics the last three or four months."

They had? Man, if that was the case, he owed Vivienne big-time for getting these guys as cover for this trip. Having influence on board was one thing. Having it play right into real life was a stroke of un-fucking-believable luck.

Gloria lifted her hand to the hollow of her throat, her aged fingers fluttering as though reliving a harrowing experience. "It's been awful. Last month I was at an event and reporters started questioning me about our oldest daughter recently being released from drug rehabilitation."

"A pot-calling-the-kettle-black ploy," Randy added. "Had to hire a publicist and prove the alleged leak was bogus before the press would leave it alone." He shook his head and zeroed his attention on the agents. "I hate that the two of you had to come all the way out here for this. Though I gotta admit, whoever's behind these attempts keeps getting more creative."

"Please, go right ahead and take a look," Quinn said, motioning the agents toward the luggage area behind the restrooms at the tail of the plane. "You need to confirm what we've said is true, and we've certainly got nothing to hide."

The two agents eyeballed each other for a moment. Ms. Fuentes nodded first and stepped past them. "We'll just be a minute." They hustled off without so much as a backward glance.

"Well, that was interesting." Trevor rubbed the back of his neck and grinned at Randy. "You really get this kind of hassle a lot?"

"More than you'd imagine."

"A byproduct of public life," Quinn added. "Someone always disagrees with your agenda and wants to find a way to bring you down. The scrutiny and challenges are worth it if we do right by the people we serve in the end."

"Can't say I'd be as understanding in your shoes," Trevor said. Especially if they dared to fuck with Natalie in the process. He ducked low enough to check the high chain-link fence beyond the main gate. "How about I have my guys do a sweep of the entrance before everyone gets off the plane? If someone's out for a story, the least we can do is make it hard for them to get any pictures."

Randy wrapped an arm around his wife's waist. "We'd appreciate that."

"I just hope it doesn't blow back on your business," Gloria said. "This trip was just what we needed for the holidays. I'd hate to have any negative press cause you problems."

Tugging his phone out of his back pocket, Trevor gave her what Bonnie had always called his country-boy smile, the same one reserved for conning her out of fresh cookies or talking himself out of a tight spot. "Are you kidding me? If the press mentions I'm carting around a smuggling police chief, I'll double my bookings next month." He added a wink for good measure. "You all have a seat and relax. I'll get Susan to have our guys comb the perimeter for press."

Striding out of hearing distance, Trevor punched a call through to his office.

Not surprisingly, Susan answered after little more than one ring. Her voice was an unnatural version of its usual chipper tone. "Phoenix Charters, this is Susan. How may I help you?"

Trevor chuckled. "I see we're entertaining a different class of clientele this afternoon. You entertaining the two that belong in the brown sedan?"

Her strained voice went a few notches higher. "Oh, hello, Mr. Raines. Is everything going okay?"

"Going just fine, darlin'. Just a misunderstanding our fine government officials are putting to bed as fast as they can. Need you to do me a favor though. Get Tony and the rest of the crew rounded up at the office. As soon as the Feds give the go-ahead, I want a thorough sweep of the perimeter. Anyone found loitering outside the gates gets called out."

"Is something wrong?"

Hardly. More like he'd been handed the mother of all get out of jail free cards and was bound and determined to take advantage, even if it meant sending his crew on a fool's errand. "Nothing wrong. Just making sure my guests don't run into any unwanted attention on the way out."

The female agent's voice cut from the back of the plane. "Mr. Raines?"

Trevor twisted and found both agents strolling from the back of the plane. "Round 'em up, Susan. I need to finish up something here. I'll be in the office as soon as I can." He ended the call and ambled back to the agents. "Find everything you need?"

Ms. Fuentes glanced at her partner and grimaced like her too-tight ponytail was giving her a headache. "It seems the tip we received was unfounded. My partner and I would like to apologize for any inconvenience caused to you or your clients."

Trevor shrugged. "No skin off my back. Kind of feel bad for you guys getting sent on an errand like this though." He glanced out the open door. "I had my secretary round up my crew so they can comb the immediate area for any reporters or photographers. You all right if I give her the go-ahead to send them out?"

"Absolutely," Mr. Lineman said. "The other agents will help us check on the way out as well and can report back if we see anything."

"Appreciate it."

The two ducked out the door and hurried down the

steps. Whether Ms. Fuentes was pissed she hadn't had the chance to play with her handcuffs, or was plotting to castrate the person who'd called in the tip was hard to say, but she covered the ground between the plane and their sedan in short order for someone with such short legs.

His guests offered their thanks and said their good-byes, lingering long enough to make sure they could exit the field without any undue attention. Only when Jerry had finally offered a mock salute and headed to the hangar did Trevor fire up his phone again.

Knox answered quickly, the speakerphone sending white noise through the line behind his voice. "Talk to me."

Pausing at the top of the Gulfstream's steps, Trevor watched the last unmarked sedan disappear around the security gate. "Think it's safe to say, Wyatt made his play."

"And?" Axel demanded.

A strong gust of wind whipped around the plane, the chill behind it as sharp as Trevor's focus. "He struck out. Now it's my turn at bat."

Chapter Twenty-Six

God, Nat loved the holidays. As a kid, she'd always anticipated the exciting stretch between Halloween and New Year's. The sights. The sounds. The delicate approach of cooler weather and the anticipation of memories accumulated with family. Since Levi had been born, they'd become even more precious. Like the universe had offered up a chance to relive the joys of her youth from a whole different perspective.

Outside the passenger window, the streets of her neighborhood crept by, the heavy Friday-afternoon traffic making Trevor's task of getting them to Levi's school twice as cumbersome. The skies were overcast and the promise of impending rain hung thick in the air, but even the humidity couldn't douse her mood. Even working a six to three shift so she could be the one to pick Levi up after school and processing twice as many irritated customers as usual, she was still on cloud nine.

Trevor's rich voice slipped through her thoughts. "You got a problem with my driving, or did you drink a pot of coffee for lunch?"

Natalie ripped her gaze from the crowded convenience store on the corner and shook her head to clear it. "Huh?"

He grinned and dipped his head in the direction of her lap. "That leg of yours has been jangling since we left the parking lot. Tryin' to figure out if you've developed a fear of my driving, or if you're overdosed on caffeine."

Well, damn. She forced her heel against the floorboard to still her leg and shrugged. "Sorry. I'm just excited."

"About the holidays?"

"Yes. But more than that. I thought this Christmas was going to be torture, but now it's got a chance to be extra special. Our first big holiday where we can be who are we and enjoy the time together."

"I take it holidays with Wyatt were something else?"

Boy were they. Formal and tied to rigid agendas prescribed by Wyatt's mother and her burgeoning social calendar. "At first they were okay. The first year we were together—before I got pregnant—we only joined his parents for a few holiday events. Otherwise, we kept to ourselves. After that, things changed. We spent more time at social events and abiding by his mother's agenda than we ever spent enjoying each other."

She rubbed her shaky hand atop her jean-clad thigh. "Levi's never known the kind of Christmas I grew up having. An easy Christmas Eve, watching Christmas classics, making our own food in the kitchen. Heck, even waking up Christmas morning to see what Santa brought and opening gifts was a structured event. I hated it."

Trevor reached across the console and covered her hand with his. "We'll change it."

We. As in the two of them. The concept added a fresh layer of giddy to her already euphoric spirits.

She twisted her hand, laced her fingers with his and squeezed. "I can't wait!"

His low chuckle filled the cab, mingling with the strains of a bluesy country ballad as he turned onto the school's block.

Her phone rang and she hefted her purse onto her lap. "When you get to the far parking lot, just get in line behind the other cars in the far right lane. The attendants won't recognize your truck, so we'll give them Levi's name when we get to the front and they'll walk him to us." She swiped the answer button without checking to see who it was, wedged it between her shoulder and ear and zipped her bag. "Hello?"

Wyatt's voice volleyed back in the harsh, unbending tone he seemed to reserve for her and Levi alone. "Are you picking Levi up?"

"Yes, of course. I told you I'd get him from school today. Is there a problem?"

"I need him at my house at six o'clock. I've decided to take him with me to my event tomorrow night and spend the holiday at my parents'."

Everything froze, the music in the background dimming to a hazy drone while her mind scrambled to catch up. "What?"

"I need him at my house at six as we'd originally planned. You had him for Thanksgiving. Christmas is mine."

"But you said—"

"I know what I said. I've also realized my boy needs to be with me for the holidays and I've decided to put his best welfare first."

Trevor squeezed her thigh, a silent yet comforting

show of support even as his mounting tension filled the truck.

"His best welfare?" Her shriek ricocheted off the windshield and her cheeks fired with enough heat they tingled. "His best welfare is not getting jerked around by his father. We made plans, Wyatt. Plans Levi was looking forward to. Things he'll be crushed if he learns aren't going to happen."

"Like spending the whole time at your new fuck's ranch?" What followed couldn't be called a chuckle. More like sinister pride garbled up in audible form. "Yeah, Levi shared all about it last night before he went to bed. If you think I'm going to let that bastard play father to my kid over Christmas, you are sadly mistaken."

God, she hated that phone. Hated it almost as much as the man who'd given it to him. "Trevor's not trying to play anything. Levi likes the horses and wanted the room to run and play."

"Then he'll have ample time at his father's and his grandparents'. Your cowboy can play wannabe dad the next time he's with you."

Anger shifted to prickling dread, and the heat wafting from the floorboard vents blanketed her in a suffocating grip. He wouldn't waver. Wyatt never did when he started in with that tone. "Please don't do this. Think about your son."

"I am thinking about my son. I'm thinking about what kind of impression it makes when his mother spends the night with a man she's not married to. Now, you have him at my place at six in accordance with our divorce decree, or we'll deal with your failure to comply in court."

"But we had an agreement."

"Prove it."

And there was the crux of it. She'd trusted Wyatt and his generosity and had failed to get anything confirmed in writing. Now, Levi would be the one to pay in broken promises and disappointment.

Trevor's hand tightened on her thigh. "Shut him down, Nat. We'll deal with this later. We're almost to the front of the line and Levi doesn't need to hear this."

"That man's with you right now?" Wyatt barked through the phone. "Jesus, you just couldn't wait to get your fairy-tale bullshit going could you?" He scoffed and something in the background thudded against a hard surface. "At my house, Natalie. Six o'clock sharp or I'll file for sole custody first thing Monday morning. Don't think I won't get it." He hung up before she could argue, the coffin finality of it resounding clear through to her soul.

She powered off the phone and gently set it on the center console. Three minutes. That's all it had taken for Wyatt to upend everything without the slightest drop of remorse.

"I gather he's changed his mind about Christmas."

Natalie nodded, the weight of her disappointment too thick and muddy to let any words bubble to the surface. What had she ever seen in him? Worse, how had she missed everything he kept hidden beneath his polished surface? She was a nurse—or at least she had been before she'd foolishly given up her career. They were trained to look for details. To be watchful and follow their instincts. But she'd ignored all the signs. Stuffed them deep and pretended to be something she wasn't for a man who willingly hurt his own child out of spite.

Trevor pulled into the far lane, easing behind the

long line of cars. Like her, his demeanor had shifted from light and easy to somewhere just shy of volatile. "He's not gonna win this, Nat. He might take this round, but he will *not* win long-term. I'm done sitting on the sidelines and watching him jack you two around. One way or another, I'm wading in and making this right."

Her head snapped up. "You can't, Trevor. That's the whole reason he's doing this. He's jealous. Levi told him how we were spending the holidays and he's changing the plans out of spite. If you get involved, it's just going to make it worse."

Trevor's face hardened, the cold fury behind his blue eyes plummeting the temperature in the truck to nearly arctic levels. "You're fucking kidding me. He said that?"

"Yes! He said he wasn't going to let you play daddy to his kid, and I'm setting a bad impression for our son."

The muscles at the back of Trevor's jaw twitched. "I brought this on you."

"Yes." She shook her head and fisted her hair on the top of her head. "I mean no. I did. I should have thought about how Wyatt would twist it and made sure we made arrangements to come home."

Trevor pulled to the front of the line and slammed the gearshift in park. "No." He shifted in the seat to face her. "This isn't on you. It's on me, but I'll make it right. Swear to you, Nat. I'll make it right, and we'll make it up to Levi. He'll get a second Christmas as soon as he's home. Twice as long and better." He forced her chin up and met her gaze straight on. "Promise you, darlin'. This is the last time that fucker jacks with you and your son."

Chapter Twenty-Seven

This was why Trevor avoided Christmas shopping at all costs. Too damned many people and not nearly enough patience to go around. Four hours he and Gabe had canvassed the mall, zigzagging between stores and exercising Trevor's credit card with a gift-giving enthusiasm only a woman could muster. What little calm he'd wrangled while curled around Natalie while she'd slept the night before was nearly gone, but he'd happily endure twice as much shopping torture if it brought a smile to his woman's face.

He still hadn't shaken the sound of her sobs from his head. The deep, gut-wrenching way her torso had shaken against his and the death grip she'd kept on his shirt. Wyatt might have won the battle, but he'd earned himself a full-scale war. "Sole custody my ass," he muttered to himself.

Gabe glanced up from her perusal of a huge display of silk robes in every vibrant color imaginable and frowned. "I thought our mission was to wow Natalie with so many gifts she was too busy opening presents to cry, not rehashing all the ways you're gonna gut her ex."

"No, *you're* on a mission. I want her to actually like her gifts, so I'm just handling the bankroll."

"Oh, she'll like them." Pulling the coral option from the rack, she held it up high for Trevor to see and waggled her eyebrows. It was short enough it would barely cover her ass and the slick fabric would no doubt cling to her luscious curves. "I doubt she'll be the only one."

The minx. Gabe might have struggled with public places and social situations once upon a time, but with her new yet significantly extended family behind her and the way she'd tackled therapy, she had a lot fewer problems doing her female comrades proud at the mall. "Starting to think I might have been smarter to bring Viv with me and leave you to planning the party."

"Oh, yeah. That's a swell idea. Let the mechanic plan the surprise instead of the event planner who does it for a living."

For a second, the niggling doubt he'd wrestled since the mothers and Vivienne had suggested tonight's surprise party billowed up full force. "You sure this is a good idea?"

Gabe hesitated mid-grab for a sheer teddy made of ivory lace and glanced down at the pile of clothes draped over her arm. "You don't think she'll like it?"

"Not the robe. The party. I'm not sure distracting her like this is a good idea."

"It's a great idea." A holiday flip, Viv had called it. New Year's Eve first with all the adult perks, and Christmas a week later when Levi was back. "You'll make it special for her and him. Trust me. It'll work out."

He hoped like hell she was right. One thing was for sure. If time, care and attention counted toward healing a woman's heart, his brothers and the rest of their motley brood would have her fully recovered by the time the clock struck midnight. Even Frank and Maureen were committed to the mission, Maureen in particular taking on the task of prying her daughter out of the house if that's what it took.

His phone vibrated in his back pocket. Worried it was Natalie, he dug it out so quickly he nearly fumbled it while juggling all the Christmas loot. "Yeah?"

Instead of Natalie, it was Knox's smart-ass voice that greeted him. "Man, for a guy that demanded we kick our shit into high gear twenty-four hours ago, you're awfully hard to reach with news."

Trevor checked the side of his phone, scowled and flipped the ringer back to active. "I'll be outside," he murmured to Gabe. "Knock yourself out."

The wicked grin she shot him said his bank account was about to take another serious hit, but in this store the payback would be more than worth it.

He ambled out of the fancy lingerie shop into the chaotic flow of people along the main hall. "What news?"

The tone in Knox's voice shifted, the lowered pitch and the lack of background noise indicating his focus was squarely on the call instead of drawn between too many monitors. "Early this morning, Wyatt Jordan withdrew a rather sizable payment from one of his investment accounts. We're talking three times what he paid the last time. About two hours ago, three boxes with our trackers ended up directly in his office…delivered in person."

"My middleman?"

"Yep. Same guy that picked up the product when Beckett dropped it off in Fort Worth. Beck's had a man on his tail ever since. How the guy stayed a shadow this long, I don't get. He's sloppy as hell."

"And Wyatt paid him triple?"

"Yep."

"So, my middleman's the leak."

"That's what it looks like."

"I want him."

"How'd I know that was gonna be your first response?" Knox laughed and the muted taps from his keyboard sounded through the phone. "Beckett's already contained him, but I'm not sure you're gonna get first crack at him. You know how fired up Beck gets."

"Don't care. He's mine."

"Yep, I get it."

Across the massive hallway was a jewelry store with only a quarter of the people milling in the other nearby stores. Not surprising really. The place looked pretty damned swank and probably had a high price tag to go with the décor. He ambled that direction. "Gia set up with the sting yet?"

"She didn't have to. Someone from Wyatt's office called about thirty minutes ago. She's got an appointment on Tuesday."

The second he stepped inside the fancy shop, the crowd's roar dimmed to dull background noise, replaced with soft classical music designed to comfort patrons as they whipped out their Amex cards. "I want him loaded up. He put down three times the normal pay, so let's make sure his inventory matches the payment."

"Already on that, too. Beck and Danny are going in tonight, but they're taking extra goods courtesy of Otter's crew."

"I thought Otter stuck to the lighter stuff. Not sure that's gonna make sense in a plastic surgeon's office."

"He does. Doesn't mean he can't get access to the

kind of designer dope Wyatt's patients would be interested in. If we're takin' Wyatt down, we need to make sure standing up afterward's not easy."

It made sense, and the fact that he hadn't been the one to think of it rubbed him all kinds of wrong. Then again, he'd been preoccupied with fantasies of smashing the fucker's face.

The glass case in front of him sparkled with at least two dozen diamond rings in every shape and size. Soft spotlights shimmered off their many-faceted surfaces in a mesmerizing glimmer.

A masculine voice punched through his thoughts. "Is there something I can show you, sir?"

Trevor's head snapped up and he took a huge step back. "Maybe in a minute." Or in another month. Maybe a year. However long it took for him to get that close to the display again and be able to draw a steady breath.

"You still shopping?" Knox asked.

"Gabe's shopping. I'm financing."

"Man, you're braver than me. I'm an online only guy. That many people makes me kitchy." The rumble of Knox's chair wheels against the tile floors echoed through the line and his voice shifted like he was mid-stretch. "You need anything else from me? I've got to dig through my contacts and find a decent hookup for tonight's big shindig. No fun being alone on our modified New Year's Eve."

"You can tell me where my rat's holed up. I'm thinking a little pre-party stress relief's in order."

"Already texted the address. Beckett and Danny are on standby to meet you." He paused a second and his voice dropped. "Three more days, brother. Three days and you'll have all the leverage you need to make sure Wyatt never hurts Natalie again."

Translation: Keep his shit in check and don't do anything stupid. "Yeah, I get it."

Across the crowded mall thoroughfare, Gabe hustled out of the lingerie shop, scanned up and down the hall until she found him, and strode his direction. The pink and white bag she'd added to her already hefty stash walloped her thigh with every purposeful step.

Trevor paced down the long row of glass cases. The shop really did have nice stuff. Classy like Natalie. Necklaces, bracelets, earrings…every bit of it looked top-notch. Not that he had a clue about jewelry outside of his platinum Tag Heuer and his Haven tags.

Rerouting back for another lap, he paused at the section singled out for engagement rings, then moseyed on to the next.

"See something you like?" Gabe said as she bustled into the store.

"Just looking. Quieter in here."

The sales clerk kept his silence, but stayed poised and ready for action. No way the guy had missed the number of bags he and Gabe were carting, so he was probably too busy mentally calculating potential commissions.

Gabe sidled up to the case he'd paused beside and snickered. "Just looking, my ass. Come on back over here and look."

A whole tray of pretty bracelets covered the section in front of him, the ivory felt beneath it accenting the rainbow of gems on display. "You think she'd like a bracelet? Something casual she could wear every day? Or are those annoying?"

"Trevor," she said softly. "Come over here and look."

He held his place and kept his focus in front of him. "Sweetheart, they won't bite. I promise."

He shifted his weight and stuffed one hand in his pocket. She was right, really. Looking didn't mean anything. And when would he have another chance to get a woman's perspective on something like that? Still, not meeting her gaze, he eased that direction.

The diamonds winked up at him, but there was one that snagged his attention first. The oval stone in the middle was huge, not so big it was gaudy, but still large enough it said, *"This is my woman and I can take care of her just fine, thank you very much."* Around it were lots of smaller diamonds, creating a classy yet traditional look.

He forced his gaze to the clerk, swallowed, and pointed to the ring. "I want to see that one."

Chapter Twenty-Eight

Soft colored lights drifted across Crossroads' mostly empty dance floor, and tiny white shimmers danced across the shadowed corners and black walls. Natalie should have been at home. Would have been curled up in the fetal position with puffy eyes and tearstained cheeks were it not for the wonderful man holding her close and swaying them to the slow song pulsing through the club's sound system. Instead she was celebrating. Finding solace and comfort from people she'd only begun to know and unearthing a strength inside herself she hadn't known existed.

Beneath her cheek, Trevor's heart thrummed a steady rhythm, and his earth and forest scent surrounded her with the same confident strength of his arms. She still couldn't believe how he and his family had rallied around her. Turned what Jace had assured would have been a dreadfully slow night into a beautiful gesture she'd not soon forget.

He'd been right about the turnout. The few real patrons that had shown for a Christmas Eve night out on the town had been obviously confused by the New Year's banners and party hats, but they'd gotten into the swing of things once the booze had kicked in. Drinks, dancing, and general hilarity had kept her occupied from the moment her mom had all but dragged her out of her room and forced her to get dolled up, until now, well past midnight and creeping toward 1:00 a.m.

The only somber point of the night had been her goodnight call to Levi. She'd checked her watch at a quarter to nine, a silent tell Trevor had spied and led her straight up to Axel's quiet office for her routine check-in. While Levi had still sounded a little off, he'd rebounded far better than she had, asking questions about her night and sharing details on all the icky food he'd had to suffer through at his grandmother's house.

She chuckled low and smiled. That was Levi. Whatever curveballs life threw him, he processed quickly and moved on, ready to uncover whatever bright sides to life he could find. He'd especially perked up when she'd promised bigger, better plans for the following week when he was home. Being Levi, he'd begged, cajoled and sweet-talked her for a full five minutes trying to learn more about what was in store, but had finally acquiesced on a precious little-man huff. Of course, Wyatt's voice had registered in the background around the same time, so his reluctant acceptance might have been based more on lessons learned than resignation.

Trevor's hand slid up her back, the heat of his touch radiating through the ivory silk of her strapless, fitted gown. He cupped her nape and nestled his lips against her ear. "You ready for your next surprise?"

She snapped her head up and her heart jolted. "There's more?" She glanced behind her where Trevor's brothers, Viv, Gabe, and the rest of their dates were gathered round a huge table. Like her and Trevor, they were decked out in their finest, pushing the New Year's theme to full tilt.

Axel sat at the head of the table with a buxom redhead sprawled across his lap and yet another tumbler of Scotch in his hand. Clad in a blue-and-green-plaid kilt and a formal jacket, his loose russet hair and full beard made him look like a barely tamed Highland warrior come to life.

"'Course there's more. We're ringing in the new year. You don't think I'm gonna do that half-ass, do you?"

Oh, no. Trevor and his family clearly didn't do anything half-ass. Even her mom and Frank had teamed up for the event, only bailing from the festivities shortly after the midnight countdown and required glass of champagne. "Trevor, I think you bought me half of the Galleria. You raced past half-ass about four hours ago. And even if you hadn't bought me a thing, watching my mom blush when Frank kissed her cheek at midnight was precious enough."

"He's smooth, I'll give him that."

"Like father, like son."

He grinned, eyes sparkling with a pleased-with-himself glint. "You liked the gifts?"

What wasn't to like? He'd loaded her up with everything from top-of-the-line black Luccheses, to ridiculously sexy lingerie—the latter being a surprise that had seared her cheeks when she'd opened the package in front of everyone. "I love them. I just wished you'd told me we were exchanging gifts. I'd have brought yours with me."

"Those aren't Christmas gifts. They're New Year's gifts. Totally different."

Totally different, her ass. More like an indulgent ploy to take her mind off the fact that she was spending her first Christmas without her son. While she'd still trade every second to have Levi with her, the effort everyone had put forth on her behalf was hands down the most amazing gift she'd ever been given.

"So what do you say?" Trevor squeezed his arms around her and splayed one hand over the curve of her ass. In one smoldering second, his lids grew heavy and sensual, and a predatory air coiled around them. "Ready for the next part?"

Her breath caught, and her sex clenched, the power of his gaze blasting through her in one consuming inferno. "Does the next part involve people watching while I unwrap sexy lingerie?"

"Someone's unwrapping sexy lingerie, but it'll be me unwrapping what's under this dress, and there won't be an audience." He speared his fingers through her hair, palmed the back of her head and angled her face for his lips. He teased his mouth against hers. "That the answer you're looking for?"

"Oh yeah," she whispered back.

He smiled against her mouth. "Good answer." Instead of giving her the kiss she craved, he pulled away, clasped her hand in his, and ambled toward his crew. Man, but he could wear a suit. In jeans, boots and Ts or button-downs, he was bona fide yummy, but dressed to the nines in a black suit and shirt, he was a midnight prince come to life. Reaching Axel, he held out his free hand. "We good for Wednesday?"

Axel shook the hand he offered and grinned in a way that didn't look friendly at all. "Locked and loaded, brother." His gaze slid to Natalie and his expression shifted, mirth and mischief deepening his forest-green eyes, but his words still directed toward Trevor. "I trust you've got ample ways to occupy our lass until our boy's home?"

"I've got a few." Trevor scanned the table, resting his attention on each of his brothers with an intensity so potent the air crackled. "Appreciate tonight."

Knox raised his glass in salute, and Zeke, Jace, and Beckett answered back all at once.

"Always."

"Happy to do it."

"Happy New Year."

"You ask me, we need to do this every year," Danny finished out.

"I'm thinkin' he's right." Jace tucked Vivienne tighter in the crook of his arms, but gave his undivided attention to Natalie. "You need anything and can't get Trevor, you call us."

Trevor's hand tightened on hers and he nodded in answer to some question she'd apparently missed. "Time to go," he said before she could figure it out, steering her through the mostly empty lobby and out into the silent night. The streets were nearly deserted, and except for the 7-Eleven at the end of the block, Crossroads was the only building lit up for business. The same limo that had brought them to the club idled at the curb, and Trevor guided her to it with a hand low on her back.

The chilled air swept against her flushed skin and lifted her hair off her neck, a welcome relief from the anticipation burning beneath her skin. Something had changed in the last few moments. Something important, but so subtle she'd missed it between the promise of his kiss and the swirling lights. She settled on the soft leather seat and splayed her hand against his hard thigh the second he slid into place beside her. "Everything okay?"

"You're not curled up and crying your eyes out, so

yeah. I'm great." He covered her hand, laced his fingers with hers and lifted her hand to his lips. "Got another gift for you."

The limo pulled away from the club's bright lights and the darkened streets pressed their intimate shadows around them. "Trevor, I don't need any more gifts. What you've done tonight—what your family's done—was gift enough. More than I'll ever be able to give back."

His thumb shuttled against the back of her hand, and the calm, confident veneer he kept in place for everyone else slipped enough to show the vulnerable man underneath. "There's no such thing as enough when it comes to you."

The space behind her sternum tightened, and her throat clogged on a surge of joy so powerful her blood sang with it. "You make it all worth it. Every day I was afraid…every day I thought I'd never overcome my bad choices…those days were worth it because I ended up here. With you."

He studied her face, his gaze absorbing every detail as though searching for the answer to some unspoken question, then released her hand and reached inside his coat pocket. The box he retrieved was long and slender and wrapped in thick white paper with a simple gold ribbon. "I've got to be honest. Gabe did most of the shopping today, but this one I picked out." He handed it over with a sheepish grin. "Jewelry's not really my forté, but I thought it was cool."

The package lay light against her palm, the ribbon trembling with the car's vibrations as it trundled toward their destination. "Something tells me this far exceeds anything I got for you. Heck, the wrapping paper alone probably cost double what yours are wrapped in."

"You can't credit me for the wrapping. I'm a guy. We'll pay crazy amounts of money if we can escape anything to do with tape and bows."

She slipped the ribbon free and carefully pried the taped ends loose. The box beneath was just as fine, the gold base and black box of such quality it could have gone without any wrapping at all and still been a thing of beauty. Jiggling the top, the lower half slipped free. A delicate charm bracelet lay nestled atop black felt, three charms already affixed to the center—a heart shaped out of angel's wings, a circular one with a picture of Levi in the center, and a cell phone. She gently freed the bracelet and fingered the cell phone, the accidental trigger that had brought them together. "It's lovely."

"It's platinum, not gold, so the links will hold up better if you want to wear it every day. Or that's what the guy said." He shrugged, showing more uncertainty in the simple gesture than she'd ever seen before. "I thought it'd be nice for you to have something to add to as you hit your goals. You know, mark the milestones while you rebuild."

She traced the length of the intricate band, the sentiment behind his gift breathing fresh air into the dreams she'd left behind. "You really think I can do it."

"I know you can. Your mom and Levi believe you can. But it's *you* who needs to remember. I thought this might be a nice reminder."

Tears swelled and blurred her vision, the knot in her throat blossoming so large she could barely whisper. "I can't top this. Not your gifts. Not tonight. Not ever."

He cupped the side of her face. "You top it every morning. The way you feel next to me. The sleepy look on your face when the alarm goes off and you don't want to get up. The sweet way you kiss me before you roll out of bed. For me, that's heaven."

God, this man. This amazing, honest, genuine man. "I used to think Wyatt's harassment was punishment. A consequence I had to endure because of my bad judgment. Now I'm grateful."

He frowned. "Not thinking I can ever muster any gratitude for the way he's treated you and Levi."

"I can." She skimmed her fingertips along his jawline. The blond stubble was barely detectable in the darkness, but it tickled the pads of her fingers and sent delicious tremors down her arm. "If he hadn't hammered on my door that night, you'd have never followed me home."

His face hardened, an unyielding resolve sparking behind his gaze and drawing his body up tight.

Before he could get ramped up and refocused on plans to hire lawyers like he had the day before, she handed him the bracelet. "Will you help me put it on?"

His chest rose and fell. Behind him, highway lights zoomed past in a lulling, dizzying rhythm, but he stayed locked in place.

"Let it go, Trevor." She lifted the bracelet higher. "Don't let him come between us tonight."

He swallowed and his shoulders relaxed on a slow exhale. Carefully, he took the delicate band and draped it over her wrist. Once the latch clicked into place, he spun the platinum around, his attention centered on the charms against the back of her hand, but his gaze distant. "I want to ask you for something, but want you to know up front there's no pressure. You decide when or if you're ready."

"Anything."

He lifted his head. "Think you ought to hear what I want before you agree."

A mix of flutters and unease scampered beneath her skin. "Okay. I'll listen."

The limo exited the highway and the road noise dimmed, surrounding them in fragile silence.

Trevor covered her hand. There was warmth in the touch, but a hesitancy, too. "Never taken a woman without protection."

She frowned. "Never taken a woman where?"

He grinned and huffed out a chuckle. "To bed, darlin'."

Oh. *Duh.* "You mean no condom."

"Yeah, that's exactly what I mean."

She bit her lip. "Never?"

"Never. Frank browbeat me about gloving up from the first day I woke up with wood. I never forgot. Not once."

She dipped her head and shifted her hand beneath his, lacing their fingers together. "But you don't want to with me?"

"When you're ready. If you're comfortable with the idea."

Comfortable with it? She loved it. Loved the intimacy of it, but even more so, the unspoken commitment behind it. She lifted her head and whispered, "Okay."

He shifted in his seat, the same nervous check Levi always got when he wasn't 100 percent sure if he'd tiptoed into dangerous ground. "I checked with Zeke. He ran all my tests. I'm clean. I've got reports I can show you, too."

She pressed her hand above his heart, the rhythm thrumming faster than normal. "Okay."

"I mean, I didn't go ahead of time to pressure you.

I just wanted to show you I was taking it serious. To make sure you felt safe and—"

She silenced him with a finger to his lips. "Okay."

He blinked back at her, the dumbfounded expression on his face probably not unlike the night she'd first asked him to dinner and they'd traded a similar exchange. "You're sure?"

"Very sure." She slid her hand around the back of his neck, tugged his band holding his hair back free, and threaded her hands in his hair. "After Levi, Wyatt demanded I start taking pills and I've never stopped. I suspected Wyatt screwed around while we were married so I had myself tested after I moved out. I'm fine."

"What are you telling me?"

"I'm telling you I haven't been with anyone but you since I got a clean bill of health and that there's a less than one percent chance of pregnancy on the pill."

"You don't want to wait?"

The limo pulled to a stop. Dimly, her mind registered that the scenery outside the window behind him didn't belong to the parking lot outside her apartment, but in that moment the only thing that mattered was him. What it had taken them both to get to this point in their lives. "I spent eight years waiting to feel like I do right now. I think I've waited long enough."

The door beside him opened and a burst of lights and bustling noises from outside filled the interior.

Trevor glanced at the waiting driver, scanned the surroundings outside, and shifted back to her. His gaze ran the length of her from toes to shoulders, slow as though marking every detail to memory. He held out his hand palm up. "Think I'm tired of waiting, too."

She laid her hand in his and his strong fingers curled

around it. In only seconds, he was out of the car, guiding her from their dark cocoon and into the chilled December night. The wind whipped their hair, the wildness of it matching the storm building between them. Behind him, Dallas's historic Adolphus Hotel stretched toward the dark sky, its ornate Beaux-Arts architecture a classic snapshot of elegant eras gone by. "I love this hotel."

"I know."

One time she'd mentioned it. An innocent ramble in the quiet moments alone after Thanksgiving when she'd shared a treasured memory of her and her mother dressing up for afternoon tea just after she'd graduated from nursing school.

But he'd remembered.

He whisked her inside, past the registration desk in the main lobby and the legendary Steinway grand piano rumored to have missed a fateful calling with the *Titanic*. Beyond the soaring twelve-foot tree laden with classic ornaments and twinkling lights and the elegant staircase that led to the shadowed lobby bar, to the elevator landing with its ageless gold doors.

Inside, he punched the top floor and pulled her back against his chest, one hand cupping her shoulder while the other splayed possessively above her abdomen. The numbers above the elevator clicked higher and higher, excitement and anticipation soaring as the floors raced by. Against her stomach, his thumb shuttled back and forth against her silk dress, the mix of his firm touch, her soft flesh, and the slick fabric a subtle reminder of what was to come.

The doors swept open and he led her to the door at the end of the hall, keeping his silence with every step. He swept the key card through the lock and the mechanism chirped as it disengaged. Pushing the entrance wide, he stood back and waited for her to enter.

"Oh, my." She strolled across the gleaming white and gray tile covering the entrance, her heels clipping against the fine surface and echoing off the towering ceiling. Four more steps in, the space opened up to a massive room at least fifty feet wide. A wall of windows looked out over the gorgeous Dallas skyline, its pristine white curtains drawn back for maximum impact and reflecting her awestruck gaze. Two massive crystal chandeliers hung overhead, one over the eight-person Chippendale dining room set and the other over the refined seating area at the far end of the room. "This isn't just an ordinary room."

He swept her hair off her neck, settled his hands on her hips, and kissed the tender spot where her neck and shoulder met. "It's not an ordinary night."

No, it wasn't. But then nothing about her life had been ordinary since the day she'd walked into Trevor's office. More like extraordinary. The stuff of dreams and fantasies the likes of which she'd had in high school, only much, much better.

His hands slid up her bodice and cupped her breasts. "Took me about two seconds into our first dance tonight to figure out you didn't have a bra on under this." He grazed his thumb back and forth over her nipples. "Been dying to stroke you like this ever since."

A shudder slid through her and her knees trembled. She gripped his forearms to steady herself and let her head drop back against his shoulder, arching her back in encouragement. Her voice came out husky, the room, the night and all her worries melting away beneath his touch. "That was five hours ago. I'm surprised you made it that long."

"Toying with you in public is one thing. Doin' it with my dad and your mom a stone's throw away is too kinky even for my tastes." Taking advantage of her exposed shoulders and neck, he kissed, licked, and nibbled a tantalizing path across her skin. He tweaked her nipples and pressed his very ready shaft against her ass. "Planned on letting you have some fun exploring the suite first, but seein' as how we've got it until Monday morning, I'm thinking me exploring what's under all this silk's a higher priority."

Reaching up and behind her, she threaded her fingers through his hair and rolled her head, offering more access for his talented mouth. "I'm all for efficiency and prioritization."

She felt his smile against her flesh and his warm chuckle coasted down her back. "You're such a team player." He drew in a deep, sexy breath, splayed his hand just above her ass and urged her forward. "How about we get you to the bedroom before I change my mind and start exploring on the dining room table."

Now there was an intriguing idea. If they had the suite until Monday, maybe she could initiate a little fun of her own later on.

A sense of weightlessness moved through her at the thought, joy and a liberating sense of freedom blossoming until her footsteps seemed whisper soft. Two months ago, she'd have never considered such a thing. Not because she wasn't open to such ideas, but because she'd have worried over how she looked or how a partner might perceive her. Trevor had given her that. Shown her intimacy wasn't about presenting an image or meeting any expectations. It was a connection. Two people appreciating and accepting each other as they were. It didn't matter how it happened. Playful, intense, awkward, or clumsy—with him the moment could be whatever it needed to be and it was still perfect.

He ushered her into the bedroom, shrugged off his jacket, and tossed it to the plush chenille couch along the far wall.

Where the main room was all class, the bedroom was old-world opulence. The armoire and dresser echoed the same rococo style prevalent throughout the hotel, and the dove-gray carpet was thick beneath her feet, but the king-size poster bed with its soft yellow and coral canopy hinted of castles, knights, and whimsical days gone by. She paced closer to it and ran her fingers along the satin comforter.

Trevor's light footsteps sounded behind her. He traced the line from the base of her neck to the top of her zipper. "Saw that bed after I checked in and gave serious thought to skipping the party and heading straight here." A gentle tug and a soft hiss, and her gown's bodice loosened, held upright only by her arms at her side. He teased his fingers down her exposed spine. "Turn around, sweetheart. Want the full impact when that dress hits the floor."

She did as he asked, her breasts swelling in anticipation.

He stood close enough to touch, but not enough to bar his view. Like his jacket, he'd shucked his shoes and socks, leaving him in just his slacks and black shirt. He traced the sweetheart neckline of her gown, gently scraping the tops of her breasts with the tips of his fingers. "Let it go."

Goose bumps lifted across her skin. Two months she'd been with him and still her body reacted like it was the first. Eager. Ready and wanting. Humming with excitement. Only now she wasn't afraid. She pushed her shoulders back and relaxed her arms. The silk slithered down her body in a wicked caress, pooling around her ankles and leaving her bared in nothing more than her heels and an ivory lacy thong. The room's cool air ghosted against her flesh, drawing her nipples to tightly puckered points. "I think you forgot my shoes."

She'd expected a grin. Maybe even one of those naughty chuckles that sent her insides swirling with delight. Instead he stared, the stark appreciation and hunger in his expression sparking electric zings against her flesh. "I didn't forget anything." He inched closer, dragged his knuckles down her belly and dipped his fingers beneath the waistband of her thong. His fingertips skimmed the tightly trimmed curls atop her mound. "Been planning on seeing you like this since you crossed your legs in the limo and I got a glimpse of those heels."

Crouching in front of her, he peeled the lace down her hips and slowly raked his gaze up from her toes to her face. "Totally worth the wait." He splayed his hands just above her knees, smoothed them along the outside of her thighs and up her hips. He kissed the scar above her womb then eased back and lifted his gaze to hers. His hot breath fluttered against her sex. "Crawl back on the bed, sweetheart."

"Um." She twisted and gauged the height of the bed. While the thick mattress and raised platform was no big deal for someone as tall as Trevor, she'd have a heck of a time hopping up on it barefoot, let alone in three-inch heels. "With the shoes?"

That time he did grin, stepping in as he did so and lifting her so her butt ended up perched on the bed. "You uncomfortable in them?"

She bit her lip. "A little."

He stepped between her thighs and thumbed each of them off without a beat of hesitation. They thumped against the thick carpets as he nuzzled her neck. "You'll wear them for me later?"

An image of her at the dining room table in nothing but the strappy sling backs flashed inside her head. "How about for breakfast?"

"Sold." He stepped back and gave a playful smack to her hip. "Now scoot back so I can lose these clothes and get back between your thighs."

She pushed back on her arms and cast him a sexy look beneath her lashes. "Yes, sir."

"Minx." He worked the buttons on his shirt, those talented fingers of his making much faster progress than her shaking hands ever could. Even when he tossed the dark fabric aside and shifted to his pants, his stare stayed locked on her. "Smart move you gettin' on my good side before I get out the rope."

Her gasp slipped out before she could catch it, and she squeezed her thighs around the unexpected quiver between her legs. "You brought rope?"

"Thought ahead enough to have your mom pack clothes for you to go home in. You really think I'd miss a detail that took up a whole lot more mental space than making sure you were dressed on the way home?" He shoved his pants and briefs to the floor.

The last of her coherent thoughts scattered, too focused on the prime display in front of her. God, he was magnificent. The room's dim lighting flitted across his muscled body, shadows accenting the ridges along his pecs, abs, and hips. His platinum dog tags rested above his sternum, the soft metal glow and etched black markings accenting his golden skin, but most of her focus stayed rooted to his thick cock jutting tall and proud toward his belly. "I guess not."

He crept onto the bed, a predator with the eyes of an angel. "The rope's soft." He cupped her knees and splayed them wide enough to kneel between them, his thumbs drawing enticing circles against her skin. "Smooth so you can wiggle and buck all damned night and not walk away with a mark." He ran his fingers along the inside of her thighs and his gaze dropped to her exposed core. "That's for later. Right now I want your hands free so I can feel them on me when I take you."

Lightly, he skimmed her labia, slowly increasing the pressure until his fingertips were slick with her wetness.

She covered his hand at her hip and squeezed, needing the connection to ground her. To hold her steady while reality gave way to the burgeoning pleasure he created. "Trevor," she whispered.

"Right here, darlin'." He eased over her, bracing himself above her with one hand beside her head. The cool metal of his dog tags fell like ice against her fevered skin, branding her as he pressed one finger deep.

She flexed into the thrust and let her hands roam against his sculpted pecs. The faint hair along his sternum tickled her palms and his heart galloped as wild and untamed as the fire burning behind his eyes.

"Gonna feel this on my cock." Adding another finger to his assault, he upped the rhythm. "Feel your heat. Fill you up. Mark you."

Tremors racked her thighs and the muscles surrounding his fingers fluttered. "Trevor."

"You want that?"

"Yes."

"Need it?"

"Yes." She let her eyes slip closed and rolled her hips in time with each surge, chasing the release he offered.

"That's it." His lips skimmed her cheekbone. Her jaw. Her lips. "Build it for me. All the way to the edge."

"No building." She clumsily threaded her fingers through his hair, her mouth too parched and desperate for his kiss to manage much more. "Already there. Please."

He nipped her lower lip and growled. "No better sound than that. Broken and husky. Begging for my cock." He slipped his fingers free, circled his shaft, and coated himself in her desire. And, God, was it beautiful. His big, powerful hand squeezing and pumping his heavily veined length and coating himself with her essence.

Before she could overthink the action, she followed her instincts and curled her hand around his, gliding her fingers above his and savoring his slick, velvet length. Her hips lifted and fell with each stroke. "I love this. Love to watch you." She guided him into place. "But, I want this more."

His glans notched into place and his head dropped back, eyes closed as though he'd just stumbled on nirvana.

She undulated against him, urging him with hands at his hips and heels in his flanks. "Now, Trevor." Gone were all her inhibitions, trampled by incessant need and thundering desire. She slipped her fingers between her legs and stroked either side of his shaft, circling her clit on each upward rasp. "Give me this."

The muscles at the back of his jaw twitched and his eyes flashed open, blazing with possession. "Anything." He inched deeper, claiming her with a sweet, delicious stretch. "Everything." Another inch. So perfect. Raw and primal. "Always."

He thrust himself to the hilt and his eyes flared. "Nat."

She smoothed her hands up his arms and over his shoulders. Her hips rolled against his, a faultless rhythm that moved between them as smooth as the ocean's lap against the sand. "I know." She coiled her arms and legs around his neck and waist. "It's beautiful. Right. Just us."

"Us." The simple echo whispered like a promise between them, reverent and thick with wonder. His gaze trailed down their bodies. "Christ… Natalie." He pounded harder, his cock hammering deep while his tight sac slapped her sex. "I'll never get enough. Never."

The sights, the scents, the sound—it all coalesced at once, catapulting her up and over the edge to the blinding white of release. "Trevor!" Her sex clenched, fisting Trevor's cock in a greedy pulse that echoed clear to the arches of her feet.

"Fuck, yes. That's mine. All mine." He surged to the root and buried himself at the end of her, his cock jerking against her spasming sex.

Complete. In that one, unparalleled intimate moment, they were one. One flesh. One need. One heart.

Beneath her heels, his flanks flexed and released, drawing out the pleasure in long, tender strokes. Powerful yet tender. Possessive yet rich with surrender. Sweat lined their torsos and the musky bite of sex drifted all around them. Arms shaking, Trevor gave her his weight, ghosting kisses over her brow, her eyes, her nose, her lips.

"Best New Year's ever." She sighed, tickling her fingertips up and down his spine.

He lifted his head, his tousled hair framing his face and blue gaze brimming with solemnity. Cupping one side of her face, he smoothed his thumb along her cheekbone. His voice grated low and broken, but so rich with emotion it streamed sunshine-bright into her soul. "I love you."

Tears swelled in little more than a second, blurring his handsome face before spilling down her cheeks. "Trevor," she whispered.

Panic filled his expression and he wiped the tears away. "Shit, Natalie. I didn't want to make you cry again."

She smiled and barked out a laugh, the harsh jerk of her torso pushing more tears free. "I'm a girl, Trevor. We don't just cry when we're sad. We cry when we're happy, too."

His gaze roved her face, searching. Studying. "I didn't freak you out?"

"God, no." She caressed his jawline, savoring the stubble beneath her touch. Her lips trembled and the space behind her sternum felt as though her heart had ballooned to twice its normal size. "You made me happy. Relieved." She traced his lips. "I love you, too. I was afraid it was just me."

He smiled and smoothed her hair away from her face. "It's not just you. Not anymore." He rolled his hips against hers, an intimate reminder of how they were still joined. His eyes slid shut and he hung his head as though the sensation was too great to do more than hold on for the ride. When he finally lifted his head, his mouth was cocked in a goofy grin. "Feel like I should get a towel and clean you up, but damned if I want to."

She sighed, stretched, and wrapped her arms around his neck. "I've got a big strong man starting my pseudo New Year off with a stellar orgasm and a declaration of love. I'm not in any hurry to change a thing."

He cocked his head, surprise and maybe a little shock widening his eyes. "It doesn't bother you?"

Urging his mouth to hers, she whispered against his lips. "It's natural and it's part of you, so no."

He groaned and deepened the kiss, a languid appreciation of all they'd shared and a promise of what was to come. Only after long, heartfelt minutes did he shift, kill the bedside light, and situate them beneath the covers. The darkness surrounded them in a soft cocoon, her torso half-on and half-off his and their legs comfortably tangled.

His fingertips drifted up and down her arm in a lazy, haphazard pattern. "Nat?"

"Mmmm?"

"Whatever worries you had about today—about matching what me and my family did for you—let 'em go. I might have given you a night, but what we just did…you telling me you love me with me still inside you and nothing between us…" He inhaled slow and deep, almost bracing. "Darlin', you just gave me the world."

Chapter Twenty-Nine

Another flight done and only two more hours until the brotherhood's plan kicked into high gear. Trevor paced the length of his Falcon's cabin, double-checking for anything left behind or unsecured. The last twenty-four hours had been hell on his focus, the nonstop cocktail of tension and adrenaline leaving him as strung out as a junkie twenty-four hours into detox. Of all the risky shit he'd tackled in his life, what was about to go down had to be the most important. Not so much as it pertained to him, but because the outcome meant Wyatt wouldn't have the sway over Natalie with Levi's life he used to. If this route didn't work, Trevor was going to have to bring Wyatt Jordan in line the old-fashioned way, even if it meant Trevor might land in jail for murder.

Satisfied all was in place and his plane ready for a trip to the hangar, he ambled down the plane's steps to the tarmac. The gray and blustery midday weather was typical for late December in Dallas, the wind gusting hard enough to yank a few chunks of his ponytail free before he'd made it ten feet from the plane. What was a bit of a shocker was finding his dually parked outside the main charter office instead of behind the hangar where he'd left it and Zeke and Axel loitering beside it.

He shook his head and headed their direction. God, they were a meddlesome pair. For that matter, all of his brothers were when they felt a need to look out for their own. He strolled up to his truck and the dynamic duo waiting for him on the passenger side. "Don't you think you're taking this alibi thing to extremes?"

Axel grinned and pushed off the back fender he'd been leaning on. "Brother, in about an hour, the Feds are going to swoop in and find a shitload of bootleg pharmaceuticals and designer drugs in Wyatt Jordan's medicine cabinet. You can bet your ass the first thing our good doctor is going to do is point a finger your direction."

"He's gonna do that no matter what happens."

"Which is why it's a good thing you've been in Chicago for the last thirty-six hours, but Zeke and I are gonna make sure you don't muck up a stellar alibi by disappearing from the public eye right before shit goes down."

Much as he hated to admit it, Axel had a point. He rubbed his knuckles against his chin. "All right then, what's the plan from here?"

"We head to The Den," Zeke said. "We'll hang out in full view and have a few beers while the rest of the guys monitor Dr. Feelgood's head-on collision with the Feds."

"Last time I checked, I could navigate all the way to my pub without tour guides. Pretty sure I can keep myself in plain sight without a chaperone, too."

"Getting there and staying in plain sight, we'd buy," Axel said. "Showing restraint and not picking up the phone every five fucking minutes is another thing entirely."

"I restrain myself just fine."

Zeke gaped at him. "Really? 'Cause I'm not thinking your middleman feels the same way right about now. The poor bastard's going to drink through a straw for at least a month and won't take an easy breath for longer than that." He tossed Trevor his keys. "Don't be a stubborn ass. Get in the truck. We'll help you wait it out."

Meddlesome. Fucking. Bastards. If he got through the next few hours without losing his cool, the first thing on the agenda was to pay both of them back bigtime.

Axel chuckled. "Don't fight it, brother. Besides, I have it on high authority your pretty young lass got called in to work this afternoon. By the time we get there and settled at our table, she'll only be twenty minutes behind you."

"Natalie's not off from her day job until four. Plus, I gave her the rest of the holidays off. She's had enough shit to deal with." That and the idea of any man pawing her without him there to smash their faces made him livid.

"Well, she's on now," Axel said. "Jace and I stopped at The Den for a drink on the way home last night and had a nice little chat with Ivan. Somewhere along the way he got the impression an extra set of hands for tonight might be a good idea."

"That chat have something to do with us exploring bringing him into the fold?"

"Gotta start somewhere. Might as well see how inclined he is for action without much in the way of answers."

"Yeah? How'd he do?"

"Only thing he was concerned about was pissing off the man who signed his checks every month."

"And?"

Axel grinned huge. "Jace told him if you canned him, he'd start him at Crossroads the next day and double his pay."

Figured. Jace knew good help when he saw it. Though if he thought he could steal Trevor's most solid employee, he was in for a huge surprise.

Axel boxed him on the shoulder. "Stop scowling and get in the truck or I'll take over drivin'."

"Jesus, that's a dangerous proposition in this monstrosity." Zeke reached for the front passenger side door.

"What the bloody hell do you think you're doin'?" Axel jerked his thumb toward the back cab. "Yer aff yer heid, if you think I'm ridin' bitch."

Zeke scoffed, but shifted to the back door. "Scottish fucking prima donna."

Trevor shook his head and rounded the hood. Every damned one of his brothers were nuts and protective as hell at all the worst times, but he had to admit, having them close wasn't a bad idea. God knew he'd had some insane impulses since he'd taken off this morning, the bulk of which vacillated between checking Natalie back into their hotel so they could pick up where they left off two days ago, and taking Wyatt out of the equation with his own two hands.

The trip to The Den went as fast as traffic in south Dallas would allow, every mile filled with Axel's random chatter on everything from his Super Bowl predictions to a new live music venue he'd been toying with developing. Thirty minutes later, they were loaded up with round one and headed to the isolated table reserved for the brotherhood.

For a late afternoon on a Tuesday, the crowd wasn't

bad, most tables taken up by men and women dressed in business casual clothes and haggard expressions that spoke of a work week off to a rough start.

Zeke tugged his phone from his back pocket, checked the screen, and stopped on a dime.

Axel took one look at him and halted as well.

"What?" Trevor said.

Zeke handed over his phone, the text application pulled up with a long running conversation from Knox on the screen.

Trevor read it. Then read it again.

The line was long but we finally got tickets to the show. Waiting for the previews.

He frowned and handed the phone back to Zeke. "What the hell is this?"

Zeke stuffed the phone in his back pocket, chin-lifted toward their table, and ambled that direction. "That's Knox being technically paranoid. It means Gia just got called back for her appointment. He gave me a whole string of phrases before we left to pick you up at the airport."

Axel tromped up the four steps to the raised platform. "If I didn't respect Knox's skills, I'd swear he does that shite just to mess with us."

Trevor was just about to follow his brothers up the stairs when Ivan hustled out of the back hallway. "Yo, boss. Hold up."

With a quick nod to Zeke and Axel, Trevor redirected and met Ivan halfway. Judging from the look on his face, someone had either screwed up royally, or his manager had a serious case of guilt. "Something up?"

"Yeah, uh…" He glanced at Axel who just grinned and raised his glass. "I just wanted to give you a heads-up. Your brothers were in last night and said they were sending some rowdy convention-goers our direction for happy hour. They thought Natalie might appeal to the crowd and give us a helping hand."

"You call her in?" Sure he already knew, but how Ivan answered would tell a lot about how things might roll in the months to come.

"They're your brothers, and you trust 'em. I figured that meant I should trust 'em too, so yeah. I called her. She said she'd come straight from work."

Now *that* was a damned good answer. Hell, if he'd have scripted it out for the guy, Ivan couldn't have done better. He clapped him on the shoulder. "Don't sweat it. You made the right call." He turned to walk away, then stopped. "And for the record, I don't care how much Jace offers to pay you, you bail for Crossroads, we'll have words."

Ivan smiled huge and splayed his hand over his heart. "Ah, man. You already knew."

"'Course I knew. They're crazy as hell, but they're my brothers. We tell each other everything." He paused long enough to make sure Ivan heard the next part of his message loud and clear. "You keep that in mind. Hard to step into my world when you're holding secrets."

For a second, Ivan's smile slipped, a stunned look leaving him with an uncustomary loss for words. "That mean what I think it means?"

"Depends. You figure out how much you're willing to share and we'll play it from there." Whether or not it was enough of a nudge to get Ivan to come clean on what

Trevor suspected was an ugly past, only time would tell, but he'd given the guy the only chance he'd get.

Before Ivan could follow up with any questions, Natalie whisked through the opening that led from the front part of the bar and beelined it for the tables up front. Nothing ever slowed her down at work. Not her troubles at home. Not how many customers were assigned to her section, or the hassles said customers doled out. She was all point A to point B. Get it done and don't mess around. Funny how he saw so much more to her now though. The softness behind the determined mask she showed everyone else. The tiny kindnesses she offered complete strangers. How her smiles weren't just geared for tips, but held genuine warmth.

Yeah, looking at her today took on a whole different perspective than that night he'd nearly canned her. Talk about your silver linings.

As if she sensed him watching, she whipped her head around, caught his gaze, and shot him a blazing smile. Even with thirty feet of bar space and six rows of tables separating them, he couldn't miss her pretty blush.

Forcing his gaze away from Natalie, Trevor cleared his throat and focused on Ivan. "Do me a favor. Change up the table assignments. Make sure Nat's on the brotherhood's table."

"Already did." Ivan fought back a canary-eating grin and shrugged. "Figured that's how things were gonna roll with you two."

Of course, he had. The guy had an uncanny ability to read situations. Not exactly a leap for him to figure out where things were headed with him and Natalie. "Just keep that in mind when those handsy college boys start getting too close to her. Getting crosswise with you, they've got a chance of living through. If I see them so much as think dirty thoughts her direction, them breathing long-term will be a sketchy proposition."

"You got it, boss." And then he was off, swaggering toward the bar with a confidence a man could only earn the hard way.

Trev prowled back toward his table. Only two steps up, he got a load of Zeke and Axel's tight expressions and slowed his gait. "What happened?"

"We're waiting." Zeke handed over the phone.

Showtime.

Fuck but he hated waiting. Hated it even worse when he couldn't so much as lay eyes on what was going down. He jerked the chair next to Axel out from under the table and dropped onto the seat. "Appreciate all the alibi logistics, but you gotta know, me sitting here with my thumb up my ass goes against the grain. I could send Vicky home and at least stay front and center tending bar."

"True." Zeke waggled his cell phone and grinned. "But then you'd miss Knox's play-by-play, and coded or not, it's not the kind of conversation that needs to happen near the bar."

Axel tipped his Scotch toward Natalie at the far end of the room. "Not thinkin' the view from here's such a hardship either."

Hell no it wasn't. If they had any clue how good the package was beneath Natalie's snug jeans and fitted T-shirt, they'd take pity and find a way to get Trevor some much-needed alone time.

For about the seventieth time that day, his thoughts

shifted to the ring locked up in his office safe. Waiting was the right thing to do. At least that's what logic kept telling him, but his gut kept arguing back and calling him a coward. "Our next rally still on schedule for Friday?"

"Yup," Zeke said. "Everyone's in town and juggling night shifts so we're meeting at two."

Axel chuckled in that sinister way that promised a whole lot of heckling. "You got something you're planning to add to the agenda? Maybe something about the woman with the killer rack that's headed our way?"

Sure as shit, Natalie meandered through the occupied tables toward their end of the bar, an empty tray tucked under her arm while she carefully scanned who was close to needing another round. She twisted just in time to catch his gaze and cocked her head as if to ask if it was all right for her to head up. On anyone else, the action was expected. No one—absolutely no one—approached their table without a nod first. The fact that Natalie thought she still had to ask felt sixty different kinds of wrong.

He crooked a finger at her. Not taking his gaze off Natalie and the sway of her hips, he muttered to Axel, "You like your eyes in your head?"

"Well, the lasses tell me they're one of my finest assets, and they're handy for getting around, so yeah, I think it's best they stay put."

Trevor grinned and scooted his chair far enough away from the table to make room for Natalie in his lap. "Then do me a favor. Be smart and don't look at or comment on my woman's rack."

Axel and Zeke both barked out a laugh just as Natalie took the last of the steps.

"Well, you three seem in good spirits." She dipped her head to the drinks they'd picked up at the bar on the way in. "Anyone need a refill yet, or are you coasting on whatever's already got you buzzed?"

Loosely manacling his fingers around her wrist, he tugged her off balance, spun her on the way down, and caught her in his lap.

She whooped loud enough to draw a whole lot of attention then went stiff in his arms just as fast. She dug the heels of her hands into his shoulders and tried to stand up. "Trevor, we're at work."

He held firm and tugged her torso closer. "I know where we are." He nuzzled her neck, soaked in her light scent and lowered his voice. "You change your mind about loving me yet?"

She giggled and relaxed her arms, instinctively tilting her head for just a little more access. Her voice was even quieter than his, but filled with laughter all the same. "You've asked me that three times a day since we left the hotel. My answer's still the same."

"I'm still not tired of hearing it." He lifted his head. "Say it again."

Only for a second did she hesitate, peeking at Axel and Zeke, who were doing their damnedest to pretend they weren't eavesdropping. Her sweet smile glowed with a soft sincerity that moved through him like the sunrises on his ranch. "I love you."

He threaded his fingers in her hair, the silk of it cool against his knuckles. "I love you, too. Enough I don't care who's around me. I'm not hiding it. Not here. Not anywhere."

"But people will talk. And if anything—"

"Don't care if they talk. They so much as look at you funny, they'll be minus a job."

She frowned down at him. "Trevor, you can't just fire people for gossip."

"Darlin', you have no idea what I'm capable of doing for you." He urged her closer. "Now are you going to give me a welcome home kiss and grace everyone watching with a proper shock, or do I need to cart you out of here over my shoulder to make it clear you're mine?"

"You wouldn't."

"Try me."

For the barest second, her eyes narrowed, a hot blast of stubbornness firing behind her beautiful dark eyes before her lips curled in a sexy smile. She leaned close enough to whisper against his mouth. "I guess a little kiss wouldn't be too bad."

Her lips pressed against his, a soft but utterly perfect fit against his. This was what he'd needed. Not a drink. Not a pair of rambunctious do-good babysitters or any other inane diversion. Just Nat. Her scent. Her touch. Her genuine, heartfelt kiss.

Zeke cleared his throat in a none-too-subtle "Ahem."

Nowhere near ready to surface from the temporary solace he'd found, Trevor forced himself to pull away and scowled at his brother. "There a problem?"

"Hardly." Zeke motioned to his phone, picked up his beer, and raised it in salute. "Just thought you'd want to know. That little thing you were waiting on? Just got word it's signed, sealed, and delivered."

Chapter Thirty

One Crown and Coke, two Buds, and a house merlot. Natalie punched the button on the screen that fi-
nalized her latest order, logged out of the system and
spun—only to find Vicky looking at her funny from
behind the bar.

For a pub with only a ten—to twelve-person crew
on the busiest nights, word of her and Trevor being an
item had sure traveled fast. Granted, most had given
her purely curious looks, but a few were flat-out nasty.
Thankfully, Vicky seemed to fall in the curious category.

Natalie pasted on the same fake, over-bright smile
she had with all the waitresses and forged ahead. "Don't
think I've ever seen a Tuesday this busy."

Bless her heart, Vicky bit back the questions dancing behind her eyes and played along with the lame at-
tempt at small talk. "Yeah, Ivan said something about
a convention going on nearby."

Well, that explained the last-minute call for her to
come in, though she was pretty sure the extra set of
hands was still overkill. Stuck waiting on her drink
orders and already caught up with checking her tables,
she shifted enough to check out the TVs mounted over
the bar. Of the three, only one was tuned to a local sta-

tion. The weatherman stood in front of an animated map of Texas and did his best to showcase a promised cold front by New Year's Day.

Or in her case, Christmas Day.

Her cheeks strained on an uncontainable smile. God, she was lucky. More blessed than she'd ever thought possible. Not only had Trevor and his family helped her turn a sour and potentially devastating first holiday alone into something positive, they'd given her a beautiful memory, too. Never—not until the day she died—would she forget Trevor telling her he loved her. Some men tossed the words around like pickup lines, but not him. He'd felt them. Had shown her the depth of his statement with the utter sincerity in his eyes and grated voice.

Ivan sidled up beside her, his broad shoulders taking up what little room remained at the bar. He crossed his forearms on the gleaming honey counter, a move that made his muscles twice as intimidating. "Never seen a girl look so sappy at the weatherman."

She ducked her head, cheeks blazing. Daydreaming really wasn't her thing. Especially not at work. But in the last forty-eight hours, she'd done enough to catch up for a lifetime of slacking. "Just taking a tiny breather while Vicky works up the drinks."

Vicky glanced up from the ice bin, spied Ivan beside her, and frowned. "I'll have 'em in just a second."

Well, hell. This was exactly what she didn't need. While she'd never really developed any friendships with the people at The Den, she hadn't made any enemies. The odds of her making friendship inroads if everyone was afraid to piss her off were slim to none. "I'm fine, Vicky. My tables are all caught up anyway." She rolled up on her toes and scanned the drinks on the bar. "Anything I can do to help?"

In the two months she'd worked there, Vicky had rarely turned down an offer for help. Even when they were slow, there was always some task to be done, even if it meant self-education on how to change out soda boxes. Today, all she got was a clipped "Nope. I'm good. Thanks."

Biting back a sigh, Natalie nodded and went back to waiting for the seven-day outlook.

"They'll adjust," Ivan muttered beside her. "Just takes some getting used to. Once they figure out you're not gonna rub their faces in it, they'll level out."

Maybe. Maybe not. In the short time she'd worked at the hospital, she'd seen a lot of friendships and a few jobs go south because of nurses striking up work relationships. "I hope you're right."

She glanced back up at the TV screen rather than meet Ivan's steady gaze. Outside a high-end office complex, a reporter stood with mic in hand. The December wind whipped her dark hair in all directions. Beneath the image, a banner headline read Grapevine Doctor Arrested in FDA Drug Sting.

A bitter chill skated beneath her skin, lifting the hairs along her forearms and the back of her neck. She knew that building. Had been there countless times to meet Wyatt for lunch or to drop something off he'd forgotten at home. "Vicky, turn that up."

As soon as she said it, Ivan rose to full height, the same tension and alertness she'd felt around Trevor firing like an electric current. "Something wrong?"

The broadcast audio rose just as the live image cut to a video clip of Wyatt being led from the front of his building in cuffs, three men in suits surrounding him. "A little over one hour ago, Dr. Wyatt Jordan was taken into custody by special agents with the U.S. Drug Enforcement Agency. According to a statement issued shortly after his arrest, federal agents were alerted to Dr. Jordan's frequent use of pharmaceuticals not yet approved by the FDA on patients. However, in an undercover operation that took place today, agents uncovered other narcotics including MDMA, also known as ecstasy, and a questionable volume of the date-rape drug called Rohypnol."

Ivan's voice shot across the bar. "Vicky, get over here. Stay with Natalie." He disappeared before his words had even died off, but Natalie didn't care. Couldn't tear her eyes away from the repeated video streaming on the screen.

Her knees trembled and she fisted her hands around the edge of the bar to keep herself upright. Roofies? The injectables she'd questioned him about were bad enough, but street drugs too?

"Hey." Vicky squeezed her shoulder and tried to get her to look away from the TV. "It's going to be okay. Just take a deep breath. It's probably all a misunderstanding."

No, it wasn't. She'd seen the bootleg imports with her own eyes and found the inflated charges to patients on his books. If Wyatt was bold enough to use unapproved medicines, the leap to peddling other drugs wasn't exactly a huge one.

Behind her, heavy footsteps pounded against the hardwood floors, mingled with the rapid-fire cadence of Ivan's voice. Strong arms wrapped around her waist.

Trevor.

Even without his scent or the familiar press of his chest against her back, she'd know it was him, his presence a living, breathing strength that filled her with no more than a thought.

His lips pressed against her temple. "Hey." He paused long enough to check the television, but the story was long gone. "Ivan told me what happened. You okay?"

"No." She turned in his arms and met his worried stare. "They arrested Wyatt. They found more of the stuff I told you about, but also MDMA and Rohypnol. He could have killed someone. Hell, he may have already and just not know it. Do you have any idea how dangerous that stuff is?"

"Yeah, darlin'. I get it. But you're not responsible for him. You're responsible for you and Levi. You did what was right. You got out."

Levi.

The shock of everything she'd learned shook free, replaced with a single-minded determination. She tried to scramble out of his arms.

Trevor held tight. "Whoa, what's wrong?"

"I need my phone. I need to call Levi." The retro clock with its blue neon lights showed nearly five-thirty. "Wyatt's always home by five. Maria leaves at five-thirty. If Wyatt's in jail, there won't be anyone to watch him."

Trevor frowned and eased away enough for her to hustle toward the break room where her things were stowed, but kept beside her with one hand pressed supportively at the small of her back. "You want me to call Beck? He and Knox are closer to Grapevine. Wouldn't take them fifteen minutes to get there."

She shook her head and pushed through the door.

"No. If Levi's heard about this he'll be freaked out enough." She fished her phone out of her purse and found three missed calls from Maria. She hit the call back button.

The phone rang. And rang. And rang.

She was just about to hang up when Maria answered the phone, her voice just a little out of breath. "Hello?"

"Maria, this is Natalie. You called?"

"Oh, Natalie! I was checking to see if Mr. Jordan had contacted you. I expected him a little while ago and he's not answering his phone. I have someplace to be tonight at six-thirty. Can you come get Levi?"

So, she didn't know. Which meant Levi probably didn't either. "Absolutely. I can be there in about half an hour to pick him up. Can you stay that long?"

"So long as you're here by six, I should be fine." Maria hesitated. "Do you know what's wrong? Mr. Jordan's never late getting home. Certainly not without a phone call."

Natalie bit back a curse and tried to keep her response even. "I'm sure he just had an emergency at work." Not a complete lie. It just so happened the emergency was one of his own doing. "I'll be there as soon as I can."

She ended the call and dropped her phone back in her bag. "Maria doesn't know what's happened. She tried to call Wyatt and he didn't answer. If I'm lucky, she'll keep Levi away from the television long enough for me to get him home."

She wrestled her arm into one sleeve of her jacket, tried to catch the other side and ended up tangled in her purse strap.

Trevor tugged the purse off her shoulder, dropped it

on the bench behind her, and stilled her with hands at both shoulders. "Need you to calm down, sweetheart. No way I'm letting you leave this worked up. Matter of fact, it might be better if I drive."

"No. If you're there, it'll give Maria more to gossip about when Wyatt gets home. I don't need that. Levi doesn't need that."

Trevor scowled but nodded his agreement and helped her get her jacket the rest of the way on. He held on to the lapels, pinning her in place. Even if she'd wanted to move physically, the intensity behind his eyes wouldn't have let her budge an inch. "You know you can use this."

"Use what?"

"Wyatt's arrest."

At first, the connection wouldn't process, but once it did, a whole different level of adrenaline kicked in. "You really think this could keep him at bay?"

"I think it could get you full custody. Maybe even supervised visits. At least for a while. I've got a damned good lawyer, one that would take this on for chump change."

God, it was tempting. The past year battering back Wyatt's nonstop threats and legal hassles had whittled away what little she'd managed to save for her nursing classes and license fees and left both her and Levi in a constant state of turmoil. "I can't do that. Not until I save up more money."

"Not planning for you to pay, Nat. That's on me."

She bristled and took a step back for breathing room. "No. I'm not doing that. You've done enough for us already. The last thing I want is for you to feel like you're being taken advantage of. I'm with you for you. Nothing else."

One of those crooked, panty-melting smiles he always used when she'd stepped smack-dab where he wanted curled his lips. He prowled closer and cupped the back of her neck, more than eliminating the little distance she'd gained. "Darlin', I've known that since the day you fed me meatloaf. Everything you give me is one hundred percent, down-to-the-bone genuine. What you've got to understand is I love Levi as much as I love you. Different maybe in the way that love's built, but no less powerful. I've got money. Lots of it and connections to go with it. If I can't use it for the people I love, then what good is it?"

Words wouldn't come. Couldn't wiggle past the emotion swelling up the back of her throat. Trevor loved her son. Not just her, but Levi, too. Tears blurred her vision and a slow burn blossomed along the bridge of her nose.

Before a single tear could fall, Trevor wrapped her up tight and kissed the top of her head. "Let me do this. Please."

Her words came out shaky, as fragile as the warmth blossoming behind her sternum. "You love Levi."

"Yeah, darlin'. I love Levi. Hard not to with all that he is. That he's part of you just makes it a foregone conclusion." He squeezed her tighter. "Say yes."

She nodded, the steady thrum of his heart beneath her ear calming her otherwise riotous emotions. "Okay."

He inhaled deep and palmed the back of her head, urging her to look at him. "Told you I'd do anything for you. I meant that. For you and Levi." His gaze roamed her face, concern and relief marking his handsome features. "You sure you're good to drive?"

"Yeah. I'm sure."

He nodded. "All right. You pick up Levi and we'll meet back at your place. Maybe splurge with a dinner out somewhere before you tell him what's going on. That work for you?"

A ragged laugh rumbled up her throat and she dashed her tears from her cheeks. Leave it to Trevor to turn something ugly into a celebration. "Yeah, that works."

"How long do you need?"

"An hour? Maybe an hour and a half with traffic?"

Normally his smiles vacillated between naughty and playful mischief, but the one he gave her in that moment was far more precious. A mix of gratitude and fragile hope. He kissed her forehead, his lips lingering with solemn reverence. "All right then. You go get our boy, and I'll start making calls."

Chapter Thirty-One

Natalie waited for Levi to strut through their apartment front door then shut and locked it behind him. If he'd been surprised to see her at his dad's front door, he hadn't shown it. Had just hurried off to his bedroom and packed up the essential toys he carted between his two homes and tossed Maria a wave on the way out the door. Then again, rolling with the punches had been a way of life for Levi since the day he'd been born, so maybe her showing up unexpectedly was just his version of normal.

She plunked her purse on the coffee table and held Levi's backpack out for him. "Go unpack and plug up your phone to charge it. Trevor said he'd be here by seven to take us out to eat."

Hefting it over one shoulder, he lumbered toward his bedroom. "Can we have Mexican? I wanna go to that place Bobby told me about. You know, the one with the bird on it."

On the kitchen countertop was a yellow sticky note with her mother's tidy cursive centered at the top.

Got your message. Playing bingo with some friends at the center. Should be home before you are. Love, Mom.

Natalie ran her fingers over the words and smiled

to herself. She'd bet anything her mom announced she was moving into the same retirement village as her friends within the next six months. She never said as much, but Natalie wasn't stupid. The only reason she hadn't already moved was Natalie's dependence on her for childcare.

Levi's voice reverberated from his bedroom. "Mom?"

"Yeah, baby?"

"Can we go?"

"Go where?"

"To the Mexican restaurant. The bird one."

"El Fenix?"

"Yeah! That one!" He bustled out of his room, a lock of his tousled blond hair falling halfway down his nose and his boots adding more swagger to his gait than normal. "Can we?"

Why not? If life had taught her nothing else in the last several years, it was to take the good when you could and enjoy it to the hilt. "If Trevor's up for it, I'm game."

"Cool!"

He started back for his room, but a knock on the door halted him midway. He redirected for the door, but Natalie caught him by the arm. "Remember what I said, Levi. No answering the door. Not for anyone."

"But it's just Trevor."

"I don't care who it is. No answering unless me, Nanna, or Trevor are on the other side telling you it's us. Okay?"

She hustled toward the entrance. Sure enough, the cable box showed seven o'clock straight up, which was just like Trevor. Never so much as a second late if he could help it. She'd need to get him a key. If they were sharing *I love yous* and spending more time in each other's beds than not, the last thing he needed to be doing is knocking on her front door.

She opened the door, mouth open to tell him as much, and froze.

Wyatt stared back at her, his face a mottled red and his whole body bristling with unspent rage. "You want to tell me why my boy's here instead of home where he should be?"

Cold that had nothing to do with the late December wind whipping through her door ghosted beneath her skin. This was bad. Explosive and deadly bad. Only twice in the time she'd been married to Wyatt had she seen him like this, and one of them had ended with a backhand to her face. She shifted her stance, putting herself squarely in front of the entrance and blocking Levi from sight. "Levi, go to your room. Lock the door."

"But Mom—"

"Go. Now."

She heard more than saw his quick retreat and the door as it slammed shut. Firming her shoulders, she forced her voice into a calm and easy tone. "Wyatt, whatever's got you so upset, you need to calm down. Maria called me. She had someplace to be and she couldn't get ahold of you. I'm his parent, too. She did the right thing calling me." She swallowed, terrified to utter her next words, but refusing to back down. Not this time. "I saw what happened on the news. I assumed you wouldn't be able to come home, so I picked him up."

"You saw what happened," he mimicked back. "I'll just bet you did. Probably were in on the whole thing."

"In on what?"

"Your new boyfriend's setup. Bet he'll be pissed to

know my ass was barely in a jail cell before I made bail. Probably screwed up all his tidy plans. So tell me. Did you have a hand in it?"

Tingles spider-walked down her spine and a cold sweat broke out on the back of her neck. "Wyatt, I think you should go." She tried to shut the door.

Wyatt blocked it and shoved her out of the way. "You gonna answer me, or do I need to beat it out of you?"

She took two shaky steps back, her mind scrambling for where she'd left her phone. "Wyatt, I swear to God, I don't know what you're talking about."

His lips curled in an evil grin and he lurched forward. He grasped her upper arm in a brutal vise and backhanded her cheek.

Pain exploded in wake of the contact, the vicious strike reverberating down her arms and legs. The only thing that stopped her from crumbling to the floor was his hand still clenching her arm. "Wyatt, just go. I don't know what's going on."

He shook her and bellowed back, "Don't play dumb, you uppity bitch. You knew goddamned good and well what I was doing in my office and you turned me in."

She locked her knees and tried to free herself, but there was no shaking Wyatt's hold. From the cable box's display, 7:05 glowed, neon blue fuzzy but a beacon of hope nonetheless. Trevor would be here. Soon. Dear God, she hoped it was soon. "I had nothing to do with your arrest. I never told anyone." At least no one but Trevor.

"You think I buy that shit? Think I'd believe you wouldn't spread your legs to get your revenge?" He shoved her backward.

Head still reeling from the blow he'd dealt her, the

room spun. She caught herself from falling and scrambled for more distance.

He stalked forward, crowding her further toward the kitchen. "Here I thought you were the classy type. Turns out you'll fuck just about anyone if it gets you what you want. Even a sneaky lowlife like that cowboy."

Something tripped. A trigger inside her unleashing years of repressed hurt and anguish in an all-consuming fireball of rage. She was done with taking Wyatt's shit. Anyone's shit. Especially when they tried to hurt or defame the people she loved. She forced her shoulders back and held her ground, her voice shaking with fury. "No! You don't get to talk about Trevor like that. He's a good man. More of a man than you'll *ever* be!"

"Oh, he's good all right. Good at smuggling in those dirty products you were so quick to condemn me for."

Her head jerked back as surely as if he'd dealt her another backhand.

Wyatt prowled closer and leered down at her. "What? Didn't know your latest fuck had his hands in the cookie jar, too? You gonna dump his ass the way you did mine?"

It wasn't true. Wyatt was a liar. A manipulator that twisted and abused the truth. Trevor wouldn't peddle bad goods. He was good. Honorable. All the things that Wyatt wasn't. "I didn't leave you because of what you were doing. I left you because you hit me."

"Hit you?" He chuckled low, the sound of it laced with so much evil her stomach pitched. The malevolent grin on his face slipped to show the pure ugliness underneath. "That wasn't a hit. This is a hit."

Before her brain could fully process the meaning behind his words, he reared back and slugged her jaw.

Her head whipped to one side, pain detonating out from her jaw and shearing down her spine. She fell against a wall, the smooth drywall slipping beneath her palms as her legs gave way.

Wyatt fisted her hair and yanked her up, pinning her shoulders against the wall that had broken her fall. "Tell me something," he spat. "Were you as frigid in the sack with him as you were with me?"

"Wyatt, please stop," she croaked as much as her jaw would allow. The taste of blood coated her tongue and the ache inside her skull was too great to fully open her eyes. How had she ever thought Wyatt handsome? Gentle and caring? "You'll regret this. Go away. Go home."

"Leave? Now?" Wyatt cocked his head, sneered, and squeezed one breast in an excruciating clench. "I don't think I will. I think I'd rather stay right here and take what's mine."

Trevor glanced at the dashboard's readout, scowled at the idiot who'd taken too long with their left-hand turn before the light had turned red and forced a slow exhale. If he knew Nat, she was more than ready to get on with dinner so she could get Levi to bed at a decent hour. He was good with that. Levi's bedtime meant playtime for him and Natalie, and man, did they have some playing to catch up on.

The light finally turned green and the red Prius in front of him inched through the intersection, Trevor on his ass the whole way. Oh, who was he kidding? It wasn't sex that had him fired up to get to Natalie's house, it was the ring in his pocket. The second Natalie had pulled out of the parking lot to pick up Levi, he'd beelined it for the safe and watched the clock ever since.

The only question now was if he should ask her in front of Levi, or when they were alone later.

Yeah, maybe later. He could take a hell of a punch, but if Natalie turned him down in front of Levi, his ego wouldn't surface again for days.

His phone vibrated in his back pocket and the Bluetooth ringtone fired through the truck's cab. The stereo's display showed Levi Jordan. He grinned and punched the talk button. "Hey, bud. I'm just a few minutes away. You guys ready to go eat?"

Muffled shouts sounded in the background. A second later, Levi's voice whispered down the line. "You gotta help Mom. She's in trouble."

Everything around him dropped into slow motion. The cars, the people, the businesses—everything except Levi's shaky voice and Natalie's stifled cries. "Who's there?"

"My dad." His voice was a little stronger, but still obviously trying not to draw attention. "He showed up a few minutes ago. He's really, really mad and... I th-think he hit her."

Trevor punched the gas and shifted lanes, barely missing a lumbering semi. "Where are you?"

"Mom made me go in my room and lock my door."

"That's exactly where you need to be. You know your address?"

"Yeah? They make us learn it at school."

"Then you hang up right now. You call 911. You tell 'em there's an intruder in your house and you stay put behind that door until you hear me ask you to open up. You got me?"

"Yeah."

Trevor took the next turn to Natalie's house so fast his shoulder hit the window. "Say it back."

"Call 911. We have an intruder. Give them my address."

"Good job. Now hang up and make the call."

"Hurry, Trevor."

The terror in Levi's voice ripped him from the inside out, an echo of his own voice all those years ago. "I'm coming. You make the call. I'll be there in two."

Not waiting for Levi to respond, he hit the end button and floored the accelerator. The houses and apartment buildings on the quiet side streets went by in a blur. The past blended with the present, the same thick dread he'd felt opening the door to his parents' too-quiet mobile home that day after school pooling around his heart. He should have stayed home that day. Had known how on edge his father had been. But he hadn't. The same way he hadn't driven Natalie.

He whipped into the parking lot and slammed his truck out of gear. His boot heels thundered against the concrete, as loud ricocheting off the buildings around him as his pulse in his ears.

Ahead, a woman and her daughter skittered off the sidewalk at the sight of him barreling their direction.

He took the stairs two at a time, rounded the landing, and shoved open Natalie's door.

Natalie lay pinned to the floor. Wyatt straddled her hips and manacled her hands above her head with one hand while the other squeezed her bared breast in a punishing grip.

One second. One terrorizing and fury-inducing second seared the image into his brain before instinct took over. He didn't register moving. Felt no remorse at rip-ping Wyatt off his woman and all but throwing him the opposite direction. One punch. Then another. And another. Rage poured out of him. Everything unspent from his youth and a fresh, untapped well from the present. No one touched the people he loved. Not again. Never again.

His forearms ached and his knuckles throbbed, but he couldn't stop. Wouldn't until the son of a bitch couldn't breathe. He reared back for another strike.

A hand coiled around his wrist and yanked him back, another banding around his other arm for added leverage. Voices waded through the animalistic haze, masculine ones he didn't recognize. He fought to free himself.

"Whoa, buddy. Take it easy."

Reality crashed around him, his eyes clearing enough for his brain to register two policemen restraining him, one on each arm. On the floor, Wyatt was curled in a ball, his arms around his gut. It wasn't enough. Not for what he'd done to Natalie. "I'll kill him. He hurt her, I'll kill him."

The man on the left muttered, "Think you damn near did already." He paused long enough to study Trevor's face. "Hey, Mike. This one of Beckett's boys?"

Trevor fought for air. Tried to steady the ragged in and out of his lungs and the unsteady beat of his heart. Eyes still on Wyatt, he managed a ragged "Beckett Tate's my brother."

The same cop who'd recognized him motioned to his partner with a jerk of his head. "Call him up. Let him know his buddy just went ape shit on some guy."

"That's not just some guy," Trevor growled. "That's her ex and he hurt her. Had her pinned to the ground."

His gaze shifted to Natalie, another policeman kneeling next to her.

Braced against the wall, she'd pulled her shirt down and had her knees pulled up to her chest as though she were freezing. Her elbows were on her knees and her forehead braced against her palms.

"Let me go." He tried to shake himself free, but the cop on his right held tight.

"We let you go, you gonna start pounding that guy again, or are you gonna rein that shit in?"

"You cuff his ass and haul him in, I'll leave you to it. Nat needs me." He wrenched his arm free and barked a command at the cop beside her. "I'll see to her. You call an ambulance."

He dropped to his knees. "Natalie?" Christ, he wanted to touch her. Wanted to hold her, but was too terrified he'd hurt or scare her. "Nat, sweetheart. Look at me."

Her shoulders shook on a ragged sob and she lifted her head. Her dark hair clung to her tear-streaked face, but it couldn't hide the nasty red marks at her cheek and jaw. They'd bruise. Badly. Already, the places Wyatt had hit her were beginning to swell. "I don't want Levi to see me like this," she whispered.

Unable to stop himself, he pulled her against him, careful not to jostle her in the process. "It's not that bad," he lied. "Levi's a tough kid. You'll see. Let me get you taken care of then I'll see to him." Keeping her cradled against him, he jerked his phone out of his back pocket and punched up Zeke's number.

His brother answered with the same carefree happy voice he'd used with Trevor and Axel at The Den. "Thought you'd be knee-deep in dinner by now."

"Wyatt got Nat. He hit her. Bad. They're calling an ambulance."

Zeke's tone shifted, the background noise and the way his voice modulated through the connection telling Trevor he was on the move. "I'm headed to Baylor. Have 'em send her there. Where'd he get her?"

Bile spun in his gut and surged up his throat. He swallowed it back. "Two hits to the face that I can see." He pinned the phone between his ear and shoulder and shifted Natalie on his lap.

She buried her face in his shirt, the tears coming nonstop.

"Darlin', need you to look at me." He gently urged her face to his. "He get you anywhere else? Torso? Ribs?"

She shook her head and refused to meet his gaze.

"Just her face," he said to Zeke. "They're bad though. Swelling already."

The Den's background noise died away and the chirp of Zeke's car alarm sounded through the phone line. "Any loss of consciousness? Dizziness?"

"She was awake when I got here." The image of her beneath Wyatt lashed through his mind, how she'd writhed and tried to free herself. "She fought him."

Sirens sounded outside, growing closer and closer by the second.

"The ambulance is almost here," he said to Zeke. "How far out are you?"

"I'll beat them there by a long shot. You just get your girl in the rig and we'll take it from there." His voice lowered. Calm and steady. "She's going to be fine, brother. She's strong. We'll fix her. All of us."

They would. His brothers were good that way. So

were Gabe, Vivienne, and the moms. They'd fix whatever Wyatt had broken no matter what it took.

Levi's shaky voice sounded from behind the bedroom door. "Trevor?"

Shit.

"Yeah, bud," he called out toward the bedroom door. "You stay put a minute." He shifted back to Zeke on the phone. "Gotta go. Gotta get Natalie situated and see to Levi."

He stuffed the phone back into his pocket. Arms shaking from too much adrenaline, he got to his feet, cradling Natalie tight. He lowered his voice and muttered close to her ear. "Gonna let Levi out."

She buried her face in his neck and whimpered. "He shouldn't see this."

"He's not going to see the marks. He's going to see his mom breathing and safe." He gently kissed her temple, all the fear and turmoil he'd wrestled watching his dad hit his mom surging to the surface. "Trust me. I know where he's at. He needs to *see* you. You understand?"

She fisted her hand in his shirt and gave him a jerky nod. "Yeah. Okay."

Gently, he laid her on the couch and smoothed her hair away from her face. "It's gonna be okay. Swear to you, Nat, I won't let this happen again. None of it. He'll pay for what he did."

Something flashed behind her gaze. Fear maybe. Or hurt. He stood and scowled down at Wyatt, who'd yet to make it to his feet. Four policemen surrounded him, one crouched close and barking a string of questions. Trevor focused on the cop who'd recognized him. "That bastard was arrested early this afternoon. What the hell was he doing here?"

"Was out on bail." The cop cast a disgusted look at Wyatt then gave Trevor his full attention. "Not thinking he'll be able to stay out much longer after what he did."

"I want him out of here."

"He needs a medic."

"He needs to get the hell out of my woman's home. I don't care if you have to drag him out to make that happen." With that, he strode toward Levi's room, paused outside his door, and pulled in a slow breath. He knocked on the door. "You ready to come out, bud?"

The lock *snicked* and the door inched open just enough to show Levi's worried face. "Trevor?" The second his gaze locked on the Trevor, Levi threw the door the rest of the way open and charged into Trevor's waiting arms.

Trevor hoisted him up, Levi's little arms curled in a death clench around his shoulders.

"He hurt her," Levi whimpered into his neck. "I heard him."

Smoothing his hand down Levi's back, Trevor bit back the need to rail on Wyatt all over again. "Yeah, he hurt her, but it looks worse than it probably is. You remember that when you look at her, all right? She's safe now. I won't let him near you again, not without me there. Okay?"

Levi hugged his arms tighter and nodded his head.

"Good." He eased Levi to his feet, gave him a minute to pull his shit together, then squeezed his shoulder. "Let's go take care of our girl."

Chapter Thirty-Two

Natalie closed her eyes and tried to ignore her mother's quiet chatter in the corner with Vivienne. The topics had ranged from interesting events Vivienne had managed over the last few weeks, to the latest gossip at the retirement center she spent so much time at. While she appreciated her mom's efforts to keep things light, all she really wanted was quiet. Quiet for her head and quiet for her thoughts.

The muffled voices of the nurses, doctors and aides on the other side of the closed curtain were oddly soothing, a reminder of days when she'd been proud of herself. Of her path forward in life and her judgment.

Oh, he's good all right. Good at smuggling in those dirty products you were so quick to condemn me for.

Wyatt's taunt slipped through her mind on constant repeat.

As if sensing her internal brooding, Trevor squeezed her hand. He hadn't let go of it since he'd gotten here except the times Zeke had kicked him out to check her over and when they'd carted her off for a CT scan. Through it all, not once had he let go of Levi, either holding his hand, or letting him doze against his chest. So supportive. So solid.

Surely, Wyatt's claims weren't true. Wyatt was a liar. A manipulator so skilled no one ever saw through his machinations.

Told you I'd do anything for you. I meant that. For you and Levi.

Countless times he'd said it. Now she couldn't help but wonder just how far that claim reached.

The trauma room curtain whisked to one side, and Natalie opened her eyes.

Zeke ambled in with the confident gait of a man thoroughly in his element. He'd changed out of the jeans and T-shirt he'd met her ambulance in and sported a pair of blue scrubs that looked like he'd thrown in on a few other emergencies while he'd waited for her results. "How's our girl holdin' up?"

She licked her dry lips and tried to muster the energy to talk. The Lortab he'd ordered for the pain had been a godsend, but left her mouth parched and sticky. "Pain's almost gone. You get the results?"

"All good. Just a mild concussion." He squeezed her free hand. "You know the drill. Any memory problems, confusion, blurred vision, nausea—I want to know."

Trevor sat up taller in his chair. The act woke Levi, who glanced around the room as though trying to get his bearings. "She can go home?"

"Yep. She needs to take it easy for a day or two. No heavy lifting. No wild nights out on the town. No mud wrestling." He grinned at Trevor, a touch of sympathy blending with his teasing expression. "Seriously, bro. She's fine. Tonight when she's sleeping, you'll want to wake her up a few times and make sure there's no slurred speech or memory loss, but my guess is she'll be fine."

"Well, that's a relief." Her mom let out a relieved sigh, stood, and held out her hand to Zeke. "Thank you so much for looking out for her. I'm not sure she'd have come in if you hadn't been here."

Trevor stood and hefted Levi up on his hip, but still kept a tight hold on her hand. "Yeah, she didn't get a choice in that." He motioned toward the entrance. "Can I go get the car?"

"How about you give me a few minutes with Natalie before we wrap this up. Wanna go over some things with her."

Trevor's face blanked and a prickling wariness danced between him and Zeke. "Something wrong?"

"Nothing's wrong. Just going to have a talk with my patient and I'm going to do it with her bristling Neanderthal out in the waiting room."

The wariness escalated to something closer to aggression.

"Stand down." Zeke waved him off and jerked his head toward the curtains. "Get out and let me talk to Natalie, or I'll lace all your booze at Haven with a laxative." He waited a beat for Trevor's shoulders to relax. "I'm your brother. Get out and let me do my job."

Mouth pinched in a tight line, he jerked a tight nod, leaned in to give Natalie a soft kiss on the top of her head, then held Levi aloft so he could do the same. "I'll be back." He pinned Zeke with a hard look. "Five minutes."

"That's enough."

Her mom bustled out in front of Trevor and Levi, then pulled the curtain closed behind them.

Zeke hung his head a second, chuckled low, and lifted his head to show a soft smile. "You know, I'd

feel bad for him if I hadn't watched him avoid serious
relationships for so long. All I can do now is look at
that hound dog expression of his and laugh." With a last
glance back toward the curtain, he perched on the edge
of her gurney. To anyone walking in, they'd think he
was a close friend settling in for an easy chat. They'd
be wrong. The man who stared back at her now was all
doctor, focused and gauging her every response. "Now,
you told me how the pain is. How about you tell me how
you're really doing."

"I'm fine." She took a slow, calming inhalation and
smoothed her hand across her stomach like that might
somehow unwind the knotted tension in her belly. "I just
need to rest. I'll be up and around before you know it."

He stared back at her, not giving an inch in his razor-
sharp gaze. "I see abused women every day, Natalie.
There's a lot more to what happens in cases like yours
than what's on the surface. Wyatt might not have gotten more than a few hits in, but that doesn't mean he
didn't strike deeper."

If he only knew. Though in her case it was less about
the consuming self-doubt Wyatt had created over the
years and more about the storm he'd ignited around
Trevor.

"Want you to promise me you'll talk to someone,"
Zeke said. "Trevor. Your mom. A counselor. Hell, Gabe
would be more than happy to talk with you. She's got
demons she's still fighting, but she's a good listener."

Rehashing today was the last thing she wanted. If
she had her way, she'd wipe it from her thoughts entirely and go back to that blissfully ignorant place she'd
been twelve hours ago. Still, Zeke had a point. Stuff-
ing questions and doubts never worked. The only way

to face her issues was to push forward. Whatever that looked like. She nodded. "I promise."

"Good girl." He patted her leg and stood.

Before he'd reached the curtain, Natalie blurted, "Can I ask you a question?" The second the question came out, she wished she could reel it back in. Questions came with answers. Answers she didn't necessarily want to hear.

He waited, eyebrows lifted in silent encouragement.

She swallowed as best she could and fisted the sheet across her lap. "Trevor told me he'd do anything to keep me safe."

One second and Zeke's expression blanked.

The ER's already ridiculously low temperature seemed to drop another five degrees. "How far would he go?" she whispered.

It felt like forever that he stared at her, so many thoughts moving behind his shrewd eyes it terrified her. "I think that's a question you need to ask Trevor, but I will tell you this—whatever you ask him, you'll get the absolute unvarnished truth." He paused for just a moment, then added, "And whatever he'd do for you, every one of his brothers would back him up."

Trevor stared out at Baylor's parking lot, itching to get Natalie out of this place and at home in bed where he could take care of her. In the downtime while they'd waited through Natalie's CT scan, he and Maureen had planned it all out. She'd head back to the apartment and pack up clothes and necessities for everyone while he carted Natalie and Levi back to the ranch. It was quiet there. Peaceful. Most importantly, Wyatt and what he'd done today couldn't taint it.

The comforting drone of his brothers, Viv, Gabe, and the moms drowned out all the other sounds around him, anchoring him the way they always had.

Zeke's voice cut across the room. "Yo, cowboy. How about you go help your woman get suited up so you can get her out of this place?"

Trevor whipped around and crowded into Zeke's space. "What was that about?"

Not backing down an inch, Zeke planted both hands on his hips. "It was about me doing my job. I don't tell you how to fly your birds, you don't fuck with my protocol."

"Christ," Jace's mom, Ninette, muttered from the chair beside them. "There's too damned much testosterone in this room."

Maureen snickered behind her hand while all the other women grinned with entertained amusement.

The snarky remark did what Ninette had no doubt intended it to do, slicing through the tension and giving both men the presence of mind to take a step back.

Trevor dipped his head and held out his hand. "I appreciate you seeing to Natalie."

"Like you need to thank me." Zeke took his hand and shook it. "Anything for family."

Jace pushed from his seat. "Amen to that." He clapped Trevor on the back. "Go get Natalie suited up. Me and Viv are following you out to your place so we can take stock and do a grocery run if you need one."

No one had to ask him twice. With a quick glance to Maureen to make sure she was good watching Levi for a minute, he strode back to the trauma room where Natalie waited. Careful in case she'd already started getting dressed, he slid back the curtains just enough to ease through and yanked them back in place.

No surprise, Natalie was already dressed in the jeans and T-shirt she'd worn to The Den that afternoon. Only her pretty feet were still bare, though she seemed intent on rectifying that problem in short order. "I see you're ready to get the hell out of Dodge."

She looked up and his heart seized. If the bruises on her cheek and jaw weren't bad enough, the frustration and absolute fear on her face boded for a shit storm.

"What's wrong?" he said.

Bracing both feet on the floor and her hands on her thighs, she swallowed as though a terrible sentence sat on her lips. "I need to ask you a question."

He held his place by the curtain, too afraid to move for fear he'd knock whatever fragile balance hung between them off-kilter. "Anything."

She squeezed her thighs hard enough to make her knuckles turn white, and her voice dropped to a near whisper. "Do you haul illegal substances on your planes?"

Mother fucker.

Of all the questions he'd expected, that had been the last one. Despite the thickening gravity around him, he braced and gave her the truth. "Yes."

As fast as the word had left his lips, a hard mask slipped across her face. She nodded. "I think you should go. I'll ask Mom to take me and Levi home."

Cold pierced him, the same gnawing winter desolation he'd felt when he found his mom and dad dead that day after school lancing through this soul. "That's it? You're not going to ask what kind or what for?"

"I already know." Her face pinched with bitter pain.

"You're the one who supplied the bootleg stuff to Wyatt, aren't you? You set him up."

The cold morphed to blazing fire, billowing up so fast and furious it burned his lungs. "Yeah, I set him up, and yes, I hauled the injectables, but I don't run the roofies or the ecstasy they found in his place. Those were extras to make sure your slimebag ex couldn't wiggle out with a slap on the wrist."

Her jaw fell slack and her eyes watered. "I didn't want to believe it."

"Well, believe it. I told you I'd protect you and I did. Not the way I wanted, but in a way that you could use."

"But Trevor, those drugs…they're not safe."

A haggard, ironic laugh huffed up his throat. "Not safe? I ran luxury shit that the government has no business banning in the first place if people are stupid enough to buy it. And the real truth? The real reason I do the runs has nothing to do with the injectables. I do it to bring in drugs for terminally ill people who are out of options and don't have time to wait for a stamp from the FDA. And for the record, I don't make a dime off those sales. Everything I profit I give to the families of those who are sick."

He paced closer, the inside of his throat throbbing as though he'd swallowed double-edged razors for lunch. "I've done four runs. *Four*, Nat. Not a whole damned operation. That's four lives I've helped save, so if you want me to be sorry, I'm fucking not. Less so now that your husband's got a record you can use to get him out of your life permanently."

Her head snapped back and her eyes widened.

God, she really thought he was like Wyatt. Dared to lump him in with a man who'd caused her physical and emotional harm where all he'd done was try to protect her. Hell, she hadn't even asked for details before she'd all but given him a dismissal.

He waited for her to do or say something. Change her mind or at least ask a fucking question. Instead she just sat there, staring at him like he was a stranger. He backed up a step. Then another. "You made a bad call with Wyatt. I get you questioning your judgment now because of it, but this time your bad call wasn't being with me. It was lumping me in with that piece of shit." He fisted his hand in the curtain and fought the need to rip it off its tracks. He raked his gaze over her, the woman he'd opened himself to. Trusted to take him like he was. "I appreciate you giving me the benefit of the doubt before you tossed me out with the trash."

Chapter Thirty-Three

Trevor stared at Haven's wraparound porch. With the harsh cold snap that had slipped into north Texas in the last twenty-four hours, the Adirondack chairs where his brothers sometimes milled until everyone showed up were empty. They were all inside though, one vehicle for every one of them crowding the circle drive and the driveway in front of the four-car garage.

Ten minutes he'd sat here, his mood as bleak as the gray skies and whipping winds outside, but he couldn't get out of the cab. Axel hadn't been wrong when he'd teased Trevor about having something to bring up at today's rally. He'd had plans. Huge ones he'd never thought he'd ever lay out for his brothers. Now he couldn't figure out what to do.

For over two days, he'd waited. Waited, wondered and relived the things he'd said to Natalie. He knew she was safe and getting back on her feet, a fact he'd confirmed with at least a few calls a day to Maureen. He'd also pestered Zeke into making daily house calls. Still, not a peep out of Natalie.

Out of nowhere, memories of Frank and Bonnie flooded his mind. How often she'd told him she was proud of him. How she'd stood by him through the lean times on the ranch, and how she'd supported his decisions even when she openly disagreed with him at the start. That's what Trevor had wanted. What he'd hoped he could have with Natalie.

Sighing, he reached for the ignition, hesitated, and snagged his phone from the center console instead. He thumbed up Frank's number from his favorites list and hit Dial.

Three rings in, he'd just about accepted that his dad had his hands full and was about to hang up when Frank's voice slid through the line. "'Bout time you called me. Been waitin' on a wish list for Levi so I can get my shopping done before I head up for Christmas."

Fuck, he'd forgotten about that. "Yeah…" He cleared his throat, not sure how the hell to broach everything that gone down the last few days and how their planned holiday plans were likely smashed to hell again. "I need to get with him. Kinda been sidetracked the last few days."

Silence hummed through the line.

Frank broke it first. "You gonna tell me what's eatin' you, son? Or are we gonna dance around the topic until you get up the nerve?"

Trevor huffed out a chuckle, but it came out about as tired as he felt. "I think what I had with Natalie is over."

In the background, Frank's footsteps sounded on a hard surface, the hollow echo of it placing him no doubt on his raised front porch. "Something cause it to be over, or did one of you make that choice?"

The same fury and gut-wrenching hurt he'd felt when Natalie had judged and sentenced him so quickly billowed up from the cage he'd tried to bury it in. "Something happened."

"Mmm hmmm." No guidance. No questions. Just quiet acceptance.

"I don't remember you and Mom fighting," Trevor said. "Not once."

At that, Frank barked out a harsh laugh. "Not sure you're the same kid who lived in my house then, because we fought plenty. Especially when I had an inclination to dig in my heels and she had a point to prove."

They had? Because for the life of him, he didn't remember it. Yeah, she'd shared her thoughts on things, even when it didn't line up with Frank's opinion, but she did it calm and never read him the riot act. "She might have debated with you, but at the heart of things she believed in you."

"At the heart of things, yeah. But that didn't mean we didn't hurl a few grenades at each other that took a while to mend. Your mom used to say the more you love, the deeper the pain when you fight." He paused a minute and pulled in a deep breath full of reminiscence. "You love this girl?"

Yeah, he did. Enough that walking out of that hospital and trusting his brothers to see her home had been the hardest thing he'd ever done. But if she didn't want him, he'd be damned if he begged. "Not thinkin' it matters now. Damage is already done."

"For you or for her?"

The question caught him off guard. "Not sure I follow."

"Son, you're a man with enough pride to fill up Texas and half a Mexico. I get that 'cause I struggle with it, too. But if there's one part of life where pride's got no place, it's with the woman you love. So I'm askin'— who's damaged? You or her?"

"She lumped me in with that prick of an ex-husband of hers. Automatically assumed I'd acted without honor or reason."

"She have all the facts when she made that call?"

He tightened his grip on the steering wheel and shifted uncomfortably in the leather seat. "No, but she didn't ask, either."

"You give 'em to her?"

"After she'd told me to take a hike, yeah."

"And then what?"

The look on her face when he'd shared the details behind his hauls flashed crystal clear in his head. How she'd flinched and got eyes as big as a harvest moon when he'd told her about the terminal patients. How her lips had trembled before he'd stalked out to the waiting room. He swallowed. Hard. "I hurt her."

Damn, but he was an idiot. Wounded in his own right, but not so much it excused flaying the woman he loved with a sharp tongue and uncensored words. Christ, after what he'd said, no wonder she hadn't called.

As if he'd sensed the direction of Trevor's thoughts, his dad laid out his guidance with the same black and white frankness he always did. "Then if you love her, I suggest you start fixin' the damage."

"How?"

"Trevor Raines, you don't need my answer on that. You already know it. You just need to pull your head out of your ass long enough to get shit done."

Whatever it takes.

He might not have ever heard the phrase before he stepped on Frank and Bonnie Raines's property, but he'd heard it plenty after. Had heard it echoed just as much in the years he'd been with Jace and Axel. He killed the engine and popped his door, urgency and purpose reigniting his drive with the finesse of a battering ram. "I gotta go."

Frank's knowing chuckle rumbled through the phone line. "I imagine you do. You call me and let me know how it goes. I like that girl and was looking forward to getting my hooks into Levi over Christmas. No fun bein' my age without a kid to spoil."

"You're still coming up," he said, striding through the kitchen. "I might have to kidnap the lot of them and tie Natalie to a chair to keep her here, but our Christmas in January is still happening at my place."

He hung up and jogged down the basement stairs. His brothers' random chatter died off the second he hit the room. Every one of them were already in place with drinks ranging from bottled beers and Scotch to sweet iced tea placed in front of them.

Axel spun in his big barrel studio chair and stretched his legs out in front of him, crossing one boot-shod foot over the other. It wasn't often he ditched his sophisticated clothes for jeans and a T-shirt, but today's getup said he'd be spending time tonight in territory better spent blending in. "'Bout bloody time ya got here."

"Had something I had to deal with." Like figuring out he was a knuckle-dragging Neanderthal. He scooted his ladder-back chair up to the table, wishing like hell he'd grabbed a beer on the way in. As nervous as he was, his tongue and courage could both use a little lubrication.

Jace leaned into the table and crossed his arms in front of him. "All right. Who's up first?"

"I'm claiming Nat," Trevor blurted before he could overthink it.

Jace tried to fight a smile, but lost the battle and ducked his head.

Zeke flat-out laughed, and Axel cursed.

Danny, Beckett, and Knox cast a combination of scoffs and scowls across the table.

"Pay up, fuckers," Zeke said. "I told you he'd cave in under a week."

Every damned one of them grumbled and reached for their back pockets.

Trevor couldn't believe it. The stacks of cash getting tossed toward Zeke beside him said it was real, but his head still couldn't wrap around the concept. "You bet on me?"

"Fuck, yeah." Danny slid a crisp hundred-dollar bill across the table.

Knox unfolded an unbelievably crinkled piece of paper and held it out for Trevor. "You cavin' was never a doubt, but the timing was debatable. No harm in a little good-natured wager, right?"

Trevor snatched the paper just as Zeke lifted his hand palm out. "I gotta confess, though. I might have had a tiny inside track. Or should I say a honkin' three-karat inside track. Gabe said the rock you bought her was a work of art."

Jace leaned back in his chair the same way he would settling in behind a big screen for a football kickoff. "I take it this means you patched things up?"

Glaring down at the bets laid out on the simple white paper, Trevor gritted his teeth. Damn, but he had his work cut out for him. If admitting what a fool he'd been to his brothers was hard, fessing up with Natalie would be about twenty times worse. "Not yet."

"You haven't asked her?" Beckett said.

Trevor shook his head. "I wanted to, but not before we got the deal with Wyatt behind us. Then Wyatt got bail, and the rest you already know."

"You sure she's ready for this?" Axel asked. "If she's so quick to judge, you sure she's ready for us?"

Yeah, she was ready. He knew it with the same certainty he'd felt the day he'd looked down at that ring and known exactly where it belonged. He'd just been too hot-headed to wade into facing the serious tactical error of not coming clean with Natalie before the brotherhood had pulled their operation. He wouldn't make that mistake again. "Nat's got a level head. She'll see the reason in what we do. And if she doesn't, she'll still back my play. She's solid. I'm the one who fucked up by blindsiding her."

Knox set his near-empty Corona on the well-scarred table, beads of sweat gliding down the side to pool around the base. "So what's your plan?"

Hell if he knew, but he wasn't stopping until his ring was on Natalie's finger and her whole damned clan was tucked up tight on his ranch. "What any smart man does. Stay on her until she can't say no. Whatever it takes."

Chapter Thirty-Four

Kneeling at the edge of her bed, Natalie taped down the last fold on Levi's final Christmas gift and pushed to her feet with a tired exhale. Discarded wrapping paper scraps littered her bed and the floor around her feet along with a few mangled bows. Talk about the perfect analogy for her life. If you'd told her three days ago her picture-perfect world would end up crumbled and abandoned like the litter, she'd have never believed it.

She grabbed the trash bag already stuffed with crinkled paper and set about tidying up her room. Levi and her mother's muffled voices barely penetrated her closed door, but the tone behind them promised they were both doing their best to put one foot in front of the other. She'd yet to tell Levi what was going on, but Maureen knew the details of what had happened between her and Trevor. Heck, she'd been the one to field at least two calls a day from Trevor since Axel had brought her home, answering questions about how Natalie was feeling and if they needed anything. Not once had he asked to speak with her.

Plopping down on the edge of the bed, she dropped the trash bag, anchored her elbows on her knees, and braced her forehead against her palms. God, she'd been such a fool. So caught up in her fears and sucked up into Wyatt's machinations, she'd never stopped to consider there might be more to the story. She'd done exactly what Trevor had accused her of—assumed the worst, and cast him off without so much as a chance for him to explain. Countless times she'd picked up the phone to call him, to at least apologize for her knee-jerk response, but shame and embarrassment held her back. He'd been right to be angry. The last man he deserved to be compared to was Wyatt. For crying out loud, she'd mercilessly cut him off and he'd still had the decency to check on her, even if he couldn't bear to talk to her directly.

Her mother's raised voice reached through the closed bedroom door. "Natalie? You almost done?"

Forcing herself to her feet, Natalie gathered up Levi's wrapped packages, forced the best smile she could, and opened the door.

Levi stood near the door while Maureen helped him on with his coat. Her mom's coat was already on and her purse slung over her shoulder.

"Where are you two off to?"

Maureen zipped up Levi's jacket then checked her pockets. "We just need to run a quick errand. We'll be back in about an hour. Do you need anything while we're out?"

Natalie hesitated putting the gifts under the tree. It wasn't nearly as fine as the one they'd bought with Trevor and definitely not real. The only thing good about it were the ornaments her mother had saved before she'd sold everything to help Natalie rebound from her sham of a marriage. "What kind of errand? I thought we got everything we needed at the grocery store yesterday."

"Oh, just a few last-minute Christmas items." She

ruffled Levi's messy blond hair, but avoided looking Natalie in the eye.

Levi on the other hand beamed a rambunctious smile straight at her, one full of delight and mischief. Nowhere near the guarded, confused look he'd watched her with the last few days.

Her senses prickled, rising up beyond the numbing depression that had weighted her every thought for days. "Something going on I should know about?"

Maureen twisted, an over-bright and patently bogus smile on her face. "Now, Natalie. It's Christmas Eve—for us anyway. You know better than to go digging into things on a special day. You'll ruin your surprises."

But she didn't have any surprises. She'd ruined their happy holiday together as well as what might have blossomed into a beautiful future. She forced her pitiful thoughts away and nodded her head. "You know what? You're right. It's Christmas Eve. *Our* Christmas Eve. You two go run your errand, and I'll take a shower and get dressed." Then she'd knuckle down and do what she needed to do. What she'd been too chicken to do. She might not be able to give Trevor the gifts she'd gotten him, but she could at least pony up a humble apology. Then she'd break the news to Levi and hope to God it didn't break his heart too bad.

With a quick wave and a goofy grin, Levi opened the door and bustled toward the staircase, Maureen quick on his heels.

The silence that lingered threatened her fragile determination. For who knows how long, she stood in front of their artificial tree and let her mind wander. She'd made a mistake. A bad one. But she could learn from it the same way she'd learned from all the others before it.

She'd own up to her wrongs and hope, if nothing else, she and Trevor could be friends. She'd need to quit her job though. No way could she be around him every day and not fall apart.

Shaking off her thoughts, she found her purse and rummaged through it for her locker key. She'd need to turn it in after she talked with Trevor, but she could do that when he was on a charter flight and maybe have a chance to say goodbye to Ivan and Vicky.

A knock sounded on the door and her heart jolted, the heavy depth of it the same as what Wyatt had used the last time she'd seen him. But it couldn't be Wyatt. Axel had assured her he'd not make bail this time, not so long as she continued to press charges. No way she was letting that bastard get away with what he'd done.

She crept to the front door, rolled to her toes, and checked through the peephole.

Her lungs hitched and a pitiful whimper slipped past her lips.

Standing tall and proud on the other side of her door was Trevor, his muscled torso wrapped in a brown bomber jacket and his blond hair loose and whipping in the winter wind. His gaze was pointed straight at the door, a resolute determination behind his eyes and a knowing glint that said he knew she was there and watching.

Sucking in a steady breath, she twisted the knob, the metal as chilled against her palm as the fear sliding through her veins. She squared her shoulders and opened the door. "Hey."

He nodded, but the easy smile that had always greeted her before was absent, replaced with an angry scowl when his eyes locked on to the vivid bruises on her face. His jaw clenched long enough she halfway expected him to turn and stalk off. "Need to talk with you."

Of course he did. Unlike her, he had the courage and the decency to wrap things up in person instead of escaping with a phone call. She stepped aside and waved him through, fervently wishing she was dressed in something besides two-day-old sweats and an oversized T-shirt. "Come on in."

He ambled through the entrance and scanned the apartment, his focus lingering on their tree in the corner. Even with his coat on, there was no missing the tension in his shoulders and the tight lines around his face. He turned and opened his mouth.

"I want to apologize," she blurted before he could speak. "You were absolutely right and I was horribly wrong. You're nothing like Wyatt. Not even close. I mean...the drugs... I'm a nurse and I can't condone selling things that aren't certified as safe, but I get why you did what you did. It was noble even if it was unorthodox. To cut you off and assume the wrong things like I did is inexcusable. I should have asked more questions and listened."

He frowned, eyebrows pinched in a deep V as though she'd knocked him for a loop. "You're apologizing?"

"I'm trying." It took all her strength to stay where she was. More than anything she wanted to touch him. To hold him and feel him against her again. "I wanted to call. I started to a few times, but chickened out. I'm sorry for that, too."

His expression shifted, confusion morphing to more of a guarded mask. He faced her fully and the air between them changed. Where there'd been tension before, now an electric, bristling energy made her want to take a cautious step back. "Anything else?"

Her thoughts scrambled. The worn taupe carpet beneath her bare feet blurred as she thought through their ugly conversation at the hospital. She fisted her hands at her sides, desperately searching for whatever it was he sought. Her locker key gouged against her flesh.

Her job.

So that's what he'd come here for. Not just to end things but to sever her employment, too. She swallowed and forced her gaze to his. It was what she'd wanted anyway. Was probably smart not just for them but for anyone else who'd have to work with them. She nodded and held out her hand. "I guess I should also give you my notice."

He looked at the key, then her and strode forward. He plucked it from her outstretched palm and tucked it in his pocket. "Anything else?"

Despair and disappointment weighted her shoulders. This was it. The end of what they could have had if she'd just trusted her instincts a fraction more. "No," she whispered. "Nothing else." She tried to smile, but her muscles wouldn't cooperate, what was left of her hope bleeding out of her soul. She nodded, shuffled to the door and opened it, letting in a sharp gust of frigid air. "I really am sorry I hurt you. For what it's worth, I appreciate you having the courage to do what I couldn't."

He strode to the door, but instead of walking out, gently tugged it from her grip and closed it. "You said what you needed to, now it's my turn."

Only two feet stretched between them, but the indefinable current she'd sensed before thickened and licked against her skin in a teasing caress.

He prowled closer. "First off, if I ever pull that shit with you again, you do not lay down and take it. You throw it right back at me until I pull my head out of my ass."

She inched backward, one step after another until her shoulders met the entry wall.

Trevor didn't stop, still moving forward until his body grazed hers, his heat and scent breathing life into her paralyzed heart. "Second, you might not be willing to give me the words anymore, but nothing's changed for me. Not now, not ever. I love you. I love Levi. The last two days have been the worst of my life. I'm not spending Christmas without my family, and I'll be damned if I spend the rest of my days without you either."

She gasped as if she'd surfaced from a near-fatal drowning and her body trembled on a furious surge of adrenaline. She splayed her hands against his chest, needing the familiar contact and the heat beneath her palms to prove the man and the words he'd given were real. "You what?"

"I love you. Nothing's better than my time with you and Levi. Not my planes. Not my horses. Not my ranch. Not even my brothers." He cupped the side of her face. "You seeing me as anything close to the man your ex is hit deep, and I took it out on you." His gaze roamed her face, so much sincerity in his expression she felt it like a reverent caress. "I'm sorry I hurt you. I'm prideful as hell and almost as stubborn as you so I can't swear I won't do it again, but I promise I'll bust my ass to keep it in check."

"But you left." Her lips trembled with the words, her

whole body shaking with the same terrified shudder. "I thought you were gone. That you'd never come back."

"I wasn't sure what to do. I've never been this deep with a woman before. Never wanted to be. But I can tell you this much. You and Levi will never come second with me. Not ever. No matter what you say, no matter what you do, no matter how deep you cut, I'll always come back. You and Levi won't ever be alone or unprotected. Not as long as I'm breathing."

"So…" She fisted her hands in his shirt, her heart kicking so hard it hurt. "You're not breaking things off with me?"

He grinned, that beautiful lopsided smile that sent sunshine-warmth blasting straight through to her toes and made her feel like the most beautiful woman alive. "I said I'm prideful, not an idiot. Only an idiot would let you go by choice."

For the first time in days, she laughed, the ragged sound weighted by the haggard emotions she'd wrestled since she'd watched him storm away. "Does this mean I'm not fired?"

"No, you're still fired. My wife needs to be with her kid and getting her licenses back. Not that you have to go back to nursing. Only if you want to. I've got more than enough income to cover us both."

Her mind stumbled and pitched as graceful as a nosedive down a concrete stairwell. "Your what?"

"My wife." He palmed the back of her head, fingers threading through her hair and palm firm against her scalp. "I'm giving you fair warning so you know what you're up against, but I don't care how long it takes. Next week or next year, we're getting married. And if

Levi will have me, I'll string Wyatt's nuts up until he agrees to let me adopt him."

"Trevor," she whispered. The meaning behind his words registered, but her mind refused to absorb them, the beauty of the life he'd painted as blinding as a cloudless summer day.

He dipped closer and lowered his voice. "I know the things I shared, the things we did to deepen Wyatt's troubles, made you question how I operate, but I'm telling you now we're good men. We make good decisions for the right reasons. Maybe not always the way the law might agree with, but never against our honor and always in the best interest of our family." He tightened his grip. "*My* family."

She knew that. Had known it the second he'd shared the reasons behind what he'd done and the pieces had all clicked together in her head. "If you'd just told me—"

"I can't promise that, darlin'. Not about things that could backfire and cause you or Levi problems, but you've got my word and the word of every one of my brothers—nothing we do impacts innocent people or is done without good intent. More importantly, nothing, absolutely nothing comes back on the people we love."

Could she do that? Trust him the way he asked? To show the same dogged support she'd offered Wyatt before he'd thrown it back in her face?

Absolutely.

The answer resonated clear and powerful from the very deepest part of her. She traced the line of his jaw and tears welled in her eyes. "I believe you." She cupped the back of his neck and urged him closer, needing his kiss more than she needed air.

He shook his head and pulled away enough to dig

inside his pocket. He pulled out a black felt box held it up in his palm.

Her breath caught and the world around her trailed to a stop. It couldn't be. Surely that wasn't what she thought it was.

"I know we're supposed to do gifts tomorrow, but I'm not waiting." He pried the lid back. Inside sat a platinum ring with a monstrous oval diamond surrounded by smaller ones. "I told you I'd work to earn you back and I meant it, but you'll save us both a whole lot of energy if you say yes now." He paused only a beat, but his voice when it came next was lower and thick with sincerity. "Marry me, Natalie. Let me love and take care of you and Levi."

So honest. So unbelievably heartfelt and genuine. That was her Trevor. The way he'd been from the very beginning. Unable to help herself, she brushed her finger along one side of the ring. She'd never seen anything so beautiful. So elegant and bold. But it was too big. As in waaay too big. "Trevor, I can't wear this."

Though he tried to mask it, his shoulders sank. "You don't like it?"

"I love it. Any woman would love it, but it's too much for me."

The concern melted from his face and the soft vulnerability he saved for her alone slipped into place. "Not for you it's not. Nothing for you is too much." He plucked the ring from its white satin pillow and slid it on her finger. "It looks good on your hand. Right." He pulled her flush against him and kissed the back of her hand. "Say yes, Nat."

The tears she'd barely held in check slipped free and her cheeks quivered on a huge but tremulous smile. Her voice came out a broken rasp, the emotion clogging her throat too thick to let anything more intelligible pass. "I picked right this time."

He chuckled at that and tucked her hair behind one ear. "Darlin', you didn't just pick me. You had me roped and tied the second I wrapped my arm around your waist that first night. It just took me a little time to figure it out." He cupped the back of her neck and lowered his head, his lips a teasing whisper against hers. "Now, are you gonna tell me yes so we can give Levi one hell of a Christmas present, or do you need me to prove I mean what I say?"

Rolling up on her toes, she speared her hands in his loose hair and claimed the kiss he'd tempted her with.

His mouth parted, eagerly accepting the advance then quickly claiming control. This would never get old. Not even if she lived to be a hundred. Everything about him fit her perfectly. The passion behind his kiss. His comforting scent and strength. The completeness that came just from hearing his voice or sensing his presence in the same room. Maybe they were going too fast. Maybe the smart thing was to ask him to wait until they had time to settle into more of a routine, but why? She'd dated Wyatt for over a year before they'd even talked about marriage and look where that had gotten her.

She eased away from him, her heart thumping with a newfound courage. No more leading with her head. This time she'd trust her heart's instincts. "You don't have to prove anything to me, Trevor. You do that every time you look at me. Every time you smile or touch me."

"That mean you're saying yes?"

She smiled and her body hummed with a certainty she hadn't felt in years. "I'm absolutely saying yes."

Epilogue

Trevor ambled back from resetting all the soda cans along the makeshift firing range toward the seven—and eight-year-olds lined up behind a row of hay bales. He still hadn't decided which picture tickled him more—the kids having a heyday with their pellet guns, or his brothers trying to keep up with the kids demanding help every five seconds. No surprise, Axel had gravitated to the three little girls on the end, which also meant he had the very rapt attention of their mothers.

Rounding the edge of the area they'd partitioned off in an open field, Trevor checked to make sure no one had moseyed into the line of fire and gave the green light. "All right, shooters. Do your thing."

No surprise, the boys did their best impression of elite operative snipers and set about annihilating the offensive pop cans on the rail. Well, all the boys but Levi. Passing his gun to Frank, who made it his job to give Levi the one-on-one treatment all day, Levi sidled up to the cute little blonde girl next to him and made sure she knew what she was doing first, then dove into action.

An easy smile in place and his customary toothpick nestled at the corner of his mouth, Jace ambled up beside Trevor at the corral's fence. "You realize you're screwed when that kid gets older, right?"

"With Levi?" Trevor scoffed and leaned his shoulders against the rails, hooking one boot heel on a lower rung. "Hell, no. That kid's got a compass like no one I've ever seen."

"Sure he does, but he's also got smoother moves than you, which means you're gonna have giggling little girls sniffing around nonstop in another few years."

A few years, his ass. Levi already got three times the phone calls Trevor did. Though, Levi only seemed to care when the girl next to him called. Still, Jace had a point. A few more years and Trevor was going to have to have that serious heart-to-heart most dads approached with a mix of pride and abject terror.

A dad.

He wasn't Levi's yet, but he could be, assuming the rest of Levi's special day came together right.

Beckett and Knox wandered up to join him and Jace, Beckett shaking his head and sporting an expression Trevor could only categorize as bewildered resignation. "Man, this is whacked." He scanned the row of kids, then Axel, Zeke, Danny, and Ivan who kept an eagle-eye out for stray shooters. "If you'd have told me six months ago you'd be shacked up and throwing kiddie birthday parties, I'd have said you were fucking nuts."

One of the doting mothers halted her none-too-covert appreciation of Axel long enough to cast Beckett a nasty look.

Knox snickered. "You might want to rein in the F-bombs for another hour or two. Natalie will skin you alive if she finds out you're swearing around the kids."

Beckett frowned.

Jace chuckled and clapped him on the shoulder. "Don't look so put out, brother. Last time I checked, kids aren't contagious."

Scoffing, Beckett tipped his head to the women pouring out of the main house's back door. Their hands were loaded up with everything from brightly wrapped gifts and plates, to a sheet cake big enough to feed an army. "You said that about women, too. With the trend you, Zeke, and Trevor are setting, I'm thinking Haven needs to go under quarantine."

Man, if Beckett only knew what he was missing. Standing next to Natalie and saying his vows had been, hands down, the best day of his life. The affair had been a quiet one at Natalie's hometown church, attended only by their closest family—Haven additions included. He couldn't have asked for anything better. Wouldn't have believed he'd actually end up so blessed after the ugliness he'd been born into, but here he was surrounded by family, married to a beautiful woman, and so damned close to being a real dad he could taste it.

Natalie skirted the long picnic tables they'd covered with bright blue tablecloths and set about laying out paper plates for the kids. Her dress might have been all the way down to her shins, but it was flowy and the color of wheat fields ripe for harvest. He'd never seen anything sexier, especially paired with her new Luccheses and her dark hair loose around her shoulders.

She glanced up from the table, caught him staring and gifted him with a knowing smile.

Knox leaned in and muttered, "Somebody's getting laid as soon as these kids are gone."

"Nope," Trevor said. "Got plans tonight with Levi and Natalie. He wants El Fenix and the new Marvel movie for his birthday night. Somewhere along the way I'm gonna give him my present."

Beckett lowered his voice and leaned a little closer to Trevor. "That present have anything to do with the conversation we had with Wyatt Jordan a few weeks ago?"

Yeah, it did. Though, Trevor wouldn't call it a conversation. More like a come-to-Jesus wake-up call in the form of eight men who'd put the fear of God in the Devil if they put their mind to it—the eighth man being Ivan's first foray into justice done Haven style. Ivan had done Trevor proud, asking zero questions and backing every play without a single hesitation.

One thing was for sure—Wyatt wouldn't be walking into any dark parking lots without a little hesitation anytime soon. Not that he got out much these days. He'd worked a plea for the drugs confiscated from his office, but had lost his license and spent most of his time trying to rebuild his reputation and a new career.

Levi lowered his pellet gun long enough to check the status of cake and ice cream, saw that all was in order and bellowed at Nat, "Mom, can we eat now?"

Guess that answered what kind of appetite all the horseback riding and shenanigans before the pellet guns worked up for a kid. Levi had been planning his shooting range for weeks, so if he was throwing in the towel this fast, the kid had to be famished.

Trevor chin-lifted toward the kids and pushed off the rail. "I think that's our cue."

Like the steadfast brothers they were, the guys all stuck through the party to the bitter end, even throwing in a hand to cart Levi's loot into the house and up to his room, then pitching in on cleanup detail. None of

them wanted to admit it, but they'd enjoyed themselves
almost as much as Trevor had.

Four hours and a Mexican meal later, Trevor strolled
along the trendy shopping area artfully disguised as
a cultural gathering area, his arm wrapped around
his gorgeous wife's waist and his other hand holding
Levi's. The theater sat about a block down the stone-
work sidewalk, and the Saturday night moviegoers were
slowly building in numbers as they meandered its direction. Their part of the sidewalk was relatively quiet,
though. The wind was just brisk enough to promise a
crisp spring night, and the sun was no more than thirty
minutes from slipping beneath the horizon.

He squeezed Natalie's hip, waited for her to look up
and cast her a questioning look.

Her lips tipped in a soft smile. "You sure you don't
want to talk to him alone?" she whispered so Levi
wouldn't hear. "I don't mind if you'd rather keep it between the two of you."

Like he had a clue what he was doing. Or worse, what
he was going to say. He'd tried to plan things out, but
every time he played things out in his head, he ended
up sidetracked racking up all the things he wanted to
teach Levi as he grew up. "No." He shook his head and
hugged her a little closer. "What we do, we do together."

To one side of the pretty thoroughfare was a vacant
bench with a smattering of saplings just planted when
the outdoor center opened a year ago. Trevor steered
them that direction.

Stymied by the change in course, Levi dug in his
heels and frowned at the theater in the distance. "I
thought we were going to the movie."

"We are, bud." Trevor sat on the bench and checked

his watch. "Got another forty-five minutes before the previews start and reserved reclining seats right in the middle. We'll be fine." He motioned Levi toward him.

Natalie sat to his right and splayed her hand on his thigh, a sweet show of support he needed more than he cared to admit.

Levi sauntered over, his little boy swagger about ten times more pronounced after the he-man antics he'd shared with his friends all day. He stopped in front of Trevor and cast a curious look at his mom. "Something wrong?"

"Nothing's wrong." Trevor covered Natalie's hand with his own, took one calming breath and prayed like hell he didn't fuck this up. "Want to talk to you about something. Something important."

With a curt nod, Levi met Trevor's gaze head-on, but the frown on his face said he was braced for trouble.

Trevor cleared his throat. "You remember what I told you before me and your mom got married?"

"Yes, sir."

God, that was cute. He hadn't let up with the *sir* and *ma'am* business since that first night he'd been to Natalie's place, especially once he learned how much the teachers and his friends' mothers ate it up.

"You said you loved Mom and you wanted to make her happy," Levi added.

"Yeah, I said that, but do you remember what else?"

Levi's brow furrowed up hard and his gaze drifted off to the side as though mentally strolling through his memories.

Taking pity on him, Trevor pushed again. "I said I loved you, too. That I wanted us to have a family. One you'd feel safe in."

Head cocked to one side, Levi said, "Isn't that what we've got?"

Natalie chuckled and ducked her head.

"Yeah, bud. We've got a family." More than anything, Trevor wanted to pull Levi just a little closer. To hang on to his hand or shoulder while he said what he wanted to say, but didn't dare for fear of making the poor kid feel pushed one way or the other. This had to be all Levi's decision or it wouldn't work. "The thing is, I'd like to make it more official."

"But you're already married."

This time Trevor was the one to chuckle, Levi's unvarnished innocence slaking a good chunk of the tension off Trevor's shoulders. "That's true. Your mom's my wife. What I want to talk to you about is seeing how you feel about being my son."

The first second, his face pinched in confusion. The next his eyebrows hopped high and his gaze shot to Natalie. "You mean…like for real?"

Natalie nodded. "Like for real."

He refocused on Trevor. "How's that work?"

"I contact some lawyers and file adoption papers. They do their thing with the judges and when the judge signs off, it'd be all official."

He swallowed and fidgeted. "What about my dad?"

"Your dad will always be your dad. I'm not out to change that, and I'll never try to keep you from him. Anytime you want to visit, we'll get it set up." So long as there were eyes on the bastard, a condition the judge had put on any future visitation for the next year. "The way I see it, you'd have two dads instead of one."

His breath coming just a little bit faster, Levi's eyes

got bright. He pinched his mouth tight for a second, obviously fighting back tears. "You really want me?"

Fuck it.

Trevor cupped Levi's shoulder and pulled him in for a tight hug. Damn, but he wished he could beat Wyatt all over again. That son of a bitch didn't deserve a son like Levi. When he could finally speak, his words came out gruff and thick with emotion. "Bud, there is nothing more in this world that would make me happier than giving you my name and having the honor of calling you son."

His face tucked against Trevor's neck, Levi jerked a quick nod.

"That a yes?"

Levi tightened his arms around Trevor's neck and nodded again. His quiet sniffle and the cool dampness against Trevor's T-shirt assured Levi's tears had won the battle.

Trevor smoothed his hand down Levi's spine and twisted enough to meet Natalie's gaze.

Tears trailed down her cheeks, too, but paired with her shaky smile they were the good kind, a distinction he'd finally learned to figure out in the months since she'd agreed to marry him. "I told you he'd say yes."

She had. Countless times, usually followed by that same happy crying thing she was doing now. He'd just had a hard time believing it. He cupped the back of Levi's head, so much pride burning through him he was pretty sure sitting through a two-hour movie was going to be the hardest thing he'd ever done. "I'm gonna have a son."

"Yeah, you are."

A son. He couldn't fucking wait to get those papers turned in.

He ruffled Levi's hair. "So, seeing as we've got thirty more minutes and I need to call my brothers and let 'em know they're gonna be uncles, how do you feel about ice cream on the way to celebrate?"

In true Levi form, his head popped up, the lure of ice cream overcoming any embarrassment that came with tears. "Can I get two scoops?"

Trevor laughed loud enough it bounced off the buildings around them, the beauty and power of it mirroring the emotions swirling inside him. He stood, planted Levi firmly on his left side, and tugged Natalie to his right. Hugging them both close, he steered them to the ice cream shop dead ahead. "Son, between you and your mom, I've got the world now. The least I can do is spring for a double scoop."

* * * * *

*If you enjoyed Trevor and Natalie's story,
don't miss the next installment in the
Men of Haven series from Rhenna Morgan.
Turn the page for an excerpt from
Tempted & Taken.*

One week Darya had waited. Waited, watched her every step and worked herself ragged. Outside the rearranged Post-it on her desk, not once had she glimpsed any indication Ruslan or anyone else had found her. In fact, her life had settled into its usual routine so easily she'd wondered if maybe she hadn't imagined leaving things askew on her desk.

Regardless, the time to meet Knox was here and hopefully, the leg up she needed to go with the introduction. Parked in front of a single-story building with plain-Jane concrete walls, she stared up at the brushed chrome Citadel Security sign and rehashed the pitch she'd spoken aloud at least twenty times a day. Cool air pumped from the car's vents against her clammy skin, barely making a dent with all the adrenaline coursing through her veins.

The clock on the dash flicked from 1:54 p.m. to 1:55 p.m. Either she could sit here until straight up two o'clock and let her anxiety climb all the way up into the stratosphere, or she could pry herself out of her car and hope a slightly early arrival showed an extra level of professionalism.

She popped the handle and shoved the heavy door

open, swinging her resale Jimmy Choo-shod feet out
onto the concrete parking lot. What the tan pumps
lacked in pizzazz they more than made up for in ac-
centuating her legs, especially paired with the matching pencil skirt that ended just above her knees and the
delicate ivory camp shirt with its mandarin collar. Putting the outfit together had been both a joy and a welcome distraction, a brief trip back to a time when she'd
been able to enjoy fine fashion instead of constantly
trying to blend in.

Before her hand connected with one of the glass entry
handles, the click of a lock being released sounded. She
pulled the door open and a wave of chilled air to make
her Challenger's AC seem weak blasted across her skin.
Even with the ample light spilling through the double
doors and windows on either side, it took her eyes a second to adjust from the bold midday sunshine.

A pretty blonde dressed in jeans and a T-shirt stood
from behind a curved reception desk stained a soft
ebony and accented in soft chrome. Her eyes were an
enviable green and her hair styled in a tousled, pixie cut.
She reached across the tops of three monitors arranged
in a perfect semicircle and offered her hand in greeting.
"You must be Jeannie Simpson. I'm Katy, Knox and
Beckett's assistant. Can I get you something to drink?"

Two or three shots of vodka would be nice. God
knew she needed something to loosen up her tongue.
While the outside of Knox's building had been nothing short of plain, the inside was jaw-dropping high-
end contemporary. Like Katy's desk, the walls on either
side of her were dark—not quite black, but charcoal
gray, and fashioned from some kind of metal rather
than paint. The wall behind Katy's desk, however, was

a beautiful dove gray that added extra depth to the limited space. Classy yet edgy cylinder pendant lights with frosted white glass hung above either end of her desk, and two impenetrable steel doors flanked her on either side. "If it's not too much trouble, water would be nice."

"No trouble at all." Katy cocked her head, curiosity glimmering behind her assessing gaze. "Your accent is amazing. I'm guessing Russian?"

For a second, Darya's thoughts flatlined. With limited daily interactions beyond her normal routine, it was seldom she met new people. So much so she'd forgotten the need for explanation. "Yes," she said, realizing all too quickly Knox would expect the same. "Not too hard to understand I hope."

"Not at all. It's actually beautiful." Katy punched a few buttons on her computer and waved Darya to the small seating area to one side of the front door. "Just give me a minute to grab your water and let Knox know you're here."

"Thank you."

"Don't mention it." She splayed her hand on a black screen beside one heavy door and a heavy clunk that sounded on par with a bank vault being released resonated through the room. Only then was Darya left alone in the intimidating environment.

Slowly, she paced toward the iron-colored leather couch and the oblong marble coffee table. Sitting was out of the question, not if she wanted to exude any kind of calm. She might be technically alone in the room, but the cameras anchored in every corner made it relatively certain there were eyes on her somewhere. She squeezed the handles on her briefcase a little tighter and pretended to study the landscape outside one picture window. What really held her attention was the glass itself, multiple layers thick and no doubt capable of stopping bullets. But then such measures made sense for a security company. As did the secured doors. At least she hoped that was the reason for such stringent measures. The last time she'd been in such a tightly controlled environment was the day she'd met Ruslan, and her world had gone from pampered to hell in all of five minutes.

The door *kachunked* behind her.

Darya turned, the pleasant smile she'd intended for Katy evaporating along with all the air in her chest. Instead of Katy strolling through the large door, Knox ambled her direction, a smile in place potent enough to disarm the most jaded woman and a bottle of water loosely gripped in one hand.

And he was gorgeous. So much more than what the pictures she'd scrounged up promised. More intensity. More charisma. More *everything*. Like in all the photos she'd seen, he wore faded Levis and military-style black boots. His T-shirt was a deep gray that accentuated his lean, but muscled torso, and tattoos peeked out from each sleeve.

It wasn't until he moved within reaching distance and held out the water he'd brought her that the white graphic on the T-shirt registered—a classic Impala and the phrase, *Get in, loser. We're going hunting.*

"You like *Supernatural*?" she blurted.

His smile deepened and he wiggled the bottle still in his outstretched hand. "Not even officially introduced yet and you're already scoring points for good taste." A rugged leather watch with a thick camel-colored band covered his wrist, while a darker brown cuff and two smaller bracelets made of turquoise and red shells circled the other. Total rock star.

She took the water, wishing she could press the ice-cold plastic against her flaming cheeks, but juggled it with her briefcase instead and offered her hand for a formal introduction. "Sorry. I'm JJ."

His grip engulfed hers, the warmth of the contact and the way he leisurely perused her from head to toe scattering her barely resuscitated thoughts. "Not a thing to apologize for from where I'm standing." His gaze settled on hers, the impact of it stoking grossly inappropriate thoughts. Vivid, carnal and deliciously wicked thoughts. His voice lowered and rasped with pure sexual promise. "I'm Knox."

Oh, yes. Definitely dangerous territory. Absolutely the worst trespass her mind could make with plans to pitch her future so close. She forced herself to relinquish his hand. "I'm very pleased to meet you."

His beautiful gray eyes sparked with mischief and he grinned in a way that said he hadn't missed the huskiness in her response. He side-stepped and swept his hand toward the door, but rather than use the movement to add more distance, he splayed his hand at the small of her back. "How about we get out of the lobby and give you a chance to get your bearings before we talk shop?"

Walking was good. Distance would be even better. Although, for the first time since she'd started wearing heels, she wasn't sure if she could put one foot in front of the other without looking like a newborn deer.

Behind the industrial steel door, the air was even colder, the steady draft tunneling between the glass walls on either side of her gently lifting the hair off the back of her neck. "You must really hate July in Texas."

"My servers hate July in Texas. I learned to tolerate it like every other native before I left the cradle."

Behind the glass, server racks stretched tall and wide in precise rows. Her heels clicked against the industrial tile, mingling with the steady hum from the machines. "This is all for your security company?"

"Some of them. The rest support the traffic from my apps."

Well, that was silly of her. The very reason she was here and she'd not been smart enough to realize he'd need a sizable infrastructure to support the business he'd built. She slowed her steps, appreciating how the wires ran in neat rows up the back of each stack then disappeared into the iron racks above. Combined with the soft blue light emanating from the ceiling can lights she felt a bit like she'd entered a sci-fi flick. "It's quite overwhelming."

He chuckled and placed his hand on yet another bio scanner beside a black wood door. "Overwhelming is when a server goes down and pissed-off customers start calling in." The lock released and he opened the door for her. "There've been a few drills I'd liken to an electronic version of a needle in a haystack, but hey. Nothin' like a challenge to keep a man sharp."

For some reason, the image of Knox knee-deep in a challenging situation sent a charge through her strong enough to power half the machines they'd left behind. True, he was handsome, but nothing captivated her more than a man's intelligence. Considering Knox had both in spades, it was a wonder she'd been able to string more than three words together, let alone remember her name.

She trailed behind him into his office. It had the same contemporary feel as the lobby, only less intimidating in its colors. A soft gray chenille sofa and two club chairs covered in a matching patterned fabric were arranged near a window on the far side of the room. In the center was what she assumed was Knox's desk, though it was far more unconventional than the standard arrangement. Where most people chose to arrange their furnishings with their back to the wall and a bird's eye view on the entrance, Knox's wide steel desk faced an astounding number of monitors mounted on the far wall, each of them streaming what she assumed was live footage from a number of businesses. Even more impressive were the four oversized computer monitors arranged in a semicircle in the center of his desk.

In the monitors hanging on the wall, people went about their daily activities, innocently working, drinking, and eating without so much as a clue they were being watched.

The muted tap of fingers on keys sounded and the screens went dark.

"They're a distraction until you get used to them." Knox spun his sleek black office chair around, rolled it toward a smallish collaboration table on her right and motioned to the guest chair behind it. "Have a seat."

She did, unpacking her laptop from her briefcase as she did so and setting it on the tabletop.

Directly across from her, he leaned in, rested his forearms on the brushed chrome surface and cupped one fisted hand with the other. "So, you mentioned a business opportunity. What's on your mind?"

So much for easing into the topic. And had she really referred to it as a business opportunity? Now he'd think she'd pulled some kind of bait and switch to earn his attention. She cleared her throat and smoothed one hand across the top of her computer. "Business opportunity might not be the right way to describe it."

His expression blanked, the warmth and lighthearted mirth that had shone in his beautiful eyes chilling in an instant. As though she'd not only angered him, but disappointed him as well. Without the vibrancy in his gaze, his eyes looked tired. Pinched and weary around the edges as though he'd gone for far too long without rest.

She forged onward, drawing from the countless rehearsals she'd spoken out loud while pacing her apartment. "You remember when I first reached out to you—when I emailed you on my tracking services—I mentioned I'd learned your name from someone you'd mentored."

He nodded, though the movement seemed cautious. "Jason Reynolds."

"Yes." She fidgeted in her seat and curled her fingers around the furthest edge of her laptop. "Jason's told me many stories about you. About the men you call your brothers and how you've made a successful career for yourself. He holds you in very high regard."

"Not sure how that plays into a business opportunity."

This was it. In the grander scheme of things, it wasn't nearly as big a risk as taking on JJ's identity or fleeing Russia, but it could still catapult her future. She pulled in a slow breath and held his commanding stare. "It's important because I want you to mentor me."

His eyes widened, a little of the emotional barricade he'd put up easing as he spoke. "Jason's a coder."

"I know. He's the one who first gave me the idea."

"And you know him how?"

"He comes to visit his grandmother every Monday. At

a retirement home. His grandmother isn't very talkative, but he always comes and brings his computer. He told me you've been known to teach people with an interest and, if they do well, give them a leg up."

"I teach people with *talent*. No matter how much interest a person has doesn't mean they can be successful in the long run."

Emboldened, she sat a little taller and leaned in. "I can't tell you if I have talent, but I can promise you I'm tenacious. I've already completed two of the self-teaching courses you recommended to Jason and have started a third."

He reclined against his chair back, one arm still draped atop the table while the other rested casually at his hip. It was a relaxed pose, but the intensity that crackled around him said she'd be a fool to assume he wasn't assimilating each and every detail to the nth degree. "You're looking to expand on the skip tracing?"

Always stick to the truth, JJ had coached her. *Or as close to it as you can get.*

"I'd like to move away from that business," Darya answered, "to build a career that's less reliant on companies but is still transportable." Realizing the unintended kernel she'd left uncovered, she clarified, "So I can travel."

For several seconds, he merely studied her, the quiet amplifying until it droned as loud as the servers in the other room.

"The skip tracing is good," she said, needing to fill the silence. "With my contracts, I can keep a steady income, but I don't like the feel of it. I don't like finding people who don't want to be found. I don't want to worry that they'll learn who found their information and take their anger out on me."

Without moving so much as a muscle, his entire demeanor shifted. A shrewd observer one second and a lethal predator on alert the next. His voice was deceptively smooth. "Has that happened?"

Not exactly. Not to her anyway, but it *had* happened. "Once. A collection company wanted to locate a man past due on his car payments. He was living at his ex-wife's address in a town only thirty minutes away. The company secured the car, but the collector inadvertently mentioned who had located the debtor's new residence."

"And?"

She shrugged, recalling the none-too-pleasant altercation that had happened only a few months after she'd gone to work for JJ. "People who lose their possessions tend to be very angry. They also want someone to blame for their misfortune, and this man in particular wanted to voice his displeasure. In person." She paused for a minute, looking for the right words to help him understand without exposing too much of her own predicament. "I don't want to experience that again. I want to create something. To build a career where my success will be limited only by my abilities."

He pulled in a slow breath, sighed as though he questioned having scheduled the appointment and sat up in his chair. "You realize there's a lot more to this than syntax and technique, right? Even with persistence, you need damned good ideas and a hell of a lot of luck if you want to be more than just a hired coder."

"I will make my luck."

His eyebrows hopped high and his lips curled in a

sly grin. "You quoting me because you believe it, or to let me know you've done your homework?"

"Because I believe it. This isn't the first time I've taken risks, and I doubt it will be the last, but every person has to make their own way. If the path doesn't exist, it's up to every individual to make one. You took your love of music and movies and made a niche for yourself. I can do the same."

"You use my app?"

Her and everyone else eager to find new leads for their playlists or Netflix binges. Lystilizer had originally focused on music only, but had been expanded to include movies a little over a year ago. The algorithm behind it was amazing, evaluating each user's individual libraries and making spot-on recommendations for new purchases. "I use it all the time."

"Music or movies?"

"Both."

"Favorite band."

That drew her up short. "Can you actually narrow your favorites down to one?"

One corner of his mouth twitched. "Fair enough. How about your top favorites in the last six months?"

"Poe, Eve to Adam and Chris Stapleton."

He cocked one eye and crossed his arms across his chest, but his grin was playful. Clearly, he not only loved music, but he was familiar with a broad spectrum of genres. "Alternative, rock and country. That's a heck of a spread. I'd have pegged you as a top forty girl."

She shrugged. "I like music that fits my mood. Why limit yourself to only one format when you can explore many?"

"True." He cocked his head. "So, what about movies?"

For a second, she ducked her head, then remembered who she was talking to and shook off her embarrassment. What difference did it make what he thought of her burning through pop culture classics? "*The Princess Bride* and *Always*."

His smile deepened. "'Wuv,'" he said, imitating the clergyman near the end of the movie. "'True wuv.'"

"'You killed my father!'" she fired back with her own impression of Inigo Montoya. "'Prepare to die!'"

He laughed loud enough to fill the room, the rich rumble of it soothing away the remnants of her fears. "A classic. I'll bet I could drop at least twenty-five quotes inside of five minutes. Maybe less."

"I'm watching *Airplane* next. Jason says it has just as many, if not more."

His laughter died off slowly, and while none of the suspicious tension she'd picked up on before returned, he studied her through slightly narrowed eyes. As if she were a puzzle he couldn't quite put together. "How long have you lived in the States?"

Every time someone asked that question all she wanted to do was bolt, but denying her heritage wasn't an option. She'd long ago accepted her accent was too prominent to eradicate it without serious training, but that didn't mean she was comfortable opening doors that might lead to more questions.

The tattoo on his forearm drew her attention. Bold and drawn only in black ink, it resembled a tree but with a tribal style and surrounded a rugged H in the center. A mark with purpose, yet nowhere near as sinister as the tattoos she'd become all too familiar with in Russia. Was Knox dangerous? Absolutely. Her instincts with people were seldom wrong and for Knox they insisted he had an intellect not to be trifled with. She'd even uncovered rumors of he and the men he called brothers having ties to criminals. But sitting with him now—watching him and interacting with him—she sensed fairness. Honor and determination paired with an indomitable courage. If she expected him to take a chance on her, he at least deserved the same willingness in return, even if it gave him a lead toward discovering who she really was.

She took a deep breath, straightened her spine and fisted her hands in her lap. "I left Russia about two and a half years ago."

Don't miss
Tempted & Taken
by Rhenna Morgan,
available wherever
Carina Press books are sold.

www.CarinaPress.com

ACKNOWLEDGMENTS

It wasn't until I was about one-third of the way through Trevor's book that I realized I was up a creek and sadly lacking in horse knowledge. Thankfully, I know this awesome-sauce equine veterinarian by the name of Dr. Jennifer Mathews who happily rushed to the rescue. Not only did she patiently correct the places I'd let Google guide me astray, she didn't laugh once. (Though I did catch her trying to hide a smile a few times.) If I bungled anything in the final product, it's entirely on me, but I sure hope Deuce, Peso, and Titan did her suggestions justice in the end.

As for editors, can I just say that Angela James is the best? Seriously, I'd cage fight to keep her. (Though I'd prefer to hire a champion stand-in to bump my odds of winning higher. My wrestling skills aren't what they used to be.)

And of course, I have to thank my rock-solid posse—Cori Deyoe, Juliette Cross, Kyra Jacobs, Audrey Carlan, Dena Garson, and, most importantly, my *amazing* family. Without each of you to keep me grounded, laughing, and overflowing with love and support, I'd be utterly lost.

ABOUT THE AUTHOR

Rhenna Morgan is a happily-ever-after addict—hot men, smart women, and scorching chemistry required. A triple-A personality with a thing for lists, Rhenna's a mom to two beautiful daughters who constantly keep her dancing, laughing, and simply happy to be alive.

When she's not neck-deep in writing, she's probably driving with the windows down and the music up loud, plotting her next hero and heroine's adventure. (Though trolling online for man-candy inspiration on Pinterest comes in a close second.)

She'd love to share her antics and bizarre sense of humor with you and get to know you a little better in the process. You can sign up for her newsletter and gain access to exclusive snippets, upcoming releases, fun giveaways, and social media outlets at www.rhennamorgan.com.

If you enjoyed *Claim & Protect*, she hopes you'll share the love with a review on your favorite online bookstore.

Get 4 FREE REWARDS!

We'll send you 2 FREE Books
plus 2 FREE Mystery Gifts.

Harlequin® Intrigue books feature heroes and heroines that confront and survive danger while finding themselves irresistibly drawn to one another.

FREE Value Over $20

Get 4 FREE REWARDS!

We'll send you 2 FREE Books plus 2 FREE Mystery Gifts.

Harlequin Presents® books feature a sensational and sophisticated world of international romance where sinfully tempting heroes ignite passion.

FREE Value Over **$20**
